"It takes a soldier to command soldiers, boy." Svarézi once again drew his savage blade.

Veltro raised his voice and screamed, cramming himself into the dust in fear.

"You're finished, Svarézi! Colletro's court is finished with you! No Mannicci bride—no council seats! No Blade Council will suffer you again!"

The blade reversed to hover like an ice pick in Svarézi's hand.

"If the council is finished with me . . . then let us finish with the council!"

Svarézi stabbed the cowering young Blade Captain through the roof of his mouth, twisting the blade down into the sand like a slaughterer. The body beneath him arched, then jerked into deathly stillness. Svarézi freed his sword and flicked the filth from the blade onto the alley walls.

Behind him, the crossbow sergeant scarcely spared a glance at his master's corpse.

"Did he speak the truth, sire? Will there be no Sumbrian bride?"

"What matter? Where a maid's door shuts, a master's opens."

Svarézi wrenched at the feathered mane of his hippogriff, dragging her beak up from a feast of carrion.

FORGOTTEN REALMS
FANTASY ADVENTURE

THE NOBLES

FANTASY ADVENTURE

The Council of Blades

Paul Kidd

THE COUNCIL OF BLADES

First Printing: December 1996
Printed in the United States of America.
Library of Congress Catalog Card Number: 95-62261

9 8 7 6 5 4 3 2 1

ISBN: 0-7869-0531-X
8564XXX1501

TSR, Inc.   TSR Ltd.
201 Sheridan Springs Road   120 Church End, Cherry Hinton
Lake Geneva, WI 53147   Cambridge CB1 3LB
U.S.A.   United Kingdom

Dedicated, with much love and laughter,
to all the folk of "Furry Fandom"
who helped us through our darkest hours.

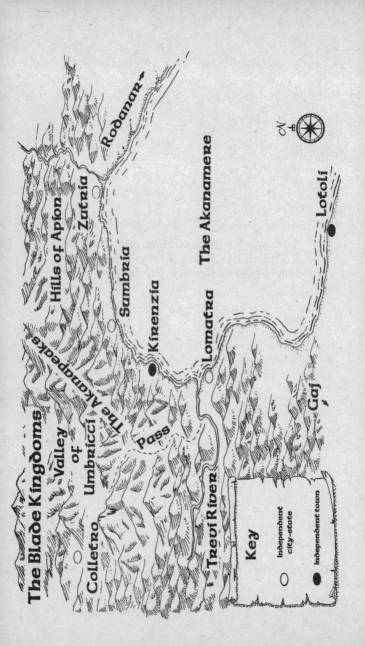

Seen from high up in the pure, sharp nighttime sky, the cool lake surface sparkled with the light of stars. A flawless, glittering carpet spread out to the horizons and beyond; the black arch of the sky blended perfectly with the waters of the Akanamere far below. The whole world seemed to be suspended in a spell of silence as the countless movements of heaven, earth and sea all blended into a timeless, frozen hush.

Suspended in a crystal ball, a flier could ride the cold night winds and dream unruffled dreams.

Hanging high above the waves, a single lonely figure rode the winds with stubby wings. Brilliant in plumes of orange, red and gold, the great bird whirred onward through a cool mountain breeze; a fantastic, addled creature fashioned from ten parts tail and two parts beak, to one part brain.

The great bird streamed like a fistful of silken ribbons through the sky, drawn by a point of light which glittered oh so brightly just above the open sea. He swirled across the inky sky, saw what lay ahead, and suddenly felt his spirits soar.

Cradled in its tiny harbor, the city-state of Sumbria shone against the darkness like a cup of fallen stars. The clean white walls shot upward from the shoreline like rearing foam, while the towers and streets seemed strung with iridescent pearls. The great, giddy bird stared down at the sight in awe, his beak hanging open as the lights dazzled his eyes. He hovered clumsily, tail dangling and great yellow feet pumping at the empty air, flicking his head this way and that as he tried to make sense out of an astonishing new world.

Suddenly the bird folded up his wings and dove. He shot low across the rooftops—across the battlements and walls. Past ranks of guards in barbute helmets of white steel and crossbowmen dressed in brigantines. Past the catapults mounted on the battlements and the silken banners streaming in the breeze. The bird rolled happily in the swirling currents of city air, his long tail swishing like noisy streamers in his wake. He turned a giddy loop-the-loop, and let out a raucous peal of joy.

All across the city, dogs began to howl. Fresh milk curdled, the chickens mislaid, and something rather unpleasant happened to all the cheese.

. . . And still the firebird sang! He caroled out a love that wrapped itself about him like a phoenix flame; he sang with a delight as pure and fresh as morning dew. He clucked, he shrieked and yodelled at frequencies far above mere mortal hearing bands, crumbling mortar on high rooftops and sending gargoyles sliding off on sudden one-way journeys to the streets below.

Great, expressive eyes suddenly fell upon a blaze of color far below; with a cry of joy, the bird dove off between two marble towers, frightened a nest of stirges half to death, and swooped to a halt outside a magnificent banquet hall.

Cracked glass panes opened out into an empty ballroom all set out for a marvelous feast. The firebird pressed himself against the windows, peering avidly within, beating at the glass like a great brain-damaged moth. Hanging there before his eyes was an immense, sparkling chandelier, its crystals ablaze with dancing points of light.

The shine of pretty baubles made the firebird's head whirl. He stared, hypnotized, at the crystal beads, each one glimmering with magic spells. His beak opened and silently mouthed a hiss of awe.

Sparklies!

Frantic with greed, the bird clawed his way high up into the skies. In a high tower beside the hall, a window stood open to the summer breeze. Like a great raffia-work comet, the bird swooped downward in a graceful arc, lofted superbly up toward the ivory window frame, and smacked himself straight into the wall.

The addle-witted bird slid like a jellyfish down the tower wall, dropped onto a balcony and sat giddily watching a cascade of stars. Lurching to his feet, the creature shook off his hurt, fluffed out his plumage and quickly scuttled in through the balcony door.

Moonlight struck brilliant sparks into the great bird's eyes and the crystal chandelier instantly fled his mind.

A mirror and dressing table stood beside the far wall. On a rosewood bust, a necklace of emeralds sat upon display; a collar of golden chain, encrusted with green gems that hurtled the light like confetti to the skies. The huge bird gaped at the thing in shock and let pure childish delight shine in his gaze.

Alone of all his race, only *he* had been clever enough to brave the empty skies! The most courageous, the most clever, the most handsome bird of all! Now a fantasy land of sparkling pretties would be his. He would line a nest with glittery baubles, and a thousand females would worship him with their sighs.

The bird danced; he stuck his head down low and his tail up high, giving a waggle to the left and a waggle to the right. He kicked his feet and trilled a busy tune, losing himself in the display of his brilliant orange tail. The firebird strutted about in celebration of his own amazing cleverness, closing his eyes and becoming quite lost to the world.

"Sofia? *Sofia!* The bath was still filled with yesterday's ass's milk! The stench was quite atrocious. Pray do not allow it to happen again!"

"Yes, milady."

Voices! The bird ceased its dance, flapped around in a mad circle, and nearly tripped over his own tail as he snatched the emerald necklace in his beak. With a great thrash of wings, he lumbered out onto the balcony and launched into the air. An instant later, the bird's streaming tail feathers had whipped across the city roofs leaving nothing but a sparkle of magic in their wake.

"Sofia! Lay out the spider-silk gown, then help me . . ."

A great, fat woman big enough to batter down a castle gate came sweeping through into the palace tower. She froze midspeech, spied the open window, then turned shocked eyes toward the empty dressing table.

"Sofia! My emeralds! My emeralds!"

"Madam?" A scrawny maid scuttled through the door like a half-drowned spider washed out of a knothole. "Perhaps they are still at the cleaners?"

"The *cleaners?*" Swelling herself dangerously with outraged pride, the massive noblewoman surged out onto the balcony. "You idiot girl—we've been robbed!"

A single orange feather had been left as the villain's calling card. The noblewoman snatched it up inside one great fist, then flowed forward like a juggernaut toward the quailing maid.

"Call the guard! Call the prince! Have the entire thieves' guild dragged out and flogged!"

A mighty mass of double chins surged like a tidal wave as a final shriek of outrage blasted up into the skies.

"My emeralds! *Bring me back my emeralds!*"

The woman shook her fists across a wilderness of empty roofs; mortar started from the tower walls as she slammed a punch against the brickwork, and soldiers scattered in panic from the courtyard far below.

High overhead, unseen against the stars, a giddy feathered figure pranced beneath the flawless moon, dancing a dance above his fabulous new home.

* * * * *

When the snows cleared from the winter passes, and summer sun gleamed down upon the Hills of Apion, it was the custom of the Blade Kingdoms to devote themselves to war.

The six kingdoms—neat, tiny little city-states surrounded by their vineyards, villages and olive groves—still showed the proud vigor of newcomers. Their gleaming new city walls had been built atop Chessentian ruins a dozen centuries old; in the valleys, there ran the aqueducts and moldering villas left from days long gone. The ruins still yielded a strange harvest of old cogs and broken statues; curiosities avoided by sensible, superstitious souls.

Two hundred years before, the grand mercenary companies of the Vilhon Reach had turned their backs on their honorless Chondathian employers and a worthless war. The huge divisions, with their traveling hospitals, mobile sanctuaries and courts, had moved slowly east into an empty land of yellow hills and fallen stone on the shores of the Akanamere.

All the sciences of the north were brought to bear upon the fallow lands; ancient aqueducts were repaired by skilled military engineers, while soldiers cleared the broken harbor mouths and roads. As years of building passed, the soldiers' tent cities became true towns, and mercenary companies changed into tiny nations. The great captains married camp followers, captives, and whores, breeding heirs to take over their commands in the years yet to come.

For two busy centuries the kingdoms had prospered—locked into the traditions of their freebooting past. Military discipline readily tucked itself under the covers of democracy. The free-voting mercenary councils became senates of nobility, each captain still having status according to the number of his men.

The free companies soon vanished, and in their place the Blade Kingdoms had been born.

The Blade Councils that ruled the kingdoms were descended from educated men; soldiers who had risen above mere passion, and who had brought the art of warfare to its greatest heights. As they grew, the kingdoms prided themselves on the triumphs of the rational mind; of law and order, sciences and art.

Men being men, disputes still arose; the Blade Kingdoms came of martial roots, and soldiers were their political heart and soul. Yet even in war, the scientific mind could rise above brute emotion; war could be confined to pure military contest, leaving the daily lives of simple subjects quite alone. And so each summer, the great armies marched across the hills in dazzling, intricate campaigns, making move and countermove like ploys played in an all-consuming game.

Thus, in the drowsy days of a golden summer, it came to pass that Sumbria and her neighbor Colletro were once again at war. The contention—as it had been in many campaign seasons past—was the ownership of the Valley of Umbricci, its salt mines, its olive presses and its prosperous cattle farms.

Burned farms and slaughtered cattle profited no man. The armies, therefore, moved through the passes and down into the valley without offering the inhabitants the slightest bit of harm. Provisions were bought and sold, and local womenfolk made the firesides of both armies merry through the nights.

The campaign progressed with intricate, energetic subtlety. By day, the hippogriffs circled overhead, their riders endlessly skirmishing and spying on the maneuvers far below; by night, cunning countermarches and surprise attacks were launched. Casualties mounted, though thanks to the laws of war, they remained blessedly light. For in "white war," wounded opponents offered ransom for their lives, and an enemy recovering with his feet tucked up in bed was worth more gold to his captor than a corpse moldering in the ground. . . .

Move and countermove, feint and strike—until finally the Prince of Sumbria and the ruler of Colletro saw fit to venture themselves upon a final throw . . .

Now, in the height of an afternoon that sparkled like warm, clear wine, the two armies spread across the valley floor in all their martial splendor. Dense pike formations stalked like many-legged insects in shells of burnished steel; the crossbowmen and pavisiers swarmed along the flanks like butterflies, covering the grass with the mad motley of their particolored clothes. Engineers scuttled back from their gigantic catapults, sheltering behind wicker shields as the machines prepared to fire. The massive engines pinned the battle lines; pikes and bill-hooks sank and locked as the soldiers rigidly dressed their formations. The valley grew still and strangely silent, quiet but for the restless stir of banners and the rustling of arms.

Beneath gay umbrellas of whirring hippogriffs, cavalry began to move: *Lanze Spezzate*—mercenary horsemen in half-armors made of burnished steel. To the rear, there rode the *Elmeti*—the noble horse, decked out in a ponderous grandeur of golden armor and nodding plumes. The horses paraded solemnly past the waiting ranks of infantry, hooves stepping high and horse-necks arching like haughty cobras in the sun. The formal parade of power passed back and forth across the fields, carefully scrutinized by the commanders of their foes.

Before the warwagon which bore the standard of Sumbria, twelve horsemen silently surveyed the enemy battle array. Big men on giant horses, they dominated the hillside with their air of magnificent scorn.

From ground to crown, the riders were sheer shining magnificence. Their horses' hides all gleamed pure silver, gold or bronze, the metallic hairs glittering to each shift and turn of summer sun. Smothered beneath armored bardings, the beasts seemed like statues animated out of burnished metal—a glory only matched by the outrageous martial splendor of their riders up above.

Each man wore an uncovered shell of pristine, perfect plate. Their helms were topped with tall cones of parchment, tubes of feathers or startling ostrich plumes; their faces were hidden beneath flawless visors of enchanted steel. Each simply sat and posed in arrogant disdain as the enemy flourished itself across the distant valley floor.

A silver god turned to the golden being at its right; the faceless head breathed cool words into the breeze.

"Their cavalry is badly mounted."

"We have the weight of them in horseflesh; they are still using southern breeds." A rider in sickly arsenic green hissed like a mantis inside his shell. "Worthless stock; mere meat before our blades!"

The golden rider's hand rose up and stemmed the flood of speech. Below them, the armies stilled themselves and locked tight into their ranks.

The rider's mount—one of the *Gens D'Or*, the golden horses of the gods—shifted sideways with prancing, stabbing motions of its metallic hooves.

"Heralds."

A single word of command sent a pair of figures strutting forward across the grass; haughty youths mounted upon pure white hippogriffs. The hippogriffs—half horse and half griffon, equipped with both equine hooves and an eagle's beak, wings and claws—made a savage, magnificent display. Ripping at the grass with razor talons, shaking feathers and arching necks like prized fighting cocks, the lithe monsters trotted out into the open ground between the waiting armies.

Coming forward to meet the Sumbrian messengers, Colletro's heralds were mounted on matched palomino beasts of their own; a most noble display. Behind the Sumbrian battle lines, the twelve horsemen watched the heralds primp and pose, viewing the whole process with professional disdain as each team cried out the pedigrees of its armies' commanders and their lists of victories. Finally the competing heralds struck their staves, signaling that parley had begun. From the Colletran lines there came a ripple of relief, with many glances toward the impressive Sumbrian cavalry. Both teams of heralds turned about and drifted back to their own battle lines, content that the peace negotiations were well and truly begun.

Sumbria's golden rider slowly levered up the visor of his helm. Within the shadows gleamed a stern, pale face framed by a close-trimmed beard. Forever calculating odds and possibilities, Cappa Mannicci, the prince of Sumbria, swiveled to gaze at his Blade Council.

"They will deal."

"My lord?" A rider in silver steel turned his helm toward the prince.

"We hold the high ground; our cavalry are better mounted. Colletro will deal." Prince Mannicci signaled with his mace, and servants drew forward bearing maps of the contested valley lands. "We can press for a minor gain—three villages and the southern mines."

"And the Sun Gem, Lord?"

"Yes indeed." The pride of the Blade Kingdoms would at last come to a fitting home! Prince Mannicci settled his battle-mace upon his thigh. "The Sun Gem shall finally pass into Sumbrian care."

The Blade Kingdoms were a military society; it was their strength, and also their strangest quirk. Each Blade Captain gained votes within the council according to the strength of his own regiments. The loss of military personnel was therefore frowned upon, since it changed the internal balance of power. Far better for men of education to fight through maneuver and deceit. Colletro had been manipulated into a poor position; rather than risk a lost battle, her generals would of necessity offer a concession and withdraw.

Peaceful war; once again, intellect would triumph over passion.

An argument in the Colletran lines drew Prince Mannicci's attention. The Colletran counsellors had gathered in anger about a single squat, gnarled figure—a man dressed in jet black armor and mounted on a black hippogriff that hacked and gouged angrily at the turf. Rather than send their negotiators forward, the Colletrans had frozen in confusion while their generals battled like a pack of snarling wolves.

Colletro's prince slashed out with a hand, ordering silence, and rode on. In reply, the black warrior spurred forward to block his leader's way. Their anger rose in volume until it could be heard clear over in the Sumbrian lines.

Sitting poised upon the edges of the battlefield, Mannicci scowled as he viewed the antics of his foes.

"Why must he forever act the buffoon?"

"My lord?"

"The imbecile in black! Ugo Svarézi." Sumbria's prince let his horse stamp down hard and slash its tail knifelike through the air. "Does he think our battle host will wait upon his pleasure through the day?"

Blade Captain Gilberto Ilégo spurred slowly toward his prince. The man wore armor of venomous green; his horse bore a matching harness, and had a hide of an eerie copper hue. Ilégo's visor glittered like a vulture's beak as it turned to meet the prince's eyes.

"General Svarézi urges the Colletran prince to fight us . . . my lord."

"Does he indeed?" Grown cool and crisp with sheer dislike, Mannicci ignored his new companion and turned toward his army's signal corps. "Svarézi has interfered in the affairs of state once too often. Sound trumpets! They have ten minutes to parley, or else we shall, regretfully, attack!"

Heralds curbed rebellious mounts, then sent a trumpet fanfare pealing through the skies. In the Colletran army, heads jerked up at the sudden noise. Colletro's prince disengaged himself from his furious counsellor, signed angrily for his heralds, and shouldered his horse forward through a sea of his own crossbowmen.

Prince Mannicci curtly signaled for his own heralds once again. His sharp eyes flicked a glance at the green-armored figure at his side.

"You may return to the ranks, Blade Captain Ilégo. I shall bring Colletro's offer to the council anon."

Ilégo swept up his visor with a smooth wave of his hand. Beneath the green metal mask, a narrow face gazed at his prince with a jackal's hungry eyes.

"Then we may declare the season's campaign at an end, my lord! Another brilliant victory for Sumbrian arms—and for your own generalship, of course." Ilégo's words, like his armor, were pure polished venom. The copper-green horse edged slightly forward as he spoke. "A reputation I am sure you will see fit to build upon."

"That the entire state may build upon." Prince Mannicci locked his helmet into a chill gaze at Ilégo's face. "A unified state, Ilégo, as I am sure your votes will continue to reflect."

"Certainly, my lord. Unlike many, I lack private family affairs that might distract me from the business of the state." The serpent gave a smile. "But then a daughter's wedding can be such a time-consuming thing . . ."

By way of reply, Prince Mannicci merely jerked his clamshell gauntlets tight. A Prince of the Blade Kingdoms— the master of three thousand swords—had nothing if he lacked his dignity.

Gilberto Ilégo, Blade Captain of Sumbria and lord of a mere two thousand swords, coolly ignored the dismissal and turned to gaze upon the narrow pass back through the mountains.

"If you wish, my lord, I can prepare the orders for our withdrawal? Perhaps my own contingent should remain as rear guard?" Ilégo's dark eyes framed themselves into a mask of genteel concern. "Surely it would facilitate your swift return to the city?"

Mannicci closed his visor with a crash of steel and coldly jerked a faceless glare at his counsellor.

"A prince is first to enter the battlefield, and last to leave it." A mace reached out to prod against Ilégo's armored breast. "Your own troops may lead the withdrawal, Ilégo; at the fore, where they belong."

Trumpets signaled the parley's opening. Prince Mannicci raked back with his spurs and sent his mount hammering across the field, sparks flying from its burnished hooves as it threw its mass of flesh and metal through the air.

Left to his own devices, Ilégo deliberately brushed his visor down until the steel locked tight. Turning his back upon prince and enemy alike, he drifted back into a forest of pikes and slowly disappeared from view.

* * * * *

"Kill them! Now, while their captains stand exposed!" Ugo Svarézi, Blade Captain of Colletro, roared in incoherent rage. "Do you fear Sumbrian steel? Charge! Charge and bring us victory!"

The captain almost foamed in anger. Beneath him, his svelte black hippogriff hissed in a dark rage of her own, seething with pent-up hate as she felt her master's spurs. The creature took an experimental lunge at a war-horse's withers, sending its victim caracolling in alarm.

"Svarézi! Control yourself. Control your beast!" Colletro's Prince Ricardo sat stiff as a wooden doll atop his gleaming silver stallion. "This is a time for wits, and not for bloodshed!"

"Then use your wits! Charge them before the army loses heart!"

"You are not our warlord yet, Svarézi." Prince Ricardo glared down a long, aristocratic nose at the other man. "I remind you that the council voted *not* to accept you as our Grand Captain of Arms!"

Colletro's dense-packed ranks of soldiers made a black ocean about their prince; hearing his words, a surge of anger washed through them like a tempest on a bitter sea. Prince Ricardo jerked at his reins, ignoring the currents crashing hard about him, and spurred hard at his horse.

"We are aware of your disappointments, Svarézi." The prince bartered insubstantial baubles with a wave of his hand. "Sumbria will want to seal a peace. I shall bespeak the hand of Mannicci's daughter for you. A princess in your bed will be acceptable to us all."

The prize of a princess would bring power to Svarézi's hands; more gold, more votes. His face sheathed within a wine-dark helmet, Svarézi glared at his prince through eyes grown black with hate.

"I will take her, and then we shall vote again, my lord. Colletro needs a Captain General. It is time Colletro ceased playing games with war."

The prince rode away without deigning to answer. Svarézi watched him go, while underneath him, the hippogriff shook out her black feathers in a venomous dance of rage.

Young cavalry commanders clustered about Svarézi; plain men in plain armor, who kept themselves well distanced from Colletro's golden courtiers. Soldiers gathered closer as one officer wrenched open his visor and rode closer to his lord.

"Captain, will a marriage bring you into command?"

"It will give me my command. It will hasten us to a new age of war."

Blade Captain Svarézi curbed his hissing mount and stalked her back into the crowd.

"And if not—then there are other ways to seize an army. One way or another, you shall have your victory."

Followed by an ebb of silent soldiers, Svarézi rode back into the ranks.

Standing his horse on open ground, Colletro's Prince Ricardo glared back at Svarézi and discarded all thought of mere promises. Svarézi's lust for power was an appetite best left unfed. The prince gathered up his reins, left all thoughts of betrothals lying just where they belonged, and rode slowly forward to the grim business of the day.

2

"Miliana?

"Miliaaaa-*naaaaaa!*"

The last syllable stabbed through Sumbria's palace like an ice pick gouging through an eardrum. Propelled by feminine lungs strengthened by untold years of gossip and complaint, the summons pealed out through the corridors and palace towers until it set the chandeliers shivering like autumn leaves.

"Miliaaaa-naaaaaa!

"Miliana! Where are you, child? In the names of all the gods, will you just learn to simply answer when you are called?"

Locked up in the third story of the palace's most obscure and ill-regarded tower, Princess Miliana Mannicci Da Sumbria heard the summons and went into an instant frenzy of activity. Slim, dusted with freckles and half hidden behind a vast pair of owlish, expensive spectacles, the girl whipped through page after page of a great, ill-smelling book inscribed on toad skin. She desperately searched for the phrases of a spell—a process hampered by the fact that her rubbery book had been written in a language that she could scarcely understand. The fact that the author had barely understood the language either simply served to make the whole process as chaotic as imaginable. Miliana hastily scanned for key words, cramming bookmarks into pages that she hoped to study in greater detail later on.

"Miliana? Miliana! Pray, do not make me walk all the way up these accursed stairs!"

A lady of the Blade Kingdoms—a real lady, complete with demure expression, flowing gown, and tall pointy hat—most decidedly did not dabble in magic. And although Miliana's expression was more often irritable than demure, and though her gowns were somewhat more ink-spattered than fashion allowed, she admittedly did have a *very* pointy hat. The heavens only knew what would happen if her assorted guardians, tutors and watchdogs found out that she had ambitions for a mere craft such as magic; some vague, horrid punishment involving pruning onions or tending the sick. Miliana avoided the awful prospect of ever finding out by keeping her studies safely hidden, deep inside her lair.

Miliana's secret hoard of spellbooks had been found while digging about in a moldy old crypt in the rose gardens; each volume now had beautiful hand-stitched covers proclaiming them to be parts one through five of *Lady Faveretti's Cookery Handbook for Erudite Young Girls (with an appendix on Poisoning for Beginners)*. Only the eerie fishy smell remained—a stench Miliana blamed on the nesting cormorants in the eaves of her tower.

After three solid years of practice, Miliana had still not yet managed to master a single sorcerous skill. The palace was continually beset with odd little accidents that she had thus far managed to explain away—although the recent fire in the west wing had stretched her powers of misdirection to their utter limit.

Three years of study! And now, finally, at the very moment of breakthrough, the very instant of casting her first spell, her idiotic stepmother had chosen to come lumbering up the tower stairs! Miliana searched for the badly scrawled syllables she needed, her freckles rippling as she screwed up her face in furious concentration.

"Miliana? Miliana—I am coming up!"

Damn! Dressed only in a silken shift, a chemise, three petticoats and a pair of fluffy slippers, Miliana scuttled crabwise about her desk, trying to dress herself while keeping her eyes riveted on her books. Sparing a quick glance for the door, Miliana hopped up and down on one foot and tried to draw a stocking up her leg while reading her spellbook upside down. She tied the stocking into place with a silken ribbon, holding one end of the bow between her teeth as she contorted herself like a mad *fakir* across her cluttered desk.

Although being a princess locked within a tower had a certain romantic charm, the locks in this case were all fastened from the inside, rather than from without. Even with a double drop-bar, the security was not enough; the tower door shuddered to a massive blow as an operatic female voice rose to a pitch of outrage just outside.

"Miliana! Miliana, open this door at once! I have never seen a child so willful, so incorrigible, and so ungrateful! Miliana? Miliana—this is beyond belief!"

Ulia Mannicci—fondly referred to as "The Hammer of the Gods" by half the Sumbrian court—had finally reached Miliana's lair. Speaking with a stepmother's authority, she shook and pounded imperiously at Miliana's door.

"Miliana? Miliana—I know you're in there! I am giving you until the count of ten, and then I shall fetch a wizard to knock this door down!" Ulia's voice warbled onward with scarcely a pause for breath. "I shall knock it down— and you shan't be allowed to have another! We shall send you to finishing school where you belong!

"I'm counting! I am counting—I swear!

"One . . . !"

Miliana spat out a curse and jammed a plain blue gown across her freckled limbs. Adjusting her lenses, she suddenly spied the spell she had been searching for—the perfect thing to grace a palace ball! Frozen to the spot, Miliana laced her bodice about her scrawny ribs and read the spell icons in breathless fascination.

"Eight . . . ! Nine . . . ! Nine and a half!"

With a groan of frustration, Miliana closed her eyes, tried to fix the spell in her mind's eye, and then buried the spellbook beneath sheet music and half finished embroideries. The girl hastily splashed her face with hot water from the kettle, threw yet more water on the tiles and artfully tossed towels across every chair-back in line of sight. As her stepmother's count reached nine and eleven sixteenths—and since further fractions were well beyond Lady Ulia's intellectual capacity—Miliana flung herself to the door, somehow kicking her fluffy slippers out of sight. She ripped aside two iron bolts, a padlock and three security chains, then heaved open the door and assumed a mask of absolute, innocent surprise.

"Why Ulia! Dear Ulia—why ever didn't you knock?"

Lady Ulia Mannicci, wife of Prince Cappa Mannicci, stepmother to Miliana, and First Lady of Sumbria, sailed into the room like a gilded pleasure barge. Dressed in half an acre of silks and proceeded by a shock-front of perfumes, Lady Ulia bore her stepdaughter aside and made a stately royal progress about Miliana's rooms.

"Miliana! Miliana, what in the world are you doing sitting here like a haundar in its lair when there are visitors to be entertained?" Fanning at her face and exhausted by her journey up two whole flights of stairs, Lady Ulia heaved her mountainous bosom and tried to catch her breath. "I must say—in my youth, such things simply were not done! The daughter of a noble house—a Blade House, a princely house, and an ancient house at that—took her duties seriously! To think what would happen to this palace if the worst ever overcame me! Disaster! *Disaster!*" A silk fan stirred up a wild, perfume-sodden breeze. "Have you not a thought for your poor stepmother's peace of mind?"

Braced against a wall to weather the onslaught of Ulia's self-pity, Miliana heaved a tired breath and pushed

out into the room. An irritating stepmother seemed to be
an integral part of the "princess" lifestyle; Miliana wearily prepared to keep the peace.

"I *am* getting ready for the party! I was in the bath."

"The bath? The bath!" Ulia surged forward in a tidal
wave of indignation. "Bathing will avail you no advantages, my girl! I have it on good authority that water
against the skin introduces rude humors into the bloodstream!"

Princess Miliana—perhaps the best example of rude
humor in the kingdom—stabbed a surly glance at her
stepmother's back and muttered seething curses under
her breath. Had Miliana's skill at magic been a thou-
sandth the equal of her temperament, Ulia Mannicci
would have immediately ended up as a startling new
design splayed across the apartment walls. Instead, the
huge woman shifted the ponderous bulk of her case-hardened corsets and wheeled about to face her scowling,
scrawny little ward.

"Every gargoyle on the roof-ridge has broken clean in
two! Would you believe it? Would you believe it? Thieves on
the loose, my emeralds stolen, half the army looking for stable space, and I don't know what all these spurs are doing
to my carpets!" Ulia Mannicci zoomed about the room with
her skirts stirring like a restless jellyfish; never once did
she pause for breath or cease roving her eyes across the
room. "Now do get ready for the palace ball, there's a dear!
Your father's fanfare is just about to be rung!"

Miliana's *toilette* was essentially simple; she ran a
comb through her great streams of long brown hair and
polished up her spectacles; a sparrow perfectly happy
with her simple plumage. The girl tugged her bodice
straight, hid the ink stains on the elbow of her gown, and
clapped her favorite hat upon her head.

Stepmother Ulia watched the entire process with an
exasperated frown.

"Don't you have a pointier hat than that, dear? We *do*
have company."

Unhappy with her stepdaughter's grooming, Ulia began to tug and wrench at the poor girl's clothing. Miliana suffered it with ill grace, muttering and cursing silently under her breath.

Miliana never ceased to be an embarrassment and a mystery to Lady Ulia. In Ulia's day, young women had taken pride in their appearance; they had rehearsed the social graces, flirtation, wit and repartee with an intensity that put the martial arts schools of the Do Jang monks of Koryo to shame. They had been flowers fit to grace the most discriminating court. Miliana, on the other hand, seemed more of a nettle than a flower—a speckled sprat of a thing with far more spleen than was good for her. For three years, Ulia had tried to teach the child the elements of courtly grace; her stepdaughter's lack of progress was apparently due to a complete vagueness and an utter misunderstanding of the *real* ways of the world. Nevertheless, Lady Ulia persevered; after all, a peacock was merely a pigeon with the right feathers added to its tail.

"Very well, Miliana my dear, it is time we were on our way." Miliana's hat seemed at least six inches too short to meet the latest fashion. Despite the girl's protests, Lady Ulia plucked it from her head and tossed the thing away. A replacement was soon discovered lurking about at the bottom of a cupboard—a golden cone fully three feet high. Ulia advanced upon her stepdaughter holding out the hat; Miliana retreated away with revulsion gleaming in her eyes.

"I don't want it! I'll wear the other one!"

"The other one simply won't do, Miliana! A princess should excel all other ladies in grandeur."

"I don't want it!" Miliana glared at the ridiculous hat with a scowl. "It knocks against the chandeliers!"

"Now don't be silly! Just put it on and please your mother."

Ulia was *not* Miliana's mother—a fact which Miliana growled, *sotto vocce,* as she took hold of the ridiculous hat. She found herself swung helplessly around and deposited before a mirror as her new hat was firmly jammed down into place.

"There! Now that's better!" Ulia beamed a smile of pure, brainless satisfaction. "How on Toril do you plan to catch any of those nice young noblemen if you don't wear a pointy hat?"

Miliana could think of several ways of catching the aforementioned noblemen—techniques mostly involving nooses, spring-steel jaws, or pits lined with spikes. One fine, slim eyebrow lifted as suspicion lit her eyes.

"What noblemen?"

Ulia beamed a smile which spoke of a great, majestic sweep of dreams finally rushing to conclusion.

"A betrothal, my dear! Your father has arranged a new betrothal—and he shall be here tonight! If the young gentleman approves of you, then the match is made!"

Miliana had thus far been betrothed at least three times. Her advantages included a cute snub nose, a sharp wit, and sole heirship to the votes owned by Prince Mannicci—meaning that potential fiancés were never in short supply.

Their plagiarized poetry, feigned sobs and sighs availed them nothing. Miliana had sent her suitors packing through the use of a rare combination of deviousness and malice; it was marvelous what a well-placed bucket of earwigs could achieve. A husband would curtail Miliana's plans to become a sorceress. A husband meant a mundane fate, and an end to Miliana's passionate little dreams. Miliana tugged her clothing straight like a warrior checking his armor straps before a battle, planning her counterattack, as Lady Ulia went into raptures behind her.

"He's from dear, peaceful little Lomatra, and from a very good family! The Utrelli clan, no less. They have votes on Lomatra's Blade Council—oh, and when you're married, it will give us all access to some marvelous little vineyards!"

The marriage would also give Prince Mannicci the ability to control votes within Lomatra's Blade Council—or better still, would allow him to syphon troops from Lomatra to swell his ranks (and votes) at home. Miliana's father played a subtle game, forever struggling to edge Ilégo and his cronies out of power.

Disposing of a new suitor meant an evening of tedium. Hours of study lost, and all for nothing! With an ill-tempered growl, Miliana hitched up her hems and stomped down from her little tower.

The palace halls buzzed and bustled like a broken hive of bees, spilling multicolored servants all about the tiles. Miliana's passage was marked only by a cloud of palpable ill temper, a stream of muttered profanities, and the passage of her pointy golden hat.

Behind her, Lady Ulia Mannicci continued the monologue of her woes; it seemed that battles fought and battles won were of a minor consideration compared to bunions, the rising price of beauty potions, and the sudden disappearances of gems.

A broad promenade led past half-finished frescoes of battles, quest, and siege, finally leading down to the Mannicci family ballroom. Lady Ulia collared her stepdaughter at the doors and twirled her around in a final diligent inspection.

"Now remember: simper, be feminine, and above all, be polite! And must you always wear those wretched things on your face?" Lady Ulia removed Miliana's spectacles, leaving the young girl blinking myopically, like a freshly unearthed mole. Ulia watched for a moment, gave a sniff, and replaced the girl's spectacles on her nose. Miliana quietly removed them and polished off the greasy finger stains Ulia had left on the glass.

Ignoring Miliana's activities, Lady Ulia posed herself before the ballroom doors and puffed out her already considerable chest.

"We are about to enter. Now do behave properly this time. We have high hopes that the Lomatrans will accept this engagement. Just remember who and where you are!"

Ulia paused, scowled at Miliana's face, then laboriously licked a handkerchief and scrubbed at an imagined spot on Miliana's cheek. The princess gagged in revulsion, helpless as a bug in her stepmother's claws.

"There! Now Miliana, my dear—we shall do the best with you as we may." Plucking at the stays of Miliana's gown, her stepmother helpfully bolstered the girl's bustline by stuffing it with her own damp handkerchief. "And remember—a happy smile is a window upon a soul filled with eternal sunshine!"

Miliana hissed beneath her breath, straightened her back, and then produced a great, false, sweet smile for her beaming stepmother. Thankfully the silver panes of her spectacles hid the fury seething in her eyes. Wiggling her posterior in the manner approved by matchmaking stepmothers, the girl turned about, dropped her smile, and lunged off out of sight between a pair of potted palms.

Her escape ploy served her little good; assorted predators marked her by the towering height of her conical hat and veil, and soon the chase was on.

* * * * *

Consider a room:

A large room—open, vast and airy. A place of white colonnades and barrel-vaults, where the ceiling had been painted with cherubim and seraphim, and where the polished floor had been spread with chalk to give purchase to a dancer's feet. A place as elegant and as tasteful as centuries of refinement could allow.

Despite the restrained tastefulness of the architecture, the palace ballroom now smote the eye like a multicolored claw hammer. Hundreds of celebrants packed the colonnades and floors—nobility decked out in eyewrenching, tasteless splendor. Slashed tunics, tight hose, and loose-laced doublets adorned the strutting men, while the women cruised beneath headdresses adorned with points, turbans, battlements and horns. Music swelled and fine wines poured, as the culture of the self-obsessed luxuriated in a glorious afternoon.

The Manniccis' palace looked out across fields of grape

vines and olive groves, upon a land of rolling hills and gentle ochre-colored dust. Within the halls they had laid tables heaped with the choicest foods, serviced and maintained by waiters who were the very essence of magnificent disdain.

On the dance floor, half a hundred brilliantly clad men and women turned and stepped to the intricate measures of an arrogant *pavane*. The dancers seemed to be split evenly between demure artistes and strutting, posing figures who swung briskly back and forth to slash the other dancers with their swinging capes and sleeves.

Above the dancers, a dense crowd had converged—the elderly, the pompous, the wealthy and elite. Sumbria's Blade Captains each boasted a palace of his own—a palace well stuffed with wives and daughters, dowagers and sons, all of whom now claimed a place at the Manniccis' victory ball. Soldiers who had returned home from the wars each formed the center of a small admiring crowd; here and there a man still wore an armored gorget or kept his arm inside a sling, artfully attracting the attention of the ladies in the hall.

Hovering beside a table strewn with orange rinds, roast ostriches, and singing fish, a thin, rather unhappy young man hovered in the shadows and played with his nails. Tall and forlorn, with unfashionably long, straggling hair and a court costume smelling of mothballs, the youth clutched a leather folder to his breast and watched the festival sweep dizzily past his eyes.

Hanging between two of Sumbria's "young blades," a brash young nobleman spied the youth and veered over to his side. Helping himself to a chilled bottle of wine, the newcomer thrust drink into his companion's hand.

"Lorenzo! Lorenzo, you look like a landed fish. Dance and drink—lie to women and flash your blade!" The noble clapped a hand against his dress sword—a silly toy that would have scarcely tickled a mouse—and clung to his companion in an unsteady daze. "We are an embassy! And an ambassador must make an impression—an impression of strength."

Lorenzo saved his folder from splashing wine as his friend collapsed into a velvet-covered chair and planted his boots between the eyes of a roasted ostrich.

Lorenzo Utrelli, scion of the Blade Kingdom of Lomatra and a visitor to Sumbria's court, stared at his friend with outrage and surprise.

"Luccio! Luccio—you're drunk."

"Drunk as a . . . as an animal that drinks a lot. Indeed! Indeed." Lorenzo's friend poured himself more Sumbrian wine, managing to come quite close to actually putting wine inside his glass. "I have been fostering diplomatic goodwill."

"Luccio, if the ambassador finds you, we're both dead!" Wrenching the drunk out of sight behind a platter of stuffed hamsters in sauce, Lorenzo unsuccessfully tried to draw his friend erect. "Look—brace up! Breathe deeply or something."

"Lorenzo, Lorenzo, Lorenzo!"

Luccio swung his friend about by the shoulders and led the nervous youth back out toward the dance floor. "I'm the one in the middle, actually," Lorenzo muttered.

"Why is it? Why, why, *why* is it that you never, ever, ever have fun?" Luccio blew a drunken breath out between his mustache hairs and rolled his head to watch a stately, slender damsel wiggle past. "You are here upon a hunt, my boy! You have been offered the possibility of marrying a princess, and I . . ." Here, Luccio thumped his chest with one hand, splashing wine all across his clothes. "I am commanded to assist you upon the hunt!"

"I don't want a hunt, and I don't want a princess." Lorenzo's face fell into a scowl. "I am here to seek a haven from Lomatran . . . Lomatran . . . pedantry! Lomatran conservatism! Sumbria is a place where a scholar can breathe free."

"Then breathe, my child. Breathe!" Luccio managed to tip his glass and pour a stream of wine across the floor. "And as you breathe, think what difference an income—a *princess's* income—might make to your studies of the arts. As your boon companion, it is my duty to see you find the solaces of love."

"Love?" Lorenzo gave a sniff of scorn. "I don't even remember this princess creature's name!"

"There's no need to even ask, my boy. A princess can be spotted from a mile!"

Reeling his head back, Luccio gazed upside down across the dance floor and gave a sigh.

"Lorenzo—Sumbrian women! Have you seen them? Have you smelled them? They make our own girls seem like heifers in a barn!" He flipped open his friend's folder and prodded at a charcoal sketch scribbled on one page. "Sumbrian women! Now *there* is a subject fit for art. Find a model, my boy. Find a nude model if you can! Something brim full with enigma and charm."

Lomatra sought Sumbria as a military ally—a fact that made every devout bachelor in Lomatra's nobility feel intensely nervous. Lorenzo, scion of a noble house, was young, unmarried, and available; assets, the ambassador assured him, which made him an ideal match.

Ideal or not, Lorenzo would see to it that this lunacy went no further. He had been lured to Sumbria on false pretenses, but now that he had arrived, he would use the opportunity to its full. The libraries and schools of the city beckoned; Lorenzo's freedom had finally arrived!

Sumbrian women were everywhere—tall, stately, and threatening. Any one of them might be a predatory princess. Lorenzo flicked his eyes across the room like a rabbit scanning from its burrow for a sight of hunting hounds, and clutched his art folio protectively against his breast.

Women turned in his direction, obviously scanning for prey. Sinking into the darkness of an alcove, Lorenzo hastily retreated backward around a potted palm, and suddenly felt something soft collide against his rear.

"*Ouch!* Fool!"

A girl spilled to the floor, plunging through potted plants with a deafening crash of noise. She landed hard on her backside amidst a staring crowd of Sumbrian noblemen.

"Oaf!"

"Sorry! Oh—um—sorry."

Lorenzo tried to help the girl to rise, only to have his hands slapped irritably away. Snarling curses as she rubbed at her injured backside, the girl rose with a ripple of long brown hair. Shoving her tall hat back into place, she whipped about and spared Lorenzo a sharp stab of a glance through a great round pair of thick glass lenses.

All around the dance floor, heads began to turn. The girl seemed to draw stares like sha'az eggs drew hauns. Male dancers paused in midstep, abandoned their partners and advanced upon the girl. Other men tugged tunics straight or puffed themselves with perfume before launching into the attack. Lorenzo blinked and stared as the girl retreated back into a corner, pursued by every young buck within a hundred yards.

She retreated, leaving Lorenzo to stare dumbly after her in shock.

Eyes. The girl had the most astonishing hazel eyes!

Lorenzo dove back into the alcove. Snatching Luccio by the chin and swiveling his friend's head around, he tried to bid Luccio to stare after the girl.

"Who, Luccio . . . who under the stars is that?"

"Who cares, my friend? Who cares! We are in Sumbria— free from woes!" Luccio swung out an arm, accidentally showering passersby with wine. "Why go for a maid, when you shall have a princess?"

Long, thin, blond, and dressed in well-patched finery, Lorenzo's friend Luccio trapped the young artist under his arm.

"A princess for my friend Lorenzo!" Luccio diligently poured himself more wine, never once noticing that he had an empty bottle. "She will be blonde and fair of visage, as princesses are wont to be—and she will also have either a curse, a prophecy, or a thing about unicorns; possibly all three."

"Really?"

"Oh, it goes with the territory." Luccio spoke with culture, conviction, and pure drunken tomfoolery. "I think the unicorn thing eventually wears off. However! They are remarkable creatures, and your mission, my lad, is to catch one; possibly more than one, if you have to toss a few back that may be undersized. I shall use my incomparable powers to seek out the object of your quest.

"Now *avant*! Onward—the hunt awaits!"

Snatching his hapless friend Lorenzo by the arm, Luccio dragged the boy off across the room. Lorenzo desperately strained for one last glance toward the short, slim girl in the golden hat, and then lost sight of her behind the swirling crowds.

* * * * *

Miliana's footsteps—little white marks made by feet which had flitted across the dance floor's chalk—left an interesting trail. She had fled behind columns, ducked through potted plants, and snuck behind the orchestra and illusionists. Finally, backed against a wall and pursued by half the air-headed young blades of Sumbria, Miliana was forced to turn at bay. To the left, Lady Ulia blocked any exit out into the palace halls, and although a plunge off the high balcony was preferable to meeting with the fawning, pompous sycophants who made up the list of Sumbria's eligible bachelors, Miliana felt loath to spatter herself all over the pavement and stain her favorite gown.

A dozen fiery young nobles advanced upon her, all visibly pulling on false masks of admiration, gaiety and love. As a group, they had little to recommend them except as fine examples of noble acne.

At long last, it was time for Miliana to show her fangs to the world. Turning her back on the pursuit, Miliana licked her lips, closed her eyes and framed the concepts of her carefully rehearsed magic spell. She felt a ripple of force pass clean up through her body from her toes—a jolt powerful enough to knock her pointy hat awry.

Smiling, freckled and petite, she turned to face the noblemen—and was instantly rewarded by a look of pure terror in their eyes.

Cantrips were simple aids to social grace; they could add a sparkle to the eye or a ring to the voice at just the perfect time of need. Miliana's version of the basic spell was truly an awesome thing; as she turned a suddenly carnivorous, fang-crammed smile upon the crowd, men suddenly remembered previous appointments, heard their mothers calling, or took instant vows of chastity.

So much for Lomatran weddings! Miliana had cleared the hall in an instant. Thrilled by the success of her first real spell, Miliana reveled in their reactions like a cat rolling in a bath of cream. She stalked after her frenzied prey, sucking in a delicious breath of victory.

Triumph at last! The age of Miliana the sorceress was finally at hand! Miliana Mannicci, bespectacled princess of Sumbria, tilted her pointy hat down across her eyes and faced the world with a predatory sigh.

Feeling herself in charge of her own destiny at last, the girl took up a glass of wine, found a quiet balcony, and leaned upon the railing to gaze out at the gently rolling foothills of the Akanapeaks.

* * * * *

"All hail! All hail and salute! Meet we now as the commanders of the Grand Company of Sumbria. Let those who share in our enterprise approach!"

Twenty swords were drawn; twenty swords were raised, clashed, and then lowered down onto a table made of purest ebony. The steel blades struck brilliant sparks of light as they crashed across a tabletop vandalized by a hundred years of such abuse.

The Blade Captains of Sumbria, commanders of cavalry, hippogriffs, and battle sorcerers, stood behind their seats as the current tally of shares were read. The valley campaign had caused no voting adjustments. With a nod to the accountant-general, Cappa Mannicci settled into his chair and hammered thrice upon the scarred old table.

"By the power invested in me by the company's Articles of Association, as Grand Commander and Prince-elect of Sumbria I declare this meeting opened."

"So noted."

The second came from farther down the table, and the two-hundred-and-forty-first meeting of Sumbria's ruling body had begun.

With his three thousand blades, Prince Mannicci ruled Sumbria's council. In some kingdoms, such as Lomatra, the councils elected the weakest of their number as their prince, knowing the council's votes could overrule his decrees. In other states, a single family held troops enough to dominate the entire balance of power. Here in Sumbria, the balance remained more delicate; the Mannicci family could not quite hold power on its own. The prince needed the support of other houses, who ebbed and flowed into voting blocks as various needs arose.

Senior among those voting blocks were the nobles allied to Blade Captain Ilégo. Unable to wrest the crown from Mannicci's hands, Ilégo instead managed to act as a thorn in his prince's side.

And so, Mannicci schemed. The bride-price paid for his daughter's hand would be taken in trained soldiers, not in gold; votes enough to give sudden iron to his reign.

Outside the room, the tinkling music of the victory ball could be faintly heard. Squaring thick yellow papers against the table, the prince briskly consulted his agenda.

"Gentlemen, our first business: the campaign spoils. Twelve blade companies were deployed into active service. I propose a standard division, with double shares for the active contingents, and single shares for companies remaining in the city for garrison. How does it please?"

At the far end of the table, Ilégo—slim, lean, and calm—raised a hand to stroke at his mustache.

"The brunt of the fighting was borne by hippogriff squadrons. Surely we should indemnify those commanders who have lost fliers and breeding stock."

"A reasonable suggestion." Old Orlando Toporello,

heavy-handed captain of a thousand blades, leaned forward across the tabletop. "Reasonable, until we remember that Blade Captain Ilégo has the largest investment in these aerial novelties." The old man slammed a hand sharply down against the boards. "Let him feather his nest on someone else's profit, and not ours!"

"A word!" At the far end of the table, a noble raised his hand. "A word upon the subject of 'innovations.' I wish to query the continued and erroneous valuation of mere handgunners as the equivalent share-value as crossbowmen and pavisiers!"

An instant furor arose. The smoke powder contention had already been shelved a dozen times before. The proponents of the crossbow now rose to bellow at the top of their lungs as the firework enthusiasts matched them tirade for tirade. Cappa Mannicci heaved a sigh and hid beneath his papers as the heated debate flared into an outright brawl.

"Innovations are our life's blood! How can you not see the value . . ."

"An arquebus is a weapon for a fool! How are we profited by missiles that go only fifty paces range?"

"And within that fifty paces, they will pierce . . ."

"Pierce what? The cheeks of your bum?"

". . . they will pierce through the stoutest . . . !"

"Order! Order!"

A mace banging on the much-scarred tabletop had little effect; only a bellow from Mannicci's sergeants restored order to the melee. As a sudden silence fell, Sumbria's prince blew out a sigh through his mustache and tilted his mace-of-office toward another man.

"Blade Captain Zuro has the floor."

Not, perhaps, the best of choices; Zuro was scarcely a soldier at all, and devoted most of his days to collecting ancient knickknacks and refurbishing his library. Tall, white haired, and sporting a mustache almost six inches long, old Zuro puffed himself up like a rooster before his peers.

"Gentlemen, I think it would be a sad mistake were we

to dismiss smoke powder too lightly. A young man from
Lomatra whom I met outside, assures me that these . . .
'guns' are the future. In his sketchbook he carries some of
the most astonishing designs . . ."

"Good!" Orlando Toporello hammered both his palms
onto the table with a bang. "Then Lomatra's army will
play with firecrackers and twinkledust, and leave the sol-
diering to those who hold good, honest blades!"

As had happened a dozen times before, Prince Mannicci
forestalled the discussion.

"Remuneration of all campaign losses can be handled
from the common fund. All in favor? Good." The mace
banged quickly down before anyone had time to do more
than blink in sheer surprise. "Next item: the increase in
thievery and brigandage in the city. Please bid the com-
plainants enter."

Pleased at forestalling yet another argument, Cappa
Mannicci leaned back in his seat as sergeants opened up
the chamber doors.

The noise instantly increased a thousandfold. A piercing, operatic voice pealed forth its complaints as Prince
Mannicci's wife, the Lady Ulia, led a wedge of outraged
dames into the council room.

"It's a disgrace! An absolute disgrace! First emeralds,
and now pearls as well! It's no longer safe for a handsome
woman even to rest in her own bed!"

A clerk brought over the list of complaints—a parchment scroll so large it unrolled clear down to the floor. As
the women battled to be heard, so the debate about
smoke powder flared into life once more. Besieged on
every side and suffering from a migraine which pierced
him clean from ear to ear, Prince Mannicci rested his
head in his hands and prepared himself for a long and
tiresome day.

3

"Right! You ten men—keep half on patrol and half in the guardhouse. Check your trip wires regular, and watch out for the glue powder spread atop the battlements!" The crossbow sergeant leaned out across the high, dry battlements of the Toporello family palace—a lavish blockhouse topped by towers, roof gardens, and airy balustrades. Night had fallen once again across the city of Sumbria, and once again the streets would see the forces of law and order pitted against this new wave of thievery.

A cat burglar held the city in a reign of terror. Night after night the demon had struck, robbing the palaces and town houses of their very choicest jewels. The streets were trebly patrolled, walls were garrisoned, and the price of watchdogs had quintupled in a week. And yet still the villain managed to pursue his evil trade.

House Toporello readied itself for the onslaught. Home to an antique horse bridle studded with star sapphires, the mansion offered an almost irresistible prize. Old Orlando therefore crowned his battlements with soldiers and filled his courtyards with half-starved hounds. A hippogriff and rider perched upon the rooftops, while cunning traps were laid crisscrossed through every room and hall. Orlando Toporello, his family and friends, thus all turned to their beds and slept in peace—apart from the occasional sounds of the cleaning staff running afoul of deadfall traps, crossbow bolts, and blades.

A trip to the privies in the dead of night was more than a body's life was worth. . . .

Now, with midnight having come and gone, the guards were being changed. Satisfied with his arrangements, the guard sergeant stared down into the empty streets, flicked his glance up to the hippogriff roosting high above, and marched back toward the kitchens for a meal of chicken pie.

Time passed, and the night grew painfully still, leaving the guards gazing blankly out across an empty world. Far below, the sound of marching boots echoed back and forth between tall city walls.

And high above the battlements, up at the very ridge-pole of the roof, a tiny sound drifted in the breeze. . . .

Creeping slowly about the corner of the roof came first a great razor beak, then a silly nod of plumes followed by a single yellow eye. The firebird's face peered from cover with exaggerated cunning, rolling eyeballs left and right before wiggling his brows in glee.

The soldiers walked their beats, keeping their eyes scanning the streets below. Upon a pepperbox turret far overhead, a hippogriff dozed with its eagle-head beneath one wing while its rider diligently searched the upper skies. Infinitely pleased with his own endless cleverness, the firebird fixed his beak in an idiotic grin.

The best sparklies—the very, very brightest and the shiniest of things—came from places where many people stood on guard! With great, mincing steps, the firebird slipped out of hiding and began to creep his way along the crest of Orlando Toporello's roof. With each pace, the bird stretched his long neck this way and that, scanning cautiously about himself in a ludicrous pantomime of stealth.

The city was fun! Of all the discoveries of the bird's humdrum life, this had been the one moment of crowning glory. No more mountaintops, no more trees and fruit, and endless, dreary days. The bird had tasted a fabulous new world—a world so wonderful the creature almost couldn't help but sing!

The bird's name, Tekoriikii, meant many things to many beings. In the ancient language of his close cousin the phoenix, it translated as: "He who rises early, singing." Alternatively, in the various orcish dialects of the northern Akanapeaks, it had come to mean: "Stop that awful racket, you feather-bearing nuisance."

For generations untold, the firebirds had dwelled in peaceful seclusion across the Shining Sea. The creatures were never even bothered by predators. Some Chultan legends put this down to the extreme beauty of the birds, and the curse of the gods that must surely fall upon anyone who brought such flawless grace to harm. An alternative explanation might be that *hunting* requires *stalking*, and stalking meant staying in earshot of the firebirds for long days at a time. . . .

Perched on a roof gutter sixty feet above the ground, plumed like a mad woman's hat and utterly vibrant with glee, Tekoriikii sniggered to himself, fluffed out his great streaming tail and pranced gaily past the lines of patrolling soldiers just below. His long tail plumes dragged unnoticed behind a crossbowman's helm; men marching back and forth in armor never heard the clumsy click of talons up above.

Like most Blade Kingdom palaces, the Toporello residence was constructed as a hollow square. Inevitably enough, Toporello's guards were facing outward, scanning the surrounding streets, leaving Tekoriikii free to walk the inner courtyard roofs. Tekoriikii slid down the copper roofing on his feathered rear and landed with a thump against the palace gutters. Strutting like a gamecock, the firebird came to an apartment window, and swung his neck across the wall to peer in through the window upside down.

In a bed the size of a desert isle, a muscular old man snored boisterously in his sleep. Crushed against his chest there lay a wooden box—a box locked with triple locks and painted with every death-glyph known to the sorcerer's art.

Palace roofs were most usually made of copper sheet all soldered shut with lead. Tekoriikii scuttled busily back from the gutter, then simply pierced the sheet-metal roofing with his claws. Great yellow legs worked busily, peeling back the roof to open up a door into the ceiling space below; then, with a jump and a flourish of his plumes, the firebird disappeared into the hole.

Like most ornate buildings in the city, the Toporello home sported ceilings made of wooden boards covered over with fine plaster painted into a fantastic array of cherubs, satyrs, and woodland bowers. Wooden boards soon surrendered to Tekoriikii's eager claws, leaving only an inch-thick shell of plaster between the firebird and his prize. At any other time, the sheer volume of noise would have alerted half the kingdom; as it was, the manic *peck-peck-peck* of Tekoriikii's beak went unnoticed beneath the raucous notes of Orlando Toporello's snores.

In the middle of the ceiling, amidst a nest of painted plaster nymphs, a tiny hole began to appear. Falling chunks of plaster were caught on the great velvet canopy above Toporello's head, bouncing harmlessly as they struck home on the brocade. Finally, in a great cascade of rubble, dross and dust, the nymphs disintegrated into a thousand shards.

Dusted white with plaster, Tekoriikii's face blinked down into the room. He stuck his long neck down through the open hole; then, with a flap of ungainly wings, the firebird sailed twenty feet straight down onto the lurching canopy.

The four bedposts sagged under the weight of feathers, plaster, boards and bird. Bouncing happily up and down, Tekoriikii flopped his head across the rim and stared in rapture at the wooden box clasped in the old man's hands.

With a great puppy-shake of his head, Tekoriikii fluffed out his feathers; plaster dust instantly shot out into the air, filling the bedroom with a choking fog. Below the idiot bird, Blade Captain Toporello drowned beneath a swirling mist of white. The man gave an almighty sneeze—swiftly followed by another spasm so powerful it nearly catapulted him clean out of bed.

Clutching onto the mattress, the old man released his grip on his box of valuables. Striking like a well-greased cobra, Tekoriikii snatched the box in his great curved beak, then rose up into the air in a storm of dusty wings. Streaming his brilliant tail plumes in his wake, the bird clambered back into the ceiling space and out onto the palace roof.

Back in the bedroom, the chorus of snores went on. Covered with dust, splinters and the occasional chunk of plaster nymph, Blade Captain Toporello floundered his hands about the bed, finally striking a piece of broken ceiling board. With a broad smile of contentment, he hugged the piece of wood against his chest, heaved a dusty sigh and drifted deeper into sleep.

Outside the palace, Toporello's guards paced their beats, the hippogriff snored, and Tekoriikii the firebird sailed out into the nighttime skies like an ungainly kite without its string.

Winging past rooftops; past towers, broken gargoyles, and snoozing guards, the firebird flapped and rustled his way to his lair. In a tall white tower at the highest vantage of the city, clever Tekoriikii had made himself a home. The conical roof above the balconies and battlements had been deftly peeled away, and the whole glorious wide attic space now gave Tekoriikii a roost with a view. Backing air with his wings and sweeping the palace walls with his tail, the bird tumbled into his cozy hiding place and gave a grateful sigh.

The wooden box—his latest prize—was studded with runes designed to trigger instant, messy death once a thief raised up the lid. Knowing nothing of such formalities,

Tekoriikii simply bit through the bottom of the box, gasping in delight as a cascade of gems spilled into the room.

There were necklaces of moonstones, horse harnesses of star sapphires, and a pendant jingling with a dozen precious stones. The firebird tossed his prizes high into the air, beginning a delighted dance to celebrate his place as the most wonderful of birds. He stepped to the left, then stepped to the right, waggled tail and wings while bobbing his head to a self-invented tune. Puffed up and dizzy with his own startling cleverness, the firebird danced his dance around an ever-growing mound of sparkly things.

Night by night, the treasure trove grew. There were old silver mirrors and chips of glass, pretty rocks and banners stolen from patrolling guards. Best of all, there were now hundreds of brilliant, shiny gems that sparked like the hearts of stars before the firebird's eyes.

What bird could match Tekoriikii's brains? What female could resist his charms? Tekoriikii danced and danced, throwing back his head to swirl about in glee.

The sound of dancing claws went unnoticed in the world beyond.

*   *   *   *   *

In the room just below the firebird's hoard, a dull explosion lit up the night. The whole tower trembled to its very roots, and mortar spurted softly from the stones. Wheezing and gasping, Miliana Mannicci hurled open her shutters and coughed herself half to death, dragging off her pointy hat and fanning it back and forth across her eyes.

Halfway up a neighboring tower, a window shutter hurtled aside. Pealing through the darkness came a voice rich with feminine outrage.

"Miliaaaa-naaaaaa! Miliana, what was that awful noise?"

Scorched black and still suffering a bit from shock, Miliana blinked down into the night.

"It's . . . it's rats!"

"Rats?" Lady Ulia Mannicci stuck her head through a window and stared up at the girl in outrage. "It sounded like an explosion. How, pray, do rats manage to explode?"

"They've . . . um . . . been eating smoke powder!" Miliana noticed a small flame flickering at the tip of her pointy hat; she snatched off the offending headgear and hid it to her rear. "It's all right. I don't mind!"

"I have had quite enough of these fireworks and bangs!" Poised like an impending avalanche on her high balcony, Lady Ulia heaved an indignant breath which threatened to burst her flimsy night attire. "In my day, rats only ate fletching and such. We had none of this dangerous and expensive smoke powder—or exploding rodents—laying about back then!"

The shutter closed with a bang, and Miliana had the night sky to herself once more. Fuzzy slippers flopping on her feet, Miliana made her way back into her scorched bedroom and sat down wearily on a chair. Polishing her dusty spectacle lenses, she heaved a sigh, contemplated the results of her latest attempt at an affect normal fires spell, and wondered just exactly how she was going to clean up all the mess before dawn.

* * * * *

"Company! Open order—*march!*

One hundred boots slammed against the flagstones in unison, sending a violent echo rippling across the palace walls.

"Company! Stand pikes!"

Locked into open order, the Manniccis' pikemen grounded the butt ends of their weapons, braced the eighteen-foot shafts, and rested their free hands against their sword hilts in the accustomed style.

Mounted on a gigantic horse of dark burnt-bronze, Prince Cappa Mannicci watched the maneuver through cold, experienced eyes. The troops looked well; fit after a brisk campaign, and had already been issued new uniforms financed from the battle spoils. They were now clad in bright pied hose, one side candy-striped and the other side a brilliant green—the very height of fashionable good taste. Mannicci let his sharp gray-shot beard tilt left and right as he surveyed his men, then drew a breath of satisfaction. With a careless wave of his mace, he motioned his fellow Blade Captains forward to inspect the parade.

Fraudulent company rosters were as old as the mercenary's trade. To assure fellow captains of the value of one another's troops, Sumbria organized inspection parades. Each Blade Captain could settle for themselves any questions of troop strengths, training and equipment by putting their colleagues' units through their paces. Cappa Mannicci stood his horse in the shade of an olive tree and let his peers ride forth to have their fun.

The Mannicci troops formed a tiny army all their own. There were battle mages with their protective squads of apprentices and pavisiers, pikemen, hippogriffs, and crossbowmen in their droves. Billmen with their wickedly hooked blades, perfectly designed for unhorsing cavalry and deflecting pikes, marched to the fore. Prince Mannicci returned a salute from the golden, prancing lines of his own cavalry, then idly turned to watch his counsellors at play.

Fuming white with rage from some unimaginable wrong, Blade Captain Toporello watched the infantry march by and wrung his reins between his fists like a pair of chicken necks.

Prince Mannicci frowned; for parades, Toporello usually decked his horse out in a harness of star sapphires. The prince blinked at the older man's shabby leather horse trappings, scratched his beard, and decided to let the topic slide.

Passing behind a clean, gleaming squadron of hippogriff cuirassiers, Gilberto Ilégo swung his mount about to slide in beside the prince. Ilégo's horse curvetted prettily, allowing the bright morning sun to strike sparks along its copper mane.

"An impressive inspection, sire. Most enlightening."

Ilégo had hardly even spared the assembled troops a glance. He matched his horse's pace to that of his prince and posed himself in thought; an artful display designed to convey both elegance and surprise.

Mannicci ignored him, covering his hate by turning his face toward the lines of marching men. Ilégo smiled at the slight, taking perverse pleasure in swapping idle talk.

"Sire, I do believe that is your daughter on the balcony."

"Like enough." Mannicci scarcely cared enough to confirm it with a glance. "Her room is just above."

"Aaaaaah." Ilégo swiveled snake-bright eyes toward his prince. "A pretty girl, by all accounts."

"I'd like to see *whose* accounts. I'd like to hire him." Prince Mannicci stirred laggards from his baggage train with a prod of his mace. "He'd be inexpensive to keep; such a man would like his meat very plain."

"But surely, my lord, she has spirit?"

"In a sense," said Mannicci. In truth, he rarely bothered to think about his sole offspring's character. Spirit in a daughter was considered about as desirable as dorsal guidance feathers on a prize-winning merino ram. "I believe she is a quiet girl—though much troubled by rats."

"Rats, my lord?"

"So I am told."

Prince Mannicci had neither the time nor inclination to bother himself about his daughter. His first spouse had died young; Mannicci's choice of a second wife had done much to line his own coffers, but very little to increase his domestic bliss. He knew he really ought to beget himself a son; unfortunately, Ulia Mannicci was the finest contraceptive device known to the Blade Kingdoms.

At his side, Gilberto Ilégo turned his horse to face the palace balconies.

"You are hard on the girl. There are tales, my lord, of princesses whose beauty launched a thousand ships." Ilégo faced his monarch with a bow. "Perhaps your own daughter might aspire to such a thing in her own small way. "A thousand *troops*, perhaps?"

Prince Mannicci dug his heels down and halted his mighty horse, creasing the corners of his eyes as he let his mind explore the flavor of Ilégo's schemes.

A welcome diversion came in the form of a skinny youth dressed in the velvet finery of the royal court. The young man hovered nearby, wide eyed as a blushing beholder; he kept a leather portfolio clamped tight against his heart, as though he were using it to keep his internal organs from erupting out through his chest.

Prince Mannicci regarded the boy with a heavy frown; eye contact apparently won him a friend for life, and the youth instantly lunged forward and performed something that might possibly be mistaken for a bow.

"My lord! M-my lord prince." The boy almost choked himself on his own tongue as he hopelessly addled a carefully prepared speech. "Sir—I merely wished to say how . . . how invigorating your kingdom seems. How fresh, how inviting, how active!"

Insanity in a man so young seemed such a pitiable thing; Prince Mannicci leaned back in his saddle, cocking an ear toward Ilégo, who duly leaned forward to whisper quiet words.

"It is one of the young gentlemen from Lomatra, my lord."

"Oh. Oh, yes." Aha—the prospective groom! Mannicci felt a sudden surge of interest. "Lorenzo Utrelli, I presume?"

The boy took the prince's smile as instant encouragement.

"My lord? My lord, I wondered if I might speak with you awhile? That is—I wonder if I can show you . . ."

At this point, the leather portfolio flipped open; cramming the wad of papers into the bole of a tree, Lorenzo inserted himself between the two older men and proudly spread out a parchment smothered in designs.

"My lords—I have ideas! Concepts, theories and designs the likes of which the world has never seen. Designs that will thrill you, my lords. Thrill you to the core!"

Prince Mannicci, ever the diplomat, wearily prepared himself to be bored. In contrast, Blade Captain Ilégo stroked his mustache and cast an amused eye across the boy's diagrams.

"Say on, lad. Say on. It cannot be any less entertaining than the parade."

Finding himself with an audience at long last, Lorenzo seated himself in the crutch of an olive tree and used a green twig to point out the salient points of his inventions.

"Look you, sirs. I have been studying basic natural phenomena with an eye to making these phenomena work with us—for us." Paper fluttered as the boy avidly flicked through page after page of incomprehensible scrawls. "Ah! For instance . . . here—do you see? I have been experimenting with the forces that make solid objects fall."

A drawing appeared; a drawing showing a very badly rendered stick figure dropping objects from a tower. Lorenzo unleashed his excitement in measured little chunks, marking each point with a sharp wave of his olive twig.

"Now, consider the downward path of a falling object. Let us take two items identical in weight. A pound of feathers, and a pound of lead. Which of them will fall more slowly?"

"A pound of feathers." Mannicci suddenly found that he approved of the boy's logical mind—a reasonably desirable trait in a potential son-in-law. "What is your point?"

"Aaaah—but *why* do the feathers fall more slowly? The answer is, simply, air resistance! The feathers present a broad face to the air, thus slowing their descent due to the viscous qualities of the air itself."

Sitting cross-legged in his tree, Lorenzo made his points stab forward one by one.

"So, how is this phenomena useful to us? Well firstly, we have discovered that narrow objects fall more swiftly.

I feel this may be useful for making some sort of aerial dart, or what I call a 'bomb.' But, certainly more valuable than that, I believe I can now create a fall-breaking machine! A device made from cloth that will slow the speed of a man's descent through the air, allowing him to alight as safe as if he were a pixie."

This declaration was met by a confused silence from the two armored noblemen. Loath to break the lad's enthusiasm, Prince Mannicci nevertheless felt it behooved him to give the boy unkind news.

"But my dear—um . . ."

"Lorenzo, my lord. Lorenzo Utrelli Da Lomatra!"

"Yes, quite . . ." The boy had the innocent, doelike eyes of a pet fawn unaware that it was being massaged with marinade. Prince Mannicci heaved an unhappy little sigh. "Yet, you must ask yourself, Lorenzo, just why you feel such a device to be useful?"

"Think of it, my lord. We could use my fall-breakers as a safety device . . . say, for the riders of hippogriffs."

"But our hippogriff riders are already provided with magical protection for such a case." The prince indicated an overflying squadron with a pained wave of his mace. "A one-use ring of feather falling, in point of fact . . ."

"But at massive cost, my lord! Think of the savings offered by a mechanical device."

The lad's mechanical device seemed to require a huge amount of silk, a fact which rather negated any claims to cheap production. Lorenzo felt his audience's interest waver, and desperately flicked on to other plans.

"Wait, my lord! If the sciences of the air don't interest you, then perhaps the study of heat? Surely a man of your education will be interested in this." Lorenzo turned a gaze so powerful and full of fire upon the older men that they involuntarily fell back. "I have here a design for a drill that uses heat to bore a hole through steel!"

Gilberto Ilégo leaned forward with a look of cold concentration on his face. Lorenzo immediately stumbled onward with his inept sales technique.

"You see, my lords, the combination of these two chemicals creates an intense blaze of light. This light, I intend to focus using lenses like . . . like . . ." The boy's thoughts instantly conjured up an image of a short, freckled girl. ". . . like the lenses used in eye spectacles! This produces a beam of light—of heat—which can melt even the toughest steel.

"Imagine the benefits to industry, my lords! Handgun production would cheapen; we could use fire beams to drill holes into pure steel bar-stock! Smoke powder weapons would surely come into their own. We can use the beams to scribe delicate engravings . . . perhaps even to cut the finest mechanical parts . . ."

Captain Ilégo viewed the drawings with a frown.

"And does this chemical combination reliably work?"

"Um . . . essentially. Essentially, yes!" The boy cleared his throat. "The problem of explosion is a minor fault at best. Given enough funding, I am sure I can overcome the obstacles."

A logical mind in a potential son-in-law may have been an advantage. An addled mind might be even more so; Prince Mannicci narrowed his eyes, measuring the possibilities.

As Mannicci sank into thought, Ilégo flicked a calculating glance between his prince and the Lomatran boy. Blade Captain Ilégo handed back the boy's drawings with a cool, predatory smile.

"Since Lorenzo is here with an ambassadorial mission, my lord prince, I'm sure his experiments can be encouraged for the duration of his stay. We can find him a workshop, perhaps. A place outside the city walls . . ."

"No. I believe we shall house him well within our palace. We might have business with him yet. . . ."

"Oh! Oh, thank you, my lord!" Lorenzo flicked a glance toward the palace balcony, drawing in an inspired, dizzy breath as he helplessly searched for words. "I shall not disappoint you."

"Do as you like, boy. But no chemicals, and no jumping off any towers." Not until he had safely married Miliana.

"We'd never explain it to your ambassador."

"Oh, thank you, my lord! Thank you!" Lorenzo bobbed up and down like a toy spider on a string. "M—my gratitude is . . . it's . . ."

Unable to think of proper superlatives, the boy could only open out his hands, finding out too late that Prince Mannicci had taken his chance and ridden fast away. Lorenzo scarcely noticed; looking over the troops, he saw a scrawny figure leaning over a distant balcony; a figure with a bored expression half hidden behind gleaming glass and a towering, pointed hat.

Lorenzo's thoughts were jarred by a cool hand descending upon his arm. Gilberto Ilégo looked down at the boy with a reassuring, though somewhat crocodilian smile.

"Five hundred, I think."

"My lord?" Lorenzo's mind wrenched itself from a dizzy flight through a vague and rosy fairy land. "Five hundred?"

"Five hundred gold ducats. It should keep you supplied with experimental equipment during your stay." Ilégo drew a scented handkerchief from his belt and passed it under his nose. "My bursar will honor any notes that you may write."

Stunned, Lorenzo could only stare up at Ilégo in utter awe. The Blade Captain turned his horse about and saluted with a wave.

"May your experiments prove to be a profit and a delight! *Do* avail me of your progress from time to time. After all, we are brothers, you and I. Intellectually speaking . . ."

The horse reared back in a splendid caracole, pumped the air with its hooves, and then was gone. Standing alone beneath the dusty olive tree, Lorenzo threw out his arms, shook his drawings in delight and felt his spirits soar.

Finally, a patron who knew the value of true science! No longer would Lorenzo be hounded out of house and home by angry relatives and enraged cleaning staff. Sumbria would be his launching place. After this, the whole world would remember the name Lorenzo Utrelli Da Lomatra!

* * * * *

In the Valley of Umbricci, in a sighing stand of grape vines beside a mountain stream, war-horses pawed the soil while armored riders sipped lightly at the local wines.

The Blade Council of Colletro prided itself on its sophistication and elegance. Twenty-one Blade Captains had come to coolly supervise the handing over of the campaign spoils. The gentlemen made a gay pretense of absolute disinterest, commenting on the savor of the local vintages, while behind them the fruits of two years hard campaigning were casually tossed away.

Sumbrian heralds came to take formal acceptance of signed articles of peace. The cheese platter came out in perfect timing to interest the Colletran nobility. Hardly sparing a glance toward their enemies, the Colletrans complimented one another on their armorers and tailors, or stared up at the clouds and languidly predicted rain.

From the black shadows of the mountains, another figure came: a man mounted on a sour, high-stepping hippogriff with feathers of charcoal-bronze. The hippogriff hissed at a noble's horse, baring its serrated beak in spite. The horse instantly retreated like a whipped cur, spilling its rider's wine across an immaculate silk tabard.

The hippogriff's rider wore a light armor of black, velvet-covered steel. While his hostile mount spread its wings and kept the other animals at bay, the rider slipped off his barbute helmet and savaged the assembled nobles with his gaze.

Almost ignoring the man's entrance, Colletro's Blade Council continued with its wine and cheese. Curbing nervous mounts, the riders refreshed their glasses and finally bid their colleague a good day.

"Ugo Svarézi, why how good of you to come." A young, slim Blade Captain let his words drip with practiced irony. "We have so missed your refreshingly innovative conversation."

Faces quirked up into wry, venomous little smiles. For his part, Svarézi ignored the voices all around him as he would scorn the prattle of brainless little birds. Coldly leaning forward in his saddle, the man turned dark eyes toward the valley floor.

"Three villages, a salt mine—and now the Sun Gem, too. The pride of Colletro, tossed into the dust. For fear of a few sword cuts, Colletran honor is pawned."

Svarézi's speech was met with looks of amused, defensive scorn; his voice rang harsh from shouting across endless parade grounds—a voice more fit for a fishmonger than a courtier. Prince Ricardo, dark, lean, and polished by a lifetime of diplomatic maneuvers, laid an armored hand upon the arm of an angry colleague and turned patient eyes to his rebellious captain.

"The laws of war, Blade Captain Svarézi, work for all of us. This year, Colletro has lost; next year, our armies shall triumph again. You must learn to see these minor setbacks as merely part of a larger game."

"A *game.*" Ugo Svarézi turned to reveal a battered, savage face with skin as pale as carrion bone. "A game has an end. This—this yearly posturing has no purpose except its own continuance. To preserve the game, you have lost sight of its final goal!"

"Ah." The prince held out a hand and felt it filled with a chilled glass of wine. "And what, pray tell, is our unremembered goal?"

"To *win* the game, my lord. To destroy the other kingdoms and seize the board as our own."

Nobles drew in weary breaths and exchanged glances of bored despair. Prince Ricardo sipped at his wine, paused in thought, then swiveled calculating eyes toward Svarézi.

"We are aware, *Captain,* of the imperatives of our game. Pray allow us to pursue our victory in the way that suits u—"

"Through *accountants?* Through unfought battles and untried swords? Through pretty maneuvers—like lead soldiers across a playroom floor!" Svarézi's sudden violence

struck at the assembly like a storm. The man crashed a
hand against his saddle as he roared his words in rage.
"We could have taken them! *We could have destroyed their
army if any of you had been man enough to charge!*"

Young Blade Captains slapped hands to sword hilts
and surged forward to defend their honor—only to be
halted by an easy motion of the prince's hand. Duels
resulted in deaths, and deaths resulted in the realign-
ment of voting blocks. The prince preferred to keep the
peace with deterrents made of words.

"It is a pity, Svarézi, that you fail to see the true genius
of our war. A true gamesman commits to dangerous
moves only when the advantage is on his side." Ricardo,
Prince-elect of Colletro, speared a piece of cheese with the
point of his poniard. "Why risk all on a single throw, when
proper patience will bring us to our prize?"

Svarézi's hippogriff gave a sour, trilling call. Atop the
creature's back, Svarézi quieted the beast with his riding
crop.

"And what of my bride, my lord? What of my Mannicci
bride?"

Courtiers stifled smiles behind gauntlets and poman-
ders as they thought of the dreadful Ugo Svarézi falling
in love. Prince Ricardo simply ordered himself more wine.

"A marriage between your own house and the house of
Mannicci is no longer at issue, Svarézi. The Sumbrians
have too much confidence in their strength at arms to be
bothered buying peace with a bride. Particularly to a man
with such uncertain connections . . ."

Wrenching furiously at his reins, Svarézi sent his hippogriff clawing back to open ground. Without so much as
a word, he raked spurs across the creature's hide and
made the beast beat its way up into the sky. Huge black
wings spread their shadow across Colletro's nobility as
Svarézi soared away.

From the back ranks of the Blade Captains, a furious
youth brought his brass-colored horse prancing to the
fore. Blade Captain Veltro's face had flushed red with

fury under his scanty beard.

"My lord prince—I beg permission to fight him! Man to man—blood and honor!" Veltro half drew his sword. "He tasks us, my lord! He defies our honor, and he defies your name!"

Without turning to view the youthful cavalier, Prince Ricardo made a gentling motion with his hands.

"Peace. Peace. Do not let him goad you into giving him his pleasure."

The prince rested against the pommel of his war saddle and scanned the high horizon with his eyes.

"You must understand, my boy: There are certain creatures that only grow stronger as they feed on blood. Deny them their sustenance, and they must wither slowly away. But feed them what they want . . ."

The prince finally fixed the young nobleman with a quiet gaze.

"Feed them what they want, and they grow strong enough to hunt for more."

Veltro sat stiff upon his horse; beneath him, the animal tore at the rich turf with its hooves.

"And this—this *animal*. Will he not seek sustenance elsewhere, my liege?"

"Where?" Prince Ricardo smiled and opened out his hands to show the boy the open, empty world. "As long as we deny him, we have clipped his claws.

"Come, let us turn our attentions to more suitable matters."

The valley's rich, cool afternoon promised a perfect chance to course for hares with the delegates from Sumbria. Turning their mounts toward the shadows of the hills, Colletro's leaders regained their peace of mind and filed quietly away.

High above, a piercing eagle shriek echoed out across the icy peaks. A small black speck of anger faded out against the clouds, and then was gone.

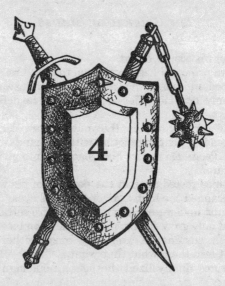

4

For Princess Miliana Mannicci, gaining access to the palace library was a process involving fiendish cunning, sly patience, and infinite subtlety.

Long days of practice were bearing fruit. Thus far, the girl had mastered (well, *almost* mastered) four whole spells. One of these seemed to allow her to store sounds inside a box; not a very useful skill, perhaps, but Miliana refused to be discouraged. For two whole hours late at night, she sat in her room and read aloud passages from *Lady Zuggi's Primer of Basic Heraldry, including appendices on Charges, Countercharges, and Trends of Modern Times*; a book so dull that the moths whirring about Miliana's candle seemed willing to hurtle themselves into the flame as their only means of escape. Finally reaching appendix three—just moments before she felt she'd suffer a lingering death from terminal boredom—the girl slammed shut her enchanted box and tied it shut with string. Locked inside was a monologue more powerful than a sleep spell, the perfect weapon for the following day's campaign.

The next step required the nicest, most intricate manipulation. Miliana unpicked an old embroidery and restitched one heraldic banner in reverse—a change so subtle, so minor, and so utterly insignificant, that only a mindless pompous pedant would give the slightest care.

Miliana left the embroidery on the loom, deliberately hiding it behind a curtain. Sure enough, not half an hour later, Lady Ulia came trumpeting into the palace solarium with the force and verve of a nomad battle horde.

"Miliaaaa-*naaaaaa!*"

Ulia's battle cry struck home like a heavy lance. Loitering noblewomen, maids and staff instantly scattered and fled like mice. Miliana simply sat in place beneath a beam of sun and closed her eyes in joy.

Lady Ulia swept into the room like a granite juggernaut. She wore her most impressive hat—a horrid thing with not one but *two* tall points, which made her look like a sort of hydrocephalic water buffalo. Sumbria's greatest lady spied Miliana's hiding place and then strode forward to confront her errant stepdaughter.

"Miliana! Miliana, I am dismayed—nay, appalled! Appalled and dismayed, that is the only way to describe it." Ulia's maid, Sophia—a scraggly little thing looking a bit like a rodent who had just been rescued from a milk jug—furiously worked a fan to sooth her mistress's brow. Ulia heaved her bosom up and down in gratitude at this simple act of kindness.

"Miliana, I have tried and tried and *tried* to establish you with all the skills a maiden should possess. What have you to say for yourself, my girl? What have you to say?"

Miliana polished her lenses and perched them back on her nose, nearly awestruck by her stepmother's command of theatrics. Predictably, Ulia never gave her an opportunity to speak; instead, she swept herself about Miliana in a grand circle, like a mighty war-galley sailing on parade.

"You shall have me faint clean away! You shall bury me from shocked disgrace, my girl. What have you to say— what have you to say about this—this . . ." Here words temporarily failed her. Lady Ulia held aloft the botched piece of needlepoint and pointed a great sausagelike finger at the reversed coat of arms.

Thick glass discs caught in window light made the most marvelous blank mask. Miliana managed to adjust her spectacles and lean toward her embroidery in beautifully feigned puzzlement.

"Oh! Is it so very important? I mean—it can't be so drastically wrong . . ."

Ulia flapped her lower lip like a landed fish and flung up a great wailing cry of dismay.

"Important? Sune bear me witness—Oh, alack the day!" A pause for breath strained her bodice lacing, which already groaned like naval hawser cables in a storm. "Heraldry is the very quintessence of the social code! Heraldry is our tool for planning every feminine campaign. What if—oh, what if one were to give a favor to the wrong champion? Can one imagine, even for an instant, what damage might be done?"

Miliana wrinkled up her nose as she polished her spectacles on her gown.

"Ulia, I can't see that it matters, since they're all going to fall off their horses anyway."

"Yes—but the wounds, girl! The wounds!" Lady Ulia clapped hands beneath her great horned headpiece in amazement. "The whole point of a tournament is for the championed lady to rush forth and kiss her hero's wounds!"

"Goodness! Well, if they land on what I think they'll land on, I certainly won't want to kiss anything of the sort!"

Ulia swelled with indignation and pointed toward the corridor with one trembling, pale hand.

"Wretch! I see sterner measures must be taken. I have been soft, but I shall be soft no longer!"

Ulia sank down onto a stool, exhausted by the wicked ways of the world.

"Whatever can you young folk be thinking of today? I ask you. I *beg* you! Our Lomatran suitor is invited here, into my own home, to our very victory ball—and does he appear? Does he make himself known to his sweetheart or his future mother-in-law? No, he does not! He disappears, like a thief in the night."

Lady Ulia stood, turned her back upon her stepdaughter and went into a magnificent huff. "I shall discharge my own responsibilities, even though the rest of Toril sees fit to let civilized manners die! To the library with you, my girl! To the library to study heraldry until your eyes can bear no more. You shall be locked inside, nor shall you stir forth until the supper has been laid.

"Now get thee gone!"

Miliana slapped her hands together in satisfaction, picked up her hems and marched gleefully off down the corridors. She ducked out of Ulia's sight, dove into the empty library, and briskly slammed shut the door.

Her tall pointy hat made the perfect speaking trumpet; removing the very tip, she placed it near her magical box of words, directing the tedious monologue toward the corridor. Lady Ulia's suspicions would thus, hopefully, be soothed, leaving Miliana free to clamber like a spider monkey along the upper shelves for many profitable hours.

In pursuing her private studies, Miliana's primary problem seemed to be basic comprehension. Not only did she hardly understand the terms used in her only source books, but she could scarcely comprehend the language in which the books were written. It seemed to be a most unusual, antiquated tongue, and although the symbols used to frame the spells needed no translation, she really did need to get a better grip on the whole wretched thing. A translation of the spellbook's index would be her best next move. Trying to cast newly discovered spells at random was proving more hazardous every day. Miliana's last attempt at sorcery had summoned a great clap of licorice-scented steam, and had created a sort of big green—furry—thing which had promptly leapt out of the window, burrowed a hole into the palace pantry, and eaten all the pickled eels.

While her own voice droned ceaselessly on and on a dozen feet below, Miliana wobbled precariously at the top of a ladder, piling her arms with books. Half an hour of devoted search uncovered treasures of the finest kind: guides to ancient languages, cabalism and folklore brimmed between her arms, along with some dust-covered scroll-ey things that must have been interesting, otherwise they would not have been so well hidden behind the shelves. Utterly engrossed, smeared with dust and teetering beneath a vast mountain of literature, the girl never anticipated disaster until it struck at her from below.

Rising over the brain-dead drone of Miliana's speaking box, there came a subtle scratching at the door. From time to time a skewer poked in through the lock, followed by curses and more frenzied activity from outside. Finally, the lock sprang open with a decisive click; the door yielded, and a tall young man strode hastily inside.

His progress was blocked by Miliana's ladder. The youth looked up in puzzlement, caught an eyeful of Miliana's frilly pantalettes, and instantly gave a leap of fright.

Inevitably, this crashed his skull against the ladder, which skittered off across the floor. Abandoned twelve feet above the ground, Miliana blinked, hung poised in midair as ancient principles of gravity took hold, and with an almighty squawk tumbled down to the rug. She was saved the worst indignities of a bruised *derriere* by having the idiot-youth's head break her fall.

Shocked, dazed and stinging, Miliana found herself collapsed upon the ground under an avalanche of fallen books and paperwork. A wild commotion began somewhere under her skirts as a struggling victim desperately called for air.

Rescuing her spectacles, which were dangling ignominiously from one ear, Miliana managed to focus her bewildered senses and draw up her skirts. Struggling up between a shapely pair of legs clad in stockings, bows, and knee-length underwear came a young man in shabby court attire—a man clutching the crushed ruins of charcoal drawing sticks. The youth pulled dark hair back from his eyes, blinked dazedly up at Miliana, and suddenly blushed, bright as a summer's dawn.

"Oh—it's you!"

Rearing up like a scruffy cobra, the young man took Miliana by the hand and vigorously introduced himself.

"Lorenzo! Lorenzo Utrelli Da Lomatra. I'm a scholar—well, an inventor, really. And an artist. You've probably seen my work here and there. I did the portrait piece the embassy brought for Prince Mannicci—'The Sea Goddess Rising From the Waves.' Not that you can have seen it yet; it's still at the embassy. But it's ever so good!"

Crawling painfully out of the rubble of unbound books, Miliana slapped down her skirts and sourly tried to snatch back some of her dignity.

"So, you're Lorenzo." The name almost seemed to ring a bell. "Very pleased to meet you, I'm sure."

"Oh—my pleasure! No really—I mean, I've seen you about the palace. You must work here." The boy tried to clamber his way up from the floor. "What do you call yourself?"

"Angry."

"Angry?" The young man screwed up his face in puzzlement, then suddenly paled as two and two made four. "Oh—oh *angry*. Oh, I am so sorry! So—so very . . ."

The boy made an attempt at dusting off Miliana's posterior, slapping her backside in a manner which made the girl peer down in alarm.

A big, black charcoal handprint now marred her dress—a handprint placed in a manner that would make Lady Ulia scream for the nearest headsman.

The corridor floor trembled; Ulia herself could be heard approaching the library door. Miliana leapt to her feet, slammed shut her "noise box" and jammed the portal back in place. As she surveyed the mess of fallen books, young man and drawings all about the carpet, a hunted look possessed her face.

Alone in a room with a man—and with his handprints all over her rump! Miliana planted her back against the door and let her breast heave in utter panic.

"Miliaaaa-naaaaaa! Miliana, whatever was that noise?"

Lady Ulia's voice struck fear straight into Lorenzo's soul. The boy dove beneath a table and scuttled about the floor on all fours like a demented rat looking for its hole. Miliana heard footsteps approaching from the corridor and nearly expired from fright.

"The chimney! Take the books and hide inside the chimney!"

"Eeerk!" Lorenzo peered up into the chimney in dismay. "There's a half-eaten pickled eel in here!"

"Just do it! Quickly!"

Lorenzo burrowed out of sight; Miliana took a calming breath, tried to still her pulse, and briskly opened up the library door. She managed to intercept Lady Ulia with a false, befuddled smile.

"Um . . . hello . . ."

"Miliana, I require nothing more of you than diligent—nay, *unceasing* effort!" Lady Ulia bowled Miliana aside and peered suspiciously about the room. "What, pray tell, is that lumpen object moving about in the fireplace?"

Young Lorenzo's backside could be seen jammed like an unseemly cork into the bottom of the chimney. With a squawk, the youth suddenly lost purchase and fell down in the cinders, almost immediately drowning beneath a cascade of books and scrolls.

"Oh . . . oh he's just . . ." Miliana blinked behind the blank shield of her spectacles, searching for a suitable set of words. "The cleaner! He's th—the library cleaner. He cleans the books . . . you know, keeps the pages all clear and sparkling."

"Sparkling!" Ulia's voice roared, rattling the plasterwork. "The boy's nothing but a mass of soot!"

Miliana crammed her backside against a wall, hiding the telltale handprint on her rear.

"Charcoal absorbs foul smells, Ulia. 'Tis a well-known fact."

"Is it? Is it indeed?" Ulia squared her shoulders and narrowed down her eyes. "Cleaner or no cleaner, his presence serves as a distraction. And I must say that I find it most unsuitable for you to be sharing a room alone with a male commoner." Ulia pulled a quizzing glass from her cleavage and used it to examine the young man as though he were a particularly noisome species of bug. "Goodness—why does he smell of eels?"

"I have no idea, milady."

"Hmmmmph." Ulia sank her lens back into its cavernous hiding place. "Well, as long as he's here, have him search the wainscoting; a large green furry thing has just made off with a dried hogfish from the kitchen shelf. The vermin in this palace are becoming quite unforgivable!"

Ulia hitched up her skirts, tried to walk through the door and managed to get her hat jammed in the doorframe. She ponderously maneuvered herself about and began to sidle past the obstacle, meanwhile fixing the hapless Lorenzo beneath her baleful eye.

"Young man, you have my permission to continue with your duties—but pray, do not be long. The young lady has research of the utmost importance to attend to. The security of Sumbria itself may one day rest upon her work."

The door closed with a titanic *slam,* leaving Miliana and Lorenzo to slump against the bookshelves in relief. The girl finally managed to peel herself away from the marble and wearily opened her speaking box; the sound of her own voice dragging its way through chapter seventy one, paragraph six: "Charges dovetail and counter dovetail and their acute relevance to social graces . . ." masked their conversation from eavesdroppers in the corridor.

Lorenzo half crouched, searching the wainscoting for signs of errant green furry things.

"What's a hogfish?"

"It doesn't matter." Miliana collapsed into a chair,

remembered the charcoal mark on her backside, and decided that she didn't care. The girl wearily rubbed beneath her spectacles and massaged her eyes. "Now look—Lothario—"

"Lorenzo! Lorenzo Utrelli . . ."

". . . Da tiddly-pom and tiddly-dee. Yes . . ." Miliana suddenly sat bolt upright in her chair. "You picked that lock! You're not supposed to be in here."

The young man—a handsome creature in an ink-stained sort of way—skittered aside like a nervous stick bug.

"Yes I am! I'm a guest! I just . . . just . . . just didn't have a key . . ."

"So you're a guest, are you?" Miliana vaguely remembered seeing the man before, but for the life of her she couldn't remember just quite where. "Well what do you want the library for?"

"Study!" Lorenzo left a trail of soot behind him as he crossed the polished marble floor. "Sumbria has some of the best books there are. It must be terribly interesting living here."

"That all depends on what you're allowed to do with your time." Miliana scowled, fixed her gaze on the intruder, and crinkled up her speckled nose. "Now, look—I'm not so sure you should be allowed in here."

The young man never even heard her. He crouched forward to inspect Miliana's magical speaking box, his face glowing with rapturous fascination.

"Oh—oh, this is wonderful! Superb!" Lorenzo turned to stare at Miliana with awe and excitement shining in his eyes. "Are you a sorceress?"

Miliana almost said "no"—and then the tone of respect in the young man's voice brought her up short. She drew erect, preened like a heron, and attempted to act terribly, terribly wise.

"Yes. Yes, I am, actually."

"And so they actually *make* you study!" Lorenzo sat himself down in a cloud of cinders and dust. "Back at home, they've banned me from every library in town. They say I'm disruptive." The Lomatran avidly examined Miliana's arrangement of the box and speaking trumpet. "This is fascinating. Now, you see, this has bearing on some of my own studies. I am exploring the possibility that sound can be translated into peaks and waves."

Miliana raised one eyebrow and peered at her companion through her pretty freckles.

"How would that be useful?"

"Ah—but perhaps it might be!" Lorenzo spread the drawing of a machine out across the table. "Here, you see? This machine uses a membrane to pick up sound, vibrating as noise contacts the membrane. The vibrations make this needle jump and change the score written on this parchment scroll, which is dragged slowly past the needle by these little springs! Now all I need to do is somehow reverse the process, find a way of reading the jump marks on the parchment, and we can make a re-playable mechanical recording of any sound we desire." The young man puffed out his chest in pride. "You see? The job's half done!"

Miliana leaned back in her chair and fixed her companion with a droll, sarcastic stare.

"You must be from the country."

Lorenzo instantly turned upon her a pair of eyes utterly alive with passion—a face so filled with fire that it welded the girl hard into her seat.

"Not *from* the country . . . *of* the country!" The boy slapped his hands onto the table and leaned toward Miliana, who leaned backward in her chair in blank surprise. "It's time to liberate the people from the tyranny of magic! Don't you see that a system of mechanics is the only means of ever freeing the world from mere autocracy?"

"You're right. I don't." Miliana speared forward, sharp light glinting from her lenses. "Magic is the one thing that *anyone* can have. The one thing that can free us from—from being ordinary!"

"Aha! *Aha!*" Lorenzo stuck a finger up into the air, dislodging a shower of grime into his cuff. "And how is this achieved? Through hard study. Through long, arduous learning and dedication! It's repression through and through!"

Moving from scorn to absolute irritation, Miliana folded up her arms.

"Look, I fail to see how my sitting on my noble backside reading books on magic represses a bunch of people that I've never even met."

"Well, that's my point, you see." Lorenzo threw open his arms, frightening the green furry thing sleeping on the mantelpiece. "Sorcery is only learned through long years of very intensive, very expensive study. Only the nobility can afford it—placing magic squarely in the hands of the autocratic classes. If there's ever going to be any real equality, we have to place a means of power into the hands of the masses!"

The girl stared at him in absolute bewilderment.

"What do you want to go around giving power to the masses for?"

"So that they can take part in the process of their own political rule!"

"Political rule?" Miliana blinked in amazement. "Have you sat back and watched what these palace dwellers do to each other all day? It's daggers in the back and internecine warfare twenty-four hours a day! If you go around getting *everyone* to carry on like that, we'll all be dead within a week!"

"Well, I don't mean that everyone should kill each other." Lorenzo ran fingers through his hair, disturbing a sooty spider which absailed quickly down to the floor. "I mean that we can break people away from the current tyranny of study!"

Miliana bridled.

"What have you got against study?"

"It is class prejudicial!"

"But *you* study!" Miliana pointed a finger straight at Lorenzo's nose. "You already admitted that you study things!"

"Um . . ." Lorenzo blinked, then hit upon an explanation. "Ah, yes, but only to serve a noble end!"

"So you're saying you're against knowledge?" Miliana angrily shoved a book across the table to crash against Lorenzo's arms. "That's what you're saying, isn't it? We should all drag ourselves down into the mire!"

"No! Look . . . you've made me forget everything I wanted to say." Lorenzo floundered about in a bog of frustration. "Study is what I want to spread! Everyone should be able to do it. It should be a basic right for every man, woman and child."

"All right then—so they can all study magic, and then everyone will be happy." Miliana gave a sarcastic, joyous wave. "What's your problem now?"

"Yes, but . . . but not everyone can do magic! I mean— the talent might not be there." Lorenzo paced back and forth like a caged animal, albeit a rather scrawny one. "What we need is an equalizer, something that can be a bit like magic for people who can't actually *do* magic, either because of poverty or inability."

Miliana heaved a sharp, irritated sigh.

"A *unique* power."

"Yes!"

"For everybody."

"Absolutely!"

The girl felt it best to let the conversation drop and lie like a dead thing on the ground.

"You're a loony."

"I'm only thinking of the masses."

"Yes." Miliana reached for a textbook and primly opened the cover. "Obviously you haven't tried *smelling* the masses lately."

She tried to dismiss him with her pose, but it seemed Lorenzo Utrelli Da thingamajig was made of sterner, dumber stuff; the man regarded her with a look of unfeigned amazement and tried to catch her eye.

"Um . . . Miss? Milady?"

"It's Miliana."

"Oh—Miliana!" Lorenzo let the name brand itself in
great steaming letters on the inside of his skull, entirely
failing to connect it with royal blood and wedding bells. "I
just wanted to tell you how much I've appreciated talking
with you. Intellectually, mind-to-mind, I mean. It's—it's
utterly amazing!"

"What?" Miliana speared her companion with one stab
of her eye. "Because I'm a mage, or because I'm a girl?"

"Well it's not as if you're actually a girl!" Lorenzo dug
his own grave with cheerful, brainless enthusiasm. "I
mean—you're a scholar."

Miliana shot the man a baleful glance. Lorenzo took it
as a sign of approval and heaved a great sigh of satisfaction.

"Well this has been fascinating. Utterly fascinating! Do
you live somewhere nearby?"

"I live in the palace. In the west tower. The one with all
the plaster falling off the walls." Miliana adjusted her
spectacles so that she might gaze down her nose at
Lorenzo. "Lady Ulia is my mother—do you understand?"

Lorenzo had rarely understood anything less; even so,
he nodded his head and attempted to look learned, cosmopolitan, and wise.

"Well, then, I can see you again! I mean—would you
mind if, from time to time, I use you as an aid for my
studies?"

"Yes, yes, whatever you like!" Miliana opened the door
to usher out her unwanted guest. "Now, please do run
along and leave me to my reading. There's only another
hour of heraldry left in my speaking box."

The girl slammed the door, then suddenly frowned,
tugged it open once again, and relieved the startled
Lorenzo of his lockpicks. Sealing herself safely back
inside once more, Miliana leaned against the shelves and
gave a great, frustrated sigh.

A Lomatran loose inside the palace? For a moment, the
concept rang vague alarm bells, and Miliana searched for
a reason.

Ah! Last night, Ulia had mentioned a Lomatran suitor. But suitors came in carriages with bouquets and minstrels singing serenades, not in scruffy hats, picking locks on library doors.

Miliana's magic noise box had now reached up to chapter eighty-eight: *The Improper Use of Propers.* Trying to regain her previous peace of mind, Miliana Mannicci perched herself on the table and began to read her sooty scrolls.

* * * * *

"Luccio!"

Lorenzo catapulted into the apartments he shared with his boyhood friend. He looked like a pixie which had spent too long buzzing around a candle flame; scorched, dumb, and dazed. The boy collided with a wall, looked wildly about the room with its easels, paintings, and half-built perpetual-motion machines, and then fought his way through a connecting door. He discovered Luccio sitting on the balcony, hard at work marking the backs of a deck of playing cards.

"Luccio—the most amazing thing's just happened!"

"Amazing?" Luccio, still suffering from the effects of a rather dodgy neutralize poison spell that didn't quite seem to quite recognize wine as a poison, peered at his friend through startling purple eyes. "Whatever do you mean, my cherub?"

"I've just met the most amazing person. Well—girl." Lorenzo blinked. "Woman. I mean—she's sort of a woman, but a person too!"

"Do tell?"

"Well, I mean, she's a girl but she's . . ." The scholar groped his hands blindly through the air searching for adequate words. "She's not like a girl at all! I mean—she only talked about real things—magic and mechanics and sociopolitical infrastructures—you know what I mean."

"Real things." Luccio shuffled cards briskly between

his palms, keeping an amused eye on his sooty friend. "Do say on! You admire her for her mind. Was this paragon of politics also, perhaps, just a touch pretty?"

"No!" Lorenzo seemed utterly offended at the inference—then immediately leapt to the defense of his new-found colleague. "Well, yes, she was. But not . . . not so you'd notice. Sort of . . . sort of *profoundly* pretty. Not just beautiful."

"But she has the appropriate dimensions, accessories—all that sort of thing?"

"Um . . . I think so." Lorenzo screwed up his brow in an attempt to recall more than Miliana's striking, intelligent eyes. "I forgot to look."

"Ah, dear." Luccio tossed aside his cards and sorrowfully folded his fingers across his breast. "That, my little chuck, is not the best of signs. It is indicative—if you will forgive me—of love."

Lorenzo Utrelli Da Lomatra drew himself up as primly as a nesting hen.

"I beg your pardon, but it is nothing of the sort! This is an intellectual challenge; a meeting of opposed philosophies and complementary minds." Lorenzo sniffed, affecting a superior air. "She has offered to assist me in my research."

"Oh, yes, of course." Luccio made a motherly expression of pouting solicitude. "I had forgotten that the pure torch of reason leaves no space for other lights within your soul."

Tall and gangly as a starving troll, Luccio reclined atop the dangerous balcony rails.

"The arrow shot, sweet triumph strikes she home
"Into the breast of heroes, who no more shall roam.
"To the winds fly wits—ambition o'er leaps the stars!
"Our court we pay to Lliira—not to Shar."

Luccio held aloft a single finger to the sky. "Who is she, what's her name, and what color were her eyes?"

"Um—well . . . well, no color! Not that I could see."

"Alas—you have the affliction. Never matter—let us

pursue it like a wild young hart and revel in the chase!"
Luccio sprang along railings, balanced carelessly beside a
drop at least three stories high. Swooping up the deck of
cards, he casually flipped two upon the table: "the lovers"
and "the fool." Accepting the omens, he fished beneath the
couch for a half-full bottle of wine. "But did you not forget, heart, that your father has his mind set upon you
wedding a princess?"

"I'll tell him she refused me. A marriage would interfere with my intellectual life—particularly marriage to
some stuck-up princess." Lorenzo dusted off his fingers,
ridding himself of his father's plans. "I shall pursue spiritual and scholarly growth."

"Aaah . . . spiritual growth!" Luccio walked a silver coin
across the back of his hand. "With your friend with the
sparkling eyes?"

"Look, Luccio—we only talked about systems of political economy."

"Aaaah! Then here's to political economy!" Luccio flung
himself into a corner and delighted himself with romantic plans. "So, what shall we do? We must construct ourselves a grand campaign. How shall we bring this flower
to your lips—this treasure to your heart?"

"I thought maybe I might send her a letter . . . something nice . . . ?"

"A letter?" Luccio rose slowly, as though facing down a
horror in the night. "A *letter?* Are you mad, my boy? Are
you addled? Are you drunken? Are you sick?" Luccio shot
up and clamped a struggling Lorenzo under his arm.
"Never! I shall show you how the deed is done. I shall
lead you to the fields of Elysium, and toss away the
plaque which reads, 'tread not upon the grass'!"

"You're a very strange man, Luccio."

"Silence! There are but a few dozen gods of love, and
Luccio is their prophet!" Luccio produced another card, "the
sun," and placed it in Lorenzo's pocket. "My credentials."

Lorenzo removed a large orange feather from a chair
and wearily sat down; his eyes were only half focused

upon the mortal world. In one corner of the room, there loomed a giant canvas—an ornate thing showing a sea goddess rising from the waves. It was to be presented to the Mannicci household at the Festival of Blades in one week's time. Lorenzo stirred himself, picked up a brush and corrected a tiny error in the painted foam.

Irritated and frustrated, he suddenly thrust paints and brush away. The boy threw himself at the balcony rails and stared in exasperation at the sky.

"I've been so tired of it! Trying to be creative, but without . . ."

"Brains?" Luccio tried to be helpful by sitting on the balcony paring his nails.

"Not brains—inspiration." Lorenzo took up his paintbrush and pallet; with fast swipes of a brush he sketched Miliana's face across a wooden board. "There's been no impetus. No ideas to rebound myself from. But now, now at last, I feel . . ."

"Distended? Bilious?"

"No! I feel . . ." Lorenzo flapped about like a fish looking for an appropriate hook. "I feel alive!"

Four more brush strokes constructed Miliana's spectacles and her eyes.

"This has been the most perfect day of my entire life! It's been . . . It's been . . ." Words obviously failed to describe it. "Sumbria! Aaaaah, Sumbria. I feel like I'm finally born into a brilliant new world."

Luccio suavely dodged beneath a waving brush that might have given him a blue mustache.

"So there'll be no serenades, then?"

"What? Oh, heavens, no." Lorenzo made a tut-tutting motion with his most disreputable pallet knife. "This is a meeting of minds."

"Still . . ." Luccio leaned forward to inspect the gaudy painting of the sea goddess at play. "You must examine all the possibilities. A romantic attachment is not impossible and, theretofore, you must be cautious. For instance— does she please your mind's eye?"

"Oh, absolutely!"

"Ah." Lorenzo's friend leaned himself waggishly against one wall. "In which case, my best advice is for you to think upon the mother. After all, that shows you how your own girl shall look in years to come." Luccio tapped thoughtfully at his pointed chin. "How does her mother look?"

A vision of Lady Ulia boiled unbidden into Lorenzo's mind; the boy instantly turned pale.

Luccio's lips made a silent O of understanding, and he went back to the balcony rails. Lorenzo paced back and forth for a while, and then tapped his chin in thought.

"I believe I must dispute your theory. The bone structures of mother and daughter would seem to be somewhat different."

"Ah, but perhaps the daughter might transmute in time?"

"It's a question of anatomy then." Lorenzo sat himself down and tucked his heels in hard against his rear. His face took on an air of intellectual puzzlement. "I don't believe there are any books covering the subject."

"Well, I should make study of it, if I were you, old chap." Luccio perched himself back on his accustomed railings, peeling a piece of fruit. "Top priority!"

"Yes. Yes—absolutely!" Lorenzo shot upright, his face rapt in absolute enthusiasm. "Well, she said she didn't mind. This is perfect. Perfect!" Lorenzo avidly shook Luccio's hand. "I'll get onto the task right away!"

Luccio gave a sigh and tried to recapture the golden peace of the afternoon. Behind him, Lorenzo busied himself with mirrors, old lenses, and bits of copper tube; just below, a rat crossing the courtyard halted, hiccuped, assumed a puzzled expression, and exploded with an almighty bang.

Young Luccio let slip another sigh and concentrated on fruit knife and orange peel; clearly the airs of Sumbria did strange things to the soul.

* * * * *

"Svarézi!"

The youthful voice stabbed out from alley shadows; Ugo Svarézi never even deigned to take notice. Leading his lean black hippogriff mare toward the garrison stables, Svarézi plodded on with his savage, troll-like gait, crushing alley refuse under his heels.

"Svarézi! Turn!"

He turned. A short, thick "cat gutter" sword glittered in Svarézi's hand as he swiveled himself around. Black velvet armor breathed in slow, sinister movements as he stood gazing back along the straight Colletran alleyway.

Behind him, his hippogriff gave a low and hungry growl.

A golden youth stood in the light: Blade Captain Veltro—young, angry, and backed up by a lounging band of perfumed swords. His young rabble draped themselves like a painted canvas across the alleyway, anticipating blood as they played with their naked blades.

Feet rustled the dust behind Svarézi, heralding the arrival of yet more of Veltro's men. The Blade Captain never turned. He began a slow, deliberate advance toward his first enemies, bringing his scarred, brutal sword into the light.

Farther down the lane, Veltro struck a heroic pose. The slim youth stood before his comrades, tossing aside the scabbard of his silver rapier.

"No bride for you, Svarézi! No general's baton—no more scorning Colletran honor. Tonight, your soul will be shrieking in Baator!"

With a feral growl, Svarézi came within sword reach and hammered the thin rapier aside. Veltro leapt back and bellowed orders to his comrades, who instantly surged into the attack.

From behind Svarézi, more war cries rang; he dropped the reins of his hippogriff and released her to the kill.

"Shaatra . . . *feed.*"

With a shuddering hiss of pure release, Svarézi's hippogriff turned to stalk back down the alleyway. The four bravos charging at Svarézi's back skidded to a halt and carefully readied their blades.

Long and lean, with an eagle's beak and claws honed razor sharp, the hippogriff mare pranced slowly sideways toward her prey.

Facing five armed men, Svarézi never slowed the pace of his advance. He stalked coldly forward toward the flushed, screaming young Blade Captain at their rear, swatting rapier lunges aside one by one. Like a black fiend, he homed in upon his chosen sacrifice, as sparks showered from clashing blades and sword points scored across his armored skull.

"Kill him! Kill him, you fools!"

Veltro's voice cracked in panic and excitement. He waved his toy sword and began screaming orders back down the empty alleyway. Svarézi advanced into the center of a hooting quartet of enemies, and finally brought his blade into play.

A courtier lunged; Svarézi cracked the man's rapier point away, trapped his forearm against his chest and wrenched the limb aside. The courtier screamed and reeled backward, his arm broken and his sword dangling from its lanyard at his wrist.

Stabbing from behind, a rapier pierced Svarézi's brigantine and ripped a fiery line across his ribs. The warlord whirled, wrenching the sword from its owner's grip, then slammed the man against a wall and stabbed him in the groin. The broad blade twisted, spilling the stink of blood into the alleyway, and Svarézi tossed the shrieking carrion aside.

Behind him, Shaatra screamed in lust for blood. A beak snapped, a wingbeat drove back a narrow sword, and suddenly the hippogriff spun to kick out with her rear hooves. A body screamed as it crashed hard against a mud brick wall. Another man gurgled horribly as the eagle beak fastened on his jaw. Shaatra shook her victim like a bloody doll, her triumphant hunting cries bubbling through the blood of living prey.

"Archers! *Archers!*"

Behind Veltro, a fresh flood of men appeared: a dozen crossbowmen in the particolored livery of Veltro's own brigades. The youth laughed as Svarézi stepped away from the embattled courtiers. Pointing with his silver sword, Veltro screamed his bloodlust to the skies.

"Fire!"

Troops knelt, jerked bow stocks to their shoulders and instantly took aim. Crossbow bolts whipped through the dust, stabbing into naked flesh and spraying blood across the alley walls.

Svarézi stooped down, wiped the blood from his blade upon a courtier's cap, and silently sheathed his sword. Behind him and beside him, dead and dying bravos clawed bloody trails though the dust—shot down to a man. Cheated of her kills, Shaatra raised a defiant scream, hurtling a corpse, shot through with crossbow bolts, aside. The black monster stared in anger at the crossbowmen, then spread her wings and rippled forward like a stream of liquid doom.

"Shaatra!"

Svarézi's command brought the creature slinking to a halt. Cowed, it ripped claws through a courtier's corpse while the black-clad general walked confidently toward the crossbowmen.

The soldiers spread out among the fallen courtiers, finishing the wounded and stripping rings from bloodstained fingers that curled like dying spiders. Their sergeant slung his weapon, faced Ugo Svarézi, and bowed.

"Forgive our hastiness, my lord. We might have hit your mount."

Svarézi waved an armored hand in answer.

"Small matter. Another one can be found."

Collapsed against a wall with blood spilling through his hands, young Blade Captain Veltro still managed a precarious hold on life. Shot through and through by his own men, the boy still tried to somehow crawl away.

Svarézi motioned the soldiery aside and walked deliberately toward the fallen man.

Veltro stared at his soldiers as if still unable to comprehend their treachery.

"They were *my* men . . . mine!"

"It takes a soldier to command soldiers, boy." Svarézi once again drew his savage blade.

Veltro raised his voice and screamed, cramming himself into the dust in fear.

"You're finished, Svarézi! Colletro's court is finished with you! No Mannicci bride—no council seats! No Blade Council will suffer you again!"

The blade reversed to hover like an ice pick in Svarézi's hand.

"If the council is finished with me . . . then let us finish with the council!"

Svarézi stabbed the cowering young Blade Captain through the roof of his mouth, twisting the blade down into the sand like a slaughterer. The body beneath him arched, then jerked into deathly stillness. Svarézi freed his sword and flicked the filth from the blade onto the alley walls.

Behind him, the crossbow sergeant scarcely spared a glance at his master's corpse.

"Did he speak the truth, sire? Will there be no Sumbrian bride?"

"What matter? Where a maid's door shuts, a master's opens." Svarézi wrenched at the feathered mane of his hippogriff, dragging her beak up from a feast of carrion. One armored fist drew a torn letter from the creature's saddlebags and crushed it like a fragile treasure in his grasp.

"Enough of petty court intrigue. It is time to raise our sights to a higher prize!"

Svarézi swung himself into his saddle and slowly rode away. Beneath him, hippogriff claws left bloody footprints in an alleyway already thick with flies.

The annual Festival of Blades brought a gay, carefree mood to Sumbria. For the nobility, the holiday celebrated the origins of families and kingdoms; a fine, defiant time where each city-state proudly shouted out its heritage. It would be a week for ambassadors and midnight balls, for tournaments and pageantry. Each noble house would strive to outdo the others in sheer magnificence and generosity.

In the drowsy warmth of a Sumbrian noon, Miliana walked through the wind-kissed colonnades. With her eyes half closed and her hair stirring out beneath her pointy hat to drift and feather in the breeze, Miliana could shut away Lady Ulia's voice and let the whole world pass her by.

Ulia never noticed; for her, life seemed to be a never-ending round of irritation and interference, and affairs never took a correct turn unless she was directly involved. Festooned in bells and ribbons, she trundled along at Miliana's side and shook the skies with her litany of woes.

"I told them! I told them all that I shall not suffer it!

The parade has always left from the gates at midday. Why should they now desire to delay it by an hour?"

Letting one bored portion of her brain handle the appropriate prods to the conversation, Miliana stifled a yawn and turned her face into the breeze.

"If it's important, why not let them delay it for an hour?"

"Delay is change! *Change!*" Lady Ulia spoke the word like a witch's curse. "It is the thin end of the wedge. Once disorder is allowed, anarchy must surely follow."

"Anarchy?" Miliana watched a bumblebee meander past, and wondered where the creature's hive might lie. "Why anarchy?"

"When people fly off upon their own affairs, despite the seasoned wisdom of their betters, that is anarchy. Only social order brings peace, and peace is the tool for happiness." Ulia stabbed a scornful glance at her stepdaughter, irritated by the play of sun across the girl's freckled nose. "Really, Miliana, I sometimes wonder if you have absorbed any of your schooling at all. I think it is high time you turned your mind to higher things." Ulia stepped over a burnt, fur-edged crater in the cobblestones. "I am quite occupied enough without attending to your affairs every hour of every day. I have the tournament seating to arrange, the caterers for the banquet have presented the most awful menu, and now we have this painting affair as well . . ."

"Oh?" Miliana's bumblebee had landed upon a sprig of foxglove; the huge weight of the insect set the weed stalk swaying wildly up and down. "What painting might that be?"

"The painting, girl! The Lomatran painting! It is the betrothal gift from their embassy to our city." Ulia waved an arm and almost knocked Miliana's pointy hat clean off her head. "All very well for your father to arrange it; but where is it to be displayed? In what light, in what way, and who shall have the privilege of first viewing? Men are so impractical about such things. . . ."

Guards were moving about the central courtyard of the palace. An engineer and a battle mage inspected windows, doors, and cobblestones, sketching notes for sinister protective spells. Miliana watched the sorcerer with mixed curiosity and utter jealousy, instantly planning an afternoon of work on her own magic.

The security arrangements seemed overly complex simply for a painting and a party, until Miliana remembered her last session of eavesdropping on her father's affairs.

"The jewel is coming here?"

"Indeed yes, child. The Sun Gem—the very heart and soul of the Blade Kingdoms!" Ulia fanned herself, wilting flowers with the strength of her perfume. "Colletro's agents must hand it over to us at the festival—their ransom for losing the campaign. But with this jewel thief running unchecked right through the town, we shall break the budget just on security for the wretched bauble!" Ulia placed fingertips across her eyes as if summoning a vision of the inevitable disaster. "It shall be the ruin of us all."

Miliana shrugged freckled shoulders in an utter lack of care.

"Why not just display a paste gem, and keep the real thing safely hidden away?"

With straightened back and a sideways sweep of her dark eyes, Ulia communicated absolute disdain.

"Really, my dear, you have no grasp of social niceties. It is a fault we shall labor to correct. Now do please leave me be. I have so much to attend to. So much to attend."

Success! Miliana closed her eyes in quiet pleasure as she withdrew. Lady Ulia bustled off like a shambling mound, leaving Miliana to spend a day in utter peace. Picking up her skirts, the girl swished off down the corridors to plan a perfect afternoon.

Reading, magic, and a bath.

Baths were Miliana's sacred times; a moment when she could lock her doors, hurtle her hat aside, and lose herself inside a universe of steam. With her chin over the edge of the tub, she would read and dream in blissful splendor until her fingertips turned white and wrinkly, and the water grew cold.

The advantages of her spellbook's rather odd construction had swiftly been demonstrated; the smelly toadskin seemed utterly waterproof. Three times now, Miliana had accidentally dipped a corner of the volume in her bath, and although the water suffered, the book itself seemed none the worse for wear.

Once safely locked inside her room, Miliana gave a gentle smile. On a warm summer's day, nothing could be more delicious than bathing with the doors to the balcony wide open. It brought in the sunlight, and helped stop her spectacles from clouding up with steam. Safe and secure with her high elevation, Miliana Mannicci, mistress of a thousand freckles, pulled the stopper from her bath faucet and began the pleasurable task of loosing her clothes.

The Blade Kingdoms were blessed by a firm grasp of plumbing technology. A gleeful team of fiery salamanders high up in the palace ceiling spent their days snacking on coal and bringing a water tank to the boiling point through the intense heat of their skins. A network of gleaming copper pipes—designed by madmen, but installed by efficient, military engineers—brought the water up across the garden wall, took a left turn at the outhouses, dripped merciless droplets into the Blade Council's meeting chambers, and finally coughed and spattered itself into Miliana's gigantic seashell bath.

The first glorious clouds of steam arose and drifted through the jasmine creepers smothering the rails of Miliana's balcony. Unnoticed among those leaves, a long tube slowly edged itself up across the balcony. The crook-topped end, equipped with a big glass lens, hunted back and forth for a while, fixed upon Miliana as she entered, singing, through her bathroom door, then settled itself contentedly into the concealing jasmine flowers.

Soothed by the sound of falling water, Miliana filled her bathroom with its essential supplies; towels, fuzzy slippers, her spellbook, and a mug of prootwaddle tea. Propping her book against a wooden washbasin, she began reading a page of confusing gibberish while beginning the wearisome task of undoing her bodice stays.

Frilly pants, gown, and pointy hat all ended up in an untidy heap on the floor, leaving Miliana naked but for a kiss of fine brown freckles. The girl closed her eyes and stretched herself, feeling the skin draw tight across her ribs, then opened one eye in puzzlement as an excited metallic clank came from the direction of the balcony.

The girl instantly ducked and scuttled like a crab for the shelter of a towel. Polishing her spectacles free of steam, she darted suspicious glances at the rooftops far and wide. The skies were free of hippogriffs, and her jasmine creepers concealed her utterly from view. With a sniff of her pert snub nose, the girl turned away and went to check on the progress of her tub.

Seen as the gods intended, Miliana seemed much like a svelte, bad-tempered, bookish nymph. Warm beneath a streaming cloak of her own soft brown hair, the girl leaned across the bath and dipped in an experimental finger, then instantly whipped about as yet another noise sent alarms chasing up and down her naked spine.

Nothing moved; no floorboards creaked, nor did any shadows move. Miliana thought of repeating her attempt to detect hostile magic with a spell, then remembered that her last attempt had instead drifted her helplessly out into the air above the courtyard. While no bad thing in and of itself, her current state of dress might make a repeat performance somewhat embarrassing.

Feathers rustled in the ceiling overhead. The noise, it seemed, had just explained itself—although the local cormorants must have reached the size of elephants, given the way they shook the plaster from the walls. With a sharp breath of self-irritation, Miliana turned back to her bath.

She eased herself into the tub one inch at a time. Hissing, sapped of energy and turning a quiet lobster pink, the girl settled her head back against the wall, closed her eyes, and let her mind wander off into a whirl of steam.

For three days and nights, Miliana had felt a hidden, watchful presence in the house, when she slept, when she dressed—even as she bathed. Experimenting with magic had brought the girl to grand new heights of paranoia; in her mind's fancies, she could imagine herself attracting the attention of unseen, unwholesome powers. Any sorceress worth her salt must surely be in constant danger.

The alternative suggestion, that Miliana was too insignificant for dire, extraplanar fiends to even waste a minute's time about, was simply too miserable a thought for her to contemplate.

Still, the thought had a certain common sense about it. Propping her cheek on her hand, Miliana heaved a great, unhappy sigh.

It would be a bewitching fantasy to consider herself even vaguely important, but the real facts were less than kind. There were no secret birthmarks on her backside, no hidden prophecies that made her the key to liberating mighty empires from evil overlords. Not even a magic talking pony as her special, secret friend . . .

It simply wasn't fair! Every other princess in the world seemed to have a damned prophecy! They were inheritors of evil dooms, magic powers, or the fates of empires. Instead, Miliana had an untranslatable book made from the skin of a dead toad (actually, a number of dead toads), and an attic full of overweight birds. The girl hurtled a pewter jug across the room in helpless frustration, hitting the jasmine creepers on the balcony and making an instant noise of breaking glass. Bits of lens and bent brass pipe went spinning to the courtyard cobbles—all unnoticed as Miliana flung her dripping arms about her knees and hugged herself in impotent misery.

She felt stifled, trapped by a world of rules. How much longer could she escape being forcibly married off to some half-witted Blade Captain? How long would it be before Lady Ulia drove her stark raving mad—or worse, taught her how to think and act just as they felt she should?

Marriage constantly threatened; a life spent shackled to the Lomatran court, or Colletro, or some other gods-forsaken who-knows-where. Magic was the only key to Miliana's prison door. All she needed to do was learn a spell or three; then she could run away somewhere and take adventure by the horns!

Sly and persuasive, Miliana's paranoia perched upon her shoulder and whispered dreary poison in her ear: A *real* heroine wouldn't have to go out and search for adventure. Adventure would simply tumble down into her lap! And would a wandering heroine have access to baths and slippers? Where would a girl find food and drink—a roof from the rain?

Real female adventurers all had skin-tight chain mail, fabulous blonde hair, and magical talking swords and battle-axes and the like. Miliana held out a damp strand of her long brown tresses, bowed her head and closed her eyes in miserable silence.

Remembering page twenty-seven of her spellbook with sudden, gorgeous clarity, Miliana gave a curse and violently splashed her bathwater at the walls.

The results were quite instructive. The spell syllable left Miliana's lips, images of runes burned hot and bright in her mental eye, and the entire world seemed to jump like a grasshopper. Miliana's bathwater rushed out of the tub all in one solid, speedy block—hit the wall and plowed clean through the flimsy plaster. Miliana blinked at the newly made door to her bedroom in surprise, then shrank helplessly back as a wooden structural beam resoundingly split itself in two.

There are few moments in life when a shy, downtrodden individual can truly feel possessed by the gods; time slows, the mind steps into overdrive, and the body moves with a speed, a surety and suppleness that has never been known before. A sword blow is dodged, a falling baby saved, an arrow parts the hangman's rope. These are the times when a mortal being feels utterly alive.

Sadly, for Miliana, this was not one of those times. With a melancholy sense of certainty, Miliana watched the wall collapse and the roof above her bath begin to sag. The ceiling quietly disintegrated into a storm of falling plaster, all of which descended straight down on Miliana's head.

Boards bounced, Miliana squawked, and untold tons of dust and rubbish thundered in from above: plaster, dead insects, live insects, bat guano, and rodent husks. As the *piéce de résistance,* a warm, soft, heavy mass landed hard in Miliana's lap, thrashing and wailing in outrage and surprise.

After the storm, there came the lull. Plaster dust swirled in the air with a curious gentility. Miliana peeled free her spectacles and rubbed the smeared lenses clean using her own bedraggled hair. She put them back in place upon her nose, and stared dully down into the far end of her bath.

A rather surprised-looking bird had landed in the tub—a gigantic orange thing shaped like an over-elaborated peacock. It had a body at least as big as Miliana, coupled with a long neck, a curved beak, and great, razor-sharp claws.

The bird sat in the bathtub and looked at Miliana; Miliana sat in the bathtub and looked at the bird. Both creatures hit on the same inspiration at the self-same time, leaped madly out of the tub, and frantically ducked behind the nearest door.

Stuck all over from head to foot with plaster dust and insect husks, Miliana gave away her hiding place with a sneeze that almost blew her rib cage out. The girl crammed herself into a corner behind a dressing table, peering blindly out through filthy spectacles as she searched for a sign of the missing bird.

Beak. Big beak! The thing had to be a predator. Miliana flicked an eye toward the bedroom door, planning a very slow, very cautious retreat into the palace halls. Nervously wrapping herself inside a soggy towel, she began to edge her way toward her bedroom door.

"Tekorii-kii-kii! Tekorii-kii-kii!"

A great, giddy head—all feathers, dust, and daze, shot out from around the doorframe behind her and gave a hoot of glee. The girl gave a rabbit-squeak of fright, lunged into cover behind the bathtub, and crouched, peering at the intruder across the enamel rim.

Flapping ridiculously stubby wings, the huge bird waddled out onto the open floor; the creature seemed to be constructed mostly of tail, which dragged behind it like the train of an empress's wedding gown. It ducked its head up and down, left and right in mindless eagerness to inspect Miliana from all sides.

Entrenched behind her bathtub, Miliana tried her best to keep the beast away.

"I'm a sorceress! Oh boy—a really powerful sorceress!" The girl raised a hand and tried to encourage a blaze of power to swirl about her fingers. Unfortunately, whatever small store of magical energy Miliana possessed seemed to have spent itself in ejecting her bathwater.

Delighted by Miliana's feeble sparks, the bird vaulted up onto the edge of the bathtub. Fixing Miliana with a giddy smile, it flapped its wings, hurtled back its head, and set the rafters ringing with a ghastly, raucous cry.

"Tekorii-kii-kii!
"Tekorii-kii-kii!"

Gaping its beak open in joy, the bird beat itself in the chest with one wingtip and proudly struck a pose.

"Tekoriikii!"

Sitting on her rump in a pile of debris, Miliana heaved a weary sigh. She reached out a hand to the bird and solemnly shook the outstretched wing.

"Miliana," said the disheveled princess. "Terribly glad to meet you."

* * * * *

A suspicious burbling sound in the iron boilers at the far end of the apartment made Luccio Irozzi look up from his reading with a frown. The untidy mass of tubes and spheres shuddered, bulged, then leaked out a cloud of fragrant purple steam.

"Lorenzo? Lorenzo, come and see to your toys."

Nothing could be heard except the excited scratching of a pen somewhere in the adjoining room.

"Lorenzo?"

Luccio set aside his parchments and glided bonelessly over to the door.

"Lorenzo—if that contraption explodes and slaughters me, I must warn you that my will names you as inheritor of all my debts."

Lost to the world, Luccio's companion sat at a table covered with pieces of thick yellow paper.

"Lorenzo?"

The youth kissed charcoal across the pages with bold, brilliant sweeps of his hand, outlining curves and shadows in an almost random array. Luccio crept closer, watching in fascination as the random lines crept together into pattern, shape, and form, and finally meshed to make the figure of a slim, exquisite maid combing out great sheets of silken hair.

Sitting quietly on the edge of the table, Luccio gave a wry smile and drew the sketch into his hands.

"Drawn from memory?"

"What?" Lorenzo half-surfaced from his artistic frenzy, drawing with his left hand while scribbling notes mirror-wise with his right. "No no—observed. It's all live-drawn."

"Well she must be most accommodating. Either that or stark raving mad." Luccio held aloft a frontal study and raised an incredulous brow. "Are you sure she's a suitable model?"

"Why?" Lorenzo looked up at his friend in utter incomprehension. "What's wrong with her?"

"Um . . . she does lack . . . aaah . . . That is, she seems to have a certain sparsity of . . ."

"Of what?"

"Nothing." Luccio let the subject die a hasty death. "I'm sure this look will come into fashion someday soon."

Thrilled by a good afternoon of work, Lorenzo tossed aside his charcoal and began to briskly wipe his hands on a rag, somehow managing to actually make himself dirtier. His eyes never once left the intricate array of figure drawings on his tabletop: sketches of hands, of elbows and ankles, necks and feet, and all the numerous bits of terrain held in between. The youth picked up one heavy sheet and held it up to the light to admire the best, most subtle portraiture he had ever done.

"She's fabulous! If only you knew, Luccio, just how remarkable she is. Look at the cleanliness of that line."

"Quite." Luccio gave a shake of his head and let the drawings slide, mumbling: "It's certainly a rather straight line . . . *Lorenzo,* O scholar of mine, my dearest and truest of friends, I must now ask you to leave this paradise of artistic forgiveness, and answer for me four questions. That is—four questions of the simplest kind."

Lorenzo squared a velvet cap across his brows, and adjusted the rapier that fashion dictated he wear at all times.

"Do ask. You know I am ever at your disposal."

"In which case . . ." Luccio opened up the connecting door and waved a languid hand in the direction of the tables with their maze of liquids, tubes, and spheres. "At what point in your ancestry was a *gnome* involved? Should this device be leaking? Is it dangerous? And why does it smell of cherry fondue?"

Lorenzo gave a sharp wail of dismay. He flung himself through the door and frantically began twirling valves and beating out braziers with his hat. Luccio watched the process from the safety of the door and drew his brows into a genteel frown.

"Well?"

"Well what?" Lorenzo burned fingertips as he rescued a pot of foaming liquid from the top of an oil burner.

"What are the answers to my four questions?"

"To the first—none of your business. No, it should not be leaking. And no, it isn't dangerous."

A metal sphere burst with a thunderous bang; chemicals lashed across the room, chewing into the stonework wherever they chanced to land. Luccio shook pieces of smoking shrapnel from the crown of his hat, and used a rapier blade to clear himself space upon a chair.

"I see. And the cherry smell?"

Emerging from the wreckage with a heavy sigh, Lorenzo glumly contemplated the ruin of his pipes and tubes, vats and valves.

"It's from over there. The igniter chemicals for the experiment." The young scientist propped his cheek on his chin. "They don't want me using chemicals in the guest rooms, so I disguised the volatiles with the essence of cherry."

Luccio leaned back in his chair with comprehension dawning in his eyes.

"Aaaaah. And might local vermin have . . . eaten this concoction?"

"I suppose they may have." Lorenzo swept broken plumbing from his tabletop with a great, almighty clang. "Why do you ask?"

"Just curious."

There was a brisk rap at the door and Luccio, stepping through smoldering debris, swept the portal open with a bow.

"The volcanology emporium . . . may we help you?"

Bent almost in two, Luccio found himself eye to eye with a petite, freckle-spattered girl. She replied with a hurried little curtsy and a nervous glance left and right along the empty palace hall.

"Greetings, my lord." The girl's spectacles were blank sheets of reflected window light. "I'm looking for a Lomatran."

"Faith, then you have found one." Luccio made his most elaborate of genuflections. "Did madam have anything particular in mind?"

"An idiot with a big drawing pad?"

"Madam, I do believe we can help you." The lanky nobleman ushered his guest in through the door. "Lorenzo—it's for you!"

Stalking into the ruined apartment, Miliana spared a glance at the steaming scars gouged into the fine wood paneling and declined to make a comment. She lifted up her hems, stepped across a tangle of broken pipes, and went in search of a fool.

She found him on the floor, frenziedly decanting a vile cherry-colored liquid into a big glass jar. Lorenzo caught sight of her, instantly tried to leap to his feet, and banged his head painfully on the underside of the table.

"It's you!"

"So I'm told." There were times when Miliana's spectacles gave her a stare like a basilisk. "Does Lady Ulia know you're brewing cherry fondant in her good guest rooms?"

"Um . . . well . . . yes . . ." Lorenzo's skills at falsehood would have done discredit to a wingless fruit fly. "It all comes off with water!"

Miliana inspected a decayed patch of marble paneling. "It's eating into the walls!"

"Only a bit . . ." Lorenzo tried to buff a scorched tabletop, which began crumbling to pieces in his hands. "No one minds. We all make a little mess from time to time."

Catching her foot on a piece of shrapnel, Miliana yelped and fell, only to be caught in Lorenzo's arms. The girl readjusted her pointy hat and scowled down at the debris in scorn.

"What is all this?"

"A light projector! It's going to be an engraving machine—or maybe a lathe." Lorenzo tried to kick broken pieces of steel tankage out of sight. "I'm having trouble with the right mix of chemicals."

"So I see." Briskly straightening her damp robes,

Miliana let the subject drop like an overripe haddock. "Anyway—I came to ask you for some help. Do you know anything about birds?"

Lorenzo blinked in absolute incomprehension. "Birds?"

"Yes, birds. Birds?" Miliana stuck out her fingertips and wagged them frenziedly in the air. "Feathers, beaks, claws—*birds!*"

"Oh, as in avians." The young scholar puffed himself up in pride. "Actually, as it so happens, I am an expert on the subject."

"Truly?"

"I am conducting a close survey of wing structures as a basis for designing my flying machine." Lorenzo reached for a thick leather-bound volume lying on a rapidly disintegrating shelf. "My lady—you have a specimen you wish me to identify?"

"If it's no trouble." Miliana watched Lorenzo as he tried to tuck debris out of the way behind the drapes. "Just leave that. I'll have someone clean it up and repair the walls."

Lorenzo balked at this airy indication of Miliana's hidden powers.

"You can do that?"

Miliana turned about and looked at the young scholar in confusion.

"Well, of course I can do that." The girl looked at the damaged room and shrugged. "Anyway—it happens to me all the time."

"Oh."

"Yes—now come on. I don't want this 'specimen' running loose about my room unattended!"

Lorenzo gathered up his books, a butterfly net and a small magnifying glass, then struggled out into the corridors in hot pursuit of the girl.

He observed his companion as she walked, fascinated by the interplay of wistful expression, subtle line, and seething irritation. Passing by the kitchen door, Miliana stole one of Lady Ulia's fruit carts, trundling the collection of oranges, melon slices and cheese off along the halls to her tower. Keeping an eye out for passing stepmothers, Miliana opened her locks and hastily crammed Lorenzo through the open door.

"Tekorii-kii-kii! Tekorii-kii-kii!"

A raucous screech joyfully heralded their entry. Lorenzo hefted his butterfly net and moved to the fore, ready to snare Miliana's wild bird. Behind him, Miliana rolled in the fruit cart and nudged the door shut.

"I'm back!" Miliana whirred her cart past the startled Lorenzo and moved out into her room. "I brought you fruit—you know, to eat? Mmmmmmm! Yummy yummy!"

Lorenzo heard the flap of wings from deep inside the girl's boudoir. With a heroic flourish of his net, he stepped into the doorway, saw the creature sitting on Miliana's worktable, and froze as stiff as if he had walked in on a medusa in her bath.

Flapping happy wings in greeting, the titanic, silly bird rose from the table and floundered forward toward Miliana. A mixture of bright orange, golden yellows and rich flame reds, the creature's plumage smote the eyes. Cooing and cawing to itself, the bird strode waggishly forward to inspect the fruit cart with avid, hungry eyes.

In essence, the bird consisted of a long length of neck, a stubby body, and acres of glorious tail. This magnificence had then been garnished by adding a beak thick enough to sever a man's hand, and great hooked talons at the ends of cheery yellow feet. Lorenzo stared at the creature, felt the blood drain from his head; then drew his rapier and took an instinctive step to place himself between the fair damsel and the great carnivorous bird.

The movement took the feathery being all aback. The bird looked from Miliana to Lorenzo, flapped its wings in indignation, and suddenly seemed to swell up to enormous size. Feathers fluffed and neck arching high above Lorenzo, the bird shuddered with appalling rage and hissed its way across the floor.

Faced with a monster, Lorenzo crouched, desperately trying to decide whether to flee or fight. Seeing its rival cowed, the bird halted its rush and loomed above the young man, beak agape and wings shaking to and fro as it strutted back and forth in glorious majesty. Finally content with its display, the bird flattened down its feathers and waddled back to Miliana.

Lorenzo recovered slowly, like a garden snail emerging cautiously from its shell. The bird gave itself very superior airs, lowering its eyelids to look back across its shoulders in scorn.

Miliana watched the whole affair in wry silence, and then planted a fist upon her hip as she addressed the giant bird.

"Finished?"

"Nonk nonk!" The bird settled its feathers.

Without the slightest trace of malice, the bird happily sidled over to Lorenzo and inspected him from head to toe, seeming to approve of everything he saw. Lorenzo returned the creature look for look, studying it in speechless amazement. Bird and nobleman circled one another in a dizzy parade until Lorenzo pulled away and fixed his hostess with an incredulous eye.

"Where in the name of the Binder of What is Known did you find it?"

"Oh, it found me." Miliana busied herself peeling an apple, using a ridiculous amount of concentration and crinkling up her freckled, upturned nose. "Or rather *he* found me. He dropped in through the ceiling, just over there." The girl pointed with her fruit knife at a chaotic wreck of plaster, ceiling boards, and dirt. "I think he's been living up there in the attic for quite a while."

Lorenzo picked his way through the rubble, cautiously climbed onto the rim of Miliana's filthy bathtub, and used the perch to see up into the attic. The filtered light showed the conical space to be largely empty, except for a great pile of wrack and rags which Lorenzo took to be the creature's nest.

"Well, there doesn't seem to be any more of them."

"One's quite enough, thank you." Miliana passed each of her companions a slice of apple. The bird held the fruit delicately in his beak and rotated it around and around with flicks of a hard, horny tongue. "I've never heard of anything like him, have you?"

"No. No, not at all." Lorenzo hoisted his reference book onto his hip and opened the cover, jamming his apple in his mouth. " 'Ot do 'ou call 'im?"

The bird replied with a great, eager flapping of wings.

"Tekorii-kii-kii!

"Tekorii-kii-kii!"

Miliana peeled another apple, her brows creasing themselves behind her spectacles. ". . . Tekoriikii."

"So I hear." Lorenzo tried to take measurements of the uncooperative Tekoriikii's skull. "There's quite an extensive cranium. Unusual for an avian, wouldn't you say?"

"Oh, he's intelligent." Miliana looked over at the bird, which was in danger of getting his head caught inside a flower vase. "Well—sentient, anyway. He does have a language."

"Truly?" Lorenzo inspected the patterns on the bird's tail feathers with his magnifying glass. "How can you tell?"

"You just have to watch him for a while. One picks it up eventually."

The bird stood on one foot, using his other claw to hold a big round cheese; he seemed to be consuming the hard rind and letting the soft center fall in pieces to the carpet. Miliana sighed and wondered how she was ever going to make the room seem clean. A maid would run wailing straight to Ulia; the only thing for it was to sweep up the filth herself, then see about patching the ceiling. Miliana stood to survey the damage, fists on her hips and her pointy hat tilted far back from her brows, while behind her Lorenzo and Tekoriikii deepened their acquaintance.

Using his magnifying glass, Lorenzo inspected Tekoriikii's talons, feet, and eyes; he flipped though pages of his book, thoughtfully holding drawings up against the light, then solemnly shaking his head in disappointment.

With her sleeves rolled up and a broom in hand, Miliana came to peer across the young noble's shoulder and scan his current page.

"Well, have you discovered what he is?"

"Absolutely!" Lorenzo closed his guidebook with a great, satisfied bang. "Master Tekoriikii is a phoenix."

The announcement was met by an unconvinced adjustment of Miliana's spectacles. Lorenzo decided that his professional judgment was being belittled, and opened up the pages of his book by way of proof.

"Here—see? *Phoenix Nobilus Conflagrata*—the sacred, or fiery, phoenix."

Miliana looked down at the picture in Lorenzo's book. It detailed a lean, elegant creature with willowy proportions and a haughty air sitting on a nest of crackling flames. The girl pushed her spectacles down her nose, peered across the rims toward the happy-go-lucky Tekoriikii, then swiveled hazel eyes back to Lorenzo's hopeful face.

"I think not."

"But milady, it's the same color. Look, do you see? Orange pinions and highlights of flame red hue."

"He is *not* a phoenix!" Miliana prevented the bird from swallowing a ball of potpourri. "Phoenixes are big on spontaneous combustion and very big on brains."

"Why does that rule out this specimen?"

Tekoriikii went avidly on about his affairs; Miliana irritably shifted the potpourri out of reach again. "Just call it woman's intuition. I think we can rule out the phoenix thing."

Lorenzo paused, sucking on the wrong end of his pen.

"We could always set fire to him and see."

"Not with *my* giant bird you don't!" Miliana threw protective arms around Tekoriikii's neck, and the bird blinked in surprise. "Now just search the book. Doesn't it say anything?"

Lorenzo sat cross-legged in the plaster dust and flipped through the pages of his references. Miliana swept the floor all around him; the bird soon came to her assistance and began carrying broken boards and plaster in his beak—usually depositing his loads on the patches of floor Miliana had just finished sweeping. Unseeing and uncaring, Lorenzo kept on with his studies, calling out possibilities through the legs of the fruit cart.

"Peacock?"

"A *peacock?*" Miliana's voice pealed loud in shock. "He's two yards long! Twelve if you count the tail."

"Maybe he's a *giant* peacock. Anyway, his tail's nowhere near ten yards. Maybe as many feet, but. . . ."

Tekoriikii couldn't help a glance at his backside, then something like a shrug.

"Maybe." Miliana began dragging her bathtub over to her balcony. "Keep looking."

Lorenzo flipped a page, oblivious to the girl's surprising display of strength.

"Here's an axe beak. A sort of flightless carnivore. Would you say he's flightless?"

Tekoriikii obligingly extended a short, feathery wing. Lorenzo sighed and went back to his books.

"It would help if we knew where he came from. He can't possibly be native to the Blade Kingdoms. I still feel the red coloring indicates an affinity for fire." A drawing slipped from Lorenzo's volume, a detailed drawing of a falcon's wing. "Ask him if he came from an area of pronounced volcanic activity—like the Smoking Mountains of Unther or the Lake of Steam."

Miliana cocked an eyebrow at the bird, who threw back his head and began to play out a little dance.

"Tekorii-kii-kii! Tekorii-kii-kii!"

The creature danced a little to the left, danced a little to the right; shook his tail high while bobbing his head down low. Finally he extended one great yellow talon and made a ghastly noise reminiscent of a wet leather trombone.

Miliana turned back to Lorenzo with a sigh.

"He says he doesn't know."

Every other princess in the world managed to win themselves a magical talking horse or a pegasus or even a blink dog as their companion. Instead, Miliana seemed to have just acquired a giant, crazed, orange bird-of-paradise.

Lorenzo closed his books with a helpless shrug. The two young humans sat side by side on Miliana's bed and watched the bird preening the feathers under his wing.

"Will you make him a cage?"

"Certainly not!" Miliana was utterly outraged. "What a wretched suggestion. He's not doing anyone any harm up in the attic."

Lorenzo watched the busy bird with a blossoming sense of awe.

"I'd like to study him some more. Still—maybe we ought to make him feel more at home."

"How?"

"Maybe we could make an enormous seed bell?"

The bird had taken an interest in Miliana's picture books. He stood with his head cranked over to one side staring at a painted fairy tale. Handsome as a cast bronze god, the bird settled itself down and began to happily turn page after page.

Miliana regarded the creature with loving fascination; the expression lit her from within like a pure, new summer's dawn.

"This isn't so bad. I mean, how much trouble can a big orange bird be?" Her face suddenly innocent and eager, Miliana turned bright eyes upon Lorenzo and trapped him in her gaze. "Hey! Have you ever heard any prophecies about birds and princesses?"

"No." Lorenzo swayed, trapped by Miliana's brilliant gaze. "No, I can't say that I have. Why?"

"It was just a thought."

Evening was falling. In the palace courtyard, Lady Ulia's voice could be heard as she harassed decorators, servants, cooks and guards. The starlings swirled high above Miliana's balcony heading for their noisy beds.

Lost in peace and quiet, maiden, boy and orange bird all sat to watch the sky stream with tints of rose.

Lorenzo turned to watch the young woman at his side; her whole being seemed to shimmer as she smiled.

"Milady? How are you going to explain the broken ceiling?"

"I'm working on it." Miliana propped her chin on her knees and watched the glorious bright bird. "Let's just take one thing at a time. . . ."

Skies darkened, starlings whirled, while in Miliana's room, Tekoriikii the firebird posed for Lorenzo's sketching charcoal with every appearance of joy.

*   *   *   *   *

Smeared with dust and cobwebs, Orlando Toporello thundered in through the Mannicci stables and slung his cloak across a stall. Mice squeaked and skittered from his path as he chased grooms out from hiding and bid them attend to his mount. Prince Mannicci watched all from his perch atop his own great golden horse, then swung himself down to greet his friend man-to-man.

"No sign, Toporello?"

"No sign, my lord!" Old Toporello slashed at a nightspider's web with his riding crop. "Another necklace stolen last night, right from under the eyes of the patrol. I have men combing every street, and there's not even a footprint to this cat-burglar's name."

"The festival will calm him." Prince Mannicci fell in step beside his oldest friend. "The parties will fill the palaces and give our thief too many eyes to dodge. We have a week in which to think of better plans."

Plans. Toporello sat and rested his weary bones on the edge of a fountain, cracking shoulders stiffened by long, hard years of drill and war.

"Speaking of plans, my lord, have the Lomatrans made any offers for your daughter's hand?"

"The bridegroom has asked to stay in the palace. He

must be pressing forward with his suit."

"And what of the girl? Does she find the match worthwhile?"

"If it keeps Ilégo from the door, it's well worthwhile."

Prince Mannicci had given his daughter his own sharp wits, clear mind, and stubborn will. The only thing he had refused her was his time. Toporello cast a glance toward the princess's little tower and chewed a strand of his own mustache.

"I see a pattern forming. Unless this boy is a better specimen than the last, I fear he shall soon discover the special joys that earwigs can bring."

"Earwigs?"

"Merely a reflection, lord, that clever sparrows can have sharp beaks." Toporello gave a sigh and heaved himself erect. "In any case, my lord, 'tis time for bed. Tomorrow brings the festival—and the dance with Ilégo can grow tiring for old bones."

"I intend to see that we both make old bones." Prince Mannicci tightened the fit of his gloves. "Goodnight, old friend. Guard your back well."

Toporello faded into the evening gloom, leaving his monarch standing alone inside the fountain yard. Tugging his gloves hard down across his wrists, the prince stood and stared in silence at his daughter's balcony before stalking back inside the palace halls.

6

In the last flickers of the evening light, when the horizon swam stark with streamers of eggplant purple and shimmering gold, a convoy of carriages made their way in through the gates of Sumbria. Creaking softly, their dray beasts plodding slowly with the fatigue of a long day's travel through the burning hills, the overdecorated coaches passed by the city gates, then moved down toward Sumbria's busy inns.

Lords and ladies alighted: Colletro's gentry come to do duty by the victors of this year's campaign. They were handed down from their carriages by Sumbrian footmen, then met by lines of heralds, torch-bearers and trumpeters. With stiffly formal manners, hosts and guests made bows; then the purely theoretical enemies went together into the great hollow squares of palaces to while away the nighttime hours.

Preparations for the Festival of Blades were gaining momentum day by day; jugglers and puppeteers were installed at every plaza, while children ran about the streets fighting ferocious mock battles with painted wooden swords. Watching the melee swirl past, Blade Captain

Gilberto Ilégo leaned idly against a tavern door, breathed in the nocturnal airs, and heaved a contented sigh.

The evenings of late summer always seemed to sizzle with the delicious scent of hot, scorched dust. Dressed in bonnet and plume, jerkin and tight hose, Blade Captain Ilégo savored the night's bouquet as though it were a primrose bloom. He watched the carriages winding inward through the gates, watched the delicate ladies and swaggering gentlemen enter their palaces and towers, and let his face draw into a slow, cool smile.

The city brimmed with guests—creatures of a hundred different races. The festival drew them as moths gathered to a candle flame. Slim elves could be seen watching the puppet booths and games, bulb-nosed dwarves from the Great Rift came to trade for surveying instruments, and a gnome illusionist astonished children with clever magic tricks. Most astonishing of all, a nixie damsel—a sharply beautiful water maiden with scales of pink and rose—was borne down the street in a glass-sided sedan chair filled with lake water. As she slid past, the creature gave a smile and locked with Ilégo's eyes.

A shadow fell across the streets; wing feathers beat up a storm of dust as a great black form settled down into the central plaza of Sumbria. Ilégo tossed aside his musings as though casting a flower out into the road, and settled back to watch Colletro's senior Blade Captain scanning Sumbria in scorn.

The man wore the most elemental of costumes: a brigantine of black velvet lined with silver studs and a barbute helmet covered in wine-dark cloth. His hippogriff—a shrewish, violent mare with elongated claws and a wicked eye—luffed its eagle wings and searched the streets for handy prey. Finding nothing worth killing close at hand, the creature muttered softly to its rider, then sank onto its haunches to let the man slide to the ground.

The Colletran noble had an escort, four of Sumbria's air cavalry all armed with light crossbows. Their prim white mounts shook out their feathers in disapproval of their guest's surly beast, stepping pointedly aside as the creature hungrily eyed their haunches.

Ilégo detached himself from the tavern door. The motion caught the Colletran's eye, who turned about to stand posing in the open shadows with one hand upon his blade. Ilégo moved himself deliberately out into the open street, placed one foot behind the other and spread his arms open in his courtliest of bows.

"Honored Blade Captain Svarézi. How very good of you to come."

Ugo Svarézi—armored, armed, and squat—glared at the intruder with eyes of watered steel.

"Why am I here?"

"Surely to enjoy the festival." Ilégo stood, his dark eyes missing nothing as he drank in the foreigner at a glance. "I have come to meet you. To extend Sumbria's most gracious hospitality.

"Pray, let your beast be stabled, and we shall walk the streets a while."

Svarézi flicked a glance at the crowded streets, the rooftops and the shadows, then judged himself to be under little threat of assassination. Ilégo, he dismissed as a lighter, less armored man with a blade fit only for tickling boys. With a side glance at his host, the Colletran bowed slightly forward in acknowledgment.

"Shaatra. Follow."

The black hippogriff answered with an evil-tempered hiss, gave up her attempts to snatch a piece out of passing pedestrians, and favored her master with a series of beak clicks and caws. The man answered in kind, the hippogriff regarded Ilégo through seething ice-blue eyes, and then Svarézi took his place at Ilégo's side. Followed by a lean and hungry monster, the two nobles moved down a street filled by puppet plays, sausage stalls and dust.

Gilberto Ilégo—tall, smooth and suave—tried his level best to begin a conversation.

"Your beast, sir—the hippogriff. I cannot help but

notice that it speaks."

"She does." Svarézi's armor clanked stiffly as he walked; no further explanation seemed forthcoming. "I have business in Colletro. I have no time for foolish festivals. Why was I invited here?"

"Why?" Ilégo led the way into a long, deserted alleyway beside a quiet graveyard. "I suppose because your presence would be a diplomatic nicety. You were, after all, at the famous 'defeat'." Ilégo twisted the words home like a nicely sugared knife. "I'm sure the surrender of the Sun Gem will be made all the sweeter by your cowed and conquered presence."

Svarézi growled, turning on Ilégo like a rat baring its fangs. Ilégo raised a questioning brow as though caught in innocent surprise.

"What? Were you not part of the defeat, brother? You do, of course, agree that it was a defeat?"

"It was a parlor game! Nothing more!" The Colletran shifted his weight as if preparing for battle—echoed by the venomous hiss of his hippogriff. "Not a soldier was man enough to risk meeting us blade-to-blade."

"Ah." Ilégo paused, elegant and sly as he laid another sally neatly at his companion's feet. "Until now, perhaps? Surely you and I could be said to be meeting blade-to-blade." The Sumbrian nobleman came to a bare knoll overlooking the city cemetery. "Ah—and here we are at last! Do please keep your beast sitting nicely at the verge."

The open knoll formed an island in a sea of drab two-story houses, a place surrounded by walls of black and empty windowsills. The cobbled streets emptied out into the dirt like gaping mouths, spilling tongues of dust that glimmered pale against the grass.

It was a place of thistledown and rattling weeds, of hard-packed soil and serpent coils of shadow. A ring of torches lit the hillside with an ebb and flow of light, while silent watchers rimmed the clearing with sharp, unwinking eyes.

Two young men fenced at the center of the knoll, rapier and dagger against rapier and buckler. Blade Captain Ilégo handed off his outer jacket, keeping a critical eye on the combatants as they strove blade against blade.

"What, colleague, is your opinion of the swordplay?"

"Swords should not be things for play." Ugo Svarézi watched the thin rapiers lunge and sweep with undisguised contempt. "Toy swords for toy soldiers."

"Lethal toys—although it hardly ever comes to death. One or the other usually capitulates before the final curtain can be drawn." Ilégo draped his jacket casually across a broken tree. "Still, I find honor to be such a delicious tool, don't you?"

The fencers seemed to notice the two Blade Captains simultaneously. As one they went stock-still, staring rigidly at the Sumbrian nobleman, then parted and reluctantly opened out the space between them.

In the center of a field of grass, a young man waited—a lean, brooding figure clad in scarlet velvets that swirled like flowing blood. He put out his right hand to receive a long silver blade, then his left, taking a metal buckler the size of a dinner plate.

Gilberto Ilégo virtually ignored the man. He drew two weapons from his belt: the first a wicked rapier with a long, whip-thin blade, and the second a short, thick swordbreaker notched all down its leading edge like a lethal comb. He passed them to a gray-bearded dignitary, who inspected the steel in the light, sniffing like a bloodhound at the blade. Satisfied, he passed back the weapons; Ilégo saw that the old man's breath had clouded up the flawless steel and frowned, polishing the rapier against his shirttails until it shone.

Ilégo strode out toward his opponent, never even deigning to go on guard. He made a swat at the other man's sword, walked casually around his enemy and let his face droop in a sneer.

The aged umpire had never bothered to signal for the combat to begin. He watched with arms folded and black eyes glittering like beads as the two nobles circled one another with crossed blades.

The young man swept his blade at Ilégo's calf and swirled forward hoping to punch his buckler into his enemy's face. Ilégo, standing crouched and square with his blades held tight, simply shook his weapons and brought his opponent to a halt. Spitting with contempt, he straightened up and once again began his casual circling, letting his sword droop almost to the ground.

His enemy lunged. Ilégo paid no attention to the blade; he whipped his sword across his opponent's forearm, raising the barest cut across the flesh. The blow minutely deflected his opponent's blade, causing the rapier to flicker past Ilégo's ear. The young man leapt wildly back, fearing a brutal stab from Ilégo's swordbreaker. Yet for his part, the Blade Captain scarcely seemed interested at all.

Gritting his teeth, the youth flickered into the attack. Finally he engaged Ilégo's attention. The young man hammered at Ilégo's sword with his tiny buckler, jabbed, lunged, and jerked his sword back from Ilégo's reach. A second stab was met by a sharp flick of the swordbreaker; the comblike blade rasped against the rapier, nearly trapping it between the tines. Parrying wildly with his shield, the youth forced Ilégo's rapier aside, staggered back from a slash of the swordbreaker, blocked a lunge at his bowels and stumbled free.

Ilégo pursued him, and the young man could only meet attack after attack. The blades stabbed home time and time again, clashing against one another in a splash of sparks. Hissing evilly, Ilégo rammed his opponent far aside, sending the dazed youth staggering back across the grass.

Fighting for breath and whipping sweat back from his eyes, Ilégo's opponent drove himself lurching back into the fight. He stabbed low, skipped forward, stabbed and lunged again. With a cry of hate he stamped his foot, then tried to disengage and lunge, his blade moving clumsily aside. Ilégo let the young man run clean onto his outstretched blade, ramming it unerringly through his opponent's heart. He whipped free his steel and turned aside to wipe his blade clean on a silken handkerchief, not even deigning to watch the body fall.

Seconds ran forward to the young man's corpse. Ilégo walked casually away across the dead, dry grass, made a sardonic salute of his swordbreaker toward the old man in the shadows, and strolled to rejoin his guest. The Sumbrian sheathed his sword without a trace of triumph or satisfaction.

"The Riturba family is such a bore. I foreclose on their loan, and what do they do but cry me up as a cheat?"

The nobleman favored Svarézi with a smile.

"I do find honor to be a fascinating thing. If I had killed him with a dagger in the back, I should surely have hung. Instead, I run him through before two dozen witnesses, and am reckoned to be a gentleman." Ilégo adjusted the set of one glove. "With luck, his brothers will raise challenge, and I can clean out the whole gutless brood within the week."

Ugo Svarézi laid a hand upon his hippogriff's feathery mane.

"Unless they stumble on to your treachery, Sumbrian."

"Stumble on it? Quite unlikely." Ilégo gave a smile. "The poison, of course, was merely a soporific, something to slow his reactions and allow a killing blow. I do find it quite untraceable." The noble retrieved his jacket from its tree limb, still not even bothering to spare his dead opponent a glance. "Naturally enough, the venom was impregnated into the tails of my shirt."

There followed a pause—a time where both men gazed at each other in the shadows of the killing ground. A cool night wind came to stir Gilberto Ilégo's hair.

"You have *desires,* colleague. Desires thwarted and choked by rules." Framed against the graveyard, Ilégo fixed Svarézi with a snake's black, calculating eye. "I can show you how to fashion the rules into your tool, colleague. *Our* tool."

Ilégo drew forth a parchment—the torn lower half of the same letter Svarézi carried against his heart. The torn pieces were a perfect match.

"You have asked, colleague, why you are here. The answer is simple. I have asked you to come in the interest of our mutual advancement. It is high time that we men of potential moved our sights beyond the bounds of a single city's walls."

In the darkness beside them, the black hippogriff gave a sharp hiss of desire. Behind her, the moon rose across the killing grounds and stained the dry grass with lifeless gray.

* * * * *

"Tekorii-kii-kii!
"Tekorii-kii-kii!"

Miliana looked up from her books and charts, smiling as she saw the great long neck dangling down from the hole in the bathroom ceiling. Tekoriikii's giddy, crested head announced itself with pride.

"Tekorii-kii-kii!"

"Well, hello!" Miliana closed her books and leaned upon her elbow to regard the bird. "Where have you been?"

"Glub glub!"

The bird jumped down through the broken ceiling in a swirl of feathers and landed on the blue-tiled floor. Thus far Miliana had kept the portal secret by ruthlessly chasing all maids and servants away from her room; a ruse that would only work until Lady Ulia freed herself from the distractions offered by the Festival of Blades.

Tekoriikii warbled happily and marched himself into Miliana's study room. The bird walked with a rolling seaman's gait, trailing a vast mass of gorgeous orange tail behind it. Silly plumes above his head bobbed and nodded as he walked, waggling like a gaudy helmet comb as he ducked his head about in avian curiosity. He sidled over to Miliana, cocked an eye at her books, and offered her a delighted smile.

Miliana unwrapped a rock-hard salted ship's biscuit, peering warmly at her guest.

"Did you eat? Here's something for dinner, if you want it. Just as a warning—don't eat any of the palace rats. They smell like cherries, but they're behaving very, *very* strangely. . . ."

The bird extended a genteel foot and fastened it about the biscuit. Tekoriikii gnawed the tidbit with an air of concentration, keeping one golden yellow eye on Miliana's face.

Miliana ruffled her scrolls and settled the toadskin sheets back into order.

"You've been very quiet up there. Were you asleep, or did you go off for a flight?"

Aaaaah! Tekoriikii instantly launched into an attempt to relate his evening's adventures. The bird danced high, the bird danced low—he gaped his beak and wobbled his backside up and down as though it came equipped with springs. A slap on his chest and a proud puff of feathers ended his announcement, and the firebird clucked his tongue and let smug self-satisfaction shine like fire in his eyes.

Miliana adjusted her spectacles across her freckled nose.

"No . . . I didn't quite catch that. Actually, languages don't really seem to be my strong point." The girl scowled in concentration. "I will keep trying, though. See here? I think I've managed to assign sounds to the first three ideographs on page seventeen. . . ."

The princess had been hard at work over her puzzling collection of toadskin scrolls. Tekoriikii helpfully came over to inspect the results of her day's labor, darting his head erratically this way and that as he examined the pages with their absurd calligraphy and diagrams. Miliana spread the pages open for him, pleased to at last have someone with whom to discuss her ideas.

"It's not orcish, and it's not elven. It looks like a southern language—sort of an early dialect of Akalan, maybe—

but it isn't." The girl paused, then waved a finger over the cryptic texts. "I'm trying to turn them all into something I can understand. Some of them are magic chants, but others are mental images I have to frame in my mind if I'm going to cast the spell . . . maybe spell ingredients, or possibly phases of the moon . . ." Miliana flipped a clammy page of her collection and gave a frustrated sigh. "I just can't find the key! I have to stare and stare at a page for hours and hours. Sometimes I seem to understand, and sometimes I just can't."

"Glub glub?" The bird flipped a toadskin over with his beak, scanning the page beneath. *"Onk honk?"*

"No, I thought of that. If I hired someone to cast a spell which would allow me to understand the scrolls, he'd tell my father. There's nothing for it but to break the code myself."

Tekoriikii coiled his head back on his neck to look the girl in the face with his astonishing golden eyes.

"Krrrrrrrk?" Wings wagged, and a foot spread its toes into a complex little sign. *"Grook awk?"*

"Well, yes—if they find out I'm doing it, it's all over. They'll burn the books and toss me out to some finishing school somewhere; no more Miliana." The girl hissed a sharp sigh for the injustices of her world. She then brightened up, pulled out her pointiest of hats, and held it open to the bird.

"Aaaah—but see? Even in finishing school, I'd still bring my pointy hat! So what I'm doing is copying the scrolls in miniature and hiding them inside the hat lining. You see? Always anticipate disaster, birdie my friend. That's what makes a great thinker a great thinker!"

It had been a long, frustrating evening of close-written work. Miliana reached fingers under the frames of her spectacles and wearily rubbed her eyes. Stifling a yawn, she leaned back in her chair and absently scratched the warm, soft feathers of the giant bird.

"Ooooort ooor! Ooooort ooor!"

Proud, pleased, and pampered, Tekoriikii began a

song—a melody that started like the nighttime murmur of priceless, winsome hummingbirds, then changed into something reminiscent of a live narwhal being fed backward through a sausage machine. The awful row set bats starting up out of the eaves, caused nearby flowers to wilt, and set guard dogs howling for miles around. Feeling her hair loosen at the roots, Miliana gave a squawk of panic and frantically clamped the bird's beak shut with her hands. Tekoriikii's throat pouch bulged, and his eyes almost burst out of his head.

"Miliaaaa-naaaaaa! Miliana, what's that noise?"

The imperious summons cut through solid stone to stick right into Miliana's heart. Tekoriikii flattened himself against a wall, his chest panting and his eyes mad with fear—the usual reaction to one's first encounter with Lady Ulia's voice. Miliana sped to the door and frantically ran her eyes across the room.

The door pounded to a hammering fist.

"Miliana! Miliana! Open up this door and speak to me at once!"

Tekoriikii began to flap madly about the room, rebounding off the ceiling, cupboards, walls and floors in panic as Ulia's voice pealed through the air. Miliana stuffed her toadskin scrolls inside her pointy hat; then helplessly tried to latch her hands onto the bird.

"Tekorii-kii-kii! Tekorii-kii-kii!"

"Miliana! Miliana, what's that sound?"

The princess managed to grab Tekoriikii's yellow feet and anchor him to the floor. Her clothing whipped backward in the breeze of frantic wings.

"It's—it's just me looking for clothes!"

"Clothes? What do you mean clothes?"

"I can't open the door!" Miliana hurtled her arms around Tekoriikii and wrestled his writhing bulk to the ground. "I—I'm unsuitably dressed!"

"Not dressed? Sooth, girl! I am your stepmother, not your sweetheart!" Ulia's fist pounded at the door until the tower foundations began to quake. "Now open this door!"

Miliana stuffed the firebird under the covers of her bed and pathetically tried to smooth the blankets down. It was a little like hiding a landshark in a china teacup. Backing frantically toward the door, the girl tried to motion Tekoriikii to stay hidden, then whirled about and ripped open the door locks.

"Ulia! Stepmother, what a surprise to find you up at this late hour."

"And when can I be expected to sleep?" Ulia sniffed in indignation. "The palace has over thirty guests. Thirty!" Pulling up her hems to reveal ankles like oak trunks, Lady Ulia Mannicci stepped across the threshold. "This festival shall be the death of me yet. Now, what was all this chaos and cacophony I heard from the corridor just now?"

Miliana twittered her fingers in the air with a devil-may-care wave.

"A sneeze . . . it was just a sneeze."

"A *sneeze?*" Ulia swelled like a mushroom after a summer rain. "What made you sneeze?"

"Um . . ." Not dust! Dust would make Ulia send for the cleaners. Miliana desperately tried to wrench inspiration out of thin air. "It was . . . feathers!"

Eyes narrowing in sharp suspicion, Ulia swept about the room. Miliana tried to guard the way into her bathroom, feeling a sweat of fear break out all along her spine.

Disorder attracted Lady Ulia like honey drew flies. She spied Miliana's disheveled bed, and before the girl could even squeak, her stepmother had whipped away the covers. There, sitting on the mattress for all the world to see, was a giant peacock/rooster/phoenix creature with giddy golden eyes.

Tekoriikii had frozen in pure fright, rooted to the spot by his first face-to-face encounter with Sumbria's most notorious secret weapon. Lady Ulia turned her back, waved an imperious hand over the paralyzed bird, and glared her stepdaughter straight in the eye.

"Well? I trust there is an explanation for the presence
of this . . . this . . . *thing?*"

Tekoriikii went from mere paralysis into a boneless
state of limp, abject terror. Miliana picked up his neck
and felt it hang like boiled spaghetti in her hands.

Her thoughts came very, very slowly—dragged through
a thick curtain of dismay.

"It's . . . a . . . costume."

Lady Ulia slowly raised an eyebrow.

"Yes?"

"For the ball tomorrow night." Miliana's lie finally
found its feet. She shook out the comatose Tekoriikii like
an old blanket across her bed. "I thought I'd wear it for
the masque."

"But my dear, I though you'd wear your little fairy costume. I did so like the wings." Lady Ulia picked up
Tekoriikii's head. "What an amazingly stupid face! You
operate it as a sort of puppet, I suppose?" Miliana's stepmother hoisted up Tekoriikii's tail. "Do you put your hand
up here?"

"*No!*" Miliana lunged forward in alarm. "No . . . it's . . .
the glue's still drying."

"Oh, of course. Please don't mind me, child. The
evening has me so very, very tired." Ulia rolled her eyes
and sighed. "Thirty guests. Did I tell you? We have thirty
guests!"

"Have we really?"

"Yes—now what did I come in here for?" Lady Ulia bustled herself out into the palace corridors. "Now do get
some sleep, child. The ball is tomorrow night. There's the
Sun Gem to receive, elven ambassadors to welcome, and
I still have no idea where I shall show this silly painting
from Lomatra. . . ."

The great lady cruised off into the darkness in a confused babble of her own woes, and Miliana gratefully
slammed the door shut behind her. Miliana wearily
wiped sweat back from her eyes and prayed that Ulia had
been mollified for yet another day.

From beneath Miliana's pillow, a muffled voice nervously explored the air.

"Glub glub?"

"Yes, she's gone." Miliana peeled herself away from the wall. "You can come out now."

Tekoriikii had hidden himself by the simple ruse of stuffing his head under the eiderdown. Inch by inch the creature cautiously emerged; his beak now looked a distinctly ashen shade of gray.

He had been lucky; a close encounter with Ulia could age some creatures by twenty years.

A light tap came at the sealed shutters of Miliana's window. The girl ignored the noise and made her way over to the bed, where she tried to prop up the bird and bring the life back into his limbs.

"Well it's your own fault, you know. All princesses are guarded by monsters. This one's just a bit louder and more powerful than most." Miliana removed her spell scrolls from inside her hat, which now had a pungent smell of sun-dried toads. "Come on—cheer up, eat your biscuits, and we'll go and have some fun."

A sharper rap came at Miliana's window. She briefly scowled, removed her spectacles, and polished the lenses on Tekoriikii's tail.

There it came again! Sharp and brief, like a night bird smacking into the shutters, or a branch flicking at the walls. Miliana heard the sound for a fourth time, rose, and opened her shutters to scowl out into the night.

A stone smacked her right on the brow. With a curse that would have made a drill sergeant blush, the girl fell back from the window half blinded in pain. Like the well-brought-up young lady that she was, Miliana furiously snatched the rock and pitched it straight back down into the dark. A rich, meaty thump followed by a piteous wail of pain rose from the courtyard below.

Lorenzo staggered out into the lamplight, looking up at Miliana with accusing, wounded eyes.

"What did you do that for?"

The girl leaned from her balcony, wondering if she should let down her hair; Lorenzo could then climb into reach so she could strangle him. Miliana rubbed ill-humoredly at her smarting forehead and glared down at the young man.

"Did you throw rocks at my damned window?"

"I wanted to quietly attract your attention." Lorenzo drew stares from three passing gardeners, a night watchman and a maid. "I want you to come out with me, in secret!"

Miliana glared at the staring servants through spectacles that shone blank as ice.

"He's the jester for tomorrow night. He's just practicing his routines." A maid looked at a gardener, seeming timid and unsure. Miliana sent them scuttling for cover with a roar. "Haven't you people got work to do? Or does Lady Ulia have to come on another inspection tour?"

The courtyard cleared with unbelievable speed and Lorenzo was left alone amidst a cloud of dust left by fleeing servants. He looked about himself in awe, then stared happily up at Miliana's face.

"I'm planning a fact-finding tour of the city. Will you come? We could take our feathery friend . . ."

"Shut up!" Miliana pegged her shutters open one by one. "Just climb up the jasmine creepers before somebody sees you!"

Shouldering an untidy parcel—his sketch pads, books and pens—Lorenzo made a creditable show of swarming up into the princess's balcony. He sprang into Miliana's rooms without the slightest hint of terror or embarrassment.

"Isn't it the most incredible night? The moon looks utterly entrancing. I've been doing that anatomy work I discussed with you, and so I suddenly just had to see you." Lorenzo tipped his cap to the girl and lit the room with an innocent, boyish smile. "Hello old bird! How do you do?"

Tekoriikii warbled, lowered his lashes, and fluffed up his plumes, obviously feeling his old self once more.

Lorenzo unshipped one of his books and spread it out across Miliana's tabletop.

"I've found him, by the way, in *Groonpeck's Field Guide to Terrifying Denizens of the Air, with special appendices for Acheron, the Elemental Planes, and the Abyss.*" Lorenzo swept open the volume and proudly pointed to the page. "He's a firebird!"

Miliana, Lorenzo, and the bird all craned to stare at the book; it contained a picture of a handsome orange bird with a great overabundance of tail plumes. Even Miliana couldn't fault the likeness. She polished her spectacles, leaned over the book, then lowered her frames down her nose to regard the bird across the wire rims.

"Is that what you are? A firebird?"

"Gronk nonk!" Tekoriikii flapped his wings, then lifted his beak up in pride. *"Kadoodle gronk nonk!"*

"He says yes." Miliana bent down to examine the book with a frown creasing her speckled brow. "It has firebirds listed as 'sacred, untouchable, and extremely dangerous; avoid at all cost.' "

"Well . . . Groonpeck was never the greatest of scholars." Lorenzo closed up the dusty old tome with a bang. "Anyway—there we are! Let's take him out and show our firebird the city-state of Sumbria."

"How?" Miliana recoiled in surprise. "Everyone will see him. I don't want Ulia to find him and serve him up for tomorrow's evening meal!"

"Just tell people he's a pet. Have you seen some of the things people are dragging about on leashes out there?" Lorenzo briskly slung his pack across his back. "Anyway, no one will even know we're out. We're going to sneak over the walls."

"And just why have you decided on this little expedition?"

"Well, I have to let my chemicals brew. Tomorrow I've been asked to demonstrate my new light lathe for the kind gentleman who patronized the project." Lorenzo swaggered in pride. "The mixing tanks don't explode anymore. The fault was in having metal storage tanks; the acids slowly burned right through. I've just had two glass ones blown, and it's all holding just perfectly. I think the results might surprise you."

Miliana rolled her eyes toward the apex of her hat with a sigh. "Pray, please don't do anything to ruin the ball tomorrow, or Lady Ulia will use your tanned hide as a hearth rug!"

"Lady Ulia?" Lorenzo let his mind search through the neglected cupboards of his short-term memory. "Oh yes—your mother . . . A most fascinating woman. I've been trying to determine her bone structure for my comparative anatomy project, but I'm not strictly sure that she actually *has* any bones."

"She doesn't need them; her arteries are stiff enough to hold her up." Miliana met Tekoriikii's eyes, and the firebird nodded in eager agreement. "You still haven't told me why we're going out into the city in secret."

"It's traditional." Lorenzo innocently spread open his arms. "We're supposed to go *in mufti*."

"What's mufti?"

"I think it's a type of cart." Lorenzo looked to Tekoriikii, who only shrugged his wings. "Since you're not allowed out of the palace, I thought we'd secretly drop a rope from the rooftop and go see the street festival. You seemed scornful that I knew so little about the masses—so I think it's high time we ceased bickering and met the masses face-to-face!"

The argument had a certain moral supremacy about it that forestalled any objections Miliana might have made. Sniffing at the nighttime breeze, Tekoriikii waddled over to Miliana's meager wardrobe and fetched her a decent cloak.

"Thank you, Tekoriikii."

"Gnub gnub!"

Miliana slapped her pointy hat on her head and led the way to her windowsill. Aided by Lorenzo, she edged out onto the railing of her balcony, then made her way along the guttering of her tower. Inch by inch, Lorenzo and the princess edged their way around the tower roof until they found themselves standing high above the streets. With her hair stirring softly in the wind, Miliana looked down from her perch and stared at the cobblestones some sixty feet below.

"Right—there's the bottom of an old gargoyle here. You can use it to attach the rope."

"Rope?" Lorenzo clung to the wall stones like a great gape-eyed gecko. "I thought *you* had the . . . "

"Oh, lovely." Miliana rested her head against the ice-cold tower wall and wearily closed her eyes.

A quiet rustle of wings announced the arrival of Tekoriikii, who seemed more than just a little pleased to finally have company out on the rooftops. The bird settled on the gutter between Miliana and Lorenzo, gripping on with talons that almost pierced clean through the stone. He looked at his new friends and gave a great, happy flurry of his wings—a buffet that almost dislodged Lorenzo. The man squeaked like a field mouse and closed his eyes, trying to somehow force his flesh clean through the tower wall.

Standing unconcernedly on her tiny ledge, Miliana leaned an elbow against the tower and signaled to the firebird.

"Tekoriikii, could you go and fetch us a rope? You know—long and thin?" Miliana made measuring motions with her hands, then pointed a finger at the cobblestones. "We need to get down. Down there onto the streets. You know—down?"

Tekoriikii followed her finger, offered a smug little warble, then lofted up from his perch. His great yellow talons seized Lorenzo by the tunic, and the man found himself hanging in midair.

The bird's silly short wings could not possibly bear Lorenzo's weight; instead, the linked creatures smoothly fell to the ground at an agreeable turn of speed. Lorenzo landed with a thump, and Tekoriikii rose awkwardly from the alley and flapped noisily back up for Miliana.

The princess cleared her throat and felt sweat break out across her brow.

"Um . . . yes . . . now, Tekoriikii, this may not actually be our best possible plan . . .

"Tekoriikii?"

The bird latched on to her bodice, jerking her off the ledge and almost making her lose her last three meals. Miliana plunged sickeningly down to the street, lost inside a happy whir of Tekoriikii's wings. She landed with a thump straight upon Lorenzo's head, toppled over in the street, and ended hard upon her rear.

She clambered to her feet and resentfully rubbed her smarting backside, glaring at the beaming, happy bird.

"So how do we get back up again, beak face? Did you think of that?"

"Glub glub!"

"Oh wonderful."

Lorenzo was briskly dusted off by Miliana and the bird. With Tekoriikii proudly strutting at the fore, the trio made their way into the city streets and left the hill of palaces far behind.

Once away from the grim, blank battlements of Sumbria's stately homes, the city seemed to come cautiously to life. A few sausage booths spread light into the spaces between jumbled terra-cotta roofs; the first pedestrians appeared, all happily sipping ale, bickering wildly, or picking each other's pockets in the light of the silver moon. Breathing in the sharp smells of dust, frying onions, and summer ale, Miliana closed her eyes and walked on into a sensation that lifted her spirits like silk into the breeze.

Lady Ulia had been left far behind, along with palaces, pointy hats, and rules. Miliana heard the bustle of a street crowd open out before her, turned a corner, and wandered out into the heart of a dream.

In a portable puppet booth, a puppet with a great hooked nose was being noisily consumed by a crocodile.

Jugglers and charlatans performed prodigies for the passing swarms, while magicians filled the air with illusions, images, and spells. Despite the late hour, the city's central plaza flocked with untold hundreds of citizens and visitors, all here to take advantage of the festival stalls.

There were soldiers from a dozen households relaxing in wine gardens, wandering elves and dwarves, barbarians and dancing bears—even some bewildered elephant-headed men trading chunks of amber for alcohol and steel. At the plaza's central fountains, a group of swaggering young blades posed before the crowds, drinking and arguing and hooting calls at the passing girls. All in all, it was a scene that whisked Miliana's breath away.

In all the chaos of the multiracial crowds, a young man, a skinny woman, and a giant strutting bird raised little interest. Miliana stood entranced before a little puppet show, watching marionettes clash wooden swords in competition for their lady fair; behind her, Tekoriikii's long neck jerked this way and that as he goggled in fascination at the crowds.

A lightning flash of his beak, and a silver necklace left the neck of a passing courtesan. The bird avidly swallowed his prize, cramming it into his crop for later regurgitation. Tekoriikii's innocent gaze met Miliana's as she grabbed him by the wing and dragged him on toward yet another fascinating display.

Lorenzo surveyed the city crowds as an artist contemplating his latest canvas. He applauded with Miliana as a magician brought a rain of roses showering down into his hair. The Lomatran threw open his arms and delightedly dragged all the scents of the festival into his eager lungs.

"Fantastic! Light and color, life and motion!" The young man avidly reached out to take Miliana's arm; he found her warm, strong, and vibrant to the touch. "This is where scholars like you and I belong—with our fingers upon the very pulse of life!"

From the corner of her gaze, Miliana caught sight of Tekoriikii swallowing something. The firebird noticed her attention and quickly jerked primly upright, innocently rolling one golden yellow eye. Arm in arm with Lorenzo, the girl took hold of the bird, smelled roasting sausages and let her stomach growl.

"Well, O scholar, does your command of life's pulse extend to eating from eerie street stalls?"

"Of course!" Lorenzo dragged the girl over to a booth made largely out of striped canvas and hairy string. "I have almost a hundred gold pieces left over from my experiments."

A suspicious current rippled through the crowd as these words left Lorenzo's lips. Unseen and unremarked, a hand reached out for the purse dangling from Lorenzo's shabby belt.

With a blur of speed, the purse disappeared, incidentally dragging a string out from Lorenzo's belt. As the line whipped free, it sputtered into life with a sizzle of flame. Purse, thief, and hissing fuse disappeared off into the crowd to the accompaniment of a cackling burst of laughter.

Curiously unhurried, Lorenzo hopped up to the rim of the fountain and stared after the thief as he dwindled merrily away.

"See? This is partially what I mean. Now, a warding spell for a purse can cost upwards of five hundred gold pieces—which is more than the pouch could possibly be worth. A noble can afford the spell, but everyone else just has to take their chances."

Far down the street, the cutpurse had dwindled to a halt, wondering at Lorenzo's strangely interested stare. Suddenly he noticed the hissing fuse attached to the stolen goods, gave a scream of abject terror, and threw the pouch away. The thing exploded with an impressive blast, bowling the thief down an alleyway and straight into a squealing horde of alley cats. Lorenzo shrugged, descended back down to Miliana, and met her wry stare with a shrug.

"I don't know whether the false purse concept is really viable; the smoke powder is too susceptible to damp and still actually a bit more expensive than the spell." Lorenzo produced his real money pouch, which hung beneath his shirt from a thong around his neck. "Shall we go and have a meal?"

A tavern had taken advantage of the festival traffic, extending its premises out into the street. Tables, chairs, and waitresses crowded out one whole corner of the plaza, and a crowd of thirsty soldiers—young recruits wearing the colors of the Toporello family—were celebrating the festival with innocent energy. Lorenzo led Miliana past a vulgar, strutting crowd of young nobles at the plaza fountain, found a clean table, and handed Miliana down into a chair. With the plaza at their feet, the young scholars settled down to watch and enjoy. Behind them, Tekoriikii happily waddled over to the fountain and found himself a perch atop a vomiting stone lion, where he sat surrounded by an astonished audience of pigeons.

The tables were served by an innkeeper who bustled over in answer to Lorenzo's hail and performed a series of nodding, bobbing bows; Miliana's pointy hat drew his attention like a moth to a flame.

"Patrone! May I offer you the finest viands of my house."

"Yes! Yes, why not?" Seeing the carefree young soldiers, Lorenzo indicated the black wine bottles scattered all over their tables. "Drinks and dinner! What are those gentlemen drinking?"

The innkeeper flicked a worried glance to small, slight, be-freckled Miliana and stroked his greasy mustache in alarm.

"Patrone! Ah, patrone, it is soldier's champagne—half slivovitz, half common wine. I cannot truly suggest such a thing for the young lady . . ."

"Nonsense. She is a scholar of the highest caliber—a sorceress supreme!" Lorenzo clicked his fingers in the air in contempt for silly weaknesses and woes. "Bring us each a bottle of soldier's champagne, a meal, and a basket of salty biscuits for my feathered friend up in the fountain."

"As you wish, patrone. The meals shall be . . ." The innkeeper tried unsuccessfully to mold the raw stuff of time with his hands. ". . . a few minutes, maybe more. The drinks—forthwith!"

At a side table, a pale, haughty elven woman dressed in diaphanous green robes adjusted a heavy pearl pendant between her breasts. The woman favored Miliana with a brief, disdainful glance, then went on with her complaints to her entourage of flunkies. Miliana ignored the elf entirely, leaned back in her chair, and watched the stars.

A bottle appeared at her elbow, and the innkeeper capped the thing with a pewter cup. Miliana decided to forestall Lorenzo's possible attempts to play the host, took up her bottle, and poured herself a full measure of the pale pink liquid. Playing at being the cosmopolitan lady, she took a sip and held it on her tongue.

Soldier's champagne could have stripped paint off walls or powered Lorenzo's light lathe. Since Lorenzo's eyes were upon her, the girl forced herself to swallow; the blank panes of her spectacles managed to hide the tears of pain. Unable to speak, she nodded slowly as though appreciating the wine's afterglow and carefully set her cup back down.

The wine clawed and sizzled its way down her gullet. Never having been allowed anything but new-pressed wine, the effect upon the girl was both immediate and alarming. Miliana's little turned-up nose flushed bright cherry red, and a buzzing sound took root somewhere deep inside her ears. She took a second sip and drank it slowly down, feeling the pressure of Lorenzo's watching eyes.

Biscuit crumbs scattered onto the pavement as Tekoriikii made his meal; at the fountain, the noble bravos harassed a pretty girl and blocked her way, laughing cruelly as they deliberately tripped up her feet. Ignoring the whole affair, Lorenzo watched some Aglarondian folk dancing on the far side of the square, then turned his bright gaze innocently back to Miliana.

"Is the wine all right? I can get rid of it if it's too . . . too lower class for you."

"The wine is fine." Miliana coughed, then haughtily poured herself another glass. "I can take anything you can."

"Kadoodle!" Tekoriikii warbled in agreement and then stole the bread basket from a passing tray. *"Squonk kadoodle!"*

Long minutes passed as both young aristocrats watched the plaza crowds stroll by. Princess Miliana tossed back her drink and slammed down the cup to draw Lorenzo's attention to the act.

"Why are you always on about this 'class' thing, anyway? Class just *is*. Everyone's happy here, so what's the problem?"

"The problem is that the division of power is unjust."

"Ha! It's only unjust if people complain that it's unjust." Miliana helped herself to a third glass. "No one's asking for anything to be changed."

Lorenzo accepted a piece of bread from Tekoriikii's beak.

"But someone *within* the system will understandably perceive it to be natural! Only the upper echelon will realize what a delicate game they play in order to keep total control of power."

With her nose and freckled cheeks flushed bright pink, Princess Miliana began fanning herself with the hem of her dress.

"I'm in the upper echelon, and *I* don't see anything."

"Yes—well, you're not *really* upper echelon." Lorenzo once again waved his hands. "I mean, it's not like you're an actual autocrat."

"I am too an autocrat!" Miliana swelled her meager chest in indignation. "I'm a princess!"

"Don't be silly."

"I bloody well am, and I can prove it!" Her freckled

cheeks now glowing cherry red from the unholy mixture of slivovitz and wine, Miliana drove giddily to her feet and leaned over to the nearby soldiers. "Hey, who has a Mannicci coin? Anything from last year . . ."

Soldiers began to consult their spare change. Miliana used one young man as a leaning post as she held coins absurdly close to her nose, frowning at them one after another until she found the one she wanted.

"Aha! There you are. My co-coming of age coin! Minted 'em last year." Miliana tripped over something invisible on the pavement and held a coin up beside her face. "See? It's me!"

Lorenzo looked dubiously from the coin to his companion, wrinkled up his nose and pulled away.

"That's not you! It looks nothing like you. It doesn't even have a sight-intensifying device!"

"That's coz it's a—thingie—an ideal . . . izashun." Miliana fished a knife off one of the tables. "Here—I'll put in the spectaculars."

Soldiers split their opinions, half crowding around the coin seeking proof, and half of them enthusiastically upholding Miliana's claims. Lorenzo took hold of the coin and examined it with suspicion in his eyes.

"Have you had too much to drink?"

"What?" Miliana swayed as she pompously stuck out her chest. "It's only champagne."

The coin disappeared as Tekoriikii slyly reached out, took it in his beak, and swallowed it whole. Meanwhile, Lorenzo blinked in bemusement; his new friend had suddenly transformed into Sumbria's princess!

A soldier passed the girl another brimming glass; she half drank it, then seemed to remember a point, and whirled unsteadily around to Lorenzo.

The motion spilled part of her drink onto the ground, where it promptly began to scorch the soil.

"And another thing! You don't believe I can really do magic, do you? Well, I can. I'm a real . . . honest . . . shorceress."

The girl had consumed several cups of the malignant soldierly concoction on an empty stomach. It was clearly time to go home. Lorenzo tried to take Miliana by the elbow, but she fought him away, appealing to the crowds of soldiers for support.

"Hey! Hey everyone . . . so am I a princess now?"

Drunken hoots of support rose from the crowd. Miliana tilted her pointy hat across her eyes.

"Right! And princesses do magic!"

A hand slithered across Miliana's rear. The girl lurched about and slapped the greasy paw away.

"Don't touch the royal rear!"

The noble bravos had descended from their perch upon the fountain. A dozen young noblemen arrogantly planted their feet upon the steps and tables, leering at Miliana. They ringed the girl and pushed her back against the soldiers' table.

"Hey, little weed—we can show you some magic!"

The innkeeper hovered in the shadows wringing his hands; he was powerless to interfere with gangs of noble youths, who could wreck his tavern on a whim and remain above the law. Soldiers, forbidden weapons larger than a poniard inside the city walls, watched the bravos' long rapiers in dismay.

Seemingly oblivious to the very real chance of a brawl, Miliana fixed upon the bravos' leader and blew the trailing veil of her hat out of her eyes.

"What was that, pumpkin pants?"

The noble thug did indeed have puff-pantaloons which looked remarkably like he had sheathed his upper thighs with a pair of prize-winning squashes. Stabbed by the laughter of the soldiers, the man confronted Miliana and made an obscene gesture with his hand.

"I said, come with us and we'll show you something!"

Miliana settled her hat on her eyes and snapped a cantrip toward her foe; the man's pants temporarily tightened by three sizes, making his eyes bulge in alarm. Miliana gave a drunken laugh and gaily reeled aside.

The bravos—twenty young blades armed to the teeth—all started forward; here and there, a nervous soldier toyed with the idea of rising to his feet. Miliana laughed in rosy-cheeked scorn, too tipsy to care, as she and her friends were overshadowed by certain doom.

Into the center of attention, there rose a slim figure dressed in ink-speckled velvet, who held the chief bravo at bay with an elegantly pointed sword.

"I believe you owe the lady your most profound apologies."

Lorenzo held his rapier competently *en garde*. It was a strangely hilt-heavy weapon, and it never wavered as the bravo ripped out his own blade and advanced.

"Come then! Let's fillet the rooster, then rob the hen!"

He slapped his sword against Lorenzo's blade—and it proved to be the worst mistake he'd ever made. The man screamed as a spark leapt the gap between the blades and sizzled up into his hands. He jerked backward like a puppet tugged by its strings and ended up in the fountain at Tekoriikii's feet.

Miliana adjusted her spectacles and looked at Lorenzo's sword with addled respect.

"S'great!" The girl waved a hand with an eager, drunken laugh. "How did do do dat?"

"Bottled lightning! The charge is stored in the hilt." Lorenzo seemed to forget the stunned crowd of bravos and tilted his sword hilt toward the girl. "See? Science at work again. We can replace magical blades with these."

"Izzat so?" Miliana seemed to be having trouble focusing. "Are they cheap?"

"Oh, yes, I just drained the charge out of a blue dragon one night when it was asleep. Anyone could have done it." Lorenzo swelled his chest with pride. "I have three more bottles at home. They screw into the hilt after every use. You see, one bottle only works one time."

"Lorenzo!"

Miliana crammed her hat over her ears in rage, but it was too late; the secret had been sprung. The horde of

wealthy street thugs instantly lost their fear and began
to close in upon the isolated pair. Lorenzo paled and tried
to hold the tide at bay with rapid little flickers of his
blade.

A great whir of feathers suddenly filled the sky. Lofting
up from the fountainhead, Tekoriikii came into the fray.
The creature landed on the pavement between Miliana
and Lorenzo and the encroaching horde, hissing like a
viper as he began his display.

Head held high, the bird advanced. The sight of a giant
orange peacock/rooster/phoenix in an angry mood served
to check the attack, as arrogant young nobles lowered
blade tips in surprise.

"What is it?"

"Is it a phoenix?"

One boy, deliberately slipshod in his expensive dress,
jabbed in the direction of the bird with a golden sword.

"It's a table bird—nothing more." The boy signaled to
his companions to attack. "A beak's no match for a blade!"

The bird danced high and the bird danced low, shuddering its tail feathers in a fearsome display. A man took
a step toward the princess only to be met by a ferocious
hiss and a swelling of the great bird's breast. Another
step, and a bigger intake of breath from Tekoriikii.
Nervous nobles lost their fear and formed themselves up
for a charge.

"Kill the thing! Kill it and take the girl!"

With a roar, the nobles ran at Tekoriikii. Standing his
ground, the bird hurtled forward his head and gave vent
to a terrifying scream.

The noise made the whole world jerk in fright. In front
of Tekoriikii the flagstones blasted apart. Tiles shattered
on rooftops far across the square, windows burst into a
mist of fragments, and a woman's diamond earrings
cracked clean through. Even from behind the bird,
Miliana's spectacles abandoned their grip on this life as
the lenses promptly crumbled clean away.

For the bravos, the effects were more catastrophic. The

men spun back in agony, with blood spurting from their
ears. They shrieked and writhed across the cobblestones,
dropping one by one as Tekoriikii stalked after them in
rage. The last man fell, and the bird shook out his feathers and scratched dirt on the unconscious bodies in contempt.

Lorenzo stared at Tekoriikii in shock.

"Yes, well, I suppose you *could* call that 'sacred,
untouchable, and extremely dangerous.' "

Ignoring the astonishing display of power from the
bird, Miliana stumbled forward, ruffled Tekoriikii's
crown, and waved merrily to the soldiers.

"Let's take 'em to the honey barge!"

Every evening, the offerings from Sumbria's many outhouses and "seats of ease" were collected by the honey
carts and driven to the riverside. Here, a stinking, reeking barge took the glutinous mass far along the shore of
the Akanamere as a gift to distant farmers' fields.
Miliana and the strutting bird led a procession to the
barge, which bobbed on the docks at the center of a
wheeling storm of flies. A few coins to the attendants, and
soon the unconscious bravos were buried neck deep in the
manure; Miliana stood waving a handkerchief as the soldiers and Tekoriikii cheered the barge on its way.

Heaving out a wine-sodden breath of satisfaction,
Miliana slung an arm about Tekoriikii and another about
Lorenzo and crushed them tight against her heart.

"A drink for Lorenzo-o an' a drink for Tekii-thingie!"
The girl dragged her companions into the midst of the
soldiers with a hoot of pure glee. "Justice! Ol' Lorenzo was
right. We all gotta make it as we find it."

"Maybe we had just better go home?" Lorenzo plucked
timidly at Miliana's sleeve. "It's getting late, and . . ."

"Late?" Miliana crowed like a morning cockerel and lit
the streets with a pure sound of joy. "No! I wanna *dance*
for justice!"

A bottle was uncorked, and soldiers called for their
sweethearts and their wives. Someone with a lute struck

up a tune, and Miliana tried to dance an Aglarondian folk dance with the happy bird. Free of Ulia and deliriously at ease, Miliana lost herself in a whirl of joy.

Lorenzo could only watch and give an anxious sigh.

* * * * *

"*Squaaaaawk!*" Tekoriikii flapped his wings in alarm, sending shadows chasing far along the empty, moonlit streets. "*Squaaaaawk!*"

Miliana loosed an urgent groan, and Lorenzo took her down off his shoulders and helped her over to a wall. For the fourth time since her disappearance beneath a table at the tavern, the girl was thoroughly sick; great soul-rending heaves tried to clear her of the alcoholic poison crawling through her brain.

Lorenzo simply sat down at her side and helped to support her through her suffering. When she had finally done, he pulled her small, frail body into his lap and wiped her streaming eyes and nose. Tekoriikii passed him a water gourd and Lorenzo made Miliana rinse her mouth, then cradled her softly as she shivered in his arms.

"Wh—why can't I be . . . magical?"

The girl whimpered the words into Lorenzo's hair, clawing her little fingers through his clothes. With an anxious expression in his eyes, Tekoriikii nudged at her and made a whistling sound.

Lorenzo agreed.

"You *are* magical! We both saw you cast a spell." He tried to coax Miliana's face out of the shadows. "Hey— you're a sorceress!"

"No . . ." Miliana hung weakly in Lorenzo's arms, hiding away her freckles and her tears. "If I were magical— really magical, then maybe I might get a wish."

"What wish?" Bird and nobleman both hung close, locked anxious gazes, and tried to coax the girl out of her shell. "What wish, Miliana?"

Miliana emerged—small, brown, and crushed by one inarguable misery.

"If I had a wish, then maybe I could be pretty. Really pretty."

The girl hid her face away from Lorenzo and the bird.

"Someone beautiful. Just—just not *Miliana*. Just for one single day . . ."

The girl clung against Lorenzo's chest and wept. Locking tortured glances, Tekoriikii and Lorenzo quietly stroked at Miliana's hair.

"Princess Miliana *is* beautiful. And I'll prove you wrong. Tomorrow I'll show you just exactly what I see.

"I'll show you. I'll make you open your eyes."

"Glub glub!"

Sick, swaying, and miserable, Miliana's whisper barely carried to Lorenzo's ears.

"I'm just so frightened. So frightened . . ." The girl curled fingers into Lorenzo's tunic. "I wanted to be like my father. I wanted to be . . . to be . . . proud.

"But I'm just so scared of the . . . futility. The dances and the husbands." Miliana swallowed back another surge of nausea. "Don't let them put me in the finishing school. I'd rather die . . . I'd rather die . . . I'd rather die . . ."

Crying herself to sleep, Miliana hung like a rag doll in Lorenzo's arms.

Tekoriikii spared the girl a long, sad gaze, and then quietly led the way back home. Behind him, Lorenzo hoisted Miliana like a treasured child and wandered carefully back to the palace doors.

From his perch high up in Miliana's attic, Tekoriikii had most of the Mannicci palace under his muddle-headed gaze. Holes in the roofing gave him a splendid vantage point for viewing the central courtyards and the stables, the kitchen doors and the colonnades. He saw the slim, gray-headed Prince Cappa Mannicci escaping for his early morning ride before his wife could stir from bed and exercise her tongue. Soldiers marched and servants cleaned; bright bunting was wound about every object found readily at hand. All in all, the Festival of Blades had begun with a flawless summer's day.

Waddling happily across the floor of his gloomy kingdom, Tekoriikii bathed in beams of light and listened contentedly to the dawn chorus of birds. A marvelous new treasure had come into his life, and the bird need only close his eyes and sigh just to savor its gentle glow.

His journeys had first brought him to a treasure trove of people and places, songs and lights; it had brought him a bounty of shiny baubles, and day by day Tekoriikii's collection grew.

And now, most miraculous of all—the journey had

given him a friend.

Hanging his head down through the broken ceiling, Tekoriikii watched the human girl in her sleep. She fed him food and taught him songs; she had shown him magic picture books, and recited aloud from the pages for hours on end.

And yet last night the little female had been so very sad.

Her lack of plumes was a terrible, crippling disfigurement. The male human Lorenzo kept a feather in his hat as though making up for the lack. Tekoriikii turned his head this way and that, regarding Miliana as she slept off her wine, and pitied her for her naked, unsightly skin.

She needed cheering—and Tekoriikii had just the thing!

With a bright burst of inspiration, the bird jerked his head back up through the hole. He warbled happily, and did a little dance to celebrate his own magnificent cleverness—Tekoriikii, the handsomest and smartest of all the birds!

Tekoriikii's sleeping nest consisted of green branches, leaves and twigs all lined with the finest silk taken from a massive set of underwear found hanging from the palace washing line. The bird upended a great sack made from a set of Lady Ulia's frilly pink drawers and spilled a dragon's hoard of jewelry out across the wooden floors.

Spread out in all their glory, Tekoriikii's gems simply stunned the eye. There were great rubies and strings of emeralds. Zircons and costume jewelry rubbed shoulders with sapphires and pearls. Bits of mirror and polished glass had caught his eye just as surely as platinum and gold. All in all, the bird's collection made an eccentric display.

Rooting happily about amongst a king's ransom in jewels, the bird pulled out a few choice pieces and hung them up from rusty nails to turn and sparkle in the sun.

Three offerings glittered before the bird's giddy yellow eyes: a looking glass, a rope of emeralds, and a single, gigantic rose-pink pearl.

In addition to being the most handsome creature ever to stalk the world, Tekoriikii was an educated bird. He knew that nothing could cheer a female quite so much as finding herself being courted and so, therefore, secret advances would make Miliana smile.

She must be given a gift—enough to let her know how deeply she was honored, for few females were ever chased by a male. It simply wasn't done. The flattery would raise her spirits, and Tekoriikii would be glad.

The bird considered his potential offerings. The mirror? Too bright and shiny. She must not be overwhelmed by the very nature of the gift. The bird peered this way and that at his own reflection, and moved on.

The emeralds? No. Too dull; too common. Although they sparkled, they were the same color as fresh new leaves and, that being the case, she might not value them. The bird regarded the gigantic pink pearl with pleasure, and then took the offering up into his bill.

The pearl had been regurgitated from his crop this self-same morning. With a brisk wash beneath a rainwater pipe, the gem sparkled bright as morning dew. Tekoriikii hopped down the broken hole in the ceiling and landed on the bathroom floor with a distinct, feathery thump.

Miliana turned over in her bed, groaning in distant agony. Beside her bed there lay a bucket as well as a pointy hat, which presumably was for use if the bucket should grow full. Tekoriikii crept toward the girl with exaggerated stealth, cunningly laid the pearl pendant on her pillowslip, then withdrew to gaze down at her in love.

Very, very small, and speckled delicately with brown; she should not let her lack of feathers distress her so. After all, not everyone could be a handsome firebird.

Tekoriikii drew the blankets up around Miliana's slender neck, clucked like a broody hen, then hopped back up into the ceiling to go about his own affairs.

* * * * *

The Palace of the Manniccis decked itself out gaily for the Festival of Blades. The ritual never failed to amuse Miliana, who thought the candy daggers and swords now being hung from all the roof beams were particularly inappropriate for a happy festival.

Passing along the courtyard, Miliana maneuvered oh-so-carefully, balancing her head atop her neck as though it weighed five hundred pounds.

Miliana had just been through the most unspeakable experience of her life. She had awoken to find herself still thoroughly drunk; the whole bed had been spinning, and the room shifted like a child's kite blown willy-nilly through the sky. She had somehow made her way to the palace shrine and had begged a blessing against poison from the family's private priests, claiming that she had eaten Lady Ulia's infamous blowfish casserole. Now, with her bloodstream purged but her body still feeling as delicate as glass, the girl took a quiet turn about the palace and tried to gather strength for the evening's affairs.

The breeze blew cool and calming; the promised headache never came. All she needed was a few moments of absolute peace, and she would feel her old self again.

On a fine silver chain about Miliana's neck, there swung a single rose-pink pearl—a large, teardrop-shaped affair that perfectly complimented her coloring. Feeling its unfamiliar weight settling on her skin, the princess drew out the pendant and eyed it with a soft, fond smile.

"Miliaaaa-*naaaaaa*!"

The piercing summons caused the girl to close her eyes and freeze, waiting for a migraine headache to begin; luckily, the priest's spells had been first class. With an air of deep and quiet calm, Miliana managed to face Lady Ulia and her father with a smile.

Plucking out her skirts and sinking a wee curtsy, Miliana nodded her tall hat in gentle greeting to her stepmother. Her father—rigid, dignified, and foreboding—gave a brisk nod of his gray beard to his daughter.

"Ah. Miliana." The prince gazed at his daughter without any real interest. "You appear to be well. How do your lessons go?"

The man had hardly spoken more than five sentences to his daughter in her entire life. Cowed, Miliana made a set of suitably dutiful noises—the lessons went well, she found needlepoint occupied most of her time, and the lavender smoke which yesterday exploded from her fireplace was most definitely the result of diseased firewood. Her father nodded, not bothering to listen to a word she had to say.

Her duty done, Miliana turned herself to the ziggurat of silk that was Lady Ulia. Swallowing carefully, Miliana congratulated herself on her survival thus far, and wished Lady Ulia the best of the day.

"Lady Ulia—is it not a perfect evening? I trust you find the airs as pleasant as I?"

"Pleasant?"

The cry caused Miliana to draw a little breath in pain. Coiling her head backward atop its great abundance of chins, Lady Ulia Mannicci blinked in horror at the girl. "Have you heard what the caterers are doing to my feast? There is still no centerpiece for the table. I desired a great bird, and what am I offered? A cuttlefish of the most revolting size! I can hardly have a mass of tentacles splayed out amongst the silverware before all of our guests!"

The tirade of woes quickly lost its force; Lady Ulia had dragged in the whalebone and case-hardened steel of her corsets several inches too tight, and the constriction left her short of breath. The woman retreated into the solace of her waving fan and cast her eyes across her step-daughter's décolletage.

Spying the pearly pendant about Miliana's tender neck, she suddenly snatched up a quizzing glass and bent her head down to examine the object in suspicion and alarm.

"A *pearl?*" Ulia blinked in blubbering surprise. "Sooth, it is a pearl. A pearl of the first quality!" Miliana's step-mother drew in a breath and examined her smiling stepdaughter with a great, foreboding eye. "And just where, my lass, did this come from?"

Something stirred under Miliana's hat. Feeling a dizzy swoop of headache threatening to emerge, Miliana attempted to turn her face into a model of unconcern.

"It just came from . . . an admirer."

"And *who*, pray tell, is this admirer?

"Well—I don't actually know." Miliana felt a warm glow as she felt the pearl between her breasts; she polished one of her reserve pair of spectacles to cover her unconscious blush. "Just . . . someone."

"A young lady does not accept gifts from unknown sources." Lady Ulia reexamined the pearl with a mixed air of outrage, pomposity, and scorn. "Particularly not young ladies who already have approved, valid suitors seeking for their hand!"

Suddenly, the entire palace shuddered to an enormous bang. Miliana staggered, went green, and clapped her hands across her aching brow.

Prince Cappa Mannicci stared in the direction of the guest quarters in alarm.

"Great Lords of Baator! What was that?"

Miliana looked up in alarm.

"It wasn't me!"

"Of course it wasn't you! How can a mere girl make an explosion?" The Prince separated himself from Lady Ulia. "It's from that boy's quarters . . . the one from Lomatra . . ."

Lomatra. The thought made Prince Mannicci turn a cold gaze to the palace's west wing.

"Tonight, daughter, you shall devote an evening to our errant suitor. This time next year, I wish you to be a Lomatran bride."

"Father!" Miliana's eyes blinked wide; appalled, she took a step closer to the prince. "Father, no!"

"I wish it. It shall be done."

Face set and angry, Miliana used the mask of her great lenses to hide her cold, determined eyes. Headache forgotten, the girl gave an obedient curtsy, then smartly turned about and marched herself away.

A Lomatran bride indeed! Miliana clenched a hand about her brand new pearl—Lorenzo's pearl—and felt it spread a spell of warmth past the fury in her soul.

She had a friend now—a real friend. And a more-or-less magical bird monster-thing to stay by her side. Between them, they would blow her father's plans straight to the Abyss!

Back in the courtyard, Lady Ulia watched Miliana leave and let a crease of suspicion gouge a line across her brows.

"Why, my dear, do you suppose your daughter is so *compliant* today?"

The Prince of Sumbria focused his attentions on the girl.

"Perhaps the seriousness of life has finally sunk home."

"Yes—or, perhaps, a *double* life . . ." Lady Ulia turned the horns of her great lime-green hat belligerently toward her prey. "There have been some very strange things going on within this palace.

"I think Miliana's activities deserve a closer scrutiny, my dear. It may prove to be the very—pearl—of the problem."

* * * * *

"Lorenzo? Lorenzo!"

Moving with all due caution, Luccio Irozzi peeked his head about his apartment's door, then edged into his quarters at the head of a band of nervous palace workmen. Moving like men venturing into a dragon's lair, the little procession scanned the room's bewildering array of pipe work, burners, and bubbling pots; they crept across the floor as though expecting pitfalls or showers of burning oil.

No new explosions seemed imminent. Luccio strode across the pitted carpet to Lorenzo's bedroom door, tried the lock, then rapped lightly on the woodwork with his fist.

"Lorenzo? Lorenzo, it is I!" The man's knuckles rippled as he drummed a dirty ditty on the door. "Be a good little

pyromaniac and open up the door before I blow your
house down . . ."

Movement came from behind the door—a hiss, an eerie
flicker of light from under the doorjamb, and a sudden
smell of scorching metal. A muffled and somewhat dis-
tracted voice wafted through to Luccio from the far side
of the wall.

"Not now! I need five minutes."

"Five minutes?" Luccio puffed out his chest like a fighting rooster and nearly capsized a pile of glassware with
his waving arms. "Lorenzo, my dressing routine has been
disturbed. The delight of a hundred eager young damsels
hangs in the balance! I have not a minute to spare, let
alone five!" Pained by the potential disaster, Luccio hurtled
himself against the portal in theatrical dismay.

"Think, Lorenzo, *think!* Consider their anguish; the
screams, the wails, the suicides! Temples swamped as
vast columns of poor, disillusioned girls sorrowfully line
up to take their chastity vows."

The door opened just a crack, and a vague, disoriented
Lorenzo stuck his head out into the room.

"I am trying to prepare a demonstration. Can't you
leave me in peace?"

"Alas, O Lord of Soot, I wish it could be so." Luccio performed a bow and elegantly indicated the workmen
ranked at his rear. "These noble minions of mine host
wish to take possession of the famous painting of the sea
goddess. It is to be prepared for display."

With a frustrated sigh, Lorenzo withdrew back into his
room.

"It's in the sitting room, just by the door. Don't lift the
covers if there's any dust around—the varnish is still not
completely dry. And don't take the easel!"

With a flourish of his hat, Luccio allowed the door to be
slammed shut in his face. He indicated the sitting room
to his tail of servants, then threw himself into a chair to
relax as the workmen maneuvered the awkward canvas
out into the corridor.

Luccio's preparations actually required very little work; why bother trying to improve on perfection? The man's clothes were deliciously and scandalously slipshod; marked cards were in his pocket, weighted dice in his belt. The Mannicci's reception offered gaming tables, business contacts, and an endless ocean of curvaceous companions. A secret note had been slid beneath his door in the wee hours of the dawn—a note in feminine hand-writing carved upon a sheet of purest mother-of-pearl. All in all, Luccio's evening promised glorious possibilities.

Again a flash of light came from beneath Lorenzo's door; a spot on the wall glowed cherry red, and the wall plaster flaked off with a disappointed little sigh.

"Damn!"

Lorenzo seemed to be having his own troubles. Luccio rested his feet on a table and helped himself to a half-empty bottle of wine.

"Lorenzo, O heart and soul of science, do be careful with your toys . . ."

Luccio sipped his wine, then almost catapulted clean across the room; some suicidal varlet had laced the stuff with raw liquor. Luccio could already feel his lips turning numb. He raced for the water jug, rinsed his mouth, and prayed for sensation to return before the evening began.

"Lorenzo—what in Talona's name have you been drink-ing?"

"What?"

"This—this paint stripper, this vile incendiary—this distilled sunfish urine left upon your desk!" Luccio made a face and searched for a piece of fruit to help drive any lingering taste away.

"It's not mine . . ." The door latch fumbled itself open, and Lorenzo's face appeared in the door. "It's left over from last night. Miliana drank about two bottles of it."

Luccio flicked his gaze from the bottle to his compan-ion in alarm.

"Dear gods! Do you mean to tell me that the woman you've been mooning over drinks *this* by choice?"

"Well . . . not by choice." Lorenzo emerged from his room, bringing with him the smell of scorched metal and cherry fondant. "It was more sort of an accident. I coaxed her into escaping from the palace with me last night, and we went to a tavern. She just started, well . . . drinking it. First she laughed a lot, and then she told us she was a princess. Finally, she just fell over and threw up for most of the rest of the evening."

"Miliana?" Luccio sat bolt upright in his chair. "*Princess* Miliana?"

"Yes, that's the one."

Discomforted and somewhat alarmed, Luccio raised his brows.

"We are speaking, dear heart, of the flower of the Mannicci house? The woman, I believe, I once *begged* you to pursue?"

"Oh, I couldn't pursue *her!*" Lorenzo scowled in clear disapproval. "She's my friend."

A knock came at the door. Lorenzo frantically dusted off his clothes as though he had one chance in a million of restoring the ravaged cloth back to life.

"They're here! Now Luccio, please keep out of sight and keep your comments to yourself. These people are very, very nice, and very, very important to me."

Carefully hiding the bottle of soldiers' champagne, Luccio regarded his companion in puzzlement.

"My dear Lorenzo—what on Toril are you doing now? You can't possibly entertain guests. We have a party to attend in half an hour!"

Lorenzo raced about the apartment, dragging rugs across the worst of the scorch marks on the floor.

"It's my patron. The one who gave me the money for all those chemicals. He's come to see my progress on my light lathe. The results will totally astound him. The device is an absolute, unqualified success!"

"As are its explosions?"

"That particular problem is now—relatively—under control." Lorenzo drew on some singed leather gauntlets and made his way to the door. "It is merely a tiny hiccup in the tube design. What are you doing now?"

"Hiding." Luccio lifted up a curtain inside Lorenzo's workshop with a droll, professional aplomb. "A man who has spent an evening plying Sumbria's princess with hard liquor clearly has need of some intelligent paranoia. Since you lack the quality, I shall happily provide you with my own."

Luccio faded out of sight behind a curtain, wiped his dagger blade with distilled venom from a hidden hip-flask, and froze himself as still as death within his hiding place. His friend Lorenzo shook off the incident and bustled forward to open the apartment door.

"Patrone! Blade Captain, what a pleasure it is to see you once again!"

Blade Captain Gilberto Ilégo, immaculate in a garb of harlequinade velvets, greeted the young nobleman with an easy bow.

"My dear young man, I was so very pleased to hear from you. Will you permit me to present my colleague, Rufo, a commander of my guards."

A squat, heavyset man with arms of knotted muscle stalked in over the threshold. Dressed in darkest black, his party clothing had quite clearly been lined with mail, not an unusual thing to find in a cautious man-of-affairs. Lorenzo greeted the stranger with an affable, excited wave and led the way into his inner sanctum.

"Gentlemen, I am most pleased you could spare me the time. It will not take long, my lord Ilégo. I merely wanted to show you just how far I have come, and to thank you for everything that you have done for me." Lorenzo led the way across a threshold strewn with soot, copper tubes, and nude sketches of a girl. "Come in and make yourselves at home."

Ilégo motioned to his companion; silent, dark and watchful, Blade Captain Ugo Svarézi walked through into Lorenzo's study and carefully scanned the hangings, doors, and walls. He passed his gaze across

Luccio's hiding place, then turned his back and walked forward to examine Lorenzo's heavy brass machine.

A central table held a most puzzling contraption. Two glass spheres held bubbling brews of deadly chemicals that were fed by pipes and faucets into a central combustion chamber. Screwed onto the bench top at the contraption's forepart, there stood a spindly frame which, though empty, seemed designed to secure some vital component or another. Above the hiss and seethe of mingling chemicals, the cheerful smell of cherries set the spectators strangely ill at ease.

Lorenzo looked at his creation and beamed an innocent, self-satisfied smile.

"Gentlemen, I present to you . . . the light lathe! The wonder of the age!"

Scowling at the contraption, Ugo Svarézi spoke out for the very first time.

"All this paraphernalia, just to drive a lathe?"

Lorenzo took on a new dimension; suddenly the crisp, driven young inventor, he pointed out the salient parts of his machine.

"Gentlemen, this machine works by using a combination of optical science, mechanical pumps, and explosive chemical reaction.

"As you know, my lord, the Blade Kingdoms have established patent laws for inventions both magical and mechanical. Although the patent for this device is registered in my own name, I would never have completed the work without your confidence and assistance. Therefore, patrone, with your permission, I would like to modify the patents to include your own name. It will thus ensure a financial reward for all your infinite kindness."

Ilégo made a little face of scorn and waved the suggestion entirely away.

"No, no, no—the machine is yours. I merely hope that I have given encouragement to the arts." The Blade Captain and his brooding colleague moved closer, inspecting the machine. "This is the complete mechanism?"

"It is indeed, my lord. Now, let me explain the theory, and let me demonstrate the principals in operation."

Lorenzo made to open up a curtain and provide more light, but for some reason every time he tugged at the drapes, the drapes tugged back. Abandoning the idea, the young nobleman dragged lanterns closer to his creation and guided his two guests about the simple machinery.

"Essentially, sirs, I have discovered a series of chemicals which react violently when combined together. The light lathe has two of these chemicals stored here, in these glass spheres. By opening these valves, a precisely measured amount of each chemical is fed into these tubes, and squirted into the steel combustion chamber . . . here."

Ilégo stroked quietly at his chin.

"Why are the spheres made of glass?"

"The chemicals are extremely acidic, my lord. I have replaced my previous metal holding tanks with ones of noncorrosive glass."

Lorenzo squatted down and traced the plumbing of the machinery for his two guests.

"Now, when the two chemicals combine inside this chamber, they instantly give forth a violent blaze of light. It is this light that provides the working force of the machine.

"The principal is similar to . . . eye spectacles . . . or a simple spyglass, only in reverse." Lorenzo drew diagrams on the white plaster walls with a piece of charcoal. "Instead of gathering distant light sources, and channeling them in to the eye, this lens gathers the scattered light from the chamber and concentrates it into a single, coherent beam.

"And just as light from a lens can be used to burn paper or start a fire, so too can this machine's light be used to generate heat. Intense heat. Hot enough to melt through stone, or even steel!"

Ugo Svarézi flicked a swift look from Ilégo to the young inventor.

"What is your lens made of? Glass?"

"Oh, no, Sir Rufo, glass cannot withstand the intense heat of the combustion chamber." Wistfully removing a small white gem from his pocket, the youth squatted at Svarézi's feet to display the stone's qualities to his companions. "I have used a quartz crystal, which a gem cutter has polished into a smooth little lens. The lens is good for three, or maybe four seconds of operation—after which the stresses will shatter it clean through. A diamond would obviously be a better choice but, alas, the cost would be absurdly great."

A demonstration was clearly in order. Lorenzo propped an inch-thick plate of steel in front of his machine, carefully placed the lens in its frame, then raced over to his desk to find a battered old helm. He donned a breastplate, lowered the visor of his helm and hung himself with wet leather sacks, signaling his associates to join him in crouching behind a heavy crossbowmen's pavis. The inventor reached out to hold two leather cords attached to his machine.

Ilégo looked down at him with some concern.

"Is this device safe?"

"Oh, quite safe!" Lorenzo exhibited the inventor's eternal, doomed optimism. "We shall use a quarter-second burst. Shield your eyes!"

Lorenzo tugged at his two strings, then frantically ducked behind the shield.

A brilliant white light cracked like lightning through the room—a brightness so intense it stung the skin like a desert sun. A whipcrack noise ripped through the air, and a stench of burning metal and stone heralded an evil cloud of steam. The observers scarcely had time to jerk with shock before the afterimages were dancing in purple spots across their eyes.

Emerging from cover, Lorenzo first inspected his machine, and then firmly sealed the safety valves. Meanwhile, his two guests crept slowly toward the steel target plate and stared at it in awe.

A tiny, perfectly circular hole had been punched clean through the metal sheet. At the other side of the room, a savage puncture more than a handspan deep had been melted through the granite wall.

Young Lorenzo stripped off his gauntlets and removed his helm.

"The stonework always seems to burst. So does unseasoned wood. I think the moisture trapped inside them actually explodes, but perhaps one day I can make a less intense version of the beam for doing work with stone." With its straps untied, Lorenzo's breastplate thundered to the floor with a wild, unholy clang.

"The lens governs the range, of course. A larger crystal would accept a higher power input, but I think you can see that this size is perfectly adequate to our needs." With a sigh of satisfaction at a job well done, Lorenzo passed a folio of plans and diagrams over to the other men.

"It all seems to work tolerably well. Unfortunately, cost is still my insurmountable problem, my lord. The process is too expensive." The boy gave his apparatus an anxious little stare. "The chemicals are ruinously costly, and the crystals must be painstakingly made by hand. But the theory is sound! I'm sure that, given time, I can find cheaper sources of the needed materials . . ."

"Here, I believe, it is now *my* turn to help." Gilberto Ilégo extended a slim, well-manicured hand. "If you give me the formulas for the chemicals you desire, I shall search for other suppliers. They may have entirely common uses elsewhere in the world."

The curtains quivered in dismay; Lorenzo ignored them and instead stared in delight at Blade Captain Ilégo. Almost speechless with joy, the young man took his patron by the hand.

"Oh, patrone! Your intelligence is a rare light in a darkened, superstitious world. Indeed, one man's chemicals might be another creature's footwash!"

The formulas were scribbled out across a page, then added to duplicate plans of Lorenzo's machine and passed into Gilberto Ilégo's arms.

Bowing deeply, Lorenzo saw his guests to the door, then allowed them to fade out into the palace halls.

Ilégo led the way hastily down the corridor into a gloomy passageway. Shoving hard at a sally port, he burst into the feed stores behind the palace stables and disappeared inside.

Svarézi closed the door behind them. The feed stores were utterly deserted; towering stacks of lucerne filled the air with cloying sweetness and dancing beams of dust. Here and there a rodent flitted across the floor. In the stables nearby, the grooms could be heard discussing the serving girls' charms. Gilberto Ilégo peered through a gap in the wooden walls, cautiously retreated across the fallen hay, and pulled an amulet from about his neck and inspected the engravings on its face.

"I detect no scrying spells. We can talk in safety."

The two men drew close together, speaking in the harsh whispers of conspirators. Ilégo almost shivered with excitement.

"Did you see it? Did you see how far that machine dug into the wall?"

"Is this what you hoped?"

"Hoped?" Ilégo feared his excitement had made his voice too loud, and forcibly checked his pace. "Never! I only intended to use the boy as a sleeper agent in Lomatra."

Ugo Svarézi took a pace or two, clenching his hand about the handle of his poniard.

"Even built into a carrying case, the machine is scarcely worthwhile. It does nothing that a master sorcerer could not do."

"Then think of it built to a larger scale, brother! A much, *much* larger scale." Ilégo whirled, excitement bringing fire into his eyes. "Think of it increased a thousandfold!"

The courtyard outside the feed shed echoed to the sound of trumpets, boots, and hooves. Suddenly at ease,

Ilégo leaned against the walls and beckoned Svarézi to approach. Together they gazed through the wall boards and out into the central palace yard.

An iron-bound coach drawn by a dozen horses had halted just before the palace fountain. Priests, sorcerers, footmen, and crossbowmen rode upon the wagon, while a hundred Mannicci cavalry formed close ranks to either side. Overhead, hippogriffs could be seen circling on guard, as the great prize of Colletro finally arrived.

Cappa Mannicci was on hand to see the spoils come home. Clapping his hands with glee, he strode forward to watch his heralds receive the priceless relic from Colletran hands. As the last rays of sunlight lanced across the palace roofs, they struck against the Sun Gem and flooded the courtyard with light.

It was a diamond so large that it would scarcely fit inside a man's clenched fist—a single flawless crystal of pure, unsullied hue. Hacked from the heart of an unaging, unliving emperor in decades long gone by, the Sun Gem had come to symbolize the free spirit of the Blade Kingdoms.

To seize the gem was a symbolic triumph for Sumbria; its loss, an absolute humiliation to Colletro. Ilégo felt Svarézi's hate, then turned and disarmed it with a smile.

"Colleague—I believe that we can bring this age of sham wars to an end. It all depends upon how much your ... your old loyalties interfere with your ambitions."

Svarézi tugged his mail-lined gauntlets to a tighter fit.

"My loyalties are to a vision of the future." The Colletran soldier swiveled glass-hard eyes toward his companion. "If we move, we must move now. I cannot risk spies or servants reporting a connection between us. Do you have a plan for the boy's heat weapon?"

"Indeed, brother. And to use it, we need only place it into your good hands."

Svarézi slowly leaned back against the wall; suddenly, the future spread before him like a bird with sable wings.

"A weapon to build a new world."

"Yes, brother." Ilégo turned dark, delicious eyes upon the other man. "We can take it all. We need only agree to operate as partners."

"Aye, brother. Partners . . ."

For a while.

Svarézi flexed black gauntlets and gazed over Sumbria's city towers, feeling plans slowly nestling within plans.

Gilberto Ilégo leaned against the flimsy wooden boards and gazed out into the courtyard once more. He tapped a straw against his teeth, then quietly indicated the procession of guards beyond.

"Can you think of a way, colleague, to seize control of the Sun Gem tonight?"

"The guards are mortal. The warding spells can all be overcome." Svarézi rested a hand on his sword hilt. "With enough gold to buy diversions, it can be done."

"Good." Ilégo pitched his straw away and quietly turned around to face the other man. "Then we may begin. I see no reason to confine two intellects such as ours to a single tiny city-state. I believe that the age of the Blade Kingdoms is over at long last.

"We need only take the world's largest diamond as our own."

Grooms approached the door. Ilégo eased open the way into the palace corridors and allowed Svarézi to disappear into the gloom. Unlatching a service hatchway, the tall nobleman slipped quietly out into the palace stables and followed the chattering grooms to the palace yards.

As the Sumbrian passed, a silly, feathery head erupted out from the gables overhead. Eyes staring, Tekoriikii watched the nobleman walk by, then whipped his neck about to stare in rapture at the giant gemstone being carefully guided inside the palace walls. The bird's beak dropped open, his feathers rose, and his neck pouch shivered with absolute desire.

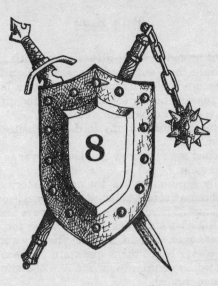

8

"My lords, my ladies, and my holders of shares . . . I
present Blade Captain Toporello of the city-state of
Sumbria, his lady, and his retinue!"

Ranked beside the ballroom door with her father and
Lady Ulia, Miliana was pinned in place as part of the
Manniccis' receiving line. Court functions always gave
Miliana a sour temper; what sweetness remained was
eroded by a headache, small talk, and the disdain of
passing haughty maidens. Miliana adjusted her spectacles, felt her favorite cantrip settle firmly in her mind,
and began to plan an evening of fun.

"Miliana, dear—do smile more brightly!" Lady Ulia
prodded a finger into her stepdaughter's ribs with force
enough to puncture a trireme's hull. "A smiling woman
radiates goodwill. A smiling woman radiates intelligence. What is more, a smiling woman can never look
plain." Ulia licked at a handkerchief and wiped an
imaginary speck from a disgusted Miliana's nose. "We
are on display, my dear, so remember that the family
reputation is in your hands!

"Now brace up—here comes the dwarven ambassador!"

A dozen booted, hooded little figures with great icebreaker noses now surrounded the Mannicci family. A small creature bobbed happily up and down in front of Miliana, shaking her by the hand while the girl replied with her very best diplomatic smile.

"Welcome to Sumbria, my lord. A pleasure to meet you at last."

Ulia raised a weary brow and leaned over to murmur in Miliana's ear.

"Actually, my dear, that is the ambassador's *wife*."

"Oh!" Miliana flushed, polished her spectacles, and took a closer glance. "I'm sorry. The beards always fool me."

Lady Ulia gave a dismissive wave of her fan.

"Oh, that's quite all right, my dear. The only words of our tongue I've ever heard them speak are 'I'll have another round.' You'd be surprised how many social situations it can see them through."

The herald sighted a new set of arrivals, and vigorously banged his tall oaken staff against the floor.

"The delegation from the elven nations of the Yuirwood! I present the Lady Lonereed Silverleaf and her escort-of-the-year!"

Miliana heard the announcement and felt her shoulders slump.

"Oh, no. Father invited the elves?"

Ulia settled herself in her dress like a peacock ruffling its plumes.

"Aaaaah . . . their age, their beauty, and their nobility unsettles you?"

"No—their utter lack of achievement!" Miliana watched a tall elven woman enter the hall. "You know, if I were eight hundred years old, I think I'd do more with my time than sitting about on my derriere singing *tra-la-la-lally*."

"The songs must have a spiritual depth of which we are unaware, dear. Now do be a good girl and smile . . ."

Miliana let her attention wander, only to have it rudely wrenched back into place by Lady Ulia's dulcet tones.

"Miliana, my dear, this is Brightlightning Dragonsbane, escort to the elven lady and Swordmaster of the Hordes of the Tangled Trees."

This title apparently belonged to a muscular, pompous elf dressed in chain mail and sporting a pudding-bowl haircut. The man sank into a pretentious bow and wetly kissed Miliana on the hand.

"Princess! How fitting that we meet at last. Brightlightning Dragonsbane, ever at your service."

Stirred into malice by the pressure of Lady Ulia's eyes, Miliana gave the man an innocent, gentling kind of smile.

"Why what a lovely name! Let me guess—you made it up all by yourself?"

"Indeed, fair damsel. Indeed!" The elven warrior whipped out his sword, instantly becoming a target for Cappa Mannicci's crossbowmen, hidden all about the hall. "For now when I cry out my name, all around me can turn and ask of me, 'Pure Knight—where come thee by such a title? Tell us of thy deeds!' "

Miliana fended off the man's imminent death with a wave to her father's sniper corps.

"Lovely! Well when you do cry out your name, do be careful not to scare the horses." Miliana peered evilly over her spectacle frames. *"Next!"*

The elven lady—a pale, spectral creature with hair that almost swept the floor, gave a grave bow to Miliana. As her eyes came level with the rose-pink pearl about Miliana's throat, the elf's eyes went wide. She sucked in a breath of utter disbelief, shot a hand up to her own throat, then numbly let herself be led away without another word. Miliana cocked an eyebrow after the departing elf, shook her head in wonder, and promptly put the incident out of her mind.

The inward traffic had ceased, and Miliana took the opportunity to escape. She placed a hand on her beautiful new pearl, felt a sudden rush of warm affection, and skipped off into the party in search of Lorenzo.

The titanic palace hall had been packed shoulder to
shoulder with dignitaries. The festival crowds had
almost tripled from the norm; the presentation of the
Sun Gem and the year's victorious campaign had
brought Sumbria a bounty of potential allies, along with
the attendant rush of saboteurs, assassins, sorcerers,
and spies. The air crackled with frustrated scrying
spells, spells of charm and mind control. In the Blade
Kingdoms, these little tools were as common as wood
lice and just about as easily squashed. Miliana wandered through the festivities, seeking for signs of her
friend. She meandered past Captain Toporello and his
anti-thievery committee, then pushed past a team of
elephant-headed loxoth who had mistaken Lady Ulia's
favorite flower arrangement for the punch.

Elves clustered together, staring at Miliana and talking in avid, animated whispers. Miliana mentally clas-
sified them as intellectual midgets and went proudly on
her way.

Passing before a jasmine bower, Miliana heard a rich
voice pitching itself into a smooth, seductive litany.

"You and I . . . two creatures almost from different
worlds. Who knows what adventures might greet the
explorer's eyes? The pounding pulse—the alien touch of
scents and dreams. We owe ourselves the experience—
let us seize it while we may!"

A sharp slap cracked out like a gunshot; surging from
the bower there came a furious young woman with a
pointy hat and veil. Miliana let her pass, then opened
up the bushes and leaned across a rail.

"Luccio, isn't it?"

Looking up from rubbing his reddened cheek, Luccio
Irozzi blindly surged up and took Miliana by the hand.

"Luccio, my flower? 'Tis Luccio indeed!" The vivacious
nobleman clasped Miliana's little hands against his
heart. "And how I have been longing for this small
moment alone. For you and I are two creatures almost
from different worlds. Who knows what adventures

might greet the explorer's eyes? The pounding pul—"

"Save it!" The girl flicked Luccio sharply on the nose. "It's me, Miliana. I'm looking for Lorenzo."

"Oh! I am so sorry, highness!" Seeing Miliana's face at last, Luccio hurriedly straightened his attire. "Lorenzo is still in our rooms. He was having trouble finding clothes that lacked scorch marks or burn holes."

With a sorry shake of her head, Miliana left Luccio consulting his list of potential trysts and marched past the guard and off into the passages that led to Lorenzo's rooms.

Behind her, the elven swordsman Brightlightning Dragonsbane swapped a meaningful glance with his mistress. The elven lady turned and thrust her way toward Ulia Mannicci with murder gleaming in her slitted eyes.

* * * * *

The palace sparkled like a beacon filled with fireflies; windows glowed, the colonnades thronged, and the courtyard fountain bubbled like champagne under a night sky sugared white with stars.

Behind the brilliant public rooms there lay the "business end" of the palace: the stables, kitchens, barracks, and armories that allowed the palace to operate as both a household and a fortress. Here the carriages and riding beasts filled the courts in patient rows as the sounds of merriment swirled past on the summer's air.

Walking through the palace gates there came a lean, strutting hippogriff bearing a silent rider. The hippogriff twitched the long equine ears atop its eagle's head, muttering irritably to itself as if resenting the ignominy of an entrance made on foot.

The creature's front limbs were equipped with talons, and its rear legs with hooves. Leaving mismatched prints across the dust, it walked the familiar path to the Mannicci stable stalls.

The Mannicci guards had been quintupled in number

for the evening revels; two soldiers supervised each bay
of stable stalls. Ugo Svarézi reined in his beast as he
approached a sergeant; the man held aloft a short wand
and scanned him for offensive magics before sheathing
the instrument and allowing Svarézi to dismount.

"Sir? Are there any special instructions for the care of
your beast?"

The Colletran passed the soldier his reins.

"No."

A blade shot out of the Blade Captain's sleeve;
Svarézi stabbed the soldier in the throat, ripped open
his windpipe, and rammed the dripping blade into his
victim's heart. The guard fell, clawing at the ground as
blood hissed up to splash stinking streams across
Svarézi's boots.

Behind him, something heavy thudded to the ground;
the hippogriff Shaatra had decapitated the other soldier
with her beak, shearing through sinew, flesh and bone
with the ease of a machine. The slim mare gave a fas-
tidious hiss, sneezed in distaste and shook the blood
free from her plumes.

She would have cleaned her feathers then and there
if Svarézi hadn't curtly ordered her into the stable
stalls. Spitting in spite, the hippogriff left bloody tracks
as she strutted out of view. Svarézi rolled the corpses
out of sight, unmoved by the simple act of murder. It
was a task he had performed at least a dozen times
before. In the Blade Kingdoms, assassination was a
uniquely personal task. The city-states had been established by mercenary companies, and the spirit of free
enterprise was, sadly, an established undercurrent of
everyday life. A wise man trusted no one but himself;
potentially, every servant could be bribed; every soldier
might be a spy.

A murderer therefore acted best when he acted
alone—unless his accomplice had an equal claim to
guilt. Svarézi moved out of the darkest shadows of the
stable doors, flashed moonlight from the mirror pommel

of his knife, and waited while Gilberto Ilégo strolled
over from the palace colonnades.

Ilégo held a large, leathery bat upon one arm. The
creature perched and chivied like a prized hunting
hawk, stropping at its master's leather gauntlets with
its fangs. Without a word exchanged between them,
Ilégo and Svarézi walked toward the palace's farthest
tower.

Within the tower, all the genius of Sumbrian security
had been brought to bear. The Sun Gem was a prize of
incalculable value; with a sneak-thief on the loose within the city walls, every precaution had been taken to
assure the safety of the gigantic diamond.

Prince Mannicci maintained a dozen sorcerers in his
personal retinue, specialists whose skills were attuned
to the arts of war. The prince had nevertheless spared
three of his best men to secure the priceless gem.

At the heart of the hollow tower, they sat; an enchanter
scanning a crystal ball, a summoner sitting in the center
of a thaumaturgic circle, and a battle mage who passed
his time reading from a huge, dusty old tome that was
substantially larger than the mage himself.

Outside the tower, hippogriff-mounted soldiers sat on
the roof scanning the skies; trained umber hulks,
hideous burrowing monsters, lay in wait inside tunnels
under the floor. Thirty crossbowmen and halberdiers
formed a ring of steel about a floor dusted with talcum
powder, caltrops, and hidden mines.

The gem itself was held in the hands of a titanic golem
made of porcelain, much like the lumpen, living statues
made of clay found in other kingdoms, only painted white
and bordered with patterns of blue flowers.

The security arrangements were painstakingly complete; all things considered, it seemed that Prince
Mannicci was in one of his less trusting moods.

Four guards stood outside the tower door—guards
augmented by a war priest armed with an array of battle spells. Ilégo led the way past the patrol, halting with

insolent ease beneath the shadows of a jasmine vine
and bidding Ugo Svarézi to huddle at his side.

An arrow slit afforded a view into the crowded tower
room. Gilberto Ilégo smoothed his mustache, then
leaned close to whisper softly into his companion's ear.

"Cappa Mannicci was never renowned for his subtlety
of wit." The Sumbrian nobleman cast an eye across the
troops, sorcerers, and giant golem just below. "In a few
minutes time, a display of something called fireworks,
imported from Shou Lung, shall begin—celebrations that
I have it on good faith will cause everyone to look skyward. The confusion should cover any number of alarms.

"Now, I have here a bag of powder—'dust of darkness'—into which I have inserted a small smoke powder
charge. When it explodes, it will spread a pall of
absolute darkness. The guards will be utterly blind and
helpless." Ilégo tickled his pet bat beneath the chin. "My
little companion here can navigate through the dark
more easily than a hawk can fly by day. He will snatch
the stone, return it to us here, and you may mount your
hippogriff and spirit the Sun Gem onward to the next
stage of our mutual project."

Svarézi—squat as a troll, silent and stinking of fresh
blood—evaluated the plan with a scowl, then gave a
curt nod of agreement. Ilégo acknowledged him with a
bow, eased himself over to the tiny arrow slit, and
adjusted the fuse of his little bomb.

They waited in the darkness for a long minute more,
until, suddenly, a peal of trumpets rose from the city
park nearby; it was the signal for a glorious new display.
A single skyrocket—a sight no one in Sumbria had ever
before seen—rose upon a tail of fire and burst above the
city walls. No sooner had the last starlets sprinkled to
the earth, when the entire skyline erupted into glorious
new flames. A thousand rockets screamed and whistled
up toward the moon, blasting open into clouds of
sparkling fire. Crowds excitedly spilled out of the palace
and crowded upper balconies. Grooms deserted the stables

and soldiers wandered from their posts to stand in the wide palace forecourt and gape up at the spectacle in awe.

Lighting the fuse of his darkness bomb, Ilégo had to shout to make himself heard above the stunning noise of the fireworks. "Fly low across the river once you have the gem—the rockets will pass overhead and cover your escape!"

The fuse sputtered, Ilégo's bomb soared out into the middle of the guards, and the tower's ceiling suddenly burst open in a shower of plaster dust.

"Tekorii-kii-kii! Tekorii-kii-kii!"

Gilberto Ilégo stared in shock as a great silly bird plunged down from the fractured ceiling in a cascade of brilliant plumes. The bird happily alighted in the arms of the porcelain golem, fastened talons about the Sun Gem, then noisily beat its wings and began to rise aloft.

Thirty soldiers, three magicians, and an animated porcelain statue all blinked in shock. They raised weapons, ignited spells, and all disappeared in a puff of inky blackness as Ilégo's bomb silently exploded in their midst.

Tekoriikii gave an odd little look of surprise and then vanished into absolute, impenetrable darkness.

"No!"

As Ilégo screamed, bedlam instantly erupted. In the pitch-black chamber, crossbows discharged in a wild storm of arrow fire, while a dozen men screamed war cries in the dark. A lightning bolt speared through the darkness and began to ricochet back and forth from the curving walls. Each flash froze a tableau of struggling men, frantic wings, and halberd blades.

Outside the tower, mere mortal senses were hammered numb by the fireworks display. Meanwhile, inside the guard room, light spells blinked on and off like fireflies at a dance party for epileptic insects. The blackness almost instantly swallowed each and every outburst; stabs and flickers illuminated a scene of absolute, outrageous chaos.

Hovering in the air above the embattled sorcerers, the giant thieving bird belabored Ilégo's trained bat about the shoulders as the mammal tried to wrest the Sun Gem from its claws. Just below them, the three sorcerers frantically beat at something with their staves; clearly spells of summoning should never be discharged in the dark. Soldiers wrestled soldiers, nursed arrow wounds, or fled, shrieking, through the windows, while the great golem strode blindly through the throng, bellowing in anger as a guard clung to its shoulders and tried to snatch the firebird's tail.

"Tekorii-kii-kii! Tekorii-kii-kii!"

The bird knocked the bat aside, bowled over a flurry of crossbowmen, and sped through the doorway and out into the palace yard. Fireworks had half-blinded the archers on the walls. A crossbow bolt shot under the bird's long tail, ricocheted from the gigantic Sun Gem and hissed straight toward Ugo Svarézi and Ilégo, making both men duck in alarm. With his fine velvet cap carried away on an arrow point, Ilégo clawed his way up from the dust and bleated in alarm.

"Stop that bird!

"Stop that bird!"

No one heard the cry; upon every roof, every balcony, and every turret in the kingdom, the people waved and cheered the starbursts in the sky. The thieving bird wheeled a somersault of sheer delight and flapped its way toward the palace walls.

Behind Ilégo, Ugo Svarézi simply turned and made a cold motion with his hand. A lean black shape whirred up from the stables and screamed a chilling challenge into the nighttime sky.

* * * * *

"Princess? May we assist you?"

Miliana paused in the guest corridors and gazed at one of her father's house patrols: four soldiers in brilliant particolored finery, and an apprentice mage in a ludicrous velvet toga. Miliana dismissed the men with an abstract wave of her hand; magicians irritated her, filling her with a stab of jealousy for the ease with which a man could study. The girl irritably stomped on her way, hardly deigning to spare the troops another glance.

A light shone from under Lorenzo's door. Miliana knocked on the lintel, frowning as a cherry-scented rat scuttled away behind a tapestry in the hall.

"Lorenzo? Lorenzo, I know you're in there—I can smell burning cherry-rat." Miliana's head gave a warning jab of pain, and the girl wondered whether the morning's neutralize poison spell had perhaps been a little rushed. "Lorenzo—aren't you coming to the party? They'll be presenting your painting in ten minutes' time. Come on ... there's a display of these smoke powder things you'll probably find fascinating out in the ..."

The door wrenched open in a trice. Lorenzo stood there before an astonished Miliana; he was bright eyed, bushy tailed, and brimming with delight. Miliana smiled and laughed, letting him take her hand and lead her into a room filled with easels, paints, and hairy brushes by the score.

Now that he had Miliana in his lair, Lorenzo seemed to stumble. The young man flushed and struggled to overcome an embarrassed silence.

"Are you well? I mean, have you recovered?"

Miliana drew herself straight, covering mortal embarrassment with a veneer of dignity.

"Um ... Oh yes yes yes yes yes ..." By pretending it had never happened, Miliana prevented herself from suffering over whatever maudlin drivel she had blabbed out to her companions. "I must thank you for taking such care to see me home, and for ... for other things." Miliana lifted up her new pearl pendant and gazed down at it with fondness shining in her eyes. "So many other things."

"Oh, we had no trouble getting you back inside. Tekoriikii flew a line up to your room, and we hoisted you through the tower window." Lorenzo seemed moderately pleased with the engineering skill involved. "So you are all right now then? You're sure?"

"Quite sure."

"Wonderful! Excellent!" Lorenzo clapped his hands with a loud, boisterous *bang*, making Miliana close her eyes and sway with the aftershock. "In which case, I have something to show you. It's something special. It's to do with what you said to me last night."

"Oh?" Miliana felt a worm of ill-ease slither stickily along her spine; she remembered vague impressions of crying her eyes out while slumped against Lorenzo's chest. "Um—there was no need to take any trouble."

"Trouble?" Lorenzo turned his clear, innocent, adoring eyes on Miliana, making her unconsciously reach up to touch the pearl hanging at her breast. "You are my friend; more than that, you are my colleague. I admire and respect you above all others. Nothing I do for you can possibly be any trouble."

He sat Miliana down in a chair and made her carefully fold her thin hands in her lap, just like a child at lessons. With an air of nervous excitement, he scuttled forward and dropped a pile of drawings on Miliana's knee.

"Now—now these are just the preliminary sketches for something which—well, which started as pure research, but ended as the profound inspiration for a work of pure and utter love." Lorenzo wheeled a great blanket-hung canvas over before Miliana. "It is my masterpiece—and I think you will be totally surprised by the insights that it shows.

The young artist whipped back his painting's cover and proudly watched Miliana's face for her reaction. To his great puzzlement, the girl leaned forward, removed and polished her spectacles, then replaced them on her nose. She stared at the painting with an expression of growing shock, and turned a strange shade of ashen gray.

She turned and regarded Lorenzo through grave, golden eyes.

"Lorenzo Utrelli Da Lomatra—I believe you may need medical help."

Lorenzo whipped his head around the corner of the canvas to see the painting; instead of the expected masterpiece, the painting was a "guesswork" sketch of Lady Ulia Mannicci in a swimming costume. The artist jerked in shock and took a second look to assure himself of what he beheld.

"No! This isn't the one!" A painting was missing; Lorenzo checked the back of the canvas to see if the lost artwork was there. "It must be in the other room!"

Miliana calmly followed Lorenzo through the door into his studio. Two easels stood by the door, one empty, and one holding another shrouded canvas. Lorenzo slumped in sudden calm as he saw the full easel; he looked to Miliana in relief, and grabbed at a corner of the cover sheet.

"I'm sorry—it's this one here. Now, just stand there and behold! I call the work simply 'Beauty.' "

The blanket flipped back, and Miliana wreathed her face in smiles.

"Why—it's stunning!" Miliana was honestly in awe. "Lorenzo, you're a genius!"

Lorenzo beamed, basking in Miliana's good opinion. He puffed up his chest in pride as the girl strode forward to take his hand. She leaned closer to the canvas to study the careful layers of brush strokes, paint, and glaze.

"It's magical!"

"It is not—it is merely . . . inspiration." Lorenzo bowed with reverence to his cherished colleague. "You said last night that if you had one wish, it would be to be beautiful. Perhaps this small token will show you how I feel. It is, of course, yours—a gift I hope that you will cherish."

Miliana regarded the canvas at arm's length with rapture shining in her eyes.

"Oh, Lorenzo, don't be silly! It has to go on display in ten minutes' time. This is something for the whole world to see."

"Really?" The artist pulled at the collar of his tunic as though it had suddenly grown too tight. "Well that is v-very courageous of you."

"Courageous? It is a celebration of art, of form! It is a thing of the spirit—not merely a painting of the flesh!"

"Exactly!" Thrilled, Lorenzo stepped forward to wor-shipfully take Miliana's hands. "Yes, that's it exactly! Oh . . . oh, Miliana, you understand!"

"Well of course I understand." Miliana Mannicci laid an adoring arm about Lorenzo's waist and gave the man a squeeze. She stood with him to regard a beautiful painting of a sea goddess rising, singing, from the waves, riding the great sea dragon of the deeps. "I never knew just how—how *sensitive* you were. This panting is utterly wonderful!"

The artist goggled at his painting in shock, and all the color drained from his face.

"This isn't the one . . ."

"What?"

"This isn't what I was trying to show you . . ." Lorenzo flung himself wildly about the room, peering behind set-tees, ripping open cupboards and setting a small green furry creature to flight. "Where is it? Where in the Abyss has it gone?"

"Calm down." Miliana made an easy gesture with one hand, playing the role of the quiet scholar as Lorenzo whirled past in a frenzy of despair. "Tell me what it looks like, and *I'll* find it for you."

"Well, the working sketches are in there!" Clambering atop a wardrobe, Lorenzo burrowed like a crazed mole through a vast wrack of scorched plaster, old papers, and half-eaten pickled eels. "I put them in your lap in the other room. Those were the drawings for the painting!"

Utterly serene at the eye of the storm, Miliana lifted up her hems and cruised gently on into the other room. Through the open windows, she saw the fireworks demonstration light the sky with stunning starbursts, streaks and blasts. She breathed a sigh of appreciation, frowned at the deafening storm of noise, then spied Lorenzo's drawings lying abandoned on a chair.

Miliana retrieved the pile of drawings, spread the top ones out across a tabletop, then looked down upon them with a ladylike little smile.

She thoughtfully adjusted her spectacles and with an expression of vapid good humor on her face, she turned toward Lorenzo.

Firework flashes lit the room as Lorenzo lunged through the door.

"Did you find the drawings?"

Miliana made a gracious, inquiring little motion over the pile of sketches.

"Lorenzo? I'm . . . naked."

"Oh, good!" The artist came forward to the table with a relieved little sigh. "Yes, those are the ones . . ."

"Lorenzo? I'm *naked!*"

The girl's voice broke in outrage as realization finally struck home. Snatching up a fistful of sketches, she flipped through them in a daze.

"You drew me naked! I don't believe it—you drew me naked!" Every detail had been recorded—every muscle group, every soft, sweet curve—every gossamer float of hair. "You drew me naked!"

Appalled at her reaction, Lorenzo timidly crept forward, wringing at his hands.

"B-but I told you I was using you to help me study. You're the one who inspired me into researching anatomy!"

"I didn't mean *my* anatomy!" The girl held up another sketch, turned it upside down and blanched quite pale. "Oh, my gods!"

"But it's a celebration!" Lorenzo waved a hand across his drawings in pride. "You thrill me—you fascinate me! You've shown me a type of beauty I've never known before. I just wanted to show the Miliana that no one else has ever seen."

"My mother's bloody midwife never saw me like this!"

The artist began a tactical retreat.

"Uh—you see, I invented a thing called a peri—"

Miliana lashed out at a tower of glass tubes and wildly crashed them to the floor. The chemicals instantly ate through the carpet, the floorboards, and into the wine cellar below. "I trusted you! I even . . . I even—*ooooh!*" The girl tore her hair in rage at her own weakness and stupidity. "You lecherous, spying little—"

"Now, now, Miliana . . ." Lorenzo pathetically held up his hands like a thief trying to hold a dragon at bay. "Look, it's all in the name of science—of art! Comparative anatomy—your mother and yourself! I just got more and more interested in you."

The girl answered with an incoherent scream. She ripped off her hat, pulled out a strip of notes, and began frantically memorizing the symbols written on the page.

Lorenzo cautiously retreated behind a padded couch.

"What are you doing?"

"I'm going to fry you like an egg, you little lump of sputum!"

Sparks raged about Miliana's hand; she whipped back her arm, shrieked in sheer, vengeful release, and flung a lethal dart of magic fire at Lorenzo's eyes.

The artist screamed like a frightened mouse and wildly dove away. The dart punched a hole clean through the furniture, sending burnt feathers blasting up into the air. Cursing like a wildcat, Miliana burst into the adjoining room in hot pursuit of her prey; a pointy-hatted psychopath, she stormed through the shadows and squealed in rage.

"Come out and die like a man, you little ball of pus!"

Something tried to race for the door; Miliana gave a predatory howl, pumping energy into a dart which stabbed like a lightning bolt clean across the room. A chair erupted, stone blew apart—and somehow a blackened but unharmed Lorenzo sped free and dove beneath a table.

"Miliana! Miliana, we can talk!"

"Go choke on your own bile!"

"Miliana? Miliana, now let's be reasonable!" Lorenzo saw the room light up with another sizzle of sparks and tried to cram himself backward into a flower pot. "N-now I realize, in retrospect, that I may be guilty of having slightly overstepped a hidden social line . . ."

"You sniveling little wretch! I'll get you for this if it's the last thing I do!" Miliana kicked over a table, powered by a seething, blinding rage; Lorenzo had scuttled off beneath a maze of furniture. "I'm going to make you eat bricks of your own sun-dried urine!"

"Miliana! Miliana, we're supposed to be getting betrothed!" Lorenzo helplessly tried to placate a monster. "I mean—you *are* the princess? So that means our parents want us to wed! You wouldn't hurt someone your parents want you to marry, would you?"

Distant lab equipment shook with fright; Miliana gave a roar of triumph and hurtled the workbench aside to reveal Lorenzo scuttling like a rat across the floor. The girl shot her firebolt and watched it streak straight at her victim's rear.

Sweat had fogged up her lenses; the firebolt missed Lorenzo, passed through a jug of cherry-flavored fluid, and instantly triggered a titanic blast of power. The chemicals exploded, blowing one whole wall out of the apartments. Blinking with amazement, Miliana and Lorenzo found themselves sailing through the sky and out into the courtyard.

They landed in the fodder pile; artist, sorceress, rubble, rats and all. Terra-cotta roof tiles slid down from the walls with a crash like a thousand breaking dinner plates. Miles of paper chains and bunting then cascaded down across the pile, festooning scorched ruins with little lights and candy swords.

Skyrockets burst and Catherine wheels blurred; overhead, Tekoriikii squealed as a great black hippogriff slammed into him from below. Miliana rose up out of an astounding pile of rubble, dust and ash, dimly reaching out to take her crumpled pointy hat. The dazed girl blinked about herself trying to remember what was wrong.

There was something she had to do . . .

Miliana felt a fluttering piece of paper land itself across her face. She peeled the paper away, saw that it was an exquisitely detailed sketch of her own naked rear, and finally felt the world jump into focus.

Yes! Kill Lorenzo!

A soldier lay half buried under fallen tiles. Miliana dazedly ripped herself up out of the ruins and took the enormous halberd from the soldier's hands.

"Can I borrow this?"

A fearful racket started overhead—screams and howls—a piercing eagle screech. Miliana ignored it all, her stunned mind fixed on a single thought as she tottered up across the ruins of Lorenzo's rooms.

A head popped up out of the rubble; Miliana took one look at Lorenzo, lifted up the halberd, and raced toward him with a manic battle scream. Wailing in abject terror, Lorenzo took off like a rabbit. Overhead, a mighty battle filled the air with feathers, wings, and screams, while a thousand skyrockets shook the heavens with a deafening crash of light.

9

"You and I—two creatures almost from different worlds! Who knows what adventures might greet the explorer's eyes? The pounding pulse—the alien touch of scents and dreams. We owe ourselves the experience—let us seize it while we may!"

One eye blackened, and the sharp mark of a woman's handprint standing sharp and red across his cheek, Luccio Irozzi wandered disconsolately through the plazas of the Mannicci palace, reciting his little litany in puzzlement. His evening had somehow gone sadly astray. Now, with the firework display lighting up the world and shuddering every windowsill, the entire party population had crowded onto the balconies to marvel at the unprecedented show. Having been beaten nearly comatose by a dozen eligible females, Luccio decided to take a break and reassess his romantic strategies.

"You and *me* are two creatures almost from different worlds?" Luccio changed the timbre of his voice and tried again. "You and *I*? Yes—you and *I* are both inhabitants of far, far different worlds . . ."

It didn't seem to work quite as well as it should. The

daughter of Blade Captain Toporello had somehow managed to pour the contents of a flower vase into his tights, and it felt as though some of the rose stems might still be down there. Dejected and defeated, Luccio made his way into the deserted courtyard and sat himself down beside the bubbling waters of the ornate fountain.

A note written on mother-of-pearl had asked him for a tryst here at midnight; Luccio scanned the deserted courtyard and hung his head with a disappointed sigh.

Fireworks burst and blasted overhead like a war between the gods; crowds made "oohs" and "aaahs" of appreciation, sounding like the ebb and flow of distant seas. The rear courtyard suddenly dissolved into a noisy chaos of bellows, shouts, and screams, while the whole palace shuddered to an unseen blow.

Having lost the party mood, Luccio ignored it all and sadly trailed a finger into the cool water at his side.

A penniless father had left Luccio the heir to an empty house and a world of debt. Without funds, there were no mercenaries—without mercenaries, no votes, and without votes, a gentleman had no influence at all. Disinclined to don a metal suit and join the troops himself, Luccio normally faced his misfortunes with a flippant smile.

Heaving a sigh, Luccio laid himself back against a marble statue of a spouting dolphin and let his velvet cap fall to the ground. Spray from the fountain kissed his cheek as he closed his eyes to the flash and glitter of artificial stars.

"It's true, really. I don't really have anything to offer. Nothing but poor old Luccio—who, frankly, is not much of a prize. No fortune, no mansion, no votes, no ties; a simple promise of devotion doesn't hold any water these days."

A stream of ripples in the fountain drifted to a halt; the whole world seemed to draw a quiet breath.

"It never really seems to work out for me. There's nothing to fall back on but myself—and I keep wondering if that's anything to offer to a girl.

"But a *real* girl—someone just . . . different. Someone

who could maybe see that there's a prize here for the taking . . . now that's a dream worth having!"

Behind Luccio, a pair of startling lavender eyes shone beneath the waters. Tall, delicate, fish-finned ears rose quietly up into the air.

With his back to the water, Luccio ran his hand across his brow.

"When I close my eyes, I can see you drifting there in front of me. You and I—two creatures almost from different worlds. Who knows what adventures might greet the explorer's eyes? The pounding pulse—the alien touch of scents and dreams. We owe ourselves the experience. Let us seize it while we may!"

A figure erupted from the water with an excited squeal and clasped Luccio in its arms. A curvaceous, scaly body, bright eyes, and wild pink hair flashed briefly in the light of fireworks as the nixie locked Luccio in a passionate, soaking kiss. With a shout, the man spilled backward into the freezing waters while the nixie damsel drew a breath, crammed his face up against her impassioned breast and happily wrapped him against her scales.

* * * * *

Cool and quiet in the darkness, Lorenzo stated his case with an admirable degree of calm.

"Look—traditionally, all beauty is judged by ultimates; the perfect figures, the studied poise . . . you know the kind of thing." Lorenzo sat cross-legged on the floor of a cupboard, trying to be the voice of sweet reason in the storm. "I merely determined that if I wanted to define the actual basics of beauty, I would have to try to discover the beautiful within a subject who exhibits absolutely none of the . . . ah . . . the actual . . . that is, none of the accepted attributes of feminine . . ." The artist stumbled, sensing himself sliding into even more trouble.

Lorenzo's refuge shuddered as Miliana's halberd blade viciously hacked its way in through the door.

"Come out of there, you—you *suitor*, you! Open that damned door!"

Inside the cupboard, Lorenzo watched his barricades and makeshift locks splinter one by one. He tried to keep himself adrift inside a sea of studied calm.

"I realize that I have behaved badly—nay, inexcusably. I can only say that what I did was done from the most pure of motivations, and that my respect for you is utterly sincere. Nor did I realize until last night that you were actually my . . . intended.

"Now perhaps we ought to get the nude painting of you back into hiding before it goes out on public display."

"What?"

Miliana hurtled the halberd aside, rammed a fist through the broken door and undid the lock with one sharp tug of her hand. She dragged Lorenzo out into the light and shook him like a stick insect in her claws.

"What do you mean it's going on display?"

"Well it's . . . it's the only painting that's missing!" Lorenzo felt the words being squeezed bodily out of his throat by Miliana's grasp. "Someone must ha-have taken the picture to put up for the ceremony!"

The girl released her victim, turning herself quite green with shock.

"Was it anything like those—those sketches?"

"Um . . ." Lorenzo tried to see a way to somehow escape with his life. "Um—no . . ."

Miliana felt a brilliant ray of hope. "No?"

"Well . . . yes." Lorenzo felt the sweat pour off him as he glanced at the halberd leaning against a nearby wall. "Um—quite a lot like them actually."

Scorched, torn, and wild, Miliana hoisted Lorenzo up to his feet, turned him about, and dragged him toward the ruins of his apartment.

"Come on! Get the painting of the sea goddess! It's going to take both of us to carry it!"

Confused, Lorenzo felt himself being propelled across the rubble by a freckled amazon in skirts.

"Aren't you going to kill me?"

"I'll kill you later. Now help me get that painting back!"

* * * * *

Standing on a balcony that faced off across the Akanamere, Lady Ulia Mannicci stood in splendor, wearing a hat that would have done justice to the goddess Umberlee herself. Puffing out her indignant bosom, the lady watched the brilliant fireworks with an air of irritation and disdain.

"Miliana should be here to applaud this display! Cappa, my dear—where has your unruly daughter hidden herself now?"

Prince Cappa Mannicci scowled and scanned the crowds, then signaled for the services of an aide.

Standing proud and hostile amidst a crowd of haughty elves, the lady of the Yuirwood threw her cloak back from her pale shoulders and pushed free from the crowds to confront her awesome hostess.

Ulia turned to face the elf like a stone giant confronting a sprite. The two women met eye to eye in a strange fellowship of mutual anger and pride.

"I am called Lonereed Silverleaf, of the Clan of Wandering Spray." The slim queen tilted her angry silver eyes. "I have come here as a guest to your house, and I claim a guest's right of justice!"

Ulia's bodice swelled like a galleon's sails before a storm.

"Justice, you ask? Then my dear, it is justice you shall have!" The human woman gazed down from the celestial heights of her pride. "How have you been wronged within my city, and under my roof?"

"Theft!" The elf drew her robes tight against her narrow frame. "My most prized of jewels—a love gift from my people—has been stolen from me. Stolen! And the thief has the insolence to wear the necklace right here before my very eyes!"

"Then this outrage shall be dealt with at once." Ulia took the elven woman by the arm and led her away from the thunderstorm of fireworks outside. "Tell me the identity of the thief."

Lady Silverleaf raised a long index finger and summoned a figure from among her courtiers; Brightlightning Dragonsbane strode forth and knelt before his lady's feet. Lady Silverleaf indicated the man with a wave of her hand.

"My bodyguard and boon companion has followed the thief to her lair."

"Good." Ulia settled her stomach in its spun-steel and adamantine girdle. "Then describe her to me."

"My lady—it is the girl who stood beside you to welcome us into your home." The elven bodyguard showed no small satisfaction in having completed his assigned task. "The short, speckled human female with eyepieces made of glass."

Half expecting outraged denial, the elves swapped cool glances as Lady Ulia swelled up like a puffer fish in imminent danger of detonation. With a look of triumph in her eye, the woman felt all her worst—and, therefore, her most cherished—suspicions confirmed.

"Miliana! I knew the little wretch had two sides to her coin." Sumbria's first lady signed for two of her own guards and two ladies-in-waiting, then beckoned the elves to follow in her wake. "Lady Silverleaf—come! We shall take back your jewel and at last uncover the whys and wherefores of this city's little cat burglar!"

*   *   *   *   *

"Tekorii-kii-kii! Tekorii-kii-kii!"

Mad with panic, Tekoriikii fought a ferocious battle in the air. A lean black javelin of feathers had lashed upward from the palace stables, crashing into him like lightning out of a storm. Claws ripped through empty feathers—Tekoriikii beat wildly at a pair of snapping jaws, and then both combatants tumbled free into a sky shot through with brilliant falling stars.

Carrying the massive Sun Gem, and trailing a hundredweight of tail feathers at his rear, Tekoriikii's flight was a thing more spectacular than speedy. Laboring his wings, the bird arced like a comet past the palace towers and nodded his head this way and that, wondering where his enemy might have gone.

"Awk!"

A black streak ripped out of the night and tried to disembowel Tekoriikii with its claws; the firebird tucked in his stomach, let his foe pass under him, then nimbly plucked a fistful of hairs from its tail.

In mating fights—the only combat most firebirds would ever know—the plucking of tail feathers was the *coup de grâce*. Tekoriikii had won a mighty victory! He swooped into a gleeful little victory roll, whirring out his wings in utter joy.

"Tekorii-kii-kii! Tekorii-kii-kii!"

The air shuddered as a skyrocket exploded fifty yards away, the bright flash illuminating a frozen scene of running soldiers, fleeing bats, and broken walls. Having outflown his opponent and snatched his precious prize, Tekoriikii folded his wings and sped away, crooning in smug self-satisfaction over being the cleverest bird in all Faerûn.

The sudden flicker of motion above him came as a surprise; his angry black opponent had returned for another round, quite against the usual rules of courtly war.

Combat between most birds is a purely ritual affair, a test of dominance with death and damage usually far from anyone's mind. Tekoriikii chuffed in annoyance as his enemy streaked in from one side; then abruptly braked to a halt and watched his outraged foe miss its intended strike by a country mile.

The creature was extremely odd in its appearance; long eagle's wings, and a slender feathered neck topped off with a cruel hooked beak. Most strangely of all, the entire rear quarters were sheathed in short, shining hair. Lacking Tekoriikii's beautiful plumes; lacking his poise, his elegance, his brains and grace, it seemed no wonder that the creature fought with such anger in its heart. Tekoriikii powered himself upward in a giddy half-loop, tucked himself into a dive, and found himself racing head to head with his shrieking, frothing enemy. The firebird made to give vent to his deadly battle scream, drew in his breath—

—and looked straight into an astonishing pair of exotic, feminine eyes.

The bird froze, the hippogriff whipped past, and Tekoriikii gave a blink of astonishment as he felt a sudden breeze across his rear. He looked down between his legs, saw his bare naked rump grinning at him without a feather to its name, and moaned a pathetic, bleating little cry.

With his unlikely aerodynamics scattered to the winds, Tekoriikii abruptly made a crash landing straight into the courtyard rubble pile.

Rummaging through the ruins of Lorenzo's apartments for his painting of the sea goddess, Miliana and Lorenzo rose and watched in bemusement as their feathery friend plunged into the ruins of an old eiderdown. Miliana adjusted her tall pointy hat—now scorched, dented, and with its veil torn all awry—and settled her grimy spectacles on her nose.

"Tekoriikii?"

Lorenzo emerged from the shards of his workroom holding a shrouded canvas in his hands.

"Who?"

"Tekoriikii? I think it's Tekoriikii!" Miliana hitched up her skirts and wended her precarious way across the rubble. "Hey, old bird, are you all right?"

"Glub glub! Yonk-squonk glub glub!"

Tekoriikii's high-plumed head appeared, swaying, dazed, and scarcely conscious. Miliana slithered toward him through a cloud of scorched duck down and frantically gathered the bird up in her arms. Tekoriikii flopped his wings and gave a croaking little cry before hanging like a limp rag against her breast.

Lorenzo fought his way through the ruins and took the

firebird's pulse, to be rewarded by Tekoriikii licking at his face. The man stared in astonishment at the bird's plucked, naked backside, a parson's nose utterly devoid of plumes.

"Where do you think all the other bits have gone?"

From the stables came the sound of running boots, rattling armor, and angry cries. Miliana stretched her small frame to its best possible height and tried to pierce the flash and flicker of the fireworks.

"Lorenzo? Lorenzo, I think we should get him out of sight." The girl took a step in retreat as the approaching charge grew in noise. "Actually, I think we ought to move him rather quickly."

Bursting into the yard from the stable gates, there came a wild-eyed Blade Captain Ilégo followed by a squat, savage troll of a man dressed all in black. Ilégo pointed at Tekoriikii and screamed out in bloodthirsty revenge.

"Kill that bird! A thousand ducats to the man who kills that bird!"

"Oh dear." Miliana took one look at the horde of soldiers who rushed past Ilégo toward the semiconscious firebird, then ran clumsily through the hillocks of fallen stone. "Quick! We'll have to carry him!"

"On what?"

"I don't know—find something flat! Hurry!"

Lorenzo's paintings had been daubed on canvas stretched tight over wooden frames; Lorenzo slammed the two paintings together face-to-face, rolled Tekoriikii onto the impromptu stretcher, and quickly hoisted up the stretcher's rear.

"You take the lead!"

"Me?" Miliana lifted up the front end in surprise. "Why me?"

"Because you know where you're damned-well going!"

They started off across the rubble, only to lose their balance as Tekoriikii suddenly surged back into life. The firebird flopped, lashed out with his neck, and plucked up a gigantic shiny object in his bill.

"The Sun Gem!"

Miliana and Lorenzo stared at the titanic jewel in shock. Before they could so much as move, Tekoriikii had thrown back his head and swallowed the jewel right down his throat. Miliana gave a scream of fright, wrenched open the astonished Tekoriikii's beak and stared wildly down into the creature's gullet.

"It's down there! He's swallowed the bloody thing!"

"What?"

"The Sun Gem! The Sun Gem!" Miliana shook the addled bird by the craw. "Cough it up! Come on—drop it—drop it now!"

The huge diamond shot out of Tekoriikii's crop and landed on the ground. Fascinated, Lorenzo tilted his head over to one side.

"Actually, that's an interesting thing; many birds are known to swallow rocks as an aid to their digestive—"

A soldier topped the rubble, gave a shriek of triumph, and clapped the stock of his crossbow under his arm. Taking rough aim on Tekoriikii, he stabbed a wicked looking bolt into the catch, laughing as he imagined a thousand golden ducats pouring through his hands.

The bow sprung with a rather disappointing twang, and the steel quarrel simply dropped off the tiller and bounced onto the ground. The soldier reversed the bow and stared down the stock in amazement, then squawked as the bow sprang the rest of the way, slapping across his nose like a whip. Nose bleeding, eyes watering, he dropped backward across the rubble pile like a falling tree.

Another soldier pounced on the Sun Gem and held it high above his head in victory. Suddenly, from the shadows, a black-clad figure stabbed the soldier from behind. The gem was snatched from dying hands; the black hippogriff appeared, and the black rider mounted and disappeared into the smoke-lit skies.

Soldiers opened fire on the retreating hippogriff, crossbows stabbing ineffective darts up into the air. In seconds they would change targets once again; stuffing Tekoriikii back onto the stretcher, Miliana and Lorenzo fled as fast as their frenzied legs could run.

Soldiers surged across the wreckage in pursuit; another group emerged from the broken gap in the palace wall, cutting off all access to the halls. Miliana changed course and sprinted to the gate that led into the palace fountain yard. Her long hair whipped back into Lorenzo's eyes, blinding him from any view of where she meant to go.

They swept through a gate, and Lorenzo almost broke a rib as Miliana came to an unexpected halt; she wrenched the stretcher hard about, kicked angrily at a lever set into the wall, and brought a spiked portcullis crashing down to seal the door behind her.

"They'll go back into the palace and find another way around. Come on—we'll hide Tekoriikii in my rooms!"

"But what about the ceremony?" Lorenzo reeled and staggered in Miliana's wake. "The painting! It's about to be unveiled!"

"Oh, dear gods!"

In the palace fountain, something struggled, thrashed, and dove. Miliana pulled the stretcher to a halt; Lorenzo's friend Luccio jerked up out of the water with a look of panicked innocence on his face. Dripping wet, breathless, and covered with some sort of welts, he stared in shock at Lorenzo, Princess Miliana, and the lolling firebird.

"I wasn't doing anything! There's no one in here!"

"Good!" Lorenzo, breathless, burnt, and businesslike pushed back his dusty hair. "Now, quickly, grab the bottom painting, get into the palace hall, and swap it for the one they're about to put up on display!"

"What?" A flushed Luccio struggled up out of the fountain, streaming water from his tunic top. "In the name of Beshaba, why?"

"Because it's the wrong damned painting! Now just do it, while we go and hide this bird!" Lorenzo, caught in the flow of panic, suddenly wrenched to a halt and stared more closely at his friend's neck. "Is that some sort of bite mark—there on your neck?"

"It's a rash!" Luccio hurriedly removed the bottom painting from under Tekoriikii. "It's nothing."

"A rash? Look . . . there's a whole lot more of them all over your . . ."

"I'll swap the paintings!" Hiding his love-bitten neck, Luccio hustled Lorenzo onward toward the palace halls. "Now—now just run along with your bird, and I'll deal with everything."

The sounds of doors bursting open came from every side. Miliana spied an open portal leading into the palace sculleries and charged off with her pointy hat tilted like a battering ram.

Luccio watched it all in bemusement and heaved a puzzled sigh. Quite suddenly, a slim, seductive shape emerged from the waters behind him and trapped him in its arms. With a brief squawk, Luccio disappeared beneath the foam as the nixie raised great passionate tidal waves with her webbed limbs.

Plunging through the sculleries with their towering stacks of copper pots and pans, Miliana collapsed in a heap to catch her breath. From her unique position under the canvas, she could see the painting staring her straight in the eye.

A slim sea-goddess riding a silvery dragon.

"It's the wrong painting!"

"What?" Lorenzo pushed Tekoriikii's plumes aside to meet Miliana eye-to-eye. "The wrong what?"

"This is the sea goddess! You've given Luccio the wrong one!"

"Damn!"

Lorenzo whipped the painting out from under Tekoriikii's belly, dropping the creature onto Miliana with a thump. He ran outside, clutching at the painting, looked about himself, and saw no sign of Luccio.

The second painting leaned against the fountain, abandoned and forgotten. Lorenzo ducked frantically back inside.

"He's gone off and left the painting out there!"

"What?" Miliana struggled out from under a great mass of limp red bird. "Well, we'll just have to do it ourselves then!" Skinny arms thrust ineffectually at Tekoriikii's bulk. "Help get this dumb thing off me!"

A cheese trolley stood beside the kitchen door. Miliana emerged from under the firebird, spat feathers from her mouth, and peered through a curtain into the palace's crowded great hall.

Up at the far end of the room, a covered canvas stood proudly on display. Courtiers, ambassadors, and Blade Captain Toporello had gathered about Prince Mannicci as he prepared to draw the cord and bare his daughter's charms to a waiting world. Miliana gave a shriek of alarm and crowded back into Lorenzo's arms.

"They're going to pull the cord!"

Lorenzo took one look at the unwieldy firebird, the cheese trolley, and the cook's hats hanging from hooks on the wall. He hoisted Tekoriikii up and slammed him atop the gurney, then jammed an apple into the creature's open beak. Tekoriikii froze in shock as he was surrounded with wax fruit stolen from a mantelpiece display.

"Tekoriikii—just stay there!" Lorenzo jammed a chef's hat across Miliana's ruined headgear, then crammed another hat across his own brows and stuffed the painting into the trolley's lower rack. "Stay there and hang on!"

The curtain was ripped aside; pushing the gurney wildly across the room, bashing aside crowds and ramming courtiers into the punch bowls, Miliana and Lorenzo clove a path across the hall. With Tekoriikii frozen in fright, the apple still gripped firmly in his mouth, they rumbled madly out into the room.

"Catering!" Lorenzo sent Toporello's buxom daughter crashing into a dwarven tunnel baron. "Catering! Coming through—excuse me, pardon me—excuse me!" Lorenzo charged straight toward the painting at the far end of the hall. "Roast ostrich for the prince! Gangway!"

The whole ensemble whipped past an astonished crowd and cracked into the painting display. Firebird, trolley, wax fruit and all went sailing like shrapnel through the sky.

Lorenzo whipped the picture of the sea goddess—this time checking that it truly was the sea goddess—out of hiding and deftly swapped it for the painting of Miliana. He jammed the newly stolen painting into the relieved princess's arms, threw Tekoriikii across his shoulders, and felt the creature croak and eject the apple in a shallow trajectory, far across the room.

"Sorry . . . this bird's off. I'll just get another!"

Leaping a hurdle of fallen men, Lorenzo led the way for Miliana through a swinging door. As outrage broke out behind them, the two thieves and their bird dropped the locking bar behind them and slumped in exhaustion against the wall.

"There, see? Now wasn't that easy?" Lorenzo raggedly caught his breath, wiping sweat back from his eyes. He briskly uncovered the painting in Miliana's hands and gazed at his creation with love.

"There—isn't it beautiful?"

"It's wonderful. Thank you *so* much for the compliment!" Behind Miliana, the swinging door was slowly being battered open. Miliana wrenched open a curtain to discover a room crowded with dwarves. "Free beer—that way!"

The effect was astonishing; with their war cry of *"I'll have another round!"* the dwarves tried to cram their way through the swinging door, pushing frantically against the efforts of the angry mob inside the great hall. Miliana tugged Lorenzo away from the wall, forced the giddy Tekoriikii to his feet, and led a swift retreat into the deepest palace corridors.

Several cunning twists and turns soon lost all signs of pursuit. Slowing her pace, discarding her disguise, and restoring her pointy hat, Miliana took Lorenzo by the hand, and Tekoriikii by the wing, and led them wearily toward her tower home.

"Now, perhaps, we can get a little peace." The girl mopped at her brow with a ragged little sigh. "And a few explanations. Tekoriikii, perhaps you might be so good as to tell me what you were doing with that jewel?"

"Glub glub!" The bird swallowed hard, put a wing up to his throat, and looked bemusedly around. *"Squonky donky glub glub!"*

"Yes, well, be that as it may . . ." Miliana creased her pretty freckled nose into a frown. "Do either of you have any idea what might have happened to you. Fiance or no fiance, they can *behead* people like you!" The girl fumbled open the latch of her apartment door. "At least the worst that can ever happen to me is to—"

The door had swung open to reveal Miliana's rooms; standing facing her in a phalanx of poisonous frowns were Lady Ulia, her maidservants, a dozen angry elves, and a squad of palace guards.

The broken bathroom ceiling had been discovered; soldiers were carrying down basket after basket of gems. It was a veritable dragon's hoard; a massive mound of glittering baubles worth a king's ransom.

Tekoriikii withdrew his head timidly behind Miliana's rump. The girl simply froze, goggling at the piles of loot in dumb despair.

Lady Ulia coldly extended her hand.

"And the pearl pendant too, I think." Miliana's stepmother snatched off the rose-pink pearl, then gazed upon her ward as though Miliana had slithered out from under a rotten log. "We, of course, await your explanation."

"I . . ." Miliana stared in absolute bewilderment at the endless tide of gems. "I . . . I've never seen them before in my life!"

Tekoriikii shivered, transmitting terror right through Miliana's back; suddenly the girl realized from whence the jewels had come.

Lady Ulia made a grand progress, moving a great, slow circle about the gathering treasure; clearly all of her worst, most cherished, most delicious matronly fears had come true.

"My emeralds, Lady Silverleaf's pearl, and every other

bauble stolen in these few weeks past. We found them up inside your loft, of course, half covered by straw. Perhaps you fancied you were making yourself a nest?" Ulia ponderously cruised herself back into Miliana's view. "I believe we have found Sumbria's secret cat burglar at last."

Ulia's eyes fell upon Lorenzo and Tekoriikii, and venom dripped out of her smile.

"Aaaah, the errant fiancé! Your mentor in crime, I presume? An inventor of . . . climbing tools? Of thievish plans?" Ulia flicked a glance across the boy and bird. "Meat for the headsman's block. Take these two wretches away! They have led this poor girl, unwittingly, into a life of crime!" Ulia gave Miliana a pitying gaze rich with self-satisfaction. "Poor child. My poor, dear child."

Soldiers clamped their hands onto Lorenzo and the bird. Lorenzo drained pale white, and Tekoriikii hid his face beneath one wing. Miliana—terrified and alone—gave them a dreadful gaze of despair, looking deep into Lorenzo's eyes.

"Wait."

Her voice, soft and husky, somehow carried through the room. The soldiers relaxed their grasp. Small, pale and frightened, Miliana dropped her gaze down to the floor.

"*I* did it. I am the cat burglar. It is my fault alone."

Lorenzo simply stared. Miliana drew a breath and raised her face, tears streaming from her eyes.

"I wasn't going to keep them; I wanted to steal all the jewels, then hang them from the city walls just to show what I could do. It was . . . It was simply out of pride."

"Miliana?" Lorenzo stared as he felt the soldiers let him go. Beside him, Tekoriikii's face emerged from hiding. "Miliana?"

"These two tried to stop me. Lorenzo Utrelli and his—his pet bird." Miliana wearily raised a limp hand toward her two friends. "I wanted to take the Sun Gem, but they dissuaded me. Sir Utrelli is a scholar, and a perfect gentleman."

Tekoriikii gave a soft trill of despair as he saw soldiers close about Miliana from behind.

The princess waited like a lamb tethered for the slaughter.

"I confess my crime. Do what you will with me."

Lady Ulia swelled her breast behind a dangerous creak of bodice lace; power was her ultimate desire, and here were all her fantasies fulfilled.

"Well, my dear. It seems our efforts to raise you as a lady have failed." The great horned hat assumed an air of absolute malevolence. "Since your crimes were motivated by pride and not by greed, I think we can apply a suitable corrective force; the owners of the gems will be pleased to cooperate now that they will have their goods returned.

"We shall return them, and we will say no more about this 'thief'—forevermore. He shall disappear into oblivion." Lady Ulia's words brought a nod from all those around her; a forest of bribes would be little enough to pay for avoiding family scandal.

"As for you, my dear: finishing school shall teach you the meaning of obedience and humility. Perhaps in a few years you will have learned the error of your ways." Ulia snapped her fingers at the guards. "Take her hence!"

Miliana needed to be half carried from the room. Her hat fell aside, and Lorenzo saw the coils of magical spell sheets hidden deep inside. He caught her hat up with a cry and tried to press it into Miliana's hands.

"Your hat!" The artist couldn't seem to make the girl take hold. "Miliana—you have to take your hat!"

"Apparently, I shan't be needing it anymore." The girl seemed as ashen as a corpse; her energy drained out before Lorenzo's eyes. Leaning forward, she brushed at the artist's cheek with a secret, tragic kiss.

"Thank you both for giving me a life—just for a little while . . ."

Her whisper left Lorenzo's cheek stained wet with tears. Walking quietly between her guards, Miliana allowed herself to be led away. Behind her, Tekoriikii and

Lorenzo could only stand locked within the shadows of her broken heart.

* * * * *

"A great tragedy. A catastrophe! But one we quite expected, I am sure." Lady Ulia had found Miliana's fall from grace utterly cathartic; even the flood of rumors that would escape her net of bribes were not too great a price to pay; she would dine out upon the story until the end of time.

The future couldn't be more perfect!

Safely ensconced in the palace once more, and with her husband leading a wild hunt on the tail of Svarézi, Ulia looked forward to the continuance of the night's ceremonies.

The gift painting from Lomatra was wheeled forward into place; the nobles and courtiers gathered admiringly around for the unveiling. If the young man trundling forth the painting was wet clean through and smelled of water weed, no one thought to comment aloud; it had, after all, been a most chaotic festival.

Luccio passed the unveiling cord into Lady Ulia's hands and escaped out into the courtyard with his head held high. Sumbria's first lady gazed out in triumph at her guests, and let her words peal forth across the waiting crowd.

"We have here the work of an unknown genius—but a man who has seen fit to encapsulate the very essence of our land." The mighty lady let her bodice swell with pride. "My lords and ladies! I proudly unveil a new masterpiece entitled 'The Sea Beast Rising from the Waves'!"

The cord tugged, silken shrouds swept down, and there before the nobles, allies, and peers of Sumbria shone the risqué portrait of the Lady Ulia herself.

It is said that in far nations, barbarians still speak in fear of the earthquakes caused by Lady Ulia falling to the ground in a dead faint. . . .

10

Hoof beats hammered at the soggy earth, deep, heavy blows that shuddered far down into the ground. The crushing weight of war steeds bearing armored men sent a shock wave rippling out into the frosty morning air.

The Valley of Umbricci was deep enough into the cold slopes of the Akanapeaks to already feel the winter's bite. From the passes, the city of Sumbria could be seen basking under a warm autumn sun, while high above the valley, the great mountains shone with crisp new snow. Across the valley floor, the fruit trees hung heavy with the last crops of fruit, while the fields had all been shorn into stiff mats of brittle stubble. The dense-packed carpet crunched and splintered underfoot, making infantry lurch and curse as they struggled out into the open fields.

The army of Sumbria marched up through the southern pass, made its way beneath the gigantic overhanging mass of rock and ice that loomed above, and thundered through into the valley like an all-destroying wave.

It was unseasonable weather for an attack; an autumn campaign had been utterly unheard of for nigh on a hundred years. Rain might dampen bowstrings, swell the

rivers, and churn the roads; snow might block the passes
and bring sickness to the men. Only the most furious,
impassioned warriors would stir themselves to war at
such a time. Few causes couldn't wait for the long winter
months to blossom bloodily into spring.

Few causes—but for the foulest insult of them all. A broken contract of peace—honor trampled, pride destroyed. At
the head of the first battle of troops, Prince Cappa
Mannicci waved his mace over the valley floor and angrily
pushed his forces on. They had marched for a day and a
night without rest, a gamble that had successfully brought
them through the pass without meeting a single Colletran
scout. With luck they would overrun the valley and pour
down the passes into the Colletran lands beyond.

After sacking the city, Prince Mannicci would see the
Sun Gem pulled from the ashes of her dead. The
Colletrans had broken the rules of civilized war; in the
name of that honorable law, the city of thieves must be
destroyed.

The terms of peace between the cities had been cast
aside; the Colletrans had reneged on their solemn word,
and had sent Svarézi to steal back the Sun Gem. Now the
laughingstock of the Blade Kingdoms, Sumbria had no
choice but to take back its pride with the point of its sword.

The *Lanze Spezzate* of the Mannicci family brigades,
all half-armored men on speedy horses, thundered down
the track to the valley floor. Prince Mannicci watched
them go and struck a fist against his saddle tree, willing
his men into even greater speed.

An approaching rattle of armor made Prince Mannicci
tug his horse into a turn. Blade Captain Gilberto Ilégo,
sheathed in his armor plate of arsenic green, drew his
mount up beside his lord and gave a gracious salute.

"My prince."

"Ilégo." Mannicci barely spared the man a glance,
choosing instead to stare with furious intensity across
the stubble fields. "Form your men up on the right of my
own. I appreciate the help you have given us in trying to

hunt this *Svarézi* down. To you I give precedence and
honor in the line of battle."

"I am most grateful for your good opinion, Lord." Ilégo
sank slightly forward in a bow, hiding his dark, black
eyes. "I shall attend to their deployment at once."

The Blade Captain turned and rode away to his own
units of billmen and archers. Mannicci watched him go,
gripping and regripping his own reins in armored
gauntlets that shook with hate.

Hate for the Colletrans; hate for the false-hearted
Svarézi, who had scorned the hospitality of the Mannicci
house to carry out his city's abominable crime. Blade
Captain Ilégo had placed the stamp of reason upon the
confused reports of the palace guard, placing guilt
squarely in Svarézi's treacherous claws. For once, political differences had been set aside as the Blade Families
became united as Sumbrians.

It had taken five frustrating days to bring the army up
to readiness, five days too long. Mannicci glared across
the fields and willed his soldiers to win through.

"My prince!"

Wings clashed and clattered as a palomino hippogriff
made a dainty landing nearby. The creature stood posed
with its neck bravely arched and its forefoot high, making a proud sight as its rider saluted with his bow.

"My prince, our air-scouts are engaged! The Colletran
army is already through the northern pass, and is deploying into battle array."

Prince Mannicci turned cold eyes to the immaculate
young scout.

"Have they prepared field fortifications? Did your sorcerers detect them tampering with the battlefield?"

"No, my liege. They move forward in attack formation
at best possible speed."

"Then let them come to the slaughter!" Mannicci signaled to his heralds, waiting behind him in a row. "The
army is to deploy into battle formation. All heavy cavalry
is to brigade here with me." Horses turned, proud trumpets

raised, and the rising challenge of the battle paean rose
into the sky. Sitting square upon his golden horse, the
Sumbrian prince stared in the direction of his fast-
approaching enemy while behind him his soldiers transformed themselves into a single, perfect instrument of war.

* * * * *

"There! I see the scum! There's a cavalry picket just
behind the mill!" Prince Ricardo of Colletro, surrounded
by his exquisitely armed and armored peers, lashed an
ivory riding crop across his saddle bow. "We've found
them right where Svarézi said they'd come!"

Colletro's army swarmed past with weapons pointed at
the slope and mud-stained boots clawing at the road. The
burgonets worn by the infantry hid the soldiers' expres-
sions; still, they gave their leaders a wide, disdainful
berth, and spoke only in low and savage growls.

They were being forced to refight a battle which
already should have been won. If Svarézi had been
prince, the Sumbrians would have been obliterated in the
summer; loot would have been taken and honor would
have been saved. Instead, the city faced a grim, lean winter, having paid a massive ransom in gold and grain to
their enemies.

Uncaring of the mettle of his men, Colletro's prince let
his fine silver horse paw at the air and thrilled as
revenge spilled into his grasp.

"A fine thing, gentlemen! A fine thing that we sent
Svarézi to the Sumbrian court. Without him, we would
never have gained word of this sneak attack. They would
have forced the passes and taken the valley in a single
day!"

Murmured agreement came from the fifty highest
nobles of Colletro, the Blade Captains and their eldest
sons, who had gathered here for war. Behind them, the
heavy cavalry collected in reserve, forming itself into a
single massive wedge of enchanted steel. The air flick-

ered as hidden lightning spat across the skies; the Colletran battle mages were busy at their spells, preparing the troops for immediate attack.

Above the stab and flash of spellfire, a new sound slowly arose: a swelling, deep, triumphant boom that made the nobles turn. All across the valley floor, tired soldiers stood to cheer. Men suddenly hoisted their helmets atop their pikes and bills. The whole army rose up with one unified roar of acclaim as a night-black hippogriff swept across the battle front, banked its wings, then sank down and clamped its claws into the ground.

The troops cheered Blade Captain Svarézi, a soldier's soldier and a man obsessed with their victory. The general raised his gauntlet in a return salute, then held aloft a severed enemy head amidst the savage acclaim of his men.

Svarézi contemptuously tossed aside his battle trophy, accepted the touch of helpful hands as he slid down from his mount, and with a curt order bid the hissing hippogriff to leave the soldiery unharmed. Immaculate in his black velvet-covered armor, Svarézi strode across the wheat stubble to his prince and peers.

Prince Ricardo acknowledged the man with a wave of his ceremonial baton.

"Valued cuz! Sweet captain!"

"My lord." Svarézi's black-bearded face glared up at his elected monarch through the eye slots of his burgonet. "The air cavalry has returned their report; Sumbria's army has not yet managed to deploy."

The announcement instantly snapped up the attention of soldiers nearby, yet failed to move the prince. Ricardo stroked slowly at his chin and gazed thoughtfully off toward the southern pass.

"It would seem to be in form to allow him to complete his preparations. We are, after all, civilized men."

"Sire, as we are civilized, *intelligent* men, we have no choice but to attack!"

Ugo Svarézi spoke with a gravel-voiced roar, a sound

more common on the parade ground than the court. He growled his words in his thick, foul common tongue, gathering an audience of noble cavalry and common foot soldiers who crowded around him in a growing throng.

"Attack, my lord! Now—before they prepare their battle lines! They have broken the truce. Sumbria is not satisfied with the little gains from treaties. Now they come to take the valley, and the city, as their own!" Ugo Svarézi let his anger soar. "Form the cavalry. Lead the lancers yourself in a single, crushing blow! Make a single strike and gut the Sumbrians before they can deploy!"

The troops greeted Svarézi's speech with a mad, incoherent roar; the cavalry horses reared in joy, pumping hooves into the air and slamming back into the ground in a stunning crash of armor plate. The army demanded an all-out attack, screaming its anger at the indecisive prince.

Ricardo and his counsellors leaned their helms together to confer, their gilded armor twinkling in the sun. Reluctant acquiescence eventually occurred; Ricardo issued his orders, heralds spurred off toward the heavy cavalry commanders, and the battle mages rode up to take positions for the charge.

The prince exchanged his baton for a heavy golden lance, allowing his pages to equip him for the attack; two servants helped to arrange his tabard skirts and helmet plumes, draping the prince's attire into clean, classical folds.

"Very well, Svarézi, we shall take your good advice. You have served the city well thus far, so we shall finish Sumbria and be done with them!" Prince Ricardo inspected his helmet as a page held it up before his eyes, nodded abstract approval, and allowed the heavy metal casing to be lowered onto his head. "Who commands the bulk of Sumbria's air cavalry?"

"Gilberto Ilégo, my lord." Svarézi coldly sheathed his bow. "Not a warrior. He commands their air forces from the ground."

"Then he should prove to be meat before your claws; support the cavalry attack from the skies."

Ugo Svarézi's dark eyes were hidden as he tilted down into a bow.

"It shall be as you command, my prince. I wish you joy of battle."

Svarézi snapped his fingers to summon his battle staff, then strode back to his waiting hippogriff. Ignoring him, Prince Ricardo raised a benedictory hand over uncaring men and spurred his mount forward to join the front ranks of armored horse.

Scarcely waiting to form, the dense wedge of armored cavalry spurred up the valley floor. The *Elmeti*, noble horsemen clad in fantastic full armor—man and horse—crashed through brush and orchards, grass and stubble with the slow-building momentum of an onrushing avalanche. Light lancers joined the flanks; mounted archers, sorcerers, and crossbowmen swarmed like clouds of gnats to the fore. The whole charge built haphazardly, collecting men and horses into an onrushing wave of solid steel.

At the forefront of his city's cavalry, Prince Ricardo thrilled to the sense of power rumbling in the air. All about him were packed the armored nobility—powerful men on heavy horses, crammed boot to boot and sheathed in flawless plate. The whole mass jammed itself tight, lances scarcely able to sink down for the attack. The cavalry reached hard footing and instantly increased its speed.

"Onward! *Onward!*"

There! On the hillside above, Sumbrian banners waved; the enemy was deploying from their march columns, pikes disarrayed and units in confusion. Warning trumpets sounded in the lines far beyond, figures churned in panic, and suddenly Colletro's cavalry felt a thrill of blood-red rage.

With a formless snarl, the cavalry stabbed spurs into their horses, raking at the creatures' flanks. The mounts screamed, and the vast formation swept forward in a maddened charge.

Trumpets pealed, and the call ran like fire in the nobles' blood. A thousand cavalry stormed ahead, screaming out in lust. Lance points sank as grass whipped past the chargers' flanks; horses pumped their legs in frenzy, hurtling themselves like meteors at the Sumbrian battle line. The faster beasts clawed to the front, slowly leaving lesser creatures behind as they stretched their necks into a blurring, deadly charge.

"Colletro! Colletro!"

A Sumbrian sorcerer fired from the hill; ice darts whipped into the cavalry, rattling from breastplates to leave a blood mist whirling through the sky. A catapult stone plowed through the ranks, crossbow bolts stabbed ineffectually across the air, and the cavalry blasted through the Sumbrian skirmish lines and crushed them to the ground.

Swarming in a thin cloud far ahead of the avalanche of onrushing knights, the Colletran light cavalry struck home like a cyclone of fire; javelins and crossbows blasted a savage volley home, plowing into knots of Sumbrian officers and men. Sumbrian arbalests sheeted darts into the churning crowd, emptying saddles, and the ranks erupted as Colletran sorcerers unleashed a wave of spells.

Lightning slashed into packed blocks of pikes, lifting men up from the grass like the blast of a volcano; fireballs flickered, wreathing magical domes of force; spirits whirled and snarled into the Sumbrian lines. Their damage done, the Colletran skirmishers frantically whirled and tried to ride away only to disintegrate as their own heavy cavalry trampled home.

"Colletro!"

Screaming horses overturned; lightning whipped through the air, and suddenly the Colletran nobles struck into their prey. With a shock front that rebounded from the mountaintops, the lancers slammed home into the Sumbrian left wing.

Infantry sprayed back from the deadly hooves like ocean foam; the horses rammed full tilt into armored men, smashing them wildly aside. Lances blasted into armored backs, ripped through helms, and shattered like glass. Pushing forward like men riding into a storm, the cavalry drove onward through a churning mass of enemies.

The dense pike formations boiled like frenzied nests of ants. Spears tangled, unable to press the attack as horsemen hacked down into the mob with axe and sword. Here and there an infantry spear lunged home; soldiers grunted as they pushed the points through horses' breasts into the guts beyond. Animals screamed, blood flew, and still the metal giants carved their swords into the shrieking mob.

Horses were crushed by the tremendous pressure of surging infantry; surrounded by the hard-packed mob, Prince Ricardo howled in frenzy as he hacked downward with a flaming sword. Here was the battle joy he had never known! The thrill of bloodshed and victory. The prince chopped down through the helm of a helpless, fleeing man; he whipped high his sword, screamed out his city's name, and thanked Tchazzar for his horse, his blade, and his beaten, shrieking enemy.

The attack had slammed home on the Sumbrian left, where Cappa Mannicci's most loyal Blade Captains had been given the vital flank command. Swept back by the storm, Orlando Toporello urged his gigantic black-bronze horse forward through the flood of his own retreating men, roaring like a maddened troll as the crush bore him relentlessly away. Finally he struggled through into the fight, smashed a Colletran noble from his saddle with a single hammer blow, and tried to fling his units back into the melee.

High above, the hippogriffs dipped and whirled as though disdainful of the muck and mess so far below. The air cavalry fought in loose, wheeling formations, exchanging arrow fire and ever ready to plunge down upon careless combatants below. From time to time a body fell— sometimes buoyed by a feather fall spell, and sometimes simply tumbling to bloody destruction through the churning fog of war.

One formation broke away from the wild airborne melee. Toporello—desperately rallying a stand of pikes to fend off another death blow from the Colletran cavalry—heard a bellowed warning and tugged his horse aside. The enemy hippogriffs slashed mere inches overhead, jerking banners with the numbing speed of their passage, then whirred low across the Colletran cavalry.

The hippogriff riders opened fire, wheeling one after another to shower arrows at a single golden figure riding amongst a press of infantry. The rider reeled as arrows scored sparks across his breast, cursed as one shaft pierced his shoulder plates to wound him, then ignored the injury and spurred his charger deep into the fray.

"My lord! My lord, the Colletran infantry advances!" One of Toporello's officers, his armor torn, blood staining his jaw, gripped his commander's reins. "They will strike us from behind!"

Prince Mannicci had ridden hard to reach the site of the disaster; he paused to let his fellow Blade Captains plunge into the midst of their own men, trying to beat fugitives back into the battle lines with the flats of their swords. Swirled and surrounded by terrified, fleeing soldiers, he ripped open his visor and somehow spied Toporello's standard. The prince raked back his spurs, sent his golden horse ramming a path through the retreating troops, and somehow shouldered the beast through to Toporello's side.

Old Toporello, sheathed in blood from head to foot and brandishing a dripping hammer, never once paused in his labors as he spoke to his lord.

"We're outflanked, and the infantry are done for! They'll break within another minute, then run straight for the pass."

"Damn! How did it happen?" Cappa Mannicci's face shone white with rage under his visor's brim. "Ilégo's scouts should have seen them before they even crossed the valley floor!"

"Then they used some sort of spell to attack us with surprise!" Toporello saw his center unit break, and readied his tiny stand of rescued infantry to plug the gap. "Do we fight it out, or withdraw?"

"Withdraw!" Prince Mannicci stood in his stirrups, careless of the crossbow bolts and spellfire still blurring through the smoke and dust. "My own ground troops will make a stand before the mouth of the pass. Flee back behind us—we'll cover the retreat!"

"Yes, my lord!"

Toporello had already turned to go on about the business of saving his men as his prince rode away to gather up Sumbria's cavalry. The old general spared a glance at the central melee, frowned as he saw no sign of the Colletran rider clad in gold, then set his heralds trumpeting the signal for retreat.

* * * * *

"Message for the prince! I bear a message for the prince!"

The Colletran herald rode in agitation back and forth through returning swarms of cavalry. The armored knights, their lances broken, horses blown, and still soaring with elation from the slaughterfest of a cavalryman's dreams, rode past toward the rear. They had broken the enemy's left wing. The loss of their own light cavalry was scarcely even remembered; now other troops could pursue Sumbria's fleeing rabble back into the pass. They had done all that Svarézi could desire, knowing that approving eyes watched them from above.

Mounted on a nervous horse—a beast of pixie breed with feathery antennae jutting up from its brow—the herald searched returning faces for a sign of his prince. His mount pranced and skittered back from the overwhelming stench of blood, shying from the brutal laughter on the air.

"A message for the prince! A message for Prince Ricardo!"

A thick, choking mist of fireball smoke and spell-fog rolled across the ground. Silent within the gloom, a knot of riders materialized: three men leading a team of pages who carried a litter made of broken spears. Lolling lifeless on the stretcher was a figure armored all in gold with a helm topped off with purple plumes.

"My lord!"

The herald surged forward in alarm; he dismounted all in a rush and flung himself at his dead prince's feet.

"My liege!"

Above him, the leading cavalryman made a face of scorn.

"You'll have to speak louder than that. He's shot his bolt and gone."

"But how?" The herald laid an astonished hand upon his prince's lifeless breast. "Who could possibly have bested such a man in battle?"

Many possibilities sprang to mind. The Sumbrian boys chorus? The guild of circus clowns? The armored horseman almost made a contemptuous reply, then thought better of it and helped himself to some of the herald's stock of wine.

"One minute he was fighting, and the next . . . he was down. He must have taken a concussion on the helm." The rider sounded too tired to make much of his prince's death. "He slowed down, missed a parry or three, and got torn to pieces like a lamb thrown to the wolves." The cavalryman nudged at the herald with a broken, filthy sword. "You'll have to go and find a real man's employment for yourself from this day on."

"You will regret this!" The herald shot to his feet, puffing up his breast in wounded pride. "His spirit can be welded back into his body! It will cost a kingdom's ransom, but it can be done! You have delivered us his body whole—so I advise you to repent your hasty words!"

The cavalryman gazed with one cocked eyebrow at the herald's face. He then slid heavily down from his horse, leaned across the golden armor, and wrenched open the helm.

Inside the armored suit, there lay nothing but empty air.

"Like a lamb thrown to the wolves. We brought this back for his widow; the rest is out there in the mess. Perhaps you're better at identifying anatomy than I." The horseman shoved the herald so that the boy fell backward into the mud. "We'll have a new prince by tomorrow dawn. One who knows what to do with his army."

The soldiers spared a glance at the sky above, where a jet-black hippogriff could be seen wheeling through the wild melee. Hoisting up the empty golden armor, the stretcher bearers trudged on into a field littered black with nameless carrion.

* * * * *

"Victory, my lords! Victory!" A Colletran Blade Captain, his voice hoarse from screaming in triumph with his men, rode a limping horse toward his colleagues as they stood their mounts under a sheltering tree. All across the battlefield, the crackle of spellfire and the ring of steel still filled the air, magnified by the close-pressing mountains into a deafening, blurring roar.

The newcomer sheathed his sword and swept his open helmet from his brow.

"The valley is ours! We need only make a pike assault on the pass, and we can spill down into Sumbria by nightfall!"

A disdainful, indolent air met the man's announcement; Colletro's inner circle of Blade Captains had little time for Svarézi's clique of coarse young men.

"There is no need for an assault." An elegant courtier who looked very much like a long-faced sheep decked out in a metal skin made a studied gesture of one hand. "Sumbria has blown the signal for a truce; they will capitulate upon our terms, surrender the valley, and a ransom. I believe the day is ours."

"No!" The newcomer, the commander of scarcely a hundred men, furiously slammed his saddle pommel with his sword. "Destroy their field army, and we can have it all! Sumbria is at the mercy of our blades!"

"Is that what Svarézi tells you?" A polite spatter of laughter tinkled out from the courtiers. "Sumbria has walls, boy! Walls and catapults, moats and sorcerers. What point in battering ourselves to death against their stones?"

High above, the black hippogriff circled. The young Blade Captain tried to will Svarézi to intervene before his victory could be frittered clean away.

Far across the battlefield, the sounds of conflict stilled. Heralds met—terms were discussed. The Sumbrian prince threw in his baton and impotently accepted fate. Pleased with the results of a well-fought day, the Colletran high command ordered itself bottles of chilled wine, watched by the disbelieving eyes of their own soldiery.

The Sumbrian troops abandoned their positions, winding off into the narrow mountain pass. Soon, only the prince of Sumbria's men remained, taking the place of honor as the last division off the battlefield. Prince Mannicci gave his opponents a heavy, stiff salute, spurred down the pass, and swiftly disappeared. Behind him, his pikemen, crossbowmen, and footmen shuffled slowly backward until they crammed the narrow passageway, watching the opposing Colletrans for betrayal.

With their general once more snubbed by his peers, the Colletran troops were in no mood to attack mere Sumbrians; the entire army converged on the hillock that held their high command. The roar of battle cries seemed dim compared to the anger of the enraged soldiery.

A battered, seething mass of bloodstained men crammed itself in a vast ring about the golden nobility. Within the ranks were the weaker Blade Captains, common soldiers, and mercenaries, all joined in shouting their generals down with a roar. Men fought through to the inner circle and gave an edge to the savage screaming of the crowd.

"Victory! We want our victory!"

One courtier rose in his stirrups, drawing a deep

breath to address the crowd in an actor's studied, flawless tones.

"Good soldiers, you have your victory! Sumbria has left us in possession of the field!" The man gave an authoritarian sweep of his armored hand. "Now go! Disperse! The task of employees is to obey, and not to howl like beasts for blood!"

The answer came as a vicious, angry snarl; one of the crossbow regiments produced a gangly camp lawyer who balanced himself upon a war-horse's flyblown corpse.

"Then we abandon your employ. The contract is dissolved!" The soldier adjusted his grimy breastplate, whipping out a stained old parchment and waving it in the air. "The Articles of Association allow us to recontract once per year! We'll hire ourselves to Svarézi or to none at all!"

"Rabble!" A Blade Captain gazed at the filthy soldier with undisguised hatred. "Do as you're ordered, or I'll have one man in ten dragged off and flogged!"

A stone whipped out from the crowd and rebounded from the Blade Captain's helm. The noble swore and then ripped out his unbloodied sword, lunging his horse forward at a suspected enemy.

The action instantly sparked off a storm. Soldiers dragged at the courtier's stirrups; he flailed at them with his sword, then screamed as a billhook snaked out to hook behind his neck. The sharp metal blade worried furiously back and forth under the gilded gorget, tearing flesh and bone until it jerked the man free from his saddle with a scream of fear. He disappeared beneath a tidal wave of stabbing dagger blades. Led on by Svarézi's carefully prepared provocateurs, the troops stormed forward, up and over the remaining Blade Captains, and simply tore the men apart.

* * * * *

On a ridgeline to one side, Ugo Svarézi watched the bloody death of his erstwhile peers. Black armor sheathed

with velvet seemed to absorb every last speck of sunlight;
not a ripple nor a highlight sheened the man's silhouette.

The city of Colletro had spilled into his hands.
Unmoved by the fruition of his plans, Svarézi turned his
back on the distant carnage and consulted his sorcerers.

"Well?"

"Prince Mannicci confers with his Blade Captains at
the far side of the pass."

"And his men?"

"They now march beneath the first overhang, my lord."
A magician bent above a crystal ball, making gliding
motions about the swirling images. "There is insufficient
snow for us to do as you command."

"I have no need for your spells here. You will go to
Sumbria and follow the instructions written here."
Svarézi passed a scrap of parchment to his chief sorcerer
without sparing the man a glance. "You depart at once.
Take a hippogriff."

"And the enemy, lord?"

"Leave the Sumbrian army to me."

Svarézi gazed coldly toward the open pass, where the
dense-packed mass of Prince Mannicci's personal troops
had finally disappeared from view. He raised a hand
without even once looking behind his back.

"Fire!"

On a hill to the rear, a hissing contraption mounted on
a vast armored wagon sputtered into life. Twenty feet
high, and so massive it had to be drawn by thirty stallions, the machine leaked a palpable cloud of cherry-
scented death. Titanic vats of glass protected by adamantine shields spurted steam as pressure valves were
wrenched open by technicians clad in armor plate. The
chief gunner sighted through a spyglass, pumped his fist,
then slammed a sealed black visor shut across his eyes as
his assistants briskly ducked aside.

Air pressure shot the contents of the glass tanks into a
sealed combustion chamber; the machine seemed to
bulge, and brilliant white light leaked through tiny rivet

holes in the armored housing. With a dazzle that left purple streamers drifting through the skies, a bolt of light blasted from the muzzle of the great machine and speared off into the pass.

The light gouged into the mountain crest—instantly turning packed ice into vapor and rock into a liquid stream. The superheated rock face exploded like a bomb. An entire mountaintop came slamming down into the narrow pass—untold tons of rubble, ice, and snow. The avalanche thundered on and on, shuddering the entire valley beneath a violent storm of noise.

Finally the rockslide began to slow; the last secondary avalanche on distant peaks drew to a close. The soldiers of Colletro stood gaping up into the pass, then turned to stare in awe at Ugo Svarézi standing at their side.

A long silence reigned; coming faintly from the rear of Colletro's battered army, there suddenly came a single tiny cheer. The first voice was joined by a second, and then a third. The noise rippled forward, then surged into fantastic life as men began to run toward the Sun Cannon—Svarézi's death machine.

The cheers turned to adulation. Svarézi, mounted on his brooding black hippogriff, reached out to allow the touch of eager soldiers' hands. The troops screamed out Svarézi's name until it became a formless, soaring litany that shuddered the very rooftops of the world.

While the cheers roared on, the technicians went swiftly back to servicing their monstrous machine. At the front of the giant Sun Cannon, the Sun Gem slowly cooled; while in the pass, three thousand Sumbrian troops lay buried under steaming lava.

11

The council chambers of Sumbria echoed to the roar of outraged voices. What had started as a postmortem of the lost campaign had turned into a maelstrom of invective and blame-passing. Blade Captains accused one another of everything from cowardice and incompetence, to outright treachery. The Sumbrian army—the finest, most expensively equipped forces in the Blade Kingdoms—had been utterly overturned. Scouts should have been sent out; cavalry should have intercepted the Colletran horse. Tactics, magic, science, or sorcery should have somehow obliterated the enemy and won the day. Battle mages and unit commanders fought to make their voices heard as they furiously tried to clear their own good names.

Everyone had another man to blame; some old enemy who had long been a secret traitor; some rival whose true colors at last were flown. The snarling madhouse shook papers, pens, and blades at one another around the tabletop, while Prince Mannicci simply sat with his head bowed in his hands.

For the prince, the battle had been more than just a military disaster. The contingents of Mannicci's closest

allies had been in the path of the Colletran charge. Worse
still, the Mannicci regiments had held the pass as it
inexplicably collapsed above them. The Mannicci family's
forces now scarcely numbered a hundred men, not
enough to qualify the prince for a vote in his own council.
He sat there upon the sufferance of the Blade Captains,
if he sat there at all.

Above the chaos, a single voice rose into a deep, com-
manding tone.

"Gentlemen! Colleagues . . . be still! We have only a few
hours to stop a disaster from turning into a catastrophe!"

Heads turned; the motion caused more men to lose
track of their arguments. The speaker stepped forward
into the lessening din with consummate timing and skill.
Sweeping open his arms, Gilberto Ilégo stood like a pristine figurehead bursting through a storm.

"We are defeated, but we are not destroyed!" Ilégo's
voice fought to overcome a reawakened roar. "No, not yet!
But division can still be our undoing!"

He spoke as though the great battle had not yet been
lost and won; flushed and bickering noblemen snatched
at the offered straw and began to listen.

"Colleagues! Sumbria is the most powerful of the Blade
Kingdoms. As an individual state, we command the
greatest wealth, the greatest intellects, and the finest
military equipment. And yet we have found ourselves
locked into a futile war for years! Rather than taking our
place as rightful leader of the Akanal, we have squan-
dered our energies in an endless war with Colletro—and
over what? A valley. A single valley." Ilégo's voice rose
suddenly into a sharp pitch of scorn. "One valley! When
the Blade Kingdoms hold a thousand such penny-plots of
land!"

Cappa Mannicci shot a sharp, deadly glance at Ilégo.
The elegant Blade Captain ignored his prince, skipping
his eyes across him to grip the crowd with his gaze.

"And why? Why have we wasted our energies on such a
futile little war?" Ilégo whirled and flung an armored

hand at his prince. "Because the Manniccis have commanded it! The Mannicci vision has locked us into a squabble only fit for schoolyard brats. A squabble with a kingdom who could just as well have been our staunchest ally all along!"

The slim nobleman had first won their attention, then eased their hurts—now he shocked them with an outrageous revelation. Men stared at him in disbelief until Ilégo passed copies of a letter out into his colleagues' hands.

"I have here a message from the Blade Council of Colletro. A *new* council! Newly elected, for new times!" Blade Captain Ilégo's voice soared like a falcon on godsent winds. "The old prince is overthrown, and Colletro offers us its blades, its science, and its sorcery. In short—their new, princeless council has asked to merge with Sumbria to form a single great kingdom! At a stroke, we can double our realm in ferocity and size!"

Prince Mannicci launched up to his feet and slammed an open hand against the table, but his angry rejoinder was drowned beneath the uproar of the crowd. Ilégo triumphantly orchestrated the furor, letting the volume build until a paid clique led the Blade Captains into howling for a vote.

A few thousand ducats had been spent, and spent well; a flood of anger—like any other flood—is best handled by carefully constructed channels. Prince Mannicci tried to speak, only to be shouted down by young captains asking to see the muster of his men. With no troops beneath his banners, Mannicci lacked the right to even take the floor.

Standing on the table, Blade Captain Furioso—stout, black-haired and wild—shook a copy of the Sumbrian constitution in Mannicci's eyes.

"We demand a vote! A new prince—one with a better plan!"

Ilégo smiled, feeling the day's events play straight into his hands. Above him, Furioso let himself be whipped on by the churning crowd.

"Two-thirds majority, Mannicci! Two thirds insist on a vote . . . an *immediate* vote. The Articles of Association demand that an election be held for the crown!"

Orlando Toporello—his armor still scarred and unclean from the battle three days before—slammed his battered sword across the tabletop.

"No! We are not a mob . . . to blame a prince when we have failed him at arms!"

"*Ha!*" Triumphant at the crest of the crowd, Furioso bit his thumb at the old man. "Can an old dog never leave off sniffing the backside of its old master?"

Toporello gave a bellow of rage and flung himself at Furioso; Furioso's page tried to block the old man's path and took a sword cut in the cheek as Toporello flailed at the packed mob of jeering nobles with his blade. A dozen arms held him back, crushing him in a press of bodies as they kept Toporello and his prey apart.

A vote was cast, yet no one counted the blades that flashed into the air; Mannicci's rule was cast away, and a dynasty lay broken. A hundred voices soared and jeered as Cappa Mannicci sank down into his chair.

Radiant, Ilégo opened his arms to the crowd.

"Then it is our will that we have a new prince! A new prince, right here and now!"

Before Ilégo could have himself nominated by his paid lackeys, Toporello slammed his sword across the table, broke the blade, and cast the shards away. He turned, signed for his sons and officers, and drove a path to the doors. Gilberto Ilégo climbed onto the table and bayed across the assembly like a wild, triumphant ass.

"Where to, Toporello? Will you not cast a vote with your brethren?"

"*Never!*" Toporello's parade-ground shout almost stripped the plaster from the walls. His huge voice stilled the rabble like a thunderous magic spell.

"To sell our honor to Colletran hands? To cast aside a prince who has served us long and well?" The old man whipped out his hands as though trying to fling them clean of dirt. "Do it if you will—but these are no colleagues of mine, nor do I care to remain within their fellowship!"

"And where will you go?" Ilégo made the question into a fabulous little joke. "Will you pack up your toys and refuse to play?"

"A free company is what we once were—a free company we remain! House Toporello takes its blades elsewhere!" Orlando cast a glance that ripped lines of fire across a dozen men. "You, Marello—and you, Ambrosi! Join the jackal pack—but make way for better men!"

Toporello turned to go. Suddenly, a young captain jerked out from the crowd and followed at his heel. They were joined by a second, then a third, all small holders who commanded scarcely two hundred men. Ilégo cast them out and let his wild voice echo through the hall.

"Then go! But forfeit your palaces, your holdings, and your lands!"

"My jewels were stolen, and the loss never killed me. We've concentrated upon fripperies and forgotten where we came from—who we are!" Standing in the doorway, Orlando Toporello rammed his old-fashioned helmet down across his skull. "Roll in your furs and sweetmeats like a pig in its own dung! A soldier's domain should be bounded by his breastplate, nothing more!"

The dissenters marched away *en masse*, leaving chaos in their wake; the contempt of Toporello had left a schism in the hall. Half the nobles shrieked out demands to give Gilberto Ilégo the crown, while others leapt forward offering their own names.

Cappa Mannicci gathered up his last few rags of dignity and left the chamber. His movement instantly stirred a new furor; for a whole lifetime, this man had ordered Sumbria's lives. Now, men shrilly clamored for advice, pawing at his robes. Ilégo saw his chances of an immediate election begin to fade away and leapt down to pursue the departing crowd.

On the steps of the council chambers, a vast mob of

citizens had collected in a swirling mass. There were soldiers and tinkers, fishwives and priests. The whole population clamored to Cappa Mannicci for their answers, parting about him like a sea of pleading hands.

Mannicci lifted a weary gauntlet, told them that he was their prince no more, and turned as a beggar thrust at him from the crowd. The beggar raised his knotted staff—Mannicci tried to hurtle himself away—and a blast of flame exploded out to rip the mob apart.

Bodies churned and voices screamed; the air stank of scorching flesh. Civilians fled in panic, trampling their own neighbors under their feet. Soldiers shouted, fighting through the tide as the city of Sumbria instantly went mad.

"The prince is slain! Prince Mannicci has been slain!"

Cappa Mannicci's body had been utterly atomized. With him had died a score of citizens, guards, and Sumbrian nobility. Burned, wounded men dragged themselves across the blackened steps, cinders crunching beneath clawed hands as they screamed out in agony. From the council chambers, the remaining Blade Captains simply stood and stared as Gilberto Ilégo wandered over to the place where Prince Mannicci had died.

"The prince has been slain by the Blade Captains!" A woman reeled across the road, clawing at passing soldiers with burned hands. "They've killed him! They've killed him!"

"Ilégo ordered it!" A young noble clutched his injured, screaming father tight against his heart. "Ilégo's killed him to secure his crown!"

"No!" Gilberto Ilégo ran blindly down the palace steps, standing amidst the ruin of his plans. "Brigands! It must have been brigands . . ."

"Brigands with a spell staff?" a soldier snarled from the foot of the steps in hate. "Aye—brigands with their pockets full of Ilégo's gold."

A dead assassin was produced—a mere rag hurtled back and forth between the talons of a growing crowd; the corpse wore Ilégo's livery beneath its beggar's rags. Ilégo screamed out his denials into an uncaring mob. He retreated as the first stones began to fly, then saw his own soldiers smash hard into the citizens. A wild melee erupted, bursting like a plague sore to spread its foul disease. Ilégo's men fought to hold the crowd back from their master's hide; soldiers from other families instantly lunged into the fight to defend the panic-stricken crowd. A crossbow fired, a woman screamed, and the fight poured through the city streets like molten fire.

Abandoned at the eye of the storm, Ilégo helplessly screamed out his innocence to the uncaring city walls.

"No! I didn't kill him!" Ilégo tore his own robes between his hands. "I would have been prince! Me! Gilberto Ilégo, Prince of Sumbria!" The man reached out to running soldiers in appeal. "Why? Why would I kill him? I would have had everything . . ."

Ilégo slumped down into the cinders, and let the last prince of Sumbria drift through his grasp like sand. He sat in blank incomprehension as he heard his city tear itself apart.

"Svarézi . . ."

Ilégo's eyes went wide as realization suddenly struck home. He lifted up his face and stared off into the empty sky. "Svarézi."

Hurtling ashes to the winds, Ilégo leapt to his feet and felt his face drain white with rage. He shook an impotent fist at the clouds and bellowed out a wild scream of despair.

"Svarézi!"

Blades clashed in Sumbria's streets, while all around, a city burned.

* * * * *

"Aaaaaaaaawk!" Tekoriikii tragically held up a small glass bottle, nudging it hopefully toward Lorenzo's hand. *"Aaaaaawk! Aaaaaawk!"*

"Um . . . look, Tekoriikii, I know what it says on the bottle, but I don't think it quite works the way you think."

"Aaaaaawk!"

Sighing unhappily, the artist took the bottle, read the label, and began vigorously shaking the pot of Old Pappa Floonbat's Patent Medicinal Hair Restorer. The bird, now miserably keeping an old gray military blanket draped across his rump, shuffled awkwardly about, then uncovered his plucked, bare backside.

Lorenzo liberally splashed hair restorer all over Tekoriikii's featherless regions, then began massaging the medicine into the poor bird's flesh. Tekoriikii whimpered and closed his eyes, slumped in apathy as he mourned the loss of his magnificent orange tail.

He could scarcely bare to look in the mirror to see if the tail feathers had begun to regrow; instead, the bird sat and stared miserably at the painting of Miliana leaning against the attic wall. He gave a soft, pathetic call deep in his throat and sadly closed his eyes.

Lorenzo turned his own face away from the painting. Bedraggled, demoralized, and crushed with guilt, the artist let his chin sink to his breast with a dull, unhappy sigh.

Tekoriikii curled his long neck around and placed his head in Lorenzo's lap. The artist scratched wearily at the bird's silly plumes while both creatures let their thoughts wander along the same sad paths.

Evicted from the palace, they now hid in cheap lodgings above a smelly old alchemist's shop—one of Lorenzo's main suppliers for esoteric chemicals. Terrified that Lady Ulia would silence them by the most obvious means, Lorenzo had managed a disappearing act and had lain low for many long, tedious days.

. . . Leaving Lorenzo and Tekoriikii all the more time in which to contemplate their failings. They gazed through the broad, wide-open window across the city roofs, and together sank into despondent, guilty gloom.

In the distance, a crowd's shouting rose into a formless

roar. Bedraggled and demoralized as they were, man and bird ignored the chaos and watched seeds spiral down from the sycamore tree that shaded the windowsill.

A bell rang as the door opened into the shop below; Lorenzo pricked up an ear in puzzlement as he heard the alchemist give out a single wild, despairing wail.

"I told you, we don't have any rings of water breathing!"

"Oh, please!" The customer seemed in a high state of anxiety. "An amulet then? Maybe a necklace?"

"No! I don't have anything . . ."

"Not even just a little one?" The customer's cultured voice wheedled mercilessly. "Maybe just some water breathing potions, then? Just two or three on account?"

"Look, why don't you just go away?"

"Just *one* potion? I can pay you tomorrow!"

Levering up the trapdoor in the attic floor, Lorenzo stuck his head through into the workshop, gasping in delight as he spied Luccio Irozzi. Luccio, now dressed in somewhat water-stained finery, shuffled on his knees as he pleaded with the shopkeeper. Luccio looked up and saw Lorenzo's dangling face; flung out his arms and shot up onto his feet in pure surprise.

"Lorenzo! Lorenzo, where in Umberlee's name have you been?"

"We've been in hiding." Luccio rapidly slid a ladder down through the trapdoor. "From Miliana's mother . . ."

"Her mother?" Luccio steadied the ladder, then swept his young friend into a hard embrace as he finally reached the ground. "You idiot—why didn't you tell me where you'd gone? I've had agents scouring the city streets for days!"

Tekoriikii hung his head down through the open trapdoor; seeing his friend in conversation, the bird clamped claws onto the ladder staves and slid backward to the lower floor. His talons peeled great bright strips of wood shavings from the ladder as he fell.

"Onk gronk!"

Luccio eyed the bird in astonishment. Lorenzo bowed and performed introductions between his human companion and the bird.

"Luccio Irozzi, I present the firebird Tekoriikii; big on feathers and small on tact."

Luccio made a bewildered bow; Tekoriikii replied with a warble, and ruffled out what feathers he still had in regal pride. The blanket draped about his backside rather ruined the effect. It began to slip, forcing the firebird to frantically adjust his attire.

The group retired back up into the attic, a place tastefully furnished with old crates and corn sacks stuffed with eiderdown. Tekoriikii turned himself about five or six times, treading himself a nest while the two humans settled themselves and uncorked a pewter jug of wine. Lorenzo nursed a tall, scorched, conical hat against his breast as he gazed in amazement at his friend.

"Luccio, what are you doing in an alchemist's shop?" The young artist sniffed at the air with a frown crossing his eyes. "Why are you in an alchemist's—and why do you smell of fish?"

"Never mind that!" Luccio snatched at his best friend's arm. "Now get your things. We have to leave the city— right now!"

"Why? Luccio, what's happening at the palace? Where did they take poor Miliana?"

"Oh—to the Velvet Gauntlet Finishing School for Wayward Young Ladies." Luccio dismissed the topic with a hasty wave. "She's safe enough—it's *we* who have to worry. The whole city is in revolt! Didn't you hear the riots outside?"

Riots! Lorenzo sat bolt upright, Miliana's image branded hard upon his heart. He heard the firebird warble something to Luccio, and kept a vague track on his friend's reply.

"Prince Mannicci's dead. The noble houses are about to fight a civil war!"

Sycamore seeds came spiraling down past the open

window—the tiny leaf-blades of the seedpods whirring around and around. Lorenzo leaned out and snatched one as it passed, then held it tight inside his hand as he stared blankly off into the sky.

"We have to rescue her!"

"What?"

"Miliana! Someone will hit on the idea of marrying her—or killing her—to control her father's men. We have to save her from this finishing school!

"Tekoriikii—we'll all escape from Sumbria together! She can finally be free!"

Tekoriikii roused himself, gaping wide his beak to give a keening scream of joy; the raucous sound set Luccio's teeth jangling. The firebird tried to flounder clean out of the window to instantly begin a rescue, but Lorenzo caught the bird and held him back, dragging him bodily across the floor.

"Luccio—we need a feather restorer. There must be something . . . ?"

"The hippogriff stables will know of some kind of spell." The young courtier scratched one fish-scented hand against his brow. "I'm sure a veterinarian might be induced to make a house call."

"Fine—fine, that's great . . ." Lorenzo opened his hand and stared at the seed lying on his palm. "Fantastic . . . all right—so, we just get Miliana out of this heavily guarded school, escape a rioting city, and all run off to Lomatra once and for all!"

"But, my dear Lorenzo—how can you get your lady love out past the school battlements?" Luccio seemed quite at a loss. "For that matter the whole city is locked in! How do any of us escape the town?"

"Tekoriikii and I will manage Miliana; you get ready and meet us by the city's water gate. I'll need probably— what—three hours?" Lorenzo turned to consult with the bird, who replied with a nod. "Three hours to prepare."

Lorenzo began gathering up charcoal, steel rulers, and an abacus. "Now, if I make us breathing tubes, do you think we can escape out by the river? We might need assistance—something to help us swim under the gate."

"Oh, yes! Yes, certainly!" The mere mention of water brought stars to Luccio's eyes. "But how do we finance the healing spell for the bird?"

"Tekoriikii—Tekoriikii, say '*aaaaaah*' . . ."

Lorenzo wrenched open Tekoriikii's beak, dove his hand down into the astonished firebird's crop, and came up with an amber necklace and a silver whistle on a string. These rather shop-soiled items were slapped down into Luccio's disgusted hands.

"There! Sell those, and use the money to buy everything we need." Lorenzo paced rapidly back and forth, maniacally ticking items off against a list in his whirring mind. "We need a long rope, pulleys, ball bearings, a water barrel, four twenty-foot-long birchwood boards, a pole, woodworking tools, and the heaviest anvil in the city!"

"Right!" Luccio slung the loot into his pockets and made his way to the ladder. "When do you need it all by?"

"Twenty minutes." Watched by a fascinated Tekoriikii, Lorenzo had begun furiously sketching plans on the back of an old shopping list left in the shop by some local sorcerer. "Meet me out front—in a wagon!"

Luccio made an exit, stage left. Tekoriikii the firebird waddled over and closed the trapdoor behind him; then leaned his neck across Lorenzo's work and cocked one yellow eye up to the page.

"*Gronk-nonk?*"

"What are we doing?" Lorenzo smudged a line of charcoal with his thumb, deftly shading his design. "We, my friend, are going to rescue Miliana from the jaws of death! We are going to save her, give her back her hat, and make a new life all our own!" The inventor held his plans up against the light and gave a wild, triumphant smile.

"Now do be a good chap and see which way the wind is blowing. We'll be rescuing Miliana before the sun goes down."

12

The Velvet Gauntlet Finishing School for Wayward Young Ladies stood coldly isolated from the temptations of the city streets; a blank, monolithic structure that spoke only of despair. Towering walls made from flawless, slick marble—utterly devoid of both window or handhold—had proved insurmountable to hundreds of lovesick suitors. The school balconies looked only inside to the open courtyard, where stood a white, empty pillar, there to remind the girls of the futility of pride.

The pillar also had a second use; disobedient girls were tethered to it through ice-cold nights. Since they acted like beasts, reason held that they should be treated as such. It served as a useful object lesson for the frightened girls.

Linked to the column by an iron chain, Miliana Mannicci stood stiffly in the dust and jammed a sewing needle through a highly incompetent piece of embroidery. Barefoot, dressed in a vile gray dress, and with her long hair stiffly braided back into a bun, Miliana bitterly kept her eyes fixed on the ground.

Needlepoint was just one more worthless female skill Miliana had never bothered to acquire; stealing a few bits and pieces from other girls had been enough to divert Lady Ulia's ire. Now well and truly under supervision, she had no choice but to stitch and sew while planning her revenge.

They had tried to beat her with a cane and had suffered the inevitable results. Watched over by a pair of female tutors, Miliana was now treated with hostility and caution. She had already managed to stab one woman with a sewing needle, and could hurtle the things with enough force to penetrate naked skin. Held tight by her chain, Miliana felt her eyes smarting with hidden tears. Her spectacles hid her eyes as she jammed the needle through her sewing cloth, twisting the tiny blade like a stiletto as she let her mind dwell on vengeance and escape.

From outside the school, there came a distant swirl of sound; crowds yelling, or possibly cheering—the dim crackle of spells, or more of the Shou fireworks. Miliana lifted her head to hunt down the sound; a tutor raised her cane and instantly advanced.

"Keep sewing! The outside world does not exist! Good can only be discovered when the distractions of worldliness and wilfulness are flensed away."

The teacher hissed with pleasure, keen to begin the flensing process anew. Miliana faced the creature like a wildcat and took a turn of her own chain between her hands—either to use as a garrote, a shield, or a flail. Her attacker balked, retreated, and began to stalk Miliana just out of reach of the deadly chain.

"Miliana Mannicci!"

The voice, which could have came from Lady Ulia's evil twin, pealed out across the courtyard like a fractured temple bell. Miliana kept her thin body facing her opponents and flicked a glance at the stairs.

Standing up above the courtyard was the headmistress of the Velvet Gauntlet, a vast woman shaped like a cavalry regiment in a skirt. The woman seared her gaze down into Miliana, then dismissed the tutors with one snap of her fingers.

"Mannicci—since you are obsessed with the offal of the outside world, then you may wallow in offal indeed." The woman stared at Miliana as though she were a particularly noisome form of garden slug. "You are a disgrace to the discipline of home economics. To the kitchens with you! You can squat there and work until supper time."

Tutors edged closer, then decided that discretion was the better part of valor and simply tossed Miliana the keys to her chain. The girl unfastened the collar about her neck, let the chain, needles, and sewing drop into the dust, and walked under the headmistress's hostile eye and deep into the school's narrow corridors.

Miliana was frog-marched down the halls, then halted as locks, chains, and slide-bolts were duly wrenched aside.

The school kitchens were a true anteroom to the Abyss. Vats of hideous porridge boiled, while ranks of pans hung like dented battle helmets on the walls. The door was flung wide open, and Miliana found herself hurtled inside.

"My special provisions have arrived." The headmistress's voice boomed like the slamming door of a tomb. "I want the meat gutted and dressed, the vegetables peeled, the wine barrels decanted into proper bottles— and get those jugs of cream whipped before it's time for my morning scones and tea!"

A trolley held a gigantic serving platter capped off with a silver chafing cover. Beside it stood a wine barrel almost six feet tall.

"It has all been thoroughly checked. The meat has been inspected, and the wine barrel has been pierced with a spear." The headmistress fixed Miliana beneath a violent, suspicious eye. "We perform the same checks on outgoing refuse—lest you think you can hide in the bins and be tossed out with the *other* garbage tomorrow morning. . . .

"Now to work! And I want that meat sizzling within the hour!"

The door slammed, the locks snapped shut, and Miliana found herself alone in a wilderness of chopping boards and tethered cooking knives. She dejectedly wandered out into the room, noted that the fireplace chimney was blocked by an iron grate, and sank into a sad little bundle on the stairs.

Trapped in her own worst nightmare, the girl cradled her head in her hands. Pale and wan, she stared at the flagstones and silently mouthed a single, silent word.

Lorenzo . . .

In an hour, the headmistress would come to inspect the kitchens. Weary beyond all words, Miliana made her way to the giant platter, reached up to grab its handles, and hoisted the silver dome up into the air.

"Tekorii-kii-kii! Tekorii-kii-kii!"

An explosion of brilliant feathers filled the room with life. Surrounded by vegetables on the massive serving dish, Tekoriikii spat the apple from his beak and whirred his wings in glee. The creature flung himself into Miliana's arms, madly twining his neck about her face. The princess crushed the bird against her heart and felt her whole world swirl with joy.

"Tekoriikii? Oh, Tekoriikii!" Miliana buried her face in the firebird's soft feather down. Words failed her as she snared fingers through her friend's silly feather crest. The bird gave a shuddering, keening song of purest joy.

Utterly careless of alerting the whole school, Tekoriikii leapt back onto the platter and began a raucous little dance. He bobbed his head over to the left and then over to the right—stuck his left foot into the air and waggled both his wings. He then proudly shook out a great mass of plumes and eagerly presented Miliana with his newly regrown tail.

The girl wept, still almost speechless, and ran the gorgeous length of tail feathers between adoring hands.

"Why, they're beautiful! Utterly beautiful!" Miliana held the velvet-soft feathers up against her face and smeared them with tears. "Tekoriikii—what are you doing here?"

The bird puffed out his breast and swaggered his head, flexing his stubby wings. Miliana blinked at him in surprise.

"A rescue?"

"Gronk nonk!"

"But how?"

The firebird strutted eagerly up and down beside the wine barrel, then made a twirling motion of his wingtip beside his brow.

Miliana scuttled forward in alarm.

"Lorenzo? In there?" The plug hole where a spear had been rammed into the barrel could quite clearly be seen. "How can he be in there? He must have drowned!"

"Nurgle-gurgle!"

The girl grabbed a crowbar, hastily climbed atop a chair and broke the wax seal about the barrel cap. She wrenched the top of the barrel clean away and found herself staring down into a pool of deep red wine.

"Tekoriikii . . . there's nothing there!"

The bird repeatedly tried to leap up and kick the barrel over; with his small weight, it was like trying to knock an elephant unconscious with a grapefruit. Miliana watched the bird, considered the consequences if she tried to help him tip over the barrel, then let her wits take the place of muscle power. She turned the tap at the barrel's base; scowling when it seemed not to work. Finally a heavy skewer managed to stab a hole into the wood, spilling a purple stream of wine across the floor.

The stinking pool of wine leaked clear across the flagstones to lap against the kitchen door. Finally the torrent slowed; hitching up the skirts of her revolting smock, Miliana stepped back onto her stool and peered down into the barrel.

A smaller barrel lay within the first, anchored firmly to the big container's base. Miliana reached down to knock three times upon the barrel top; wax caulking splintered as the hatch began to rapidly revolve. With a pop, the little barrel top flipped open to reveal Lorenzo crouched inside with a breathing tube clamped in his mouth.

The tube ran out to the big barrel's fake tap—the last place anyone would have thought to check. The artist painfully arose from hiding, shakily reached his feet, then goggled as Miliana wildly crushed him in her arms.

"Lorenzo!"

He held her in his arms, feeling her thin body bore against him. Much to Lorenzo's surprise, he felt his neck running wet with her tears. The artist blinked and timidly ran a hand across her cheek.

"Is anything wrong? Why are you crying?"

"Don't be a fool!" Miliana helped the man clamber awkwardly out from the reeking wine barrel. "What on Toril were you doing in there?"

"It's a rescue! You know . . . we've come to save our lady fair!" Lorenzo and Tekoriikii both puffed themselves with pride. "Well you *are* a princess. You have to come to expect this sort of thing."

"But the gates are closed! The walls are guarded!"

"All taken care of!" Lorenzo took a swift stock of the room, still holding Miliana in strong, adoring arms. "Good! The box is here. Now all we have to do is get the thing outside." The man reached behind himself and produced a large package from his hidey hole. "We brought this! Now get your notes and start looking for a feather fall spell!"

"Feather fall?" Miliana unwrapped the package and discovered her own dear pointy hat, a hat well stuffed with her own handwritten spells. "We can't jump from the walls! They're slick marble—there's no way up!"

"It's all taken care of . . . now just find the spell!"

Miliana clamped the hat across her head, and instantly felt her spirits soar! A grand princess once again, she flipped through her curling lists of spells, feeling sure that she could cobble together the spell effects required. She had never cast the spell before—but she was *Miliana*—Miliana the sorceress, mistress of her own destiny!

At this precise moment, the kitchen door burst open wide. The headmistress stood framed in the doorway, roaring in alarm.

"So! We have uncovered your perfidiousness at last!" The titanic woman somehow moved aside to reveal a squad of home economics tutors armed with rolling pins and knives.

"Slaughter the male, but keep the girl for punishment. *Attack!*"

With a bloodcurdling scream, a dozen shrieking female tutors charged in through the door, plunging through the lake of spilled red wine. Unconcerned, Lorenzo took the terrified Miliana and hoisted her up onto the table. Tekoriikii joined her, sitting atop a fruit bowl while Lorenzo dangled his own feet high above the ground.

"It's fascinating, isn't it? Magic creates natural forces, but it takes science to actually study them . . ." The artist touched his rapier to the pool of spilled wine, pulled the trigger, and watched as the teachers squealed, performed little somersaults, and crashed—unconscious—to the ground. "Electrical force, for instance. Blue dragons have it, magicians make lightning bolts, but did anyone ever bother to study the phenomenon of conductivity?"

"Oh, shut up!" Miliana leapt down to the floor, treading on a weakly moving domestic skills tutor. "The headmistress is still out there trying to fetch more help!"

By the shuddering and rumble of the floorboards, it seemed the massive headmistress had charged off into the academy's heart. Miliana and Lorenzo each took one end of his extremely heavy box, and with Tekoriikii helpfully perched in the middle singing songs, they struggled their burden out into the school's open courtyard.

Lorenzo flipped open the box and unshipped a pole, some boards, and a set of gigantic paddle blades. He began to busy himself unloading miles and miles of bundled rope, glancing briefly up the towering walls.

"A hundred feet tall, would you say?"

"One hundred and twenty-five . . . and faced with

marble!" Miliana was almost making handstands with fear. "Will you just hurry up! There're teachers guarding this place night and day!"

"We're working on it as fast as we can—just prepare your feather fall spell!" Lorenzo began mounting a series of brackets down the courtyard's marble punishment post. "Tekoriikii? The pulleys, if you will?"

The bird flew off with a series of pulley wheels dangling from his claws. While Lorenzo happily tested his brackets and frames, the firebird fixed a pulley high atop the curtain wall.

Yells and screams rebounded from the school corridors. Up atop the battlements, a tutor with a crossbow took aim at Lorenzo's back. Tekoriikii swooped down, plucked the weapon from the woman's hands, and sent her tumbling back in terror down the stairs.

A pole well wrapped with rope formed the centerpiece of Lorenzo's collection of parts and pieces. Lorenzo slid the pole down into his brackets, then topped it off with a ring of gigantic birchwood propeller blades. He checked the fit of the rotor assembly, then attached a pair of free-moving rings to the pole to act as handholds and a support for the passengers' feet.

"The principle is based on a flying sycamore seed." The artist began feeding excess rope off to one side. "The rope is wound about the drive shaft; a weight is dropped from a height, pulling on a rope, and the rope whips free, accelerating the rotor blades to high speed. Lift is produced; we stand on the lower ring and grip the upper while the shaft turns between us, and the whole assembly will fly up into the sky!"

"Brilliant!" Miliana was utterly impressed. "So we fly over the school walls?"

"And we'll then join Luccio in an escape—out through the city's river gate—to freedom."

Miliana watched Tekoriikii threading the pulley ropes and checking the fastenings one by one.

"So how do we drop a weight?"

"Aha! There we must trust to science once again!" Lorenzo rubbed his hands together with glee. "A feather fall spell is used to slow the descent of a falling body through the air. How does it achieve this? By reducing the specific mass of the target of the spell."

Miliana blinked. Lorenzo lectured on:

"Well, don't you see? A pound of feathers falls slower than a pound of iron, yes?"

"Um . . ." The girl felt a fallacy somewhere in the offing. "Well, yes, I suppose . . ."

"Right! So lighter objects must fall slower than heavier ones. The feather fall spell make objects lighter in order to slow their fall." Lorenzo made a proud gesture at Tekoriikii, who sat puffed like a canary beside the magnificent new flying machine. "We have with us the heaviest anvil in the kingdom—the perfect counterweight. All you do is throw the spell; Tekoriikii carries the weightless anvil up aloft across the walls and ties it tight to the rope. When the spell wears off, the anvil falls . . . and we have our motive thrust!"

The girl fixed Lorenzo with a heavy-lidded stare.

"You brought *what* with you?"

"An anvil! A gigantic anvil!" Lorenzo stuck his thumbs beneath his arms "A great big anvil we left just outside the gates . . ."

Miliana wearily hid her face inside her hands. Lorenzo bit his lip, and sensed that he had made a slight *faux pas*.

"Look . . . um . . . We invent a new type of acid that can tunnel through the school's wall—"

The girl hit him with her hat; it seemed the only thing to do.

At this juncture, the forces of the headmistress inevitably came racing back into the fray. Massed squads of teachers armed with rocks, meat cleavers, and school benches held like battering rams charged into the courtyard, whipping themselves into a lather of righteous rage.

A hundred enemies surged into the courtyard. Miliana

and Lorenzo somehow shot up the marble punishment column, where they perched aloft like monkeys shaking fists at a storm. The tutors ignored the flying machine and instead tried climbing up each other's backs to reach their prey. Miliana stuck the point of her hat into one woman's eye and cursed angrily at Lorenzo's rear.

"Use your lightning sword! Knock them all out!"

"I only have one charge left!" Lorenzo brandished his rapier, parrying weapons left, right, and center. The whole column shuddered as battering rams struck against the base. "They'd all have to be wet—unless we can somehow convince them to all join hands?"

The column shook, and Miliana ended up perched upon Lorenzo's back like an ungainly crab.

"What do you mean you came here with only one power charge?"

"It isn't as simple as it looks!" Lorenzo unsuccessfully tried to remove Miliana's bare foot from his eye. "You have to attach copper cables to the two canine teeth of a sleeping blue dragon! Either that, or fly a kite up into a thunderstorm."

"I'll fly you up into a storm in a minute!" Miliana balanced on Lorenzo's back, desperately trying to find useful spells inside her hat. "Some damned rescue this turned out to be!"

Intrigued by all the action below, Tekoriikii fluttered down and perched on a gargoyle just above the yard. Miliana punched a teetering pyramid of singing tutors, watched the amateur athletes fall, then fixed upon Tekoriikii with panic in her eyes.

"Tekoriikii! Scream! You know—scream, like you did the other night!"

The bird made a *"Krrrrrr"* of curiosity and fixed Miliana with one golden eye. The girl dodged a passing stone and opened her arms out to the bird.

"That battle scream, you dodo! The one that knocked out all those men! Come on—get angry or something!"

The bird had no real inclination to hurt anyone. To his

eyes, Miliana and Lorenzo seemed to be engaged in some sort of dance rather than a fight; each of his friends took it in turns to tread upon each other while gangs of snarling teachers shook the column back and forth. The bird ruffled out his feathers and creased his brows into a puzzled frown.

"A—all right, just sing a song, then! You know . . . like you do when you feel happy?" Miliana struck upon a sudden inspiration. "Your tail! How does it feel to have your lovely tail back?"

Tekoriikii drew a breath of excitement. He spread out his streaming tail feathers like a courtier's fan and shimmered them back and forth in glee. Filling his chest, the bird opened up his beak and caroled out a scintillating song of pride.

Lorenzo and Miliana ducked and blocked their ears; the teachers lacked the benefit of their victims' hard-won experience. With the shock front of a god-flung tidal wave, Tekoriikii's song swept clean across the open yard.

Tekoriikii's high notes loosened eyeballs in their skulls and cracked the marble facing all along the courtyard walls. The luckiest of the teaching staff simply fell from their half-built human pyramids and dropped unconscious to the ground. Those with greater stamina, but less native luck, managed to hear the second chorus before fainting clean away.

Uncorking his fingers from his ears, Lorenzo gazed about a scene taken from a hideous battlefield. A hundred women lay strewn in heaps about the cobblestones; some heaps stirring weakly as a semiconscious victim tried to knock her head against a wall. Tekoriikii settled into a magnificent sulk and turned himself away from his ungrateful audience.

Lying behind her troops was the headmistress—several hundredweight of iron-hard flesh. Lorenzo leapt down from the column and snatched up the rope which powered his flying machine.

"Excellent! We'll use *her* as a counterweight! Tekoriikii—

come over here and help." The inventor and the firebird began trussing a rope beneath the gigantic woman's arms. "She'll hit the city dung pit; she'll be all right . . ."

Lorenzo pulled the last knot tight, laughing as he heard the sound of soldiers hammering at the bolted gates.

"Right! Now all we need is that feather fall spell—Miliana?"

He looked about, only to find the princess crawling about the courtyard on all fours; an empty pair of wire frames were clamped above her nose.

"My spectacles! He broke my curse-damned spectacles!" Miliana groped her hands in front of her, as blind as a mole. "That's the second pair he's done that to so far!"

The school doors shuddered as unseen soldiers tried to force their way in. Lorenzo heard the roar of male voices, and orders calling for battering rams and heavy crossbows.

"Miliana—the feather fall!"

"I can't read!" The girl snarled in ill temper, waving a hand across her eyes. "I'm blind as a bat without my spectacles!"

"But you can't read the language the spells are written in anyway!"

"I still need to visualize the symbols in my mind!" Miliana bumped herself into a wall. "Maybe someone has a telescope someplace?"

Outside the school, fireballs and lightning bolts crashed against the gates; it would only be a matter of moments before the doors came crashing down. Lorenzo ripped off Miliana's hat and began flipping frantically through the spell sheets one by one.

"How does it start? Can you remember what the page looks like?"

"There was a sort of curly thing . . . it looked like a pot." Miliana faced Lorenzo with a nearsighted scowl. "I don't know! I've never really cast the thing before. I thought it was a spell for magic missiles . . ."

A pot—a pot-shaped symbol. Lorenzo frantically sorted tiny scrolls, each scribbled in Miliana's shocking handwriting.

"Aha!" He found something that looked like an inverted cup. "Here's a pot, but it's upside down."

"That's it!" Miliana clamped her pointy hat upon her brow. "That's the one!"

"You never said it was upside down. How was I supposed to find it if it was upside down?'"

"It doesn't matter!" Miliana tried to cuff Lorenzo on the ear, and missed him by a mile. "Now just try to retrace the symbols on something big—really, really big . . . so I can see!"

A fireball lit the courtyard with a bang; the gates sagged, hinges turning red-hot from the blast of magic flame. Lorenzo tried to choke down the panic, looked across the courtyard, and felt a new idea strike home to his mind.

"Wait—just wait. I'll only be a minute."

Capable of seeing nothing but the vaguest blurs, Miliana moved cautiously to her feet. If she strained herself, she could *just* make out the curtain walls; Tekoriikii was either the vague orange wobbly thing to her left, or else the warm surface she was currently standing on. The princess wandered slowly forward as the gates cracked clean in two, then suddenly felt herself grabbed by the arm.

"There! Will that do?"

Lorenzo seemed triumphant; the girl adjusted her empty frames out of habit, and squinted closer at the courtyard floor.

The shapes of spell symbols stood out in bold gray lines. Miliana murmured words under her breath, suddenly remembered the gestures to the spell, and felt herself light into a smile.

"That's it! I've got it!" She reached out with groping hands as she settled the spell formula in her mind's eye. "Where's the headmistress?"

Miliana was led to the great fallen whale; the Princess waved her hands, spoke a loud, triumphant syllable, and cast one of Tekoriikii's down feathers to the winds. Lorenzo saw the headmistress's body flicker with purple energies, and signaled Tekoriikii to take off into the air.

The bird latched onto the ungainly burden and effortlessly carried her aloft. The drive-rope trailed neatly behind, the slack slowly disappeared, and Lorenzo led Miliana to the flying machine to clamp herself against the steering rings.

Another fireball detonated, and the school gates exploded with a roar. Standing clasped about the shaft of his new flying machine, Lorenzo had to shout above the screams of charging warriors.

"How long does that feather fall spell keep working?"

"I don't know!" Miliana felt the desperation of uncertainty. "Someone told me it depends on the weight!"

Tekoriikii gave a squawk as his burden suddenly dropped from his claws. The headmistress plunged toward the city cesspits, the rope whipped tight, jerked the flying machine hard against its brackets, and suddenly the drive shaft began to blur with speed.

The propeller blades whirred, the rope snapped free, and the headmistress hit the dung pile with a meteoric splash. As a hundred pikemen and halberdiers came thundering across the fallen bodies of the teaching staff, Miliana and Lorenzo shot skyward and up across the school walls. A storm of crossbow bolts followed them aloft—one passing mere inches from Miliana's hat.

Clutching blindly to the handholds and feeling a storm wind blowing past her ears, Miliana could only blink her eyes and frown.

"What was that?"

"Nothing." Below Lorenzo, the dreadful school dwindled; outraged soldiers worked to break up Miliana's spell formula which had been laboriously formed from the posed bodies of unconscious home economics tutors.

The wind blew, the bright sun shone, and it felt marvelous to simply be alive. Tilting his face like a hound sniffing the wind, Lorenzo thrilled to the joys of flight.

Beneath the noisy rotor blades, the sounds of crashes, swordplay, spells, and cries of anger and fear hung loud across the city. Lorenzo gazed down across the streets far below, staring at the war-torn thoroughfares in dismay.

The flying machine worked quite well; Lorenzo confessed himself to be well pleased. The bearings whirred, the body balanced well, and the sensation of flight sent a dizzy rush of freedom through his veins. Tekoriikii circled happily nearby, noisily flapping his wings as he gave a cheery cry.

"Tekorii-kii-kii!"

Feeling her captivity sliding far away, Miliana risked loosening her handhold and groped for Lorenzo's arm.

"Lorenzo?"

"Yes?"

"Well done."

Swelling with pride, Lorenzo gazed below as he felt the craft begin to descend.

"Ah, good—there's Luccio—and there's the river now."

Miliana gave a great relieved sigh. "So we're landing by the river?"

"Um . . . not exactly . . ."

Miliana had enough time to blink, then gave a great unhappy wail. The flying machine plunged neatly into the drink—inventor, princess, silly hat, and all.

Tekoriikii watched the whole process from above, then landed gracefully on the wagon Luccio had parked on the riverbank. Luccio and the bird watched as Miliana and Lorenzo struggled damply toward them through the river mud.

"Well, all in all, Lorenzo, I think that was one of your better plans." Luccio reached down to proffer a kiss to Miliana's muddy hand. "Dear lady . . . so good to see you safe, and at liberty."

Luccio unshipped a bag of snorkels and alighted from the wagon top. "Alas, there is a swim ahead of us. The river is the only means of escape. The streets swarm with ten thousand blades."

"Why?" Miliana stood wringing out her muddy hair, then capped herself with the ruins of her pointy hat. "Is there a bread riot on? What's all the noise?"

Luccio looked at her, unable or unwilling to break ill news. Biting his lip, Lorenzo came forward to gently put an arm about Miliana's shoulders.

Her face had already drained ashen white. Creeping quietly into Lorenzo's touch, she let him quietly lead her away.

Lorenzo softly whispered to her. Luccio began to unpack his wagon, laying out snorkels, food packages, a toadskin book, and spare spectacles salvaged from the ruins of Miliana's room.

"Nurgle?"

"Just a moment, old chap. Leave them together for a while." Luccio quietly placed a hand on Tekoriikii's back. The bird mournfully strained toward Miliana, made anxious by the half-heard sound of tears.

Sunning herself on the riverbanks, there lay a long, exquisite female nixie—a curvaceous humanoid with webbed feet, webbed hands and dainty gills. Luccio introduced her to the curious firebird with a schoolgirl's blush.

"Tekoriikii? This is the Princess Krrrr-poka, of the Akanamere. She . . . ah, she owed me a favor." Luccio sealed his packages inside little wooden casks. "You can fly over the river; the rest of us will use snorkels, and she will tow us underwater past the armies and the gates."

Beside the river, Lorenzo stood with Miliana leaning on his arm. The young couple gazed in silence in the direction of Miliana's old home, which now formed the center of a distant storm of screams.

Miliana was free.

And Sumbria was burning.

13

In the city of Sumbria, the civil war between the Blade
Houses lasted for eleven savage days.

In the early battles of the first violent hours, the citizens had flocked into the streets—some to avenge their
fallen prince, and some to protect their homes from
marauding gangs of soldiers. Gilberto Ilégo, now univer-
sally acknowledged as the prince's assassin, had rallied
his supporters about him, and the city burned and shuddered as it transformed into a place of surging battle
lines.

Days passed; alliances shifted, soldiers clashed, and
the dead were left unburied in the streets. The crash of
magic spells sent rows of houses slumping into rubble,
and the citizens abandoned the nobles to their fight. The
market quarter became a place of tent ghettos and frightened families; women and children stood in the streets
and stared up the hill at the palaces of the mighty.

One by one, the great houses besieged each other. In
the first few days, a half dozen of the small fortresses
fell—until the battering rams ran short of soldiers willing to man them, and those sorcerers with the power to

breach the walls eventually fell victim to each other's
spells. The factions split, then split again as each Blade
House determined to protect its own affairs, and the
great battles of the days before dissolved into street
fights and skulking nighttime brawls.

Food supplies fell and sicknesses began; finally the soldiers themselves abandoned the fight. Some dragged themselves back to their barracks and remained slumped in apathy. Others took to looting empty houses, installing themselves in taverns barricaded into little forts. There they
drank themselves into a howling stupor, raiding the surrounding streets for women, bread, and gold; rolling in their
own filth as the city took on the stench of the damned.

Only Gilberto Ilégo's house remained at war. It was a
savage, mindless battle fought against the entire world.
Ilégo was blamed for all the nation's troubles, and so he
shut himself inside his lair and struck out at anything
that dared come near. His men made savage raids into
the market streets for food and snatched careless citizens
to use as conscripts for their unceasing attacks on other
palaces. Like a monster in its pit, Ilégo carved himself a
niche among the ruins of a better world.

Until, one cold-dawned autumn day, the sound of wondering, joyous cheers came drifting in across the city
roofs.

As the tiny sound began to spread, tired Blade
Captains ran to their battered marble towers and stared.
Soldiers crowded into gateways, looking at one another in
confusion as citizens crept forth from their homes.

The cheers turned into a roar of adulation, and suddenly the crowds began to run out into the sun.

Through the gates of Sumbria—opened by a swarm of
citizens who then flung aside the keys—came a procession more welcome than a shower of purest gold.
Colletran soldiers, all with their weapons slung and
swords sheathed, marching in column beside a wagon
train that stretched far away into the foothills of the
Akanapeaks.

The soldiers escorted cart after cart loaded to the brim with priceless food; there were bales of bread and biscuit, sacks of dried fish and flour. Whole pyramids of sausage followed barrow loads of autumn fruit. The populace of Sumbria gaped at the treasury in shock, standing in stunned amazement as the triumphant march passed them by.

And then the wagon crews began to hurtle bread into the crowds, sparking off a delirious storm of cheers.

The Colletrans had brought everything that a war-torn city might possibly need. Food and water, tents and blankets, shovels to clear rubble and five thousand hands to use them. Scores of healer priests dismounted and moved out to treat the sick. Barrels of water and beer were trundled over to a makeshift hospital. Colletran soldiers presented themselves to exhausted Sumbrian citizens, enlisting local aid in sweeping looters from the streets. Civil order restored itself in one great heady rush as food gushed out, unmeasured, into the hands of the poor.

What no one in Sumbria could possibly know, of course, was that the food and provisions had been largely stolen from Sumbria's own outlying farming hamlets, farm after farm having been left completely decimated.

Cheering swept the city as if it were a day of festival, with people swarming down the streets to behold the wonder of the age. Flowers flew through the air and landed at the feet of a black, high-stepping hippogriff, whose armored rider soothed the crowds with steady hands.

Ugo Svarézi, now prince-elect of Colletro, conferred with Sumbrian citizens, noblemen and troops. With the looting at an end and law and order restored, an amnesty was declared; but an amnesty that did not extend to the villain of the play.

Every tragedy needs a decent scapegoat for the crowd. Sealed up inside his palace, Gilberto Ilégo found Colletran snipers firing at his embrasures and Sumbrian nobles hammering at his gates. Drunk, desperate, and wild, he could only slump against his own walls and laugh as he saw Svarézi ride like a demigod through the adoring Sumbrian mob.

The palace's left wing fell beneath a hail of spells and trebuchet stones; a company of Ilégo's men deserted through the rubble and fled, only to be cut down in the streets. In the gatehouse tower, Ilégo's last surviving companies barricaded themselves behind the doors, snarling like wild animals spitting from a cage.

The entire population of Sumbria swarmed about Ilégo's lair, screaming out for blood. Amongst the combined soldiers of two cities, Ugo Svarézi rode like a heavy-hearted father gazing upon wayward children. The crowds wanted to please him, to point up at Ilégo and blame him for the war. Svarézi gave them his benediction and rode on into the storm.

Ilégo, tired almost past thinking but still capable of reveling in irony, swung carelessly from his own battlements and leaned out across the crowd. He hoisted a glass to the citizens and drank to their health with wine. He swallowed, then interrupted his drinking in pantomimed surprise.

"What? No chorus? No music heralding the curtain call?" The ragged courtier brayed like a laughing ass. "Svarézi! Surely you can stage a better production than that? You have the costuming, the timing . . . even the proper cast!" Ilégo half made to serve himself more wine. "I, of course, shall play the villain. I'm told one is needed in any proper tale.

"Sadly, I fear this is less a tragedy than a mere farce—with you, my dear little citizens, playing the sheep who take the fall."

Below him, a mob of untold thousands jeered up at him in hatred. Ilégo bowed before his audience as though idly acknowledging their cheers, and then cocked a hand up to his ear and gaped down at them in shock.

"What's that? Did he never tell you what we planned?" Ilégo clung above his gate, eyes wild above a ragged beard. "Did he never tell you I was to rule Sumbria, and he Colletro, together! Did he tell you why he stole the Sun Gem? Did you ever ask him why?"

Dragging up through the streets, there came a titanic wheeled machine; a massive armored box drawn by a dozen cartage teams. Ilégo greeted its appearance with a cheer.

"Never extend the final act, and always dazzle them with an unforeseen display!" Ilégo raised a careless bottle to the crowd. "Time's up, my friends! It seems we have our curtain call!"

Down on a cleared street, among the mob, armored gunners checked their hoses and retorts, then raised clenched fists to their commander. The master gunner jerked the valve release and slammed his visor shut across his eyes.

Mounted at the forefront of the machine, the Sun Gem blazed unutterably bright. A searing bolt of violet light spat across the air, and Ilégo's gatehouse wall blew apart. Molten stonework fountained through the sky and superheated masonry exploded in an example of demolition such as all Faerûn had never seen. In an instant, the palace of Ilégo was no more.

Svarézi surveyed the lifeless ruins with a cold, unwinking eye. Turning into the arms of an adoring, cheering crowd, he rode forth to take the city as his own.

* * * * *

"Never! He shall have neither my blessing, nor my hand." Lady Ulia Mannicci, looking like a veritable storm front in her black widow's gown, glared down across a multitude of chins. "I am the widow of this great city's rightful prince. I shall not besmirch his name by wedding myself to a foreign usurper!"

Ugo Svarézi's envoys, a Colletran Blade Captain and a representative from Sumbria, both kept diplomatic smiles as they held their bows.

"Madam, the prince's offer is sincere. He is now the prince-elect both of Colletro *and* Sumbria, and is moved to offer marriage to the greatest lady of the age.

Ulia gave a snort and cracked a cast-iron fan into her fist. The death of her husband had left her disgruntled, but not diminished. With the coming of peace, Svarézi had wasted little time in sending emissaries of his love. Lady Ulia had been found in command of one of her own palace towers, a place in which she had gathered almost a hundred young girls to save them from the ravages of the civil war. She had defended this treasure through two weeks of constant battle, keeping all comers from her door by a combination of hurtled rocks, chamber pots and invective . . . and the largest trebuchet battery in the Blade Kingdoms.

Peace had come, and Ulia's teeth had been carefully drawn. She now stood and confronted new enemies, glowering at them with the eyes of a maddened bull.

"I am aware of exactly what your master wants, and he shall not have it! I have read all the same books as he. If he wishes to legitimize his conquest of Sumbria, he may seek marriage elsewhere."

Colletro's diplomat changed his expression to a sly, calculating smile.

"Perhaps we can persuade the great lady to change her mind?" The man flipped his colleague a lazy glance. "Were she to sample our hospitality, she would surely see the error of her ways.

"Alas, the chambers we have to offer are a trifle cramped. We cannot guarantee her ladyship's total satisfaction . . ."

Ulia gazed down at the man as though about to crush him like a snake.

"You would not dare! The prince has an heir, sir. An heir who will avenge slights delivered to his family!"

"An heir?" Awake at last, the Sumbrian delegate raised a sardonic, mocking brow. "Cappa Mannicci sired no heirs."

"I refer, sir, to his daughter Miliana, who has escaped this city to organize an army to reconquer her lost home!"

"Aaaaaah . . . then it is vengeance my lord must fear!" The Sumbrian delightedly clapped his hands. "I am sure he will lie awake in terror at nights, dreading the arrival of your stepdaughter and her avenging sword."

Still pretending to a veneer of friendliness, the Colletran emissary intruded himself at Lady Ulia's side.

"Seriously, my lady, the prince's offer is the best for us all. Would you let mere pride destroy the bright hopes for our new nation?"

"I wish your new nation to the dogs, sir!" Ulia let her bodice creak with the swelling of her pride. "I can smell a despot as well as anyone, and despotism is the stench that creeps across this land. The people still cheer too much to notice it, sir, but they shall come back to their senses in time."

"By which time, my lady, it will all be far too late." The Colletran snapped his fingers and summoned a horde of guards. "With your permission, my lady, we shall install you as our master's special guest. Diet and exercise may help clear the evil humors from your mind. A good brisk run tied behind a team of horses twice each day, and a diet of bread and salad greens." The man chuckled as he saw the color flush into Ulia's face. "You may halt our little regimen at any time, of course; simply agree to become my master's bride, and you may once again return to the lap of luxury."

"Varlet! Do your worst!" Ulia shoved her guards aside and proudly hefted up her hems. "Toril itself shall expire before you manage to break the likes of me!"

Trailing a nervous procession of guards, Lady Ulia stormed away into the talons of her enemies. Outside the palace walls, the street crowds still excitedly bubbled as the new prince of Sumbria was showered endlessly with praise.

* * * * *

As far as cities went, Lomatra placed itself at the picturesque end of the scale. Overlooking the clear waters of

the Akanamere and capped off with spectacular lime-
stone promontories, the city had the look of a sleepy fishing village grown to unmanageable size. It seemed a land
of pastel colors and evening hush, of warm lakefront and
eccentric little trees bounded by a broad, deep river that
masked the city from the mountain pass above. Miliana,
who had spent her life confined to the Mannicci palace in
Sumbria and a few closely chaperoned bridle paths,
found the place utterly enchanting.

The city's general air of sleepiness and disarray were
what annoyed Lorenzo the most. Clad in bedraggled
clothing, tired and filthy from long sleepless nights
beside the road, he surveyed his native land from the
hills up above, and gave an irritated snarl.

The Blade Kingdoms were each quite tiny when measured on the scale of other lands. Each nation consisted
of a single town, a few surrounding villages, and their
supporting fields. Most could be crossed in less than a
day's ride. Even so, the escape route taken by Miliana
and her band had taken two weeks of vile, uncomfortable
tedium. They each had only a single set of clothes, and
those had been damp and muddy from their trip under
the river gates. With no money, the group had been
unable to afford food; dinner had been provided by
Tekoriikii, who had scavenged rabbits, watermelons, and
long poles threaded with dozens of dead, dried carp.
While the bird seemed to enjoy the salty fish, no one else
could bear to ever look a carp in the face again.

With brigands and rapacious refugees scouring the
hills, Miliana and her friends had hidden in a cave for
many long, boring days. Now bedraggled, scratched by
brambles, and beset with chafing itches, they had all
endured quite enough. Despite Lorenzo's protests, the
footsore humans had shambled on to the promised haven
of the Lomatran city walls.

Flying gaily overhead, Tekoriikii gave a screech of
heartfelt joy and looped toward the sun. His companions
glared up at him and muttered curses under their breath.

Miliana felt utterly exhausted; she had never walked a full day's march before in all her life. Footsore, unkempt, and smelling like a sea hag dragged backward through a sewer, she was quite ready to sell her soul for a decent bed and a massage. She watched, uncaring, as Lorenzo and Luccio exchanged conversation with the soldiers at Lomatra's gates, never even questioning why the gate commander offered her a horse.

The girl leaned upon Lorenzo for support. As she rode, Miliana nodded wearily, casting an eye up to a fine, half-timbered house that occupied the slope of a quiet hill.

"Where are we going? Is that an inn?"

"No . . . it's home." Lorenzo kept his shoulders hunched and kicked irritably at vagrant cobblestones. "My home. So now I have to crawl back in through the doors and beg for leave to stay."

"Oh?"

Miliana sensed a delicate situation in the offing, but was just too damned tired to care. She held Tekoriikii on the saddle bow before her and hugged him tight to keep him still. "What about Luccio? Does he have a house here too?"

Luccio answered with a polite cough, hiding his responding blush behind his hand.

"Yes. Ah—well . . . I suppose I am what is best called a 'boon companion.' "

"Meaning I have to convince my father to let him free-load from our kitchen once more." Lorenzo spared his own front door a bitter, reluctant glance. "All right, let's get this over with. He told me to bring home a princess—and now I'm bringing one . . ."

Pulling his ruined clothing into some semblance of shape, Lorenzo the artist, scion of the noble house of Utrelli, moved up to the thick wooden bars across the gatehouse door. An old man bearing a spiked wooden club scrabbled up from his comfortable chair behind the portal and waved the weapon back and forth above his head.

"Be off with you, ragamuffin! You'll get no charity here!"

"Oh, hush!" Miliana regarded the old man with a foul-tempered scowl. "Can't you see he's Lorenzo Utrelli?"

"He knows . . ." Lorenzo kicked at the gate in spite. "Open the gate, Alonzo, or I'll burn the damned thing down."

The old gatekeeper muttered; seething with dislike, he ripped open the locks and swung the heavy doors aside. Lorenzo led Miliana and Luccio in through the gatehouse, biting his thumb at the gatekeeper as he passed.

Just to prove superiority, Tekoriikii strutted back and forth past the old man three times, clucking to himself as he shook out his fabulous tail.

In a courtyard formed by a hollow square of half-timbered walls, Lorenzo handed Miliana down from her horse. The girl shot an ill-tempered glance back to the gate.

"Is he always like that?"

"Nasty old . . ." Lorenzo tried to help Miliana bash her hat back into a presentable cone. "I tried to replace him with an automatic door-opening machine."

"What—because it was less expensive?"

"No, because it would have offered better conversation." The young artist adjusted his rapier belt and headed for the stairs. "Come on up. Tekoriikii, leave him alone, you don't know where he's been!"

The group entered a darkly panelled, badly lit great hall that smelled of wood polish and fried onions. A pair of overfed maids took one look at Lorenzo, gave spiteful scowls, and stalked off without a word. Lorenzo ignored the scene and busied himself opening up the curtains, trying to bring some illumination to the room as he spoke for the benefit of his friends.

"Welcome to House Utrelli. Contents: One father—heavy cavalryman, retired. One brainless dolt of a younger brother—light cavalryman, *not* retired. The barracks house three hundred *Lanze Spezzate*, four noblemen, five squires, and a gatekeeper with a club. An environment tailor-made to foster hostility and hate." He turned as the sound of silks whispered down a connecting hall. "The house also contains one sister: Name—unimportant. Profession—gold digger."

The door opened, revealing the sister in question—tall, haughty, and wearing a well-stuffed court gown. She faced Lorenzo with a sweet, false smile and dropped herself into a little bow.

"Brother scribbler."

"Sister bloodsucker." Lorenzo looked at the girl with absolute, unfeigned dislike. "These are my friends. This is Princess Miliana. We've all just escaped the fall of Sumbria."

"Why, how very nice for them!" Lorenzo's sister simpered, keeping her malicious face locked into its perfect smile. "And so why have you brought them here?"

"Why do you think?" Lorenzo ignored the girl and began wrenching open doors. "Where's father?"

"Father has left word that he is not at home."

"Meaning that he *is* home and just doesn't want to see me." Lorenzo pulled open a broom cupboard and stuck his head inside. "*Father?*"

A muffled reply drifted through the wall; thrusting into the room came a massive, powerful old man. Although fully seven decades old, he towered over his own son by some six inches in height and fifty pounds of muscle mass.

Franco Utrelli, once a cavalier of the realm and now father to a nitwit inventor of a son, took one look at Lorenzo and let his nose wrinkle to a hidden smell.

"Oh, it's you." Lorenzo's father looked as though he had just trodden in something nasty. "Unless you've got a princess—get out."

"Father, it's an emergency! And anyway—I have a princess." Lorenzo flicked a glance at a man behind his father who could have been his father's younger clone. "Hello, Alberto. Father, Sumbria has fallen to Colletro. The whole city just passed into Svarézi's hands."

"Good riddance to 'em, too!" The senior Utrelli tried to

wave Lorenzo from the room. "Always cluttering things up with do-good intentions and too-clever-by-half plans . . ."

"Father—we've been allies for a hundred years!"

"And look where it's gotten us! It's turned our young fighting men into a race of worthless nancies." Old Utrelli senior prodded a finger at the dandified Luccio. "In my day, men were men. Soldiers and commanders . . . like your brother here. Now *there's* a fine figure of a man. Not some damned paintbrush-swizzling, tinker-brained, gnome-headed, leveling little freak!"

Lorenzo's younger brother puffed out his muscular chest in pride. Lorenzo sneered and jabbed at the creature in unremitting spite.

"He's *exactly* what's wrong with the entire system of social class! He has the brains of a golem and the education of a goblin; yet we're told that the lower orders have to listen to every word the damned fool says! If we're ever going to have true justice, we need to run governments through meritocracy. Set up a way to have the ruling done by those most fit to—"

"The nobility *are* most fit to rule!"

"No one has given the common folk a chance to try, so how can we possibly . . ."

Lorenzo's father stuck his fingers in his ears.

"I'm not listening!" He began to sing loudly and tonelessly, instantly attracting Tekoriikii's attention. "Not listening! Not listening!"

Lorenzo's sister tried to intrude with her sweet, genteel smile.

"Now, Lorenzo, you know how father feels about your proposition to overthrow the ruling classes."

"What would you know about it? The only thing you ever overthrew was your own virtue."

Lorenzo's brother stirred into action with an "I say, steady on . . ." The family argument settled into full swing. Watched by an innocent and confused Tekoriikii, who flicked his head from side to side and up and down like a frog at a gnat convention, all four members of the Utrelli family, their two maids, and their gatekeeper all crowded into a circle and began a wild melee of words. Invective flew like an arrow storm, accompanied by hand gestures, stamping feet, and wild bellows of rage. Miliana watched in growing fury, slowly cramming her ruined hat deeper down over her brows.

"*Shut up!*"

Miliana's voice snapped like a lightning bolt, bringing an amazed halt to the family wars.

"Shut up! I order you to *shut up!*"

Lorenzo's sister blinked at her in shock, then opened her mouth to speak. She took one look at Miliana and blanched as the princess bunched a fist.

Short, begrimed and bespectacled, Miliana kept the Utrelli family rooted to the spot as she snapped out orders like a leader born.

Her first command sent Lorenzo's brother scuttling away.

"*You!* Go return my horse to the city gate. You maids— go get a room for me and then pile some straw in a corner as a nest for the bird. He wants a box of salt biscuits, a bucket of nuts—and get me a bottle of new white wine." Filthy, tired, and angry, the princess kicked Lorenzo's brother on his way. "Move it! The rest of you—I want baths for me, for Luccio, and for Lorenzo, a change of clothes and a meal—and someone get me a map of the Blade Kingdoms, *now!*"

Trying to preserve her air of cynical gentility, Lorenzo's sister faced Miliana with lowered lashes.

"And is there nothing else?"

"I'll work on it." Miliana marked the door to the bathhouse and hitched up her filthy skirts. "I get the bath first. Just find me a decent dress and some towels."

The sister gazed down her nose at Miliana with a sneer.

"And what, my dear, should you be called?"

"I should be called when I've finished my bath." Miliana ruthlessly pushed the larger girl aside. "After that, you can call a meeting of your Blade Council, and call your troops to arms."

Miliana departed in a slap of bare, muddy feet. Lorenzo's sister kept a smile frozen on her face as she swiveled furious eyes upon Lorenzo.

"And who, exactly, is she?"

"She's serious." Lorenzo managed to pull off one mildewed boot, releasing a shower of stones across the floor. "Don't bother her until she's had her bath."

Luccio departed for the pantry, slapping his hands together in glee. Lorenzo crawled off to find himself a tin bath and a mug of beer. Watching the entire household whir like a hornet's nest, then depart, Lorenzo's sister drew in a magnificent breath of protest, only to find her audience had flown.

Exasperated, the girl stamped her foot in rage. With a toss of her head and a heave of her breast, she stormed irritably from the room.

. . . Leaving Tekoriikii in full possession of the floor. The bird looked about himself in curiosity, spied a string of pearls dangling about Lorenzo's sister's receding neck, and waddled off in swift pursuit, naked avarice gleaming in his eye.

* * * * *

"My lord? My lord, the dockyard guildmasters wish to tender their report."

Approaching nervously in the shadow of the hippogriff aerie atop Sumbria's highest tower, the Colletran chief of staff faced Ugo Svarézi with a bow. Behind the administrative head of Svarézi's new army, terrified technicians tried to hide from the bite of the first winter storm.

Forever clad in his black velvet brigantine, Svarézi ignored the interlopers and stared at the tower above him. His cold, chiseled face showed neither hatred nor joy, merely a desire for absolute, soulless efficiency.

With the winter months blooming bitter cold, the hippogriffs were restless. Svarézi ordered boilers stoked beneath the aeries, warming the floors to a springtime heat. Normally, the creatures bred in spring, the mares raising their young across the summer season, but this year, Svarézi wanted every mount upon the wing. He would breed his beasts through winter, and have the fledglings weaned before the summer campaigns began.

"My lord? My lord—the dockside artisans . . . their report i-is quite important . . ."

Svarézi turned and his expression chilled the artisans' blood stone cold.

The prince walked toward them slowly, the wind whipping through his coarse black hair.

"I require forty warships in twenty days. That is all."

The dockside guildmasters wrung their hands; already their crews were working like men possessed. Svarézi kept their wives and children under guard within his walls—to "remove the distractions they might offer to proper work."

The master of Sumbria's caulker's guild crept forward by a pace.

"Sire—the numbers required—it is far too—"

"It is what I have ordered." Svarézi placed a hand on the man's shoulder and walked with him to the battlements. "In twenty days, we will have a fleet." The cold eyes met level with the guildsman's own.

"We *will* have a fleet."

"S-sire, it is too much. You require too many hulls!"

"Then use river barges as a base." Svarézi turned aside without a care. "Commandeer them from Sumbrian docks . . . or take them from puny Kirenzia . . . wherever seems convenient."

Behind the old guildsman, his colleagues paled. One man stole forward with sweat starting from his brow.

"But the sea and river trade, sire! The barges are essential to bring produce to the cities! How will the harvest be brought in once summer—"

"Harvest is harvest; now is now." Svarézi never even spared the man a glance. "By harvest time, we will have the loot of whole cities to buy the goods we need."

Walking his underlings to the wall overlooking the port, Svarézi gazed over the dockyard and its pathetic scattering of half-built battle craft.

"I will draft three thousand peasants as your labor force; in winter, no one needs to till a field."

"We will lose men, sire. The land grows cold."

"Yes—we will lose at least half—but we will have a fleet in twenty days."

Svarézi pushed the old man forward; with a detached expression, he watched him fall, screaming, onto the rocks a hundred feet below.

"I believe you can be motivated into far, far greater speed."

Without a glance behind him, Svarézi marched into the lower stable rooms and gazed about the cluttered aerie floor.

The lean black hippogriff Shaatra had found herself a prime position. Sleek flanks gleaming, she turned around and around widening her nest; twigs and straw had been bound together with painstaking skill, and the bottom had been lined with astonishing flame-red plumes. Crooning softly to herself in age-old songs, the hippogriff prepared the cradle for her first-ever clutch of young.

Svarézi took one look at the nest, strode across the floor and kicked the little structure to the winds.

"Not you! I have need of you. Find another year for warming shells."

The warlord crushed tufts of fine black down beneath his heel as he snarled out for the grooms.

"Keep this beast out in the cold! And don't let it stare at the accursed stallions!"

Shaatra stood gaping in numb horror at the ruins of her nest. With a piercing scream of pure despair, she flung herself on Svarézi's unguarded back. Her beak tore sparks from the human's armor, spraying blood across the walls. With a vengeful, sobbing cry she whirled about to gouge him with her claws.

Bleeding great sheets of blood all down his back, Svarézi unhurriedly linked his armored hands. He swiveled heavily as the hippogriff came on, and crashed his fists clean across her brow.

The bird screamed and staggered, her head snapping sideways in shock. Svarézi struck her again and then again, hammering down blows until the beast collapsed at his feet. Careless of his wounds, he reached for a training staff and beat the creature methodically up and down its hide, crashing blows into the moaning animal as it weakly tried to crawl aside.

Finally, he left Shaatra to her pain. Tossing aside the bloody staff, he turned to the grooms.

"I care nothing for their love. Only for their fear." He met the staring eyes of his underlings with a blank, cold expression. "Life is nothing but a contest of unremitting power."

With that, the warlord of Sumbria and Colletro left the tower. Behind him, Shaatra whimpered and reached out for a fallen fragment of her nest. Black talons closed upon a crumpled orange plume, and the hippogriff wept silent, bitter tears.

* * * * *

Safely ensconced inside a massive wooden bath, Lorenzo lifted up one gleaming leg and soaped thoroughly down along the line of hairs. He stretched tired muscles, wriggled up his clean pink toes, then lounged back to let the hot water spread its soft, delicious spell.

A bath at last. Battles survived, struggles overcome, now rest at a long, hard journey's end. Lorenzo smiled; Lorenzo sighed; Lorenzo luxuriously rolled his head and came face-to-face with a pair of brilliant hazel eyes.

"Holy Ishtishia!"

He crammed himself beneath the scanty cover of a floating sponge and turned lobster pink from head to toe. Beside him, Miliana settled herself on a folded towel and made wet rings upon the polished floor with two steaming cups of tea.

With her long hair wound up beneath a towel, and
wearing a thick white bathrobe, Miliana seemed softly
serene. Smiling calmly behind twinkling spectacles, she
passed Lorenzo a steaming drink and balanced it firmly
on the edge of the tub.

Lorenzo's eyes appeared across the rim like a mouse
peering from its burrow.

"Miliana, what are you doing?"

"Oh, it's just equal time." The girl seemed utterly at
ease. With a warm yawn she patted the tall sides of the
tub. "You've seen me in my bath. I simply thought I might
return the compliment."

"But I had the door locked!"

"Your sister gave me the key." Made tired by warmth
and steam, Miliana adjusted her spectacles. "An odd girl.
Actually, I think I like her."

Caught in the warm fog that just preceded bedtime,
Miliana sat and sipped her tea. Comforted by the shelter
of oaken planks, Lorenzo emerged to lean across the
edges of his tub. He accepted Miliana's gift of tea,
propped himself up on his elbows, and fondly gazed at her
through a haze of steam.

"You seem quiet."

"I feel quiet." Miliana, damp and glowing from her own
time in her bath, looked up at Lorenzo and creased a
sweetly anxious brow.

"Lorenzo . . . am I too foul-tempered?"

Her companion fumbled a dripping hand across the
tub; Miliana caught the fingers in her own and gave a
squeeze. Lorenzo reached across to push a damp curl
back from Miliana's face.

"No. I'd say that you're just foul-tempered enough."

"I suppose so." Miliana flexed her fingers in Lorenzo's
grasp. "It's just that—back home—I've evaded, snarled,
and schemed. But until you came along, no one's ever
really been worth arguing with before."

From the pocket of her robe, Miliana pulled a borrowed
coin—a half-ducat piece from Sumbria. Her father's face

had been stamped across the electrum disk—a face that still showed its habitually cold stare.

Miliana held the coin before the mask of her spectacles.

"I try to think of all those funny little plazas—those fountains and streets we both walked through—as they were. Not how they must be now, all broken down by Svarézi's men.

"I like your home, Lorenzo. I don't want what happened to Sumbria to happen here."

"We'll fight it." Lorenzo looked quietly at Miliana's wistful face. "We'll win. Hey, you're a real princess, remember?"

For an answer, Miliana shifted the coin and stared into her father's face.

"He's really dead, isn't he." The girl looked softly at the portrait with its blank, unseeing eyes. "I loved that city, and now it's gone.

"And do you know what he'd have expected me to do about it?"

"What?"

"Absolutely nothing. The man scarcely knew I was alive."

Miliana's fist closed over the coin and clenched, slowly squeezing it until her knuckles turned white.

"We'll show him . . ."

Lorenzo gripped Miliana's free hand, changing her bitterness into a wan little smile.

"Yes. We'll show him."

They kissed softly, lips touching as each wound fingers into the other's hair. Resting forehead to forehead, they clung together in silence, companionship, and steam.

Finally, the girl rose, kissed Lorenzo's fingers, and wandered to the door.

She halted and looked back at him, her face soft and fond behind the panels of her spectacles.

"Argue with you tomorrow?"

Lorenzo smiled.

"Tomorrow."

Moving out into the hall, Miliana closed the door behind her and wandered quietly into her borrowed bedroom. A candle burned warm and yellow beside the bed, while Tekoriikii sat in a nest of straw happily reading the pages of a picture book. Miliana stroked his crest fondly as she passed, then sank onto the bed.

She lay curled on her side, staring at the little disk of gray metal in her palm. The warm scent of straw and bird spread its spell across the bedroom, and Miliana's coin hung heavy in her hand.

Minutes later, it slipped onto the covers, off the bed, and rolled across the wood floor. Craning his neck up across the bed, Tekoriikii watched his friend for a long, quiet while, then softly drew the blankets up across her freckled arms.

The girl lay calm and quiet. Tekoriikii gently snuffed the candle, tucked his head beneath one wing, and sank into a contented world of sleep.

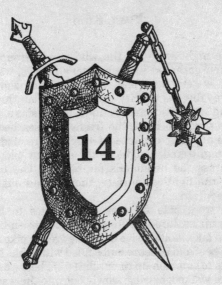

14

Winter on the shores of the Akanamere came in hard and strong. For the tiny city-state of Zutria, it was a welcome time of unprecedented harvest. For days on end, wild storms and winds would lash against the coast; the fishing fleets would shelter in the city's fine stone harbor while the crews kept the cold at bay with fried fish and hot spiced ale.

As the wind dropped—as it always did after three or four full days of violent blow—the city folk, farmers, and fishermen spread out from Zutria's walls. In the predictable calms, the bait fish swarmed in dense clouds along the shore, bringing a fabulous bounty that was netted in by wading men. Their wives and children worked the rocky beaches, raking tons of wrack into reeking piles to be carted off as fertilizer for the city fields. Zutria—poor, independent, and proud—made the most of every passing moment of the year.

And every year, just before the high midwinter's feast, the storms would hammer hard along the bay. Spectacular sheets of spray flung high across the city walls, driving sentries into shelter and sending everyone indoors.

As the night wore on, the wild winds dropped away. Fishermen gathered in each other's houses, waiting for the first watery light of dawn; as the horizon lit with ghost-gray fingers, the city emptied itself out through the gates and wandered merrily down to the shore.

In the predawn light, the freshwater sea became one vast, shimmering expanse of black. Here and there a wave cap glittered, caught by the sunlight leaking eastward across the headlands far beyond. The fishermen scanned the lightless surface, then spread out to begin the day's affairs.

There were nets to work and catches to be made. Friendly nixies, lured up from their cool green homes far below the lake, would drive away the greedy pike in return for dried beef and squeeze bulbs filled with wine. Men blew the horns to summon up their allies from below as the first nets were walked, hissing, slowly out into the waves.

The nets moved onward, then faltered as their handlers stared out across the lake.

Lit pink by the winter sun, tiny shapes lined the water out beside the headlands; low, sleek hulls which flickered in and out of sight behind the restless swells.

Zutria's citizens gathered on the beach to stare, all shading eyes against the sudden flash of dawn as daylight flooded out across the Akanamere.

The tiny slivers arrowed fast across the bay, and finally the shapes stood out sharp and clear. They were battle galleys; fast-rowed warships flying a strange new banner of purest black.

From Zutria's walls came the sound of trumpets, bells, and drums. Windlasses creaked as a boom made of chained logs and metal spines was raised up to block the harbor entrance. With the city safe behind its walls, and her port protected by engines, spells, and booms, Zutria stood immune from any mischief the attacking ships might do. The fisherfolk gathered on the shores to watch the fun, wondering what the invading fleet would do to vent its rage.

The fleet of galleys might have belonged to Sumbria, the nearest city down the coast, were it not for their black flags and clear hostility. The lean little shapes formed a swarm about a giant barge that ponderously beat into the bay. With its huge oars rippling like a water insect's limbs, the barge settled itself before Zutria's harbor mouth, just out of ballista range.

The barge backed water, the world fell into an expectant hush—and suddenly the air flickered to a blinding bolt of light.

A shaft of searing heat stabbed out from the barge. The seawall exploded like a bomb, slumping stones into the water with a hiss of scalding steam. The crash of breaking masonry sent shock waves through the air, while violet afterimages hung like wraiths before the eyes of shocked defenders.

The giant barge shifted; black figures swarmed across an armored box mounted at the bow, and the deadly light beam stabbed across the bay once more. It raked across the harbor guard towers, cutting through stonework in a searing blast of noise. Seconds later, Zutria stood open and exposed.

With insolent ease, the light beam scored across the waves, boiling water and sending up titanic gouts of steam. It snipped the boom chains clean in two like a princess opening new public baths with a pair of golden shears, and the black galleys surged forward in a triumphant, screaming wave.

Water elementals clashed as defending mages tried to hold the storm tide back; crushed aside by superior sorceries, the Zutrian spells swiftly flickered out and died. Within minutes, the attacking warships had driven hard ashore, spilling armored men into the streets.

Spells rang out. Here and there a fire bloomed, yet the invasion happened so swiftly that Zutrian soldiers scarcely had time to resist. The fishermen stood blinking as the black banners broke out above the rooftops of their homes.

Watching from the rocks beside the bay, a row of nixies stared in silence at the menacing black barge. Thin, aquatic faces swapped blank looks of shock and alarm.

Surfacing amidst her people, a pink-haired princess gazed at the city, then stared at the black-armored figure striding up through the ruined harbor walls. Lithe as a dolphin, the girl reared high up on thrashing flippers and stared at the Sun Cannon floating in the bay.

With a frantic splash, the nixies plunged back down out of view, speeding clean white wakes toward the distant south.

Toward the peaceful shores of Lomatra.

* * * * *

Winter had not mellowed moods in the fair city of Lomatra. Not only had the wet weather brought its usual spate of colds, coughs, and running noses, but it had also brought a staggering influx of refugees from Sumbria. Retainers from the households of Mannicci, Toporello, and several smaller families had joined hundreds of commoners who had run for better climes. They had crowded themselves one and all into the Lomatran city streets, where Miliana had them housed in a deserted barracks hall.

Enforced proximity between noble and common folk went unnoticed in a general gratitude for shelter from the bitter winter storms. The refugees brought tales of woe from home—wild stories of growing armies, ruthless taxes, and rapine. Although the Lomatran commoners listened to the stories in disquiet and alarm, their nobles decided that it was all merely a ploy to avoid paying rent and taking jobs.

Until the day the first official messages from Prince Ugo Svarézi arrived.

Using her pointy hat to help hold an old cloak spread against the rain, Miliana sheltered Lorenzo and Tekoriikii as they scuttled past her into the Lomatran city hall. Miliana shook out her cloak, careful not to stain her one

and only decent gown. Lorenzo's allowance would only
spread so far, though Tekoriikii's gullet provided an errat-
ic, but illegal income. Dusting off her brand new hat—tall,
blue, and sharpened like a needle—the princess ducked
beneath the lintel and strode on into the hall.

Lomatra's Prince Rosso was a small, mouselike man
who had been elected by his peers mostly because he never
argued with their plans. He commanded less votes than
any other man in Lomatra's Blade Council, and the
Utrellis were his main supporters. Lorenzo's father had
succeeded in arranging his match with Sumbria's princess
simply because his powerless family had made the perfect
candidate of compromise. Most of the other families had
considered a few hundred troops contributed to the
Mannicci bride-price a small cost, particularly if it kept
their more powerful rivals from enjoying the advantage a
union with the Manniccis would provide. The added power
of the Utrellis would hardly be noticed.

Standing alone inside the hall, dwarfed by the wooden
benches which soared giddily up the walls, Lomatra's
prince seemed nervous, short, and really rather tired. The
huge crowds of spectators that the day's meeting had
drawn were utterly unprecedented; over three hundred
nobles, merchants, Sumbrian refugees, and common folk
had crammed into the gallery. Self-consciously pulling at
the collar of his breastplate, Prince Rosso rapped upon
the council table and tried to make himself heard.

"Um . . . the meeting can come to order. If you like . . ."
The little man removed and polished spectacles at least
as big as Miliana's own. "I'd like to make a short speech,
if I may."

Lomatra sported only eleven Blade Captains, all evenly balanced, more or less, as to numbers of both votes and
men. The armored figures crashed themselves into their
seats, drowning out their ruler's voice as he unfolded a
damp sheet of parchment and began to read.

"Um . . . we have received a message—well, an ultima-
tum really—from the new prince of Colletro, Sumbria,

and Zutria. He offers us the chance . . ." The prince nervously adjusted his spectacles. "Well—*demands*, really—that we combine our Blade Council with his own—"

"And a fine opportunity, too!" A fat warrior in armor that looked to be tailored to fit a beer barrel slammed his sword against the table, bringing his prince's speech to a halt. "We should get in now, while there's still time to dominate their policy!"

A surge of violent protest bellowed from the galleries; Sumbrian and Lomatran commoners leapt to their feet and roared disagreement, echoed by the meek voice of their prince in the hall below.

"Um . . . well, I do rather think *we'll* be absorbed by Svarézi, rather than the other way around . . ."

A beery voice rose into a roar.

"So? Mannicci was already trying to place a finger in our pie! Why ally through marriage, when we can amalgamate our councils?"

Suddenly a loud, good-natured rumbling sound came from the far end of the hall; the Blade Captains turned as a sedan chair swayed in through the doors and settled by the council table. The council relaxed, the audience busied itself with a speculative roar, and Miliana steepled her fingers and gave a thoughtful frown.

"Who is it?"

"Spirelli, our only nonhuman Blade Captain." Lorenzo coldly gnawed upon his lower lip. "This could be bad; Spirelli could swing the voting either way. He's an invertebrate politician."

"You mean 'inveterate' . . ."

"No, invertebrate." Lorenzo moved to give a clear view of the speaking stand. "Still, it makes for a nice change."

Miliana kept her face frozen, unamused, as a huge, slimy snail slithered from the sedan chair and took the floor. The creature had the voice and demeanor of a village schoolmaster gargling on a mouthful of soap.

"Colleagues, colleagues, colleagues!" The snail Spirelli had an unnerving habit of looking both his supporters and detractors in the eye at once. "Pray forgive my tardy arrival. I have been gazing out across the city roofs, contemplating our luck in avoiding the recent storms. The waves bring a wealth of driftwood to the beaches; merchant ships dock in our harbor and pay our docking fees . . ." The snail puffed himself up with pompous pride, swiveling his eyes to examine the hostile commoners. "I wonder if, perhaps, we cannot learn a lesson from the storm. It is our particular strength to turn disasters into assets to us all."

Miliana shifted forward in her seat and glared at the snail in hate. At her side, Tekoriikii finished plucking the emerald out of a merchant's signet ring and turned about to stare at Spirelli in surprise.

The snail cruised silkily along behind his prince's throne.

"Lomatra has always been an ally to Sumbria. If we break with that tradition, we make ourselves seem faithless in the eyes of the world. Let us take it that Svarézi's conquest of the Blade Kingdoms is a *fait accompli*. He has the wealth of Sumbria; the population of Colletro. Zutria has shown us just how all the lesser kingdoms shall fall." The snail coiled its neck about the prince's shoulders. "By maintaining our traditional ties with Sumbria, we place ourselves in a position of unexpected power. How else can Lomatra be expected to survive?"

"With an alliance!" A sooty chieftain of the metalworkers guild shook his blacksmith's hammer as he roared. "An alliance with our neighbors against Svarézi's hordes!"

The cry was met by a storm of agreement from the upper galleries; the commoners had spent long weeks succoring refugees from Sumbria and beyond. They roared and raged, hammering fists against the railings and showering curses through the air . . .

. . . All of which the Blade Captains ignored. As autocrats, they held the demands of commoners as less than smoke upon the wind.

Rising to his feet, a slim captain clad in sapphire armor calmly addressed the hall.

"I think the council is essentially agreed. Cooperation and compliance with Svarézi's program is the most beneficial course for us all."

Despite the frantic protests of their prince, the murmured agreement of the Blade Captains rumbled around the tabletop; until, suddenly, a fierce new voice ripped out to stun the hall.

"Traitors!"

The Blade Captains wrenched about in shock, staring up at a pointy-hatted form that leaned out from the galleries to cast a giant's shadow.

"Beneficial? As nobles of a *defeated* city, you would all be nothing!" Miliana's voice twisted like a poisoned dagger from the crowd. "But as willing lackeys of Svarézi, you keep your palaces while the citizens of Lomatra are crushed by Svarézi's taxes, and die in Svarézi's wars!"

Miliana had the commoners leaping to their feet and echoing her words. Fists pumped into the air as the gallery shook to the people's rage. The Blade Captains glared up at the mob in absolute disdain, then turned back to put the seal on their affairs.

"The vote proposed: That Lomatra declare a unity between its own Blade Council, and those of Sumbria, Colletro, and Zutria. Those in favor?"

"Wait!"

Prince Rosso shook like a leaf blown by a storm. All around him, his people roared in hatred for the council, demanding courage—demanding war. The little prince, sweating, tugged at his armor's tight gorget.

"Colleagues—this decision, it seems . . . it seems unpopular. It seems . . ." The prince jittered like a captive bug. "It seems . . . cowardly. Surely an alliance with our neighbors to the—"

"I think that option has already been discussed in full." Spirelli spared his fellow Blade Captains a glance rich with self-interested irony. "Shall we conclude our business with the vote?"

"No. No, not yet!" Desperate to at least delay their

inevitable fate, the prince scrabbled with the covers of the great book which lay upon the table—the Articles of Association for the Lomatran Free Company. "Um . . . wait a minute! It—it's just in here!" The prince flipped through vellum pages almost larger than he was tall. "Here we are . . . a recess may be declared without a vote, once only, if any member so demands." The prince jumped at the noise as he let the covers slam to the tabletop. "Well, I'm a member, and I do think that this requires more than just . . . just a quick vote without even a debate. The people really don't seem very happy at all."

The fat, barrel-shaped Blade Captain stirred in his chair.

"Oh, my liege, commoners never really do know what's good for them. This is why important decisions are left in the hands of better men."

"Even so, I'd like a recess, just so everyone can think about it." The prince banged his blade upon the table, almost jumping from the violent noise. "Dismissed! I—I mean, let's break until after lunchtime. Maybe until the second hour after noon?"

The Blade Captains exchanged weary sighs; shrugging amiably, they deferred to the wishes of the prince and pushed back their heavy chairs. Walking out beneath the fury of the city's common citizens, they wandered back to the comforts of their palace walls.

* * * * *

"Those treacherous, self-seeking, backstabbing, vermin ridden . . ."

When Miliana ran herself out of invective appropriate for a noble lady, Tekoriikii's head surfaced from behind the innkeeper's bar.

"Onk gronk!"

"Thank you . . . lowlife, frog-sucking scum!" Miliana slammed her back against the tavern wall, her face beet red with rage. "They're willing to sell you all into slavery for sake of a cash reward!"

The upper balcony above Lomatra's largest tavern, the Besotted Python, scarcely managed to rise above the worst of the noise. The taproom below had packed itself with soot-smeared workers from the powder mills and iron foundries, the joiners' guilds, the seamen's guilds, and masters of apprentice halls. Despite the sheeting rain, the streets about the tavern had jammed tight with angry crowds as half the city tried to cram inside to hear the news.

A guildmaster stood on a table railing at the crowd; although the commoners thundered their agreement to every single word, the citizens were utterly impotent. The Blade Captains were the Blade Captains, and they held the power.

In Sumbria, the citizens were taxed into the ground to finance the hiring of vast companies of mercenaries. Svarézi's agents roamed far and wide seeking swords-for-hire. There were turbanned horse archers from the south, brigands, berserkers, and buccaneers. Foreign mercenaries had already swept the cattle from Lomatra's outlying fields, fuel for an army which slept beneath a field of gallows trees.

"Kirenzia just fell!"

A soldier, one of Lomatra's city sentries, fought his way in through the throng. "I just saw the dispatch! Kirenzia is no more!"

Uproar swelled through the rain-soaked crowd. The soldier's voice diminished like a child's cries against the ocean's roar.

"I saw it! I saw the dispatch! They opened their gates in surrender, and Svarézi's mercenaries sacked the town! Not a man, woman, or stone still stands!"

A hundred voices shouted questions; Miliana leaned across the railings, keeping hold of her tall hat with one slim hand.

"You! You there . . . do your Blade Captains know?"

"What?" The soldier struggled in a tide of his fellow men. "Aye! They would have heard the news at dawn!"

Miliana turned and fixed her companions with a cold, hard stare; they returned to their drinking without a word being said.

Above the pandemonium, the balcony offered a tiny scrap of peace. A giant fish tank, suspended like a sedan chair between a sturdy pair of poles occupied pride of place on the floor. The pink nixie sat just underwater sucking on a squeeze bulb of wine, occasionally thrashing at the water with her webbed feet. Luccio's lake-bound princess had brought word of Zutria's fall, and had spent the next few hours curled despondently on the bottom of her cage.

Lorenzo was utterly outraged. Cramming fingers through his hair, he took a proffered glass of wine out of Tekoriikii's claws and swirled it in his grasp.

"*My* invention! He's killing people with my damned invention . . . "

"It's not your fault, Lorenzo." Miliana hung her head between her hands and stared in desperation at a blank tabletop. "No one blames you."

"It is my fault, because I made the cursed thing!" Lorenzo rammed himself back into a corner of the wall. "My light lathe! This is all because of me!"

Playing at being a waiter, Tekoriikii collected empty glasses, waddled over to the balcony rails, and let the tray of empties simply drop into the hall. He strutted happily back to his companions, oblivious to a chorus of screams from far below.

The irrepressible Luccio tried to be the voice of sweet reason amidst his friend's despair.

"All right—we know he's using the Sun Gem as a focus for the ray. Lorenzo, how long should the Sun Gem last?"

"Long enough." Lorenzo whirled, helpless rage burning in his eyes. "Luccio, it doesn't matter. The damage has been done. He's looted enough cities to hire an army a dozen times our size."

Cries rose from below as another speaker helplessly
harangued the crowd, offering fear without solutions.
Miliana ripped off her hat and cast the thing aside, flipping out long glorious sheets of mouse-brown hair.

"Did Svarézi bribe your council, or are they cowards of
their own accord?" The girl took off her spectacles to polish them, and felt them tremble in her grasp. "That
snail's the worst of them all! How did he get to have a
seat on your Blade Council?"

Lorenzo unconsciously held Miliana's hand.

"Well it's a free company, isn't it? I mean, he just
cruised out of an enchanted forest—the Satyrwood or
somewhere—about ten years ago, bringing enough mother-of-pearl to buy himself two palaces and a golden pleasure barge. He even changed his name. It used to be
Boble-boop, or some such sound."

"So, why Spirelli?"

"I'm not sure. I always thought it was a type of pasta."
Lorenzo drained half a glass of thin white wine. "Anyway—
Spirelli changed his treasure to cash, hired a thousand
troops, and bought himself the vote."

"Ha!" Miliana's bitterness hung in the air like knives.
"So it's money. Just money. The mercenary creed." The
girl slashed scorn across her own worthless "royal" heritage. "What a race of heroes we all are."

"It can't be helped." Luccio tried to pour balm on
Miliana's hurts while holding the finny hand of his nixie
princess. "Anyone can do it—it's all written in the Articles
of Association, you see—"

"It says nothing of the sort!" Lorenzo jutted out his
chin like a badly shaven battering ram. "You have to be a
citizen first."

"The snail, one hesitates to point out, was not a citizen to
begin with." Luccio gave his friend a leveling eye. "He simply lived here a year or more and paid taxes; he who pays
taxes is a citizen; once he became a citizen, he could become
a mercenary commander. Once he became a mercenary
commander, he had the vote—and, therefore, power."

"He just *made* himself a Blade Captain?" Miliana cocked her head, echoed by Tekoriikii at her side. "Just from scratch?"

"It took almost two hundred thousand ducats, but I believe that was the case." Luccio gave a dismissive wave of his hand and went back to stroking his aquatic princess's hair. "He owns half the city now—even the city hall, though as an act of largess he lets the city have it back for a mere peppercorn's rent."

Watched by an admiring Tekoriikii, Miliana arched slowly backward in her seat, her eyes fixed upon the ceiling beams. The whole room suddenly faded out of view as Luccio's words drifted through her mind.

Peppercorn rent . . . !

She felt herself drifting to her feet; with Tekoriikii's feathered presence to support her, she walked over to the balcony and stared down at the crowd.

Men cursed and swore, shouting to each other from a foot's distance away. They screamed advice and heeded none, like ants milling upward from a broken hill.

"What makes you all so angry?"

Choleric faces turned up to her; here and there a man recognized her from the council hall, and rumor buzzed swiftly that here stood Sumbria's exiled princess.

A hush spread as the closest men tried to hear what Miliana had to say. The girl leaned over the balcony, her lenses winking like a medusa's paralyzing stare.

"What did you expect? You handed these men your fates, and they used you! What else did you think they would do?"

"They're gentlemen! They're officers!" A man stood on a table and bellowed up at the girl. "Who are you to say they're scum?"

"Who is she?" Lorenzo leaned across the balcony, taking Miliana's hand. "She's Princes Miliana Mannicci Da Sumbria!"

Miliana took a firm mutual grip on Lorenzo's hand. Below them, a man struggled to make himself heard.

"It ain't right that we don't get listened to! The nobles are special-like! They ain't supposed to treat us like we was sheep!"

Loud, angry curses of approval followed, only to be stilled by Miliana's derisive laugh.

"What's the shame in being sheep, as long as your voices are heard? Make a stand, be proud, and tell them how you demand to be ruled! If the flock roars loud enough, then the gods themselves will have to take heed!

"We're citizens—not scum! This isn't Chondath—we aren't Chessentian slaves! Every citizen has a blade, and every blade has a right to be heard!"

People suddenly cheered in approval. Behind Miliana and Lorenzo, Tekoriikii strutted up and down, adding a touch of magnificence to the occasion. As the girl teetered upright on the balcony rails, the bird spread open his tail to frame Miliana with a brilliant fan of fire.

"You want to have your opinions heard? Then why not do it? Do it legally, and make them listen to you!" The girl shook a fist, almost losing balance as her voice rose into a peal of victory. "Could you use the vote if you had it? Would you really know what to do?"

Men and women roared out a thunderous reply. Miliana blinked and disappeared as the railings shook beneath her feet. Lorenzo and Tekoriikii raced to the edge of the balcony and looked down in fright, only to see Miliana buoyed up on a sea of triumphant hands.

Keeping her hat clapped to her head and her frothing petticoats in the air, Miliana bellowed up at Lorenzo's astonished face.

"Lorenzo! You wanted a revolution? Then bring every-one from outside!" The girl bobbed as she was passed slowly backward toward the tavern's bar. "And get me a bag of peppercorns! The biggest you can find!"

Amidst wild cheers, the crowd bore Miliana away. Tekoriikii alighted on the mob beside her, bobbing up and down like a duck on a pond as Lorenzo raced off to turn a kingdom upside down.

Luccio watched his friend race by and raised a puzzled little hand.

"Lorenzo? What's going on?"

"Peppercorn rent! Don't you see?" Lorenzo the inventor launched himself gaily down the stairs. "The entire population has just negotiated a severe cut in pay!"

The young man raced off to collect his newly-announced bride, leaving Luccio and Princess Krrrr-poka blinking at the dim, deserted hall.

* * * * *

"Meeting is brought to order! Will all counsellors please prepare to render forth their vote?"

Lomatra's fat Blade Captain hammered on the meeting table, utterly ignoring his prince; men drew their blades, preparing to hold them aloft or cast them down to indicate their vote. Gazing up at the empty audience galleries, Lomatra's prince bleated in alarm.

"Wait! The audience has not arrived."

"An unneeded distraction; I have ordered them barred from the hall." Blade Captain Spirelli extended his eyestalks with a silky smile. "Our business will be easier without them.

"Vote!"

"W-wait!" The prince leapt forward as the men reached for their blades once more. "Perhaps we should read the minutes of our last session?"

Spirelli jerked his eyestalks, then let them angrily extend.

"We all remember the last meeting. It is all perfectly fresh and clear. I must insist that the vote be taken and emissaries be dispatched to the Svarézi camp forthwith!"

The sounds of a mob clamored at the council gates. A soldier shouted a warning, then babbled as he was forcibly moved aside. The heavy doors slammed open, and a mighty mob of common citizens surged into the room, hooting and cheering the strange procession of figures at their head.

A girl, an inventor, and a giant bird; a courtier and a
female nixie in a clear glass tank formed the spearhead
of the charge. Blade Captains leapt to their feet and drew
their swords, halting in place as they saw themselves
outnumbered by hundreds to one.

Gleefully adjusting her spectacles, Miliana faced the
warlords with a grin. At her side, Lorenzo made a delighted bow.

"Greetings! We have news for the Blade Council of
Lomatra!"

"Revolution!" Spirelli recoiled, a look of pure horror in
his prehensile eyes. "The guard will never stand for this.
The army will have you hung!"

"Not a revolution; a reevaluation!" Miliana held aloft a
scroll, protected by a giant bird and a brace of blacksmiths armed with hammers and quarterstaves.

Next to Miliana, a Blade Captain raised his sword with
a snarl of rage. Miliana pointed a finger and cast her
feather fall spell, then grabbed the armored man with
one small hand and effortlessly threw him through the
air.

"Odd." Luccio watched Miliana's performance with a
pained expression on his face. "You know—I don't think
real feather fall spells work quite the way she thinks . . ."

Luccio's watery companion nodded agreement from her
tank, then settled back to watch the show.

Princess Miliana, late of Sumbria, made a great production of quoting from her scroll.

"Let it be known that these, the undersigned, being citizens of Lomatra, do hereby enlist in the regiment of
infantry raised by Lorenzo Utrelli Da Lomatra—being
paid the rate of one peppercorn per year! They have all
just been paid in full." Miliana spilled the scroll all over
the floor. "There are eight thousand signatures there
right now, with another four or five thousand on the way.
The guilds are making their own regiments—and so are
the city wives! They're electing captains to represent
them in council even as we speak!" Miliana planted a fist

on one bony hip in glee. "That's more votes than the rest of the army combined!"

"There're no votes here!" Spirelli oozed indignant bubbles from his shell. "These aren't soldiers . . . they're just a rabble!"

"Not so." Lorenzo had settled himself on a table, and was helping his confused prince flip through pages in Lomatra's Articles. "According to the Articles of Association, any annually paid, armed body of Lomatran citizens who swear oath to accept the command of another Lomatran citizen are deemed to be a legitimate regiment." The citizens of Lomatra growled behind him, shaking their collection of pitchforks, brickbats and quarterstaves. "These doughty citizens are armed, they have sworn allegiance, and they have all just been given their pay!" All across the hall and back into the streets, people held aloft their token peppercorns. "The Brigade of House Utrelli is, therefore, eight thousand strong! And our voice now carries eight thousand votes!

"I believe we shall now hear from House Utrelli's new political advisor."

Miliana bowed cordially to Lorenzo, allowed Tekoriikii to sweep her clean a seat, and made a place for herself at the council table.

"And now, gentlemen, I think his highness the prince had some very, very definite views of his own as to how the city affairs should be run. And for once, I think his council will listen with respect." A growl came from the citizens flocking the streets outside, and Miliana smiled happily as Lorenzo placed his hands on her shoulders from behind.

"Gentlemen? Let us see some of your military acumen in action. We have—at most—six weeks before Svarézi's army arrives."

15

Lomatra's preparations for war turned the winter into a frenzy of activity—most of which seemed to involve shouting. Soldiers drilled with pikes and crossbows, shouted at by sergeants of the guard; militia units formed, all yelling as they argued over who got the helmets with the cheek pieces, and who had to wear the breastplate with the holes. In the council chambers, the new age of "peppercorn democracy" led to wholesale hollering as citizen delegates bandied invective back and forth across the floor. Stuck in the middle of the whole madhouse, Miliana spent her days organizing helpless soldiers and her evenings searching for a headache-curing spell.

The primary cause of the headache was the sheer magnitude of the task in front of them. The alliance of the minor Blade Kingdoms could muster quite a busy little army, but they were still greatly outnumbered by Svarézi's minions. The market had been scoured of mercenaries, and militia units were of doubtful utility. Miliana refused to panic, and instead placed her faith in the fruits of Lorenzo's fertile mind.

As midwinter passed and astral-traveling scouts reported the concentration of Ugo Svarézi's regiments,

Miliana convened a meeting in the Besotted Python's taproom. Eager as puppies, Miliana, Tekoriikii, Luccio and his watery princess sat at a table and watched as Lorenzo proudly unshipped a mighty roll of plans.

Dressed in a trim blue gown and her fine, impressive hat, Miliana steepled up her fingers and brightly awaited Lorenzo's offerings.

"Well? So what have you invented?"

"Lots of things! We can dazzle the enemy with the products of our minds."

Luccio, Miliana, and the nixie princess all gathered around an excited Lorenzo. Tekoriikii sat in the wrought iron chandelier above, hanging his long neck down to stare this way and that as the young inventor proudly spread out the harvest of his genius.

There were drawings of earth borers, of reaping machines and rocket-assisted swords. There were smoke powder guns and spears and things with prongs. Lorenzo had even designed boots fitted with little wheels for rapid troop deployment: a hundred fantastic new inventions that would win him fame for a hundred thousand years.

. . . And very little that would stop a horde of pikemen walking straight over Lomatra's walls. Overhead, Tekoriikii bobbed his plumes and fixed the diagrams with a puzzled yellow eye.

"Gronk nonk! Onkie-doodle gronk nonk!"

Lunch arrived; beans and sausages baked in a ceramic pot. Miliana heaved out a sigh and began to jam a spoon into their midday meal. Lorenzo looked avidly from face to face, wondering why he had not yet been overwhelmed with applause.

"But, don't you see? Can't you imagine what an army could achieve if it was equipped with all of these?" The inventor rose up to his feet with an impassioned cry. "The wheel-boots, and the retractable stilts for fording streams alone should be enough to bring us victory!"

Miliana irritably ground her spoon into the beans.

"Lorenzo—we need *a* secret weapon—just one, or

maybe two. We don't have an infinite number of hands."

Trying to help, Tekoriikii flexed his wings and wagged them hopefully.

"No, darling. We need something other than a flying machine—but thank you very much for offering . . ."

A delicate girl-face lifted up from its mobile fish tank and whispered shyly in Luccio's ear. The man listened, nodded in languid agreement, and then leaned back in his chair.

"Princess Krrrr-poka points out that if we can only pursue one major project, then it must cover as many of our weaknesses as possible." The slim young man made an elegant motion of his hand. "So, then, let us define what the strengths of our opponent are, and what our own weaknesses may be."

"Numbers!" Miliana excitably waved her hands. "We're outnumbered by about ten to one."

"Oh, numbers!" Lorenzo snapped his fingertips in Tekoriikii's astonished face. "Numbers are only people. People we can handle. It's their magic that's a proble—"

"Ha!" Surging to her feet in triumph, Miliana pointed a finger right between Lorenzo's eyes. "So you admit it! Magic is superior to technology!"

"No it isn't! It just happens to be a problem here and now."

"So technology is weaker, so I'm the best!" Miliana crashed her hands together, everything else forgotten in a sudden rush of glee. "You said it . . . we all heard you!"

Miliana and Lorenzo flung themselves into an animated argument. The firebird took the opportunity to claim Lorenzo's chair and help himself to his dinner bowl of sausages and beans.

Ignoring the activities of his friends, Luccio steepled his hands in thought.

"So what we need is something immune to an overabundance of enemy pike, cavalry, and crossbows. Something that uses minimum manpower to tie up a maximum number of enemy. Something proof against the normal types of battle spell." The courtier delicately plucked a sausage from the terra-cotta dinner bowl and lowered it into the nixie's mouth. "What can we create that will allow us to overcome a mercenary army ten times as large?" Luccio dabbled his fingers in his girlfriend's water tank. "Miliana? A list of common battle spells, if you please."

Abandoning her fruitless argument with Lorenzo, Miliana briskly ticked spell titles off against her fingertips.

"Well, there's magic missiles and minor projectile spells, heat metal, warp wood . . ."

"Hmmmmm . . . very good for fouling up arrows, wagon wheels and spears."

"Yes. Then there's your lightning bolt and fireball; poison fogs like stinking clouds and cloudkill . . . illusion spells, I guess . . ." Miliana crinkled her freckled nose in a scowl. "Anything bigger than that, and it's time to run like squealing weasels!"

Lorenzo, oblivious to the whole conversation, wonderingly lifted the lid from a pot of beans.

"Where do they make these things, anyway?"

"They bake them down on High Street." Luccio answered with a dismissive wave.

Miliana slapped at Lorenzo's hands as the inventor hit the pot a blow with the butt end of his rapier. "Stop that!" she scolded, "You'll get beans on Tekoriikii!"

"But the pot's tough . . . it doesn't break!"

"It's not clay, its made from ground-up shells. If it was clay, the heat would crack it." Luccio took the bowl away. "Leave it alone and tell us what you want to do."

"Do? Do!" Lorenzo suddenly whipped papers aside and drew sketches directly onto the tabletop. "I know what to do!" Moving faster than a genie, the inventor had already settled on his plans. "Brilliant! Luccio tell your girlfriend I'll need a hundred bags of sponges, and as many stinging jellyfish as her people can find."

"Right!" Luccio stuffed his head underwater and began to talk in a mumbling stream of bubbles. Lorenzo wrenched the man back out into the open air and continued with his interrupted orders.

"After that, I want you to collect cart horses, shells, and

all the spyglasses you can find. Miliana, I need the entire potters' guild and the wheelwrights' guild here within the hour."

"Right!" Luccio leapt to his feet, streaming water from his hair. "Anything else?"

"Some more beans?" Lorenzo held up his plate in dismay. "Tekoriikii's eaten all of mine."

* * * * *

"My liege?"

Ugo Svarézi stood overlooking the nighttime campfires of a mighty army. The whole bowl-shaped Valley of Umbricci had been turned into one massive military camp. The cooking fires curved high up the mountainsides where they twinkled in the dark like countless stars.

The stars twinkled because men moved between the onlookers and the flames; the army was on the move, leaving its fires burning as a decoy for any airborne eyes. Svarézi watched as his vanguard spurred off down the road, dark-skinned horse archers hired *en masse* from the hot lands far to the west. Behind them came artillery and wagonloads of hireling sorcerers; the heavy weapons were kept up at the blade edge of the march, ensuring quick deployment on the battlefield.

Svarézi was well pleased with his efforts through the months of wind and rain. He had snatched up minor kingdoms during winter lulls, picking them up like plums before his enemies realized he had struck. By stripping his conquests to the bone for ready cash, he had acquired a mercenary army virtually overnight.

Labor conscription had stripped the mines of metal; the enormous civilian casualties would breed back their numbers with time. For the moment, all that mattered was the short-term goal.

Now, with the harvest season about to begin, his enemies should be dispersed into their fields. Their armies would take many vital days to gather in from their winter quarters; Svarézi's troops would overrun the city-state of Lomatra in a matter of hours.

And with Lomatra gone, the scattering of still-independent towns would sue for peace. In less than a year, Svarézi would have accomplished what no other man had ever done; he would have welded the Blade Kingdoms into a single entity beneath a single crown.

The Akanal would lie before him like a kid for the slaughter. Decadent old kingdoms to the east—more squabbling city-states and pitiful Chondath lined the Vilhon Reach to the west—barbarian lands stretched on to the south. Within a few years, he could carve a bloody empire across the face of Faerûn.

An empire ruled by one lethal, tireless king.

Tethered behind Svarézi, the black hippogriff Shaatra stirred. The creature winced as Svarézi curbed her with a glance before turning back to his waiting officers.

"What of the errant Sumbrian companies?"

"Orlando Toporello and his followers?" A lean Sumbrian officer—one of the new breed arisen over the ashes of the old—laughed aloud in scorn. "Our agents found him; he refused your gold and silver. He says that money defiles a 'true soldier's' hands."

"Then he will make a very poor mercenary." Svarézi slowly settled his black burgonet helmet on his head. Toporello's reticence was almost annoying; two thousand fully armored cavalry would bring a solid backbone to his army's rabble of riffraff from the west. "Forget him. He will need gold to feed his horses soon enough."

Chessentian free-lancers of Helyos's Renegades rode past along the road below, four thousand strong in articulated metal shells. They would be chaff before Blade Kingdom lancers in an all-out charge, but their sheer numbers would serve to simply overawe most mortal enemies. They had a cruel streak Svarézi had come to admire. The prince of the Blade Kingdoms watched his vanguard thunder down the valley road, then clutched a fistful of feathers from Shaatra's mane and swung up into his own saddle.

"Move the main body out immediately—pikes to the fore and crossbows at the rear." Shaatra shivered, arched and flapped her wings as Svarézi raked her sleek black flanks with his spurs. "Burn the Lomatran villages at will. Kill at need; they will offer peace soon enough. We'll have no need for Lomatra—or its fields—as a base for our swords."

Kicking at his hippogriff, Svarézi clawed aloft. The black shape swept low across an army teeming through the dark like countless ants. He framed himself against the dark, then faded out into the night on silent wings.

* * * * *

Scudding low across the chalky hillsides in the light of dawn, a patrol of Colletran hippogriffs whipped just above the trees. The dawn dew hissed beneath their pale brown wings—leaves flicked at hooves and talons as the mighty beasts rippled past the boughs. Marked only by the flap and swerve of feathers in the breeze, the air cavalry made a silent race against the sun.

Their orders were to make a swift, unseen reconnaissance, to check the dispositions of the Lomatran alliance, and to confirm that their troops were still not mustered.

The scout troop's commander had other, more ambitious plans. Who could forget the air commander Otorelli Lambruccini, who had alighted on the gates of Zutria so long ago? In a single swoop he had flung open the city gates and won a bloodless victory! There was not an air cavalryman alive who didn't cherish Lambruccini's triumph in his dreams.

A silent approach, a quick sweep up onto Lomatra's walls, and who knew what the results might be? Looking back at the perfect arrowhead formation of nine hippogriffs to his rear, the commander felt cold shivers of anticipation ripple up his spine.

"Tekorii-kii-kii! Tekorii-kii-kii!"

A hippogriff screamed in fear; two more took frantic evasive action and collided in midair, spilling their riders free. The scout commander halted at his reins in fright, then felt his mount buck in pain as the hairs were plucked clean out of its tail.

A thunderbolt of orange raffia-work rattled gaily past, tossing plundered hairs into the breeze. Rustling its feathers in delirious abandon, the giant orange bird turned a lazy roll and pulled the helmet plumes clean off a rider's head.

Hippogriffs broke left and right; another pair climbed clumsily up toward the sun. Shocked almost to death, the scout commander ripped his composite bow out of its sheath and clumsily fumbled an arrow into place.

"Numbers one and six—fork left and right!" The young commander stood up in his stirrups, staring wildly at the bird. "Kill it quickly! It's some sort of predator!"

He took aim at the orange bird, led the target and made allowance for the wind, then felt his eyes cross as the fantastic bird opened up its beak and sang.

Tekoriikii was having an utterly glorious day. He had risen up to greet the sun, dancing high above the clouds while Miliana and his good friends marveled at him from below. The air was crisp, the skies were clear, and now a horde of bumbling enemies had come to offer him their tails. Singing for the pure joy of it all, the bird turned giddy circles as he whirred his way back home.

The effect of Tekoriikii's song on the air cavalry was nothing short of pure disaster. The leader's composite bow opened like a chrysanthemum flower as the music turned mere glue to water. Horn, sinew, wood, and bone all curled out into individual loops and springs, leaving the human staring at his weapon in dumbfounded dismay.

"It's a secret weapon! Fly for reinforcements!"

One glimpse at the flat fields all about Lomatra was enough. The green land was dotted with formations of troops—with wagons and haystacks in a strange, regular display. Turning sharply to the north, the hippogriff scouts fled back toward their army as a signal arrow puffed smoke from Lomatra's walls.

* * * * *

Dawn stained the Lomatran fields with a light of softest gold, sheeting pure and ethereal between a thinning hint of clouds. The mountains to the north were blocks of purple shadow; the fields were hard and flat, not yet plowed for the season's wheat. The world seemed hushed with expectation as if bathed in newborn light.

The plains had been spread with haystacks and towering bundles made of twigs. They stood in rigid, neat formations, each surrounded by teams of men and women dressed in a motley armor made from old plowshares, pots, and pans. Behind them, the professional soldiers gathered in dense ranks—Lomatra's foot and cavalry, bolstered by the small offerings of independent principalities and towns. The clashing riot of their uniforms—puffed and slashed tunics of a thousand tasteless hues—lent a strange air of festival to the morning.

Restless militia armed with makeshift spears thronged the fields behind. They clustered in their thousands, waving banners proudly emblazoned with peppercorns, restlessly watching as something moved out through the city gates.

Lomatra's Blade Council moved silently out to take the place of honor at the army's head. A giant snail on horseback and a dozen reluctant nobles made for a poor display; they looked about themselves as though seeking a face-saving escape, never once failing to notice the crossbowmen posted to their rear.

The new commanders emerged, to be met by a dutiful cheer, and the crowd's joy soared as a scrawny little figure struggled out into the light. Sitting, stunned, on his huge horse, half lost inside his armor and polishing his spectacles in wonderment, Prince Rosso of Lomatra was almost overwhelmed by a wave of adoration. The most popular prince in the history of the city-state moved hesitantly forward, a smile breaking out on his face as he felt the roaring, wild approval of the crowd.

Soldiers clustered boisterously about, slamming at his cuisses and promising unending fight. Helmets were hoisted atop pikes, drums beat, and trumpets soared. The little villages of the outer foothills shouted out their love for the little Prince of Peppercorns.

A second cry arose—thunderous approval for the city's living treasure-trove. Borne aloft on the shoulders of the guildmasters of the city halls, Lorenzo Utrelli Da Lomatra blushed at the unexpected adulation.

Bobbing up and down at his side, Miliana and Tekoriikii gazed blandly out across the churning masses of armed and armored men.

"Gronk nonk!"

"No no . . . you stay and wait for the hippogriffs. You know what to do."

"Nurgle!" The firebird chuffed out his tail and swaggered himself from side to side. *"Tekoriikii nurgle!"*

The transport committee drew to a halt as Lorenzo and his friends came level with Lomatra's prince. Lorenzo doffed his velvet cap to his elected liege and tried to shout above the chaotic noises of the crowd.

"My lord!"

"My boy!" The prince joined Miliana in a contest of spectacle polishing. "You have inspected your machines?"

"They are perfectly ready, my lord. I promise you that they will change the very face of war."

"Then I wish you all luck, and may the gods smile upon the right." The prince peered myopically toward the passes to the north. "For I see our opponents have finally arrived."

Miliana and Lorenzo struggled to turn about. From their vantage point atop the mob, they could see clear across the fields.

Spilling like a locust plague across the violet hills, there came a foul black stain. It came from the dense-packed bodies of lancers, scouts, and mounted archers—of pikemen, crossbowmen, foot soldiers, and halberdiers. Mercenaries from a dozen different lands crammed into the fields. Their lust for gold hurtled them down at the tiny little city sleeping on the shore.

The sight galvanized the allied army. The elected prince conferred with the Lomatran lords, then called for their banners to be raised.

Prince Rosso looked to Miliana for support.

"I would prefer to move immediately. That's the right thing, don't you think my dear? Deny them time to set up artillery and complex spells?"

"Meet them in the plains, my lord." Lorenzo removed his untidy cap and clapped on the scorched, blackened helm he wore in his laboratory. "We'll hit them in the center, and you can follow with the infantry." The inventor climbed atop a strangely solid haystack and bellowed out to the waiting crews. "Prepare to mount! Breach—*Haystacks!*"

Much to the delight of the crowd, Miliana allowed Tekoriikii to help her struggle up out of the arms of the infantry. Lorenzo goggled at her as she passed him on her way to the haystack's crest.

"Are you coming too?"

"Of course I'm coming. I'm not putting you out there alone!"

"It might be dangerous . . ."

"They burned my house, killed my father, and plucked my favorite bird!" Miliana took her place atop the haystack's crest. "I'm damned if I'll miss the final battle. It's time to make my father writhe in his grave!"

Tekoriikii faced the audience with a solemn little nod of agreement, and the army shook the heavens with their cheers.

Princess Miliana suddenly became the center of attention on the field. Borne up by a soaring storm of cheers, she stood forth before them like a warrior queen of old. With banners snapping at her back and a giant orange firebird at her side, she struck a pose and made a speech, her voice soaring out like a thunderbolt across the people's minds.

"Yes, I'm coming! Why should a princess hold herself more dear than the freedom of our citizens? Why should I sit idle when a tyrant comes howling at our door?" The princess snatched off her pointed hat and raised it to the sound of soldiers' cheers. "Democracy can't be made from an armchair, safe at home! Form up the citizen battalions! Bring freedom to the Blade kingdoms!

"I say the age of tyranny is *done!*"

The crowd roared and shook their weapons for their little princess. Climbing from her high summit, Miliana jammed a hand down through the haystack and ripped open a hidden hatch, then disappeared waist-deep into the straw.

"War-turtles . . . *march!*"

With a lurch, the haystack split apart. Bursting out into open view came a sinister war machine shaped like an inverted soup bowl, which rumbled slowly off across the plains. From her perch up at the top hatch of the revolving turret, Miliana waved a triumphant fist to the full-throated roar of the army.

Thirty haystacks erupted; angular, sinister, and sheathed with brilliant mirror tiles, Lorenzo's hideous inventions moved off to a jerky start. Lorenzo passed his father and his brother where they stood with the heavy cavalry and gave them a salute; shooing Tekoriikii off the port side hatch, the artist crawled into the depths of his mighty vehicle and swiftly disappeared.

Watching the formation of war-turtles depart, Lorenzo's father snorted disapproval through his beard.

"I still say it's no way to fight a war." The old man slammed down his visor and grabbed Lorenzo's muscle-brained brother by the arm. "Get mounted, boy! There'll be no end to this damned battle until we've staved in some heads in the old, traditional way. . . ."

The senior Utrelli joined the ranks of his prince's heavy cavalry. The mighty cavalcade spurred off after the war machines as the Lomatran hills turned black with the sheer number of their enemies.

16

"My liege—they've summoned earth elementals!"

A staff officer turned his golden horse to Svarézi, proffering a spyglass. "There . . . heading toward the center of the plain . . ."

Dust clouds had risen from the fields, helping to obscure the view. Svarézi bullied his hippogriff into standing still, then leveled the perspective glass and scowled down from on high. It took long moments for him to sift the confusing images into order in his mind.

The plain was dotted with giant shapes; juggernauts rolling with a smooth motion that told of wheels. Each object shone a painful silver in the morning light, almost hiding its inverted soup-bowl shape. Svarézi studied the twin wheel tracks the machines left behind in the dirt and slammed shut his telescope with a confident bang.

"War wagons."

"My lord?"

"War wagons. A common enough ploy used by peasant armies fearful of cavalry." Svarézi sat straight in his saddle with one fist proudly planted on his hip. "An enclosed wagon, armored with timber and steel; the interior is filled with crossbowmen, archers . . . even light artillery.

"They're vulnerable to magic. We'll warp the wooden wheels—use fire spells to touch off their superstructures. Keep the combat troops back, and send in the sorcerers for their sport."

Svarézi looked at his titanic army and for the first time let his face stir with pride.

"Bring up the Sun Cannon! We'll overturn their little carts, vaporize some of their infantry, then see their faces as we melt a hole clean through their city walls."

The mercenary officers exchanged low, cruel smiles as far below, the great battle was finally joined.

* * * * *

"Target left! *Left!*" Miliana took her eye away from the padded periscope and crashed her pointy hat down across the gunner's head. "There, stupid, rotate the damned turret or I'll wring your neck!"

The worst-tempered vehicle commander in the army cursed and drove her crew into obedience. Wrenching frantically at the traversing cog, the war-turtle's gunner swung the turret to the left and let his sights settle on a proud line of sorcerers readying lethal battle spells.

"I see them . . . I mean . . . target sighted!"

Miliana ferociously crammed her face against the viewing slot.

"All right—steady . . . steady . . . Shoot!"

The spring arms of the turtle's springal hammered wildly at her side; Miliana watched a cloud of heavy javelins soar out at the enemy, then all spin uselessly aside as one of the sorcerers made an easy gesture with one hand.

"Damn! He's got a spell up to protect him from normal missiles." The girl watched her target with her face set in a snarl. "Load abnormal missiles!" The gunner slammed a bundle of pre-blessed javelins into place. "All right . . . open fire!"

The turret bucked as the springal hammered out its load. Seen dimly through a haze of dust, the Svarézi sorcerers whirled brokenly aside. Apprentices dropped their books, bells, and candles, and began to run, falling one by one as a flywheel catapult spurted darts from deep inside the turtle's bows.

Other war machines in line with Miliana were having similar success. The juggernauts rolled on, crunching corn stubble under their wheels. Miliana looked down from her high seat to where Lorenzo labored in the dark; the girl excitedly wiped her sweating brow and gave a smile.

"It's brilliant! The war-turtles are actually working!"

"Of course they're working." Lorenzo prodded at a horse's neck and kept power surging through the hull. "I told you they would, didn't I?"

Lorenzo's latest masterpieces were an engineering triumph; inverted bowls of dense ceramic formed the hulls, which were modeled on the bowls used for Lomatran baked beans. Inside the hulls, six huge horses shod in insulated ceramic shoes provided motive power. The vehicle was suspended above the ground by four wide-rimmed ceramic wheels, and trailed leather curtains to seal the hull against the earth.

Atop the horses rode a platform housing two crossbowmen, a flywheel-powered dart projector, and Lorenzo, the turtle's elected driver. In the revolving turret up above, Miliana, a loader, and a gunner dispensed mayhem like children flinging rocks at nests of bees. The double springal sent shudders through the whole machine as it flung loads of missiles out across the fields.

"Earth elemental at one hundred yards . . . Damn—it's overturned number seven!" Miliana swore as a wave of living soil flipped a war-turtle completely over on its side. "Grab its attention! Load blessed ammunition!"

"Loaded!" The springal crew worked with admirable speed. "I see it."

"Shoot!"

Something made the war-turtle tingle as the great weapon fired. From his perch above the horses, Lorenzo looked up in alarm

"What was that?"

"Warp wood spell." Miliana kept her eye glued to her periscopes. "There's a bunch of druids to the left. Svarézi must have hired them in from Turmish. Good thing we used whalebone for the springals. Damn; missed the elemental! Fire again—quickly!"

The whole machine bucked as the catapult fired. Miliana clenched her fists with glee.

"Spitted him with half a dozen!" The girl looked down into the turtle's hull. "Lorenzo—got your sword?"

"Why?"

The answer came as a great heave of the ground. The horses screamed, the whole framework groaned, and a great roaring head made out of soil erupted between the wheels. Lorenzo squealed like a frightened pig, whipped out his rapier, and jammed it in the earth elemental's brow. He jerked the power trigger and sent his last remaining electric charge crackling right between its eyes. The elemental crumbled like a sand castle in the wind, leaving Lorenzo to plaster himself across the back of a trembling horse.

High above, Miliana looked down with a frown.

"Watch where you're steering, dolt, we're going to hit a tree!" The whole contraption rocked, a crunching noise followed, and Miliana scowled into her periscopes. "Oh wait . . . it's all right. It was only the druids." The girl polished up her periscope lens. "Drat! There's mistletoe hanging off the outside . . ."

A fireball enfolded the hull, failing to even singe the clever ceramic armor. Here and there a lightning bolt flickered in defiance at the far end of the battle line, ricocheting from the insulated armor. Flipping up her periscope and taking advantage of a temporary lull, Miliana sat back in her chair and heaved a great bloodthirsty sigh.

"It's not bad, this. First we invent the peppercorn vote, and now we overturn the whole basis of modern war." Poison fog from something like a cloudkill suddenly began to creep in through the vision slots. Unconcerned, Miliana slipped on a leather mask and breathed from the vehicle's stored air supply. Her muffled voice rang Lorenzo's praise.

"All in all, I think this battle's going pretty well so far!"

The war-turtles clanked ever onward, while all across the fields the last Svarézi sorcerers broke and ran.

* * * * *

High above the melee, the Svarézi air cavalry wheeled in an enormous holding pattern as they watched the unfolding drama of the battlefield. Rumbling out from the city walls came strange enclosed war wagons, closely followed by a dense rush of infantry. The Lomatran mounted corps—what few horsemen and hippogriffs they could muster—all stood their beasts before the city gates, behind a haystack barricade. Clad in scarlet armor and soaring like a war god through the clouds, the captain of Svarézi's air troops let his face split into a gap-toothed smile.

"Cousin! They have isolated their mounted men."

"Aye, cousin . . ." The captain's second in command—leaner, hungrier, and clad in a purple brigantine, flexed the sinews of his bow. "We can fall on them from behind and crush them into their own retreating war wagons!"

"Good—it is done!" The captain jabbed his laboring mount with his heels. Throwing back its head, the creature gave a piercing rally-scream. "Wings in line astern—attack dive!"

"Wait!"

A terrified voice drifted up from below. The commander hauled back on his reins, bringing an answering surge from the powerful wings beating at his sides. He peered down past the hippogriff's smooth wings to see a tiny flier desperately climbing up to join him.

"Wait! Captain, I see it! The red bird—it's over there—hiding in the trees!"

The air commander rolled his eyes; the morning's scout reports had been less than satisfactory.

"One bird?"

"No, captain! *The* bird! The red bird!" The scout finally reached a decent altitude for conversation; he seemed sweaty, shaken, and his equipment hung in rags. "It's waiting to take us in the flank as we pass!"

The ferocious killer bird in question could just be seen as it sat in the boughs of an olive tree, bouncing happily up and down like a child on a swing. It looked far too stupid to be anything other than an escapee from some noble's pleasure garden.

However, the scout commander had managed to lose almost half his patrol. The air captain and his cousin exchanged glances across the wings of their hippogriffs, then shrugged in silent accord.

"We'll make our course take us past the bird. We can try arrow shots at the beast in passing." Irritated by the delay, the commander hoisted up his bow. "Now enough! Attack formation—dive!"

Five hundred hippogriffs turned sharp wing stalls and dove in tight formations toward the city far below. Wind whistled through a thousand wings; sunlight glinted off outstretched hooves and claws. All along the battle squadrons, men added their shrieks to the bloodcurdling sound of monster eagles' screams.

Bouncing happily up and down in the branches of its olive tree, the ferocious red bird seemed utterly engrossed in its own affairs. He genially wig-wagged his wings as he saw the hundreds of horribly be-weaponed hippogriffs diving straight down his throat, then threw back his head and opened his beak in glee.

Diving in the middle of the swarm, the Colletran scout leader instantly turned a strange shade of mottled green.

"Don't let it sing! For Tchazzar's sake, don't let it sing!"

In the tree below, Tekoriikii fluffed out his tail and crooned a little song that told of the glories of his long-and-lovely tail. He warbled in brilliant counterpoint to his own complex tune, losing himself in the gorgeous complexity of his musical creation.

The upper end of Tekoriikii's vocal range achieved very little other than causing the wine in Lomatra's tavern barrels to turn instantly to vinegar. The lower notes, apparently pitched to the resonant frequency of a hippogriff's brain, had an altogether different effect. The diving battle mounts staggered as though they had run into a solid wall and began to emit weird, keening moans. Some of the beasts simply rolled over on their backs, spilling wailing riders from their seats where they frantically activated feather fall rings. Other hippogriffs drifted to the ground and tried to cram their crania far beneath the soil.

Annoyed at the lack of audience appreciation, Tekoriikii scowled, fluffed out his feathers, and flew away in a huff. High above the damaged squadrons, the scout leader unplugged his ears and rallied two hundred panicked survivors who swerved like mad canaries through the air.

"There it goes! Don't let it get away!"

Demoralized and shaken, the ravaged squadrons clattered off in pursuit. Looking slyly behind him as he skimmed low across the ground toward long rows of haystacks, the orange bird suddenly gave the lie to its apparent lack of brains. With a decidedly smug flick of its tail, the bird made its escape toward the city walls.

"Kill it! Kill the creature before it sings again!"

The bird whipped low over the ground. Following with a hue and cry in a motley line abreast, two hundred fliers crowded after Tekoriikii in pursuit.

All along the city walls, blacksmiths' apprentices tipped anvils from the battlements. Ropes whipped taught, driveshafts blurred, and suddenly a shocking forest of whirring propellers shot up from the haystacks all around.

The Utrelli Patent Whirligigs buzzed skyward like a swarm of wasps, each trailing part of an enormous fishing net. Some hippogriffs managed to somehow pull themselves aside; others slammed into the netting and tangled helplessly inside. Buoyed by the whirligigs, the captives swung like feathered herring in a net.

"Tekorii-kii-kii! Tekorii-kii-kii!"

Still somehow surviving, the scout commander heard the firebird's mocking cry. His hippogriff now shared its rider's ragged breathing and red-rimmed eyes. A dozen fellow air cavalry panted through the air, wildly searching for diving enemies.

Nothing attacked; there was nothing but the braying, hooting firebird whizzing off toward the city gates. The portcullis had been lowered almost to the ground—and the scout leader instantly sensed his victory.

"Dive right for its tail! It'll pull up before it hits the wall. Follow behind and kill it as it pulls up to fly across!"

They had speed on the bird; speed and height. A deadly dive, a flash of spears, and vengeance would be theirs. With a trilling whoop, twelve hippogriff cavalry made sharp wing-overs and sped toward the ground.

Tekoriikii blurred his silly, stubby wings, dragging his brilliant tail across the sky. He sped scarcely a wingtip's length above the ground toward a gateway now fixed at only two feet tall. No airborne creature could possibly make the gap. The hippogriffs hurtled themselves into greater speed, long wings whipping up and down as they outstretched their deadly claws.

"Tek Tek-a-tek Tekorii-kii-kii!"

As the scout leader goggled, a small sally port opened in the portcullis. The bird folded flat its wings and shot like an arrow through the little door, which instantly slammed shut in its wake.

Hippogriff riders, moving too fast to break off their manic dives, hauled at their reins and screamed. Men collided with each other, plowed into the moat, or crashed straight into the gatehouse walls. Screaming like a frightened maid, the scout leader somehow laid his hippogriff on its side; man and mount slammed into the hard-packed road and slithered on their flanks, screaming in fear as the jagged portcullis spines ripped past—a hairsbreadth overhead.

They hit a garbage barrel, showering themselves with refuse until they came to rest buried in a pile of dung. Flapping weakly in shock and pain, the scout leader and his battle steed could do nothing but collapse as a brilliant orange figure fluttered to rest at their side.

"Glub glub!"

Tekoriikii made to sing a song of triumph over his vanquished foes, but to his extreme annoyance, both man and hippogriff screamed in fright and fainted clean away. Sniffing in injured pride, the bird scraped dust over his victims with his claws, fluffed up his tail feathers, and strutted off toward the battlefield.

* * * * *

From his vantage point behind the lines, Svarézi slammed his perspective glass shut. His sorcerers streamed in panic from the field, hounded by monsters summoned by enemy magicians; his entire corps of mages had been destroyed by a peasant militia crammed into wagons.

Svarézi's brooding silence was terrible to behold. He watched the enemy war wagons halting to allow their infantry to close the gaps between the vehicles and slowly begin trundling onward toward his own battle lines.

Behind him, an officer stilled his own pure silver warhorse with a pat of one armored hand.

"We disabled almost ten of them, sire."

"Ten." Svarézi's voice remained utterly without tone. "I see."

"Rock to mud spells proved fairly effective."

Svarézi swung himself up into his hippogriff's saddle, stilling the creature's brooding backward glance with a scowl. He wrapped the reins about one wrist.

"They have demolished a sorcery corps which cost almost three hundred thousand ducats to amass—and all for the cost of ten wagons bogged in the mud." Svarézi kept his cold, professional stare locked on the advancing attack. "We shall make an all-arms assault at the center of their line. Use one third of the army and match them one-to-one. Once the Lomatran forces are committed, I will personally lead the reserves on a drive to the city gates.

"The Sun Cannon will wait until we have descended the hill slopes out of line of sight, and then have it blow their wagons clean away."

Svarézi raised one black, mailed fist, then dropped his open hand to point straight at the valley floor. Behind him twenty thousand densely packed infantry, demi-lancers, and knights surged toward Lomatra like a vast, organic wall.

* * * * *

"Here they come! I think we've jerked their chains." Miliana had been sitting perched on the upper turret hatch of her war-turtle, watching Tekoriikii's antics overhead. Her reverie came to a dramatic end as catapults began firing from the ridges overhead. "Stir up the horses, and let's get moving!"

She slammed shut the hatch, flicked mistletoe onto Lorenzo's back, and heard a muffled sound of voices from outside as militia packed themselves tight behind the war-turtle's hull. The surviving vehicles scuttled on across the ground like deadly crabs, thickening out a line of the Lomatran alliance's best infantry.

Safely inside the armored hull, Miliana frowned, crammed her eyes against her periscopes, and gave a sudden curse.

"Lorenzo—you know how I said we were outnumbered about three to one?"

"What?" Lorenzo peered through his driving slits, steering the huge vehicle by a series of cranks and ratchets. "Yes?"

"I lied. There's ten to one odds out there, or I'm a garden gnome!"

"It doesn't matter!" Lorenzo let his vision slit clank shut, the hull outside rattling to a sudden rain of arrow fire. "Is Tekoriikii clear?"

"What?"

"Did Tekoriikii get rid of all their air cavalry?"

"Yes!" Miliana had to shout above the awful clatter of hooves, springal winches, and catapult wheels inside the belly of the wagon. "When should he make his run?"

"Not until all their troops have moved away from the artillery!" Lorenzo swung the war-turtle to the left, where it jounced over the ruins of a warrior-priest of Tempus's portable battle shrine. "All we need to do is get that bird to the Sun Cannon, and we can retire behind the city walls."

Suddenly the entire universe lit brighter than a bomb; searing white light glared in through the vision slits, burning paint and scorching skin that fell beneath the beams. The war-turtle shuddered as a shock wave trembled through the ground.

Wide-eyed as an owl, Miliana gazed down at Lorenzo in shock.

"What in the name of Talos's tongue was that?"

Crew commanders flung open their hatches to stare. In the center of the alliance battle line, a smoking crater still glowed with molten lava at the rims. A scorched debris of pikes and polearms showed the fate of a company of infantry.

The surrounding regiments were milling in disarray; men who had been gazing in the direction of the blast were blinded by the dazzle. Lorenzo stuck his head out into the open air, stared at the blazing destruction, and gave a bitter curse.

"Miliana! Signal the other war-turtles!"

"Was that the Sun Cannon?" The girl still seemed

frozen in utter disbelief. "Was it? Was that the Sun Cannon?"

"Yes, it was the damned Sun Cannon!" Lorenzo abandoned his horses and crawled across the crossbowmen's firing platform to reach the rear of the vehicle. "Miliana! Signal the turtles to make smoke! We're abandoning the infantry!"

"Abandoning them?" The princess wrenched herself around, tangling skirts and frilly knickers as she tried to find the artist as he crawled under her. "We can't leave them all alone!"

"We have to!" A fuse sparked off a pot filled with a sulphurous black brew. "The Sun Cannon can't shoot at what it can't see! We'll leave the infantry in the smoke screen, and the turtles will draw its fire." Lorenzo set his smudge pot spewing dense clouds of smoke behind the tank and crawled clumsily over the backs of his draft horses. "The turtles will punch through the center of their battle line and head for their reserves."

"Lorenzo—we can't leave the infantry all alone against those . . . hordes!"

Lorenzo slipped into his seat, flipped open his vision flaps, and wrenched the vehicle over to one side.

"It's safer! Once his army closes with the infantry, the Sun Cannon can't fire at them any more!"

Once again the outside world sheeted brilliant white. This time the beam centered on a war-turtle, hit the mirror tiles sheathing the ceramic skin, and scattered wildly away. The searing light scorched soil to the turtle's front and melted the mirrors, but left the vehicle unharmed. The singed leviathan staggered but struggled on, its crew insulated from the heat by the ceramic hull.

Pulling free her spectacles to reveal a sunburned face, Miliana risked a peek at the outside world, then scowled down at Lorenzo.

"What are these damned things made out of anyway?"

"They're mirror tiles; silver sprayed over the back of clear glass."

"Really?" Miliana tried to rub the dazzle from her eyes. "Aren't they expensive?"

"Never you mind!" Lorenzo attended to his steering controls "Just make the damned signal!"

Miliana waited for the violet afterglow from the Sun Cannon to fade, then popped the upper hatch. Removing her pointy hat, she uncapped the tip and used the garment as a megaphone.

"War-turtles make smoke! All war-turtles make smoke!" Miliana's high pitched voice whirled out across the chaotic battle front like a thin bird caught in the breeze. "Form on the flagship for fast assault!"

Spewing vast billows of black smog which left the infantry coughing and frantically reaching for their sea-sponge gas masks, the war-turtles lumbered into a tighter formation. Miliana signaled the charge with her most impressive hat. Hatches clanged shut as the vehicles built up speed, rocking wildly as the horses found their footing on the solid valley floor and built up a crazy momentum. Here and there a vehicle squealed its brakes as the horses began to lose control of the runaway wagons.

A brilliant sun bolt scored the ground and clipped a war-turtle; the huge vehicle exploded like a bomb as the ray hit battle-damaged mirrors and stabbed into the hull beyond.

"Drawing its fire?" Clutching to her seat as the charge bounded wildly over broken ground, Miliana stared agog at the ruins of their fellow battle wagon. "Lorenzo!"

"I didn't say we'd survive!" The inventor whipped the horses into greater speed. "I just said it was best for everybody else!"

"Oh, wonderful!" Miliana lurched, frantically grabbing for handholds as the turtle sped toward the vast wall of enemy infantry. "Aren't you going to slow down?"

"No!"

"I thought not." The princess settled her spectacles grimly on her eyes. "Load explosive!"

"Explosive loaded—weapon up!"

"*Shoot!*" Miliana scarcely felt the twang as a pot-load of priceless smoke powder was lobbed into the enemy ahead. ". . . and then hold on tight!"

Nineteen gigantic battle wagons, all careening along at breakneck speed, smashed into a titanic formation of Svarézi pikemen. Useless spears bowed and snapped like twigs, rattling off mirror plates and shattering apart. Soldiers flew to every side like broken puppets as the vehicles impacted on the tight-packed mobs of men. Miliana retched as she felt the wheels judder across a surface that felt like corduroy paving, but came accompanied by a demented peal of screams.

A whip cracked, urging the horses on as they bogged down against the outside mass; a bucket of darts was upended over the whirring flywheel, spraying shot into the outside world. Bombs exploded, and Miliana's artillery crew fired unbidden, hammering lethal clouds of darts into the mob beyond.

Infantry scattered in terror, and the battle vehicles lurched on; a storm of crossbow fire flicked like hail from the hulls as a new line of troops compacted in front of the monsters and prepared to resist the assault.

With a sudden cry, a swarm of swordsmen raced out from behind the lines, crashing into the wagons and trying to tip them over with their hands.

Lorenzo felt the vehicle rocking and frowned at the blades and spear shafts jabbing under the hull. The enemy crammed themselves against the vehicles' fronts and jammed in their heels, braking the ponderous wagons to a halt, trying to lever the war-turtles over on their backs.

All of which allowed the choking clouds from the turtles' burning smudge pots to envelop the valley floor. Pressure eased as Svarézi's infantry scattered away to every side, fighting desperately for air.

"Don't pursue! Get in among the enemy lines so the Sun Cannon can't fire!"

Blocked from firing at the Lomatran infantry or vehicles, the Sun Cannon vented its fury on the city walls.
Whole lengths of battlements were sliced like wedding
cake, slumping into molten heaps of slag.

Watching the battle wagons charge, Ugo Svarézi
curbed his hissing hippogriff and nodded to his heralds.
The young men stood in their stirrups and raised trumpets to their lips, signaling the reserves to concentrate in
readiness for the *coup de grâce*.

The Lomatran forces were engaged, and all that was
needed for a victory was a simple envelopment—a sharp
dash to cut the enemy's route back into the city, then a
charge to take their militia in the rear. The expensive
loss of troops against the war wagons could be forgotten,
and the lives of foreign mercenaries scarcely mattered
to Svarézi's schemes. He would raise more foreign regiments on the loot from this one campaign, and the
Blade Kingdoms would prove the stepping stone to
empire. With a slash of his hand, he sent four thousand
horsemen sweeping wide around the enemy, heading
toward the Trevi River, which emptied past the walls
into the sea. The stream stood low, the path to victory
lay open, and in minutes the Lomatran alliance would
be no more.

* * * * *

Beneath a tree beside the river, Luccio Irozzi lounged
idly in the water watching the battle on the plains. Naked
save for sharkskin flippers, a loincloth, and a long snorkel
lashed to his head, he winced as he felt cold goosebumps
creeping all across his skin. He watched the dark cloud of
Svarézi's cavalry reserves begin their envelopment,
checked that their path would intersect his little haven
from the storm, and slipped an outlandish diving helmet
into place across his head.

"I believe it's time to sink beneath the drink." The
young noble slithered deeper into the water, ducking

splashes as dozens of nixies rose all around him to stand high in the water on their thrashing fins, staring at the encroaching cavalry. Princess Krrrr-poka hefted a long battle trident to signal her men, and one by one the creatures ducked out of sight beneath the river.

The water was three feet deep, a vile smoky green, and freezing cold with snowmelt from the mountaintops. Teeth chattering with the cold, Luccio eased his tender body down into the water and concealed his snorkel tube among the reeds.

In a tree above, Tekoriikii continued happily bouncing up and down, using the whip motion of the branches to give him a clear view across the field. He watched the huge infantry lines engage; saw the war-turtles bashing their way toward the mountain passes. Finally, he saw the high roads begin streaming with cavalry. The Svarézi reserves abandoned their protective stance about the Sun Cannon and descended from the ridgeline high above, forming lines and advancing at a sharp trot to the stream. Opening his wings, the bird crossed his eyes and tried to remember his instructions, then let the air shiver to a great, delighted cry.

Tekoriikii the firebird ceased bouncing up and down in his tree. His feather-brain quite clearly remembered the spectacular trick he was to play. Ascending to the now safe, deserted skies, he thrashed his way off toward the Sun Cannon, where it sat all alone above the pass.

17

"The city walls! The city walls!" A cornet of Svarézi's Sumbrian cavalry rose in his stirrups and called across the regiments with an excited cry. "Forward! On to Lomatra!"

The cavalry were already quite aware that they had drawn close to the city walls, which were readily identifiable as the tall gray stone things towering overhead. Ignoring the young officer, four thousand troopers crammed into a single eight-deep line, surged toward the tidal stream, and breasted their way into the freezing spray. In a magnificent display, the massed cavalry of Svarézi's budding empire thrust across the Trevi River to bring home his victory.

Starting from the upstream flanks, a chorus of terrible, pain-racked screams ripped out across the air. Horses began to rear and plunge, bucking in frantic agony. Riders were catapulted into the waters, where they erupted shrieking and clawing at exposed faces and hands. Every patch of immersed skin showed long red welts and burns. The horses bolted from the water, sometimes dragging fallen riders by the stirrups as they floundered free and sped toward the hills.

Downstream, the right flank of the huge formation staggered as their comrades simply fell apart. Whole regiments fled, while the waters churned with agonized men. The young cornet stared as a horse archer waded past, dripping strings of clear jelly from his brow; where the archer's hands touched the jelly, savage blisters had already started to form.

"Jellyfish!"

"Get out! Get out of the water! The stream's alive with jellyfish!"

The lucky men still untouched downstream spurred their horses from the flood. Some chose to go ahead, their frightened horses lunging up out of the plague-ridden stream. Others wrenched their mounts about and retreated to their own safe, familiar banks. Only a quarter of the horsemen emerged on the Lomatran side, where they milled about in confusion and alarm.

"That's better!" Dressed in battered, old-fashioned russet armor, Lorenzo's father slammed his visor down. "That layabout Luccio is good for something after all!"

Standing their horses before the city gates, the Lomatran heavy cavalry turned their ponderous ranks to face the enemy survivors. Lorenzo's father slapped his eldest son across the helmet and raised his heavy lance, signaling the charge. The regiment clanked off toward their demoralized opponents to sweep them from the field.

* * * * *

"Tekorii-kii-kii! Tekorii-kii-kii!"

Rowing through the air, his eyes slits and his face lit with a superior little smile, Tekoriikii passed high above the raging battlefield. The hippogriff cavalry that might have stopped him had all been neutralized, leaving the bird with a clean, untroubled sky. The bird need only swoop down upon the Sun Cannon, snatch away the Sun

Gem, and the threat of the evil machine would be gone.

The handsome firebird spied his prey. With a triumphant wig-wag of his wings, he made a spectacular
dive at his target far below. Intent on measuring their
chemicals and working at their valves, the Sun Cannon's
crew never once looked skyward or realized their onrushing peril. Tekoriikii zeroed in on the gigantic, sparkling
diamond fastened to the cannon's tip and, with a manic
hiss, opened out his claws.

On the ridgeline below, artillery crewmen ducked as
the Sun Cannon fired. A bolt of deadly light sizzled
through the air, and Tekoriikii found himself blinking
through dazzled eyes.

Much to his amazement, an arrow passed under his
wing. Tekoriikii wrenched his neck about, trying to make
sense out of the violet afterimages dancing past his eyes.

A black shadow whipped in from the left. Tekoriikii
arched his back to break his speed, and suddenly a massive wingtip cracked across his throat. The firebird spun
out of control. He clamped his claws onto a flailing black
figure, feeling the whole world spin as they clutched
together in mutual fear. The bird saw the earth rushing
straight at his face, beat furiously with his wings, and
somehow managed to land himself and his unwilling
partner smack into the turf.

Tekoriikii groaned, watching the universe spin with
whirring stars. He gave a croak from his poor sore throat
and scrabbled shakily to his feet.

The reason for his nice soft landing immediately
became apparent; Tekoriikii had landed tail-first on a
gaggle of artillery gunners. The bird stepped off the
padded hillock of flesh and dazedly looked around the
scene.

A terribly familiar lean black hippogriff flopped and
thrashed across the ground, utterly stunned by its fall.
The mare gave a pitiful squeal as she tried to move a broken wing. She opened dazed eyes and fixed them on
Tekoriikii as she felt the worst nightmares of a flying

creature suddenly become real.

Knocked even sillier than usual, Tekoriikii blundered over to the hippogriff and tried to make a motherly little sound.

His voice stuck in his throat. Eyes bulging, the bird clapped wings across his craw and staggered drunkenly aside.

A short, heavy sword swiped through the air right where Tekoriikii's head had been. Snarling like a troll, Ugo Svarézi lurched upright, pinned beneath the hippogriff, and tried to hack Tekoriikii clean in two.

To the firebird, actual violence was utterly meaningless; combat was restricted to demonstrations of supreme cleverness. Taken aback by a direct assault, the bird felt his sense of honor and propriety utterly impugned.

Svarézi lunged across his hippogriff's back, falling just short of Tekoriikii's hide. The bird tried to give an outraged scream, but to no avail; the merest hiss escaped his throat, where once an exquisite singing voice had been. Tekoriikii paddled backward out of range of Svarézi's sword, feeling his whole world swim in a giddy daze. The human hurtled a dagger, missing the throw as Shaatra rolled over him and trilled in agony.

Pinned by his injured mount, Svarézi tried to ram the hippogriff aside. The creature croaked, unable to rise, and tried a half-hearted snap of its beak at the firebird. The prince tried to shove at his mount, but the creature screamed and fought to remain prostrate on the ground. Cursing, Svarézi snatched hold of the hippogriff's neck and whipped his sword up to split the creature's skull.

With a broken hiss, Tekoriikii vaulted up across Shaatra and grappled the human to the ground. His beak fastened on Svarézi's wrist, claws gripping at the man's armored chest as Tekoriikii tried to batter the man's weapons away.

Svarézi somehow beat the firebird clear, almost tearing off his own right hand. Tekoriikii fell, and Svarézi lunged against the weight pinning him to the ground, somehow managing to battle free. Crying out in pain, Shaatra slid downhill across the grass, rolling on her side to tangle with the dizzy firebird.

Prince Svarézi clambered atop the Sun Cannon, laughing as he laid his hands on the controls. He kicked a lever, sending the spindly barrel sinking down to aim at the helpless firebird. Tekoriikii and the hippogriff both stared in horror as the Sun Gem glowed brilliant white before their eyes.

*   *   *   *   *

"Damn it!"

Miliana's spectacles had cracked clean across each lens, leaving her staring at an eerie, disjointed world. The whole war-turtle shuddered to a halt, the hull ringing like a temple bell as something crashed hard against its armored shell.

The vehicle ended on a decided list to the right. Lorenzo cut free the horses as Miliana blinked down at him from above.

"What in the name of the Abyss was that?"

"They finally got smart. They rolled rocks on us from the ridges above." Oh well—it had been a good run while it lasted. The war-turtles had done more than their inventor could possibly have dreamed. Now bogged, half buried, or broken up by catapult fire, the machines fell still as their crews abandoned them to take up the fight with crossbow, spell, and blade.

Outside the turtle, enemy infantry still swarmed like angry bugs. A sorcerer saw a chance for an easy kill and maneuvered for a shot under Lorenzo's hull. As he approached, Lorenzo gave a delighted exclamation and reached for a copper pole, which he industriously linked to the hilt of his sword.

A lightning bolt spat toward the damaged turtle. Electricity hit the vehicle's ceramic skin, blasted off mirror plates, then snaked over to the copper rod and poured power up into Lorenzo's sword. The sorcerer snarled in rage, disengaged his spell, and ripped out a long magic staff. Accompanied by half a dozen armored infantry, he rushed the disabled machine and began to claw his way inside.

The internal crew fought hard to keep the intruding infantry at bay. As the battle raged, a vision slit popped open, a copper rod waggled its way out of the hole and prodded itself up against the enemy sorcerer. A violent discharge of electricity ensued, sending the Svarézi troops jerking back like puppets tugged by the strings. Lorenzo popped his head out from under the war-turtle, decided that the coast was clear, and wrenched open the wide rear hatch to let the horses blunder free.

"That's it! Now make for the Sun Cannon—fast!"

Miliana popped out of her turret hatch, accidentally smacking a Colletran swordsman in the eye and sending him tumbling, unconscious, over the side.

"Has Tekoriikii neutralized the thing?"

"He must have." Lorenzo helped the girl clamber down across the slippery mirror tiles. "It hasn't fired for a while."

With an escort of Miliana's two artillerymen, the inventor and the princess took a swift bearing to the cliff top and climbed their way through the rocks above the melee.

Svarézi's infantry up above sniped and skirmished from a little rock fort they had made to command the crest. Deadly accurate fire drove a terrified Miliana into cover with an arrow quivering through her hat.

Crammed hard into a jumble of broken rocks, Lorenzo gave a sudden yelp as a crossbow bolt rebounded from a boulder mere inches from his face. "Miliana! Do something! What spells did you memorize this morning?"

"Um . . ." Miliana bit her lip. "Feather fall. I'm getting good at it."

"Feather fall?" Lorenzo felt himself slowly going mad. "You took feather fall spells into a fight?"

"Well I can throw it twice a day now. I'm getting better."

The inventor wearily put his face in his hands. Incensed, Miliana rolled up her long sleeves, set her pointy hat to an aggressive tilt and found the largest boulder on the mountainside. She hissed out her spell, threw a puff of Tekoriikii's feathers up into the air, and hoisted the titanic rock over her head and hurtled it up into the sky.

The boulder sailed over the Svarézi position, shuddered, and regained normal gravity once again. The enemy infantry stared at it for one long, fragile moment, then screamed and flung themselves downhill. The rock smashed their little fort to pieces and duly chased them all off toward the valley floor.

Lorenzo frowned and wiped a dirty hand across his nose.

"Have you ever had those spell scrolls of yours checked? I read up on feather fall spells—and that isn't what you're casting!"

Miliana poked a nasty tongue out at Lorenzo and made a rapid climb straight up the hill. Muttering to himself, the inventor spurred off in hot pursuit, dragging out his rapier as he climbed in her wake.

"Tekoriikii? Tekoriikii—where are you?"

Miliana topped the cliff face, searching wildly for her friend the firebird. "Tekoriikii—don't do anything stupid! Wait for me!"

The princess stopped as though she had run into a wall of rock and stared aghast at the hillcrest above.

Tekoriikii lay tangled with a skinny black hippogriff, splayed helpless before the Sun Cannon's maw. Ugo Svarézi—ragged, bloody, and half-crazed with hate—kicked the valve releases to fire the deadly light beam straight into the bird.

"Bastard!"

Miliana snatched up a rock and hurtled the makeshift weapon with all her might. Her broken spectacles made her miss Svarézi by a country mile. The would-be emperor flicked a glance in her direction, gave an ill-tempered snarl, and kicked the Sun Cannon's firing controls.

His eyes had left his two helpless feathery victims for only the merest beat of a heart. Moving with viper's speed, Shaatra snapped up from the ground, lunged beneath the Sun Cannon's barrel and rammed her back against the firing tube. The weapon raised, and an instant later the deadly light beam stabbed into the grass a dozen feet behind Tekoriikii's tail. Scorched and wounded by the barrel's heat, the hippogriff fell down to its belly and began to weakly try to drag herself away.

With a start, Tekoriikii realized that his tail had caught on fire; the bird frantically beat his backside against the grass and gave a frightened wail of dismay.

Seeing Miliana, Svarézi's eyes lit up in recognition. He sprang down from the Sun Cannon's firing platform and stalked toward her.

"So. My little Sumbrian bride." The warlord flexed black gauntlets like a vulture testing its claws. "It seems we can share a wedding bower at last . . ."

Miliana stared, felt a thrill of fear, and tried to back herself away, falling over backward as the rubble tripped her heels. Svarézi moved forward, only to check as a slim figure emerged from the rocks at his side.

Lorenzo held a bared rapier in his hand as he placed himself between Miliana and their enemy. Svarézi gave the boy a contemptuous glance, then ripped his short cat-gutter sword from its sheath.

"You want to fight me, boy, with your toy sword?" The Colletran tyrant made a swift arc of his brutal blade to free any stiffness in his wrist. "You want to fight me for your scrawny princess?"

Lorenzo flickered forward in a short, sharp fencer's step.

"Miliana! Get up and run!"

"No! Stay!" Svarézi began an arrogant, graceless advance upon the boy. "Stay and watch your sweetheart's guts spill to the ground!"

Without a word, Lorenzo skipped forward, launching across an impossible distance to spear at Svarézi with his blade. The Colletran grunted a vicious oath of shock and somehow swatted the rapier point aside.

A blinding spark leapt between the blades—the last dregs of Lorenzo's lightning bottle. Svarézi reeled, stunned and blinking as he fought away the shock. Furiously stumbling back, Svarézi blindly beat aside a frenzy of attacks; he snarled as Lorenzo's point scored a strip of velvet from his helm, lodged against his mail gauntlet without piercing home, and whipped, blurring, past his mouth to rip a cut across his skin.

Svarézi shook his head, trying to regain his wits; the lightning charge had left lights dancing past his eyes. Bleeding from a facial wound, the warlord roared and hammered Lorenzo's sword aside, missed a brutal cut with his blade, and crashed his hilt into Lorenzo's chest with all the power at his command. The slim inventor was flung back by the blow, clawing desperately to his feet to present his blade and keep the circling enemy at bay.

Lorenzo risked a brief glance across the cliff summit and felt one source of panic fly away; Miliana had scrabbled clear and hidden herself behind one wheel of the Sun Cannon. The girl crept closer to Tekoriikii and the fallen hippogriff and stared in terror at Svarézi's blade.

"Lorenzo, run! Run back down the hill!"

"I can't! He still has reserves." Lorenzo's breath shuddered with fatigue; he used one ripped sleeve to wipe sweat back from his eyes. "He can lead them around the army and crush us like an egg!"

On the roadside nearby, Svarézi lifted the back of his hand to his mouth, flicking a glance down at the resulting smear of blood.

"He's right, girl! Did you hear him? At the base of this hill, there lies enough manpower to grind Lomatra to a pulp." The black-armored nobleman rubbed his own blood between his fingertips. "Once we've killed this Lomatran puppy, we'll see to the destruction of your sad adopted home!"

He lunged forward, trying to crash past Lorenzo's guard and rip him open with an upward thrust of the short, brutal sword. The blade point scythed a line past Lorenzo's waist, bringing a flicker of blood across his shirt.

"Lorenzo!"

Miliana surged forward in panic as rapier and short sword clashed. She stumbled to a halt just short of the fight, helpless to intervene as the blades howled and slithered in a blur of rage.

Moving in a nearly senseless panic, Lorenzo somehow held his own, punching his sword hilt across Svarézi's helm to drive him back away. Tekoriikii tried to thrash forward and bring his beak into the fight—exposing himself to Svarézi's blade. Miliana wrenched at the chassis of the Sun Cannon, trying to rip free a strip of wood to make a quarterstaff or club.

Tekoriikii snapped his beak; Svarézi swore, whirled, and whipped back his weapon to finish off the bird once and for all—baring his arm to a desperate, sobbing lunge from Lorenzo's sword.

The stiff rapier pierced through velvet, mail, and silk to stab clean through the inner elbow of Svarézi's weapon arm. With a roar of rage, Svarézi spun aside. Blood sheeted from his forearm, spilling to the ground. His sword hung from nerveless fingers as he staggered blindly out of range.

Lorenzo moved forward; Svarézi spun, blurred out his free hand to snatch Miliana by the hair, and dragged her shrieking to his side.

"*Enough!* Throw the blade away or the she-witch dies!"

Svarézi wrenched his captive tight against his chest. Even so sorely wounded, he could have snapped Miliana's neck like a stick. The girl froze as he wound tight his grip, fear bulging out her eyes.

"Stop!" Lorenzo held out his sword, his face draining

white. He came a step closer to Svarézi, his eyes only on
Miliana's face. "Don't hurt her! I'll drop it. Just leave the
girl alone."

Miliana tried to speak, but Svarézi's hand ripped at
her hair, choking her with agony. Lorenzo threw his
sword far away across the road, then held out his empty
hands.

"It's gone! Now let the girl go free!"

Beside the Sun Cannon, the warlord gave a derisive
laugh.

Miliana managed to croak out a few words in fear.

"He-he'll ransom me! He's rich!"

Lorenzo blinked, stared at Miliana, then swiftly
reached a hand to his belt.

"Here! Here . . . yes, I'll ransom her! See? A thousand
ducats in gems!"

He tugged, threw his purse, and Svarézi laughed and
loosened his grip on the girl. She fell to the ground as
Svarézi snatched the heavy purse out of the air.

"A thousand ducats' prize and a princess for my bride!
A fitting crown for my victory."

A wisp of smoke disappeared up the fuse that led into
Lorenzo's patent anti-theft purse. Miliana lunged wildly
aside, diving through the grass. The prince spared a
quick glance at the heavy purse and opened his mouth to
give a terrified cry.

The blast shuddered the entire hillside. Lying flat on
his belly behind a score of rocks, Lorenzo felt debris
shower all around. He lifted his head and wildly searched
for Miliana as the smoke blew in wisps along the road.

"Miliana? Miliana!"

"I'm over here!" Legs clad in frilly petticoats waggled
as the girl struggled up from the dirt. "Is he gone?"

"Um . . . best not to ask."

Struggling erect, Miliana knelt on the grass and
instantly began searching the rubble with her fingertips.
Wiping sweat and scorch marks from his brow, Lorenzo
came over to kneel in puzzlement at her side.

"What on Toril are you doing?"

"My spectacles are gone! This war is costing me a fortune in ground glass!" Blind, scorched, and annoyed, the girl gave up on her search. "Is Tekoriikii alright?"

"The hippogriff's beating out the fire."

"Oh, good." Blinking like a newborn kitten, Miliana faced in the general direction of the din of battle. "Can you see the fight? Who's winning?"

"We're pushing his battle lines back. But Svarézi's reserves are still massed down at the bottom of the road." The young inventor stood up on tiptoes to stare ashen-faced downhill. "There must be ten thousand men down there!"

"Damn." The princess blundered over to the Sun Cannon and leaned against its hull. "We have to do something!"

Miliana froze; blinking her rather pretty eyes, she began wrinkling her nose like a rabbit and exploring the air.

"Um—Lorenzo?"

"Yes?"

"Should I be able to smell cherries?"

The two humans both turned to look up at the gigantic chemical vats looming overhead. Shaatra the hippogriff and Tekoriikii both caught the sudden aura of fear and joined them in staring at the weapon in alarm.

A hissing cloud of pink steam escaped from the armored pipes and valves, and Lorenzo instinctively backed away.

"The explosion must have cracked the vats . . ."

"You mean those chemicals are going to mix?"

"Ummm . . ."

Miliana peered through a cloud of cherry-scented death.

"How big a bang will the damned thing make?"

"Um, well, a bench model the size of your hat blew up my old room at your father's palace."

"That's what I thought." The new, improved model

weighed ten thousand times more. "Can we stop it from going off?"

"Um . . . no!" Lorenzo frenziedly sought the best route for escape. "Miliana—we have to run!"

"The hippogriff can't move!" Miliana pulled chocks from under the Sun Cannon's wheels. "Come on!"

"Miliana!"

"She saved Tekoriikii! We can't let her get blown to H'Catha!" Miliana planted her skinny shoulder blades against the back of the giant armored wagon. "Push! Come on, it'll roll downhill if we can get it moving. Tekoriikii—give a hand!"

The bird floundered up from where he had been contemplating his newly ruined tail. Ineffectually leaping and hopping up into the air, he tried to throw his weight behind the wagon. The injured hippogriff looked on in wonder as all three friends ignored the growing hiss of chemicals and tried to shove the gun downhill.

"It's too heavy!" Lorenzo searched about for a lever or a pulley. "I can't get it to move!"

Miliana stepped back, rolled up her sleeves, and sang out her last and only spell; the feather fall effect rippled the Sun Cannon with a gleaming purple skin, temporarily reducing the weapon's mass to nil.

"Now shove!"

A mighty heave sent the wagon on its way. Fifty feet long and three man-heights high, the juggernaut rolled down onto the road, picked up speed, and careened down toward the valley floor. The rearmost unit of Svarézi infantry looked back in alarm, then screamed as one as the wagon heeled slowly over and crashed down onto its side.

The entire valley floor lit with an explosion of violet light. Svarézi's reserve regiments disintegrated; others flung themselves down before a hail of debris. The Lomatran militia dove for cover, then crept slowly out to watch a cloud of reeking purple smoke fade and disappear.

Svarézi's battle lines were a crushed, molten wilderness of broken men and steel.

On the ridgeline high above, Lorenzo numbly helped Tekoriikii to his feet, then took a pace back to stare, dumbfounded, at the view.

"It does make rather a bad bang. Next time maybe I should use less cherries."

"What next time?" Miliana blinked into an out-of-focus world. "Did we win yet?"

"That just about does it." Lorenzo took another pace to his rear. "Oh! I've found your spectacles . . ."

"Really?" The girl eagerly reached out her hands. "Are they all right?"

"Um . . . not really. I've just trod on them."

Shaking her head, Miliana linked her arm through Lorenzo's and gazed off across the valley with a sigh.

Left to his own devices, Tekoriikii took a quick look left and right, then scampered off downhill and fluttered up into the reeking purple clouds.

* * * * *

"Are we too late?"

"No, no, no, sir knight! I would say you are fortuitously just in time." Spirelli the snail clung stickily to the back of a rather annoyed horse, peering his eyestalks out beneath his helmet brim. "I believe the time has come to charge and claim the day!"

Beside the snail, Orlando Toporello stood in his stirrups and signaled to his men. A thousand Sumbrian refugees, welcomed onto the battlefield by a slimy, charismatic snail, slammed down their lances and spurred into the charge. They swept past cheering Lomatran infantry—past dangling nets of snarling hippogriffs and streams filled with joyous nixies—and out into the plains to surround Svarézi's last remaining infantry.

Carried along throughout the charge, Spirelli remained close upon Toporello's heels. Toporello's men began to gather in the remains of Svarézi's army, reaping a rich harvest of prisoners from the field.

Ignoring the fracas, the snail eagerly intruded himself into Toporello's field of view.

"Sir! Sir, since you have fought for no payment at all, I wondered if I might offer you the use of my own house, my own stables, and my own rations for your men? Just as a show of proper hospitality." The snail shouted to be heard above the cheers of exhausted men. "We could sign a little receipt if it makes you feel better—just for my own records, of course."

"I couldn't impose upon you, sir." Old Toporello brushed his mustaches back into proper order as he saw his princess, the Lady Miliana, standing watching him from high above. "You are not our employer, after all."

The snail extended its eyestalks in genteel emphasis as he rode at Toporello's side.

"We can soon see to such little niceties. Perhaps your men might each take a peppercorn from me as a token piece of pay?"

"Why not?" Toporello scowled, then dismissed the whole affair as some foreign idiosyncrasy. "Why not indeed! They've already received a peppercorn apiece from your prince."

The snail cursed under its shell as Toporello rode away, then spied a dazed company of Colletran prisoners. Slapping his horse into action, Spirelli swiftly rode over to the mercenaries' side.

"I say! Would any of you men care to undertake regular work? Say, for the price of a meal tonight, a roof over your heads—and a peppercorn?"

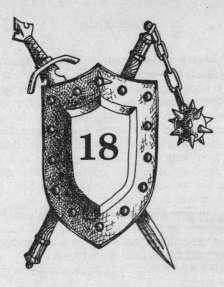

In the clean sunlight of a Sumbrian dawn, the ravaged city almost seemed at peace. Light filtered through the clouds and lit the dirty streets and cluttered wards, sheeting everything with a film of purest gold. The abuses of Svarézi's occupation still stood out like vulgar sores, but time would surely smooth the scars and blemishes away.

The age of city-states seemed dead and gone; Svarézi had ended Blade Wars for all time. First Colletro, Sumbria, and Zutria had been crushed down into one single state, and now Lomatra had helped forge a small alliance all its own. The "peppercorn vote" had swept the Blade Kingdoms in a rage; perhaps it was time to weld the tiny kingdoms into something greater overall.

Firstly, the abuses of war had to be soothed and healed. Walking the streets of her old, dear Sumbria, Miliana heaved a sigh. Palaces had burned and fallen, and the bricks had been roughly clamped together into ugly communal housing for the impoverished citizens. The river barges had to be rebuilt; hopefully with help from Princess Krrrr-poka's generous nixies, the coming harvest would not be stranded far upstream. There were streets to clean and trees to seed, a council to rebuild and lives to find. With Lorenzo, Tekoriikii and Prince Rosso at her side, Miliana walked up the ruined steps of her old home.

Here, more than anywhere, the worst changes had come. The Mannicci palace now looked much the worse for wear, still showing the scars of a night of fireworks and frenzy so long ago. The towers had been used as Svarézi's prison, and the courtyards had been made into stables for his beasts of war. It seemed doubtful that the palace would ever be the same.

Guards ran ahead into the corridors to release Svarézi's prisoners. Weak, sickened men were led aside and taken into care, while Miliana winced at the foul stench emanating from her old family haunts and halls.

"Ah! Miliana, my dear. It is so very good to have you back."

A strong, proud voice, now touched with unheard-of tenderness and gratitude, came from an opened cell. Eyes frozen and jaw wrenching sideways in disbelief, Miliana watched as her stepmother was led out from captivity.

Lady Ulia—always imposingly tall, was a mere shadow of her former self. The vast bulk of fat had gone; in its place, there stood a statuesque creature made of slender muscle topped off with long black hair. The enforced diet and savage exercise had left Ulia with the figure of an elven fertility goddess. A little weak and shaken, the gorgeous creature tottered forward and laid her hand upon Miliana's arm.

"You did us proud, my dear. A fiancé and a battle won. I always knew you would turn out well in the end." Ulia still wore her black mourning dress—now roughly stitched tight to fit a mightily streamlined frame. "It's always best to let a true hawk fly free.

"I believe your father would have said 'well done.' "

Miliana looked quietly down and took Ulia's hand.

The prince of Lomatra fixed Ulia with an astonished stare. Ulia allowed the man to proffer an arm, then led him away into the shadows of the broken palace halls.

"I hear you are not married, sir?" Ulia's posterior waggled in ways that left Lorenzo staring after her in disbelief and awe. "Perhaps you might see fit to keep me company for a while? I feel a little fragile, and things seem so
unsettled in the world."

A small green furry creature bounded like a puppy in
Lady Ulia's wake. Shaking herself, Miliana turned
around. Tekoriikii had contrived to disappear, and all the
guards had gone. She led Lorenzo hand-in-hand on an
inspection of empty rooms and hollow halls, finally stop-
ping before a tower littered with copper pennies, open
cupboards, and broken chests. Miliana gazed about herself in disappointment and let her face twist into a scowl.

"I thought Svarézi had a treasury . . ."

"Not anymore, apparently." Lorenzo gave a shrug. "The
harvest will bring in enough money to rebuild some
homes."

Miliana led the way down through the city streets, out
through the silent gates, and toward the rocky shore that
stretched out before them until it faded far from view.
The girl gazed out across the freshwater sea and polished
her spectacles on the hem of her dress, while long
streams of fragrant hair twined past Lorenzo's smiling
face.

"Why are you smiling?"

The girl adjusted her spectacles, meeting Lorenzo eye
to eye. In reply, the inventor shrugged and reached out to
take her small, soft hand.

"No reason." Lorenzo freed a strand of gossamer brown
from across Miliana's spectacle frames. "Just thinking of
a goddess rising from the sea."

Down in the foam, Luccio sat reading something aloud
to his aquatic princess. Miliana and Lorenzo kicked away
their shoes and gave the lovers a polite, wide berth, content instead to walk alone along the cool, dry stones,
threading through the occasional stand of tall brown
grass.

The mountain breeze blew fresh and clean. Miliana gazed off into the distance with a wistful eye, leaving Lorenzo in a reverie at her side.

The inventor stood in the wind and held his princess's hand.

"So what happens now?"

"Hmmmm?" Miliana kept her eyes on the horizon. "Oh—a big new council—maybe one for all the cities rolled into one."

"No . . . I mean to you and I?"

"Anything we want, I suppose. You've got your inventions—and I suppose I can have my magic now. There's no one to stand in my way. No one to tell us who we have to be with anymore."

"And what would you like to do?"

"Like?" Miliana quietly tightened her grip on Lorenzo's hand. "I'd like to revel in the treasures I've found, and find all the treasures I never thought I'd have a chance to look for."

They both stared out at the water, gazing out together into an undiscovered world. Miliana turned her face up to stare into Lorenzo's eyes, then reached out to come into his arms.

The wind blew, the tall grass sighed, and Lorenzo drifted into a gentle kiss with the woman he loved. They stood entwined together at the threshold of a world, lost inside a dawning, joyous dream.

* * * * *

Irritably dragging her splinted wing, the hippogriff Shaatra wandered along empty palace corridors. She pricked her tall feathered ears, trying to track down an elusive, haunting melody that had lured her out of sleep. Troubled, injured, and feeling utterly alone, the black mare moved through a wilderness of torn curtains and ruined tapestries, searching for the meaning of the strange sense of loss in her soul.

Pained and tired, the hippogriff finally abandoned her search and wandered up the stairs of a tall old tower. She hoped only for a place to sleep while her breaks and bruises healed. Shaatra pushed open a hanging door, walked out into an open tower room, and felt her hooves and talons sink into a softness she had never known before.

"Tekorii-kii-kii! Tekorii-kii-kii!"

The cry almost shot Shaatra clean out of her skin. The hippogriff turned to run, then stared in amazement at a towering mound that had been scraped together out of rubble, earth, and straw.

She looked down to find that she stood on a carpet made of velvet and looted tapestries. On his fine new mound up above, Tekoriikii waited with his chest puffed out in pride, coughing softly to draw attention to his beautiful, fiery plumes.

The bird felt himself at the very pinnacle of cleverness. He had found the correct mate for Miliana—and now he had finally found a perfect mate all his own, a creature elegant and black. A creature that matched him in the aerial battle of snatching tails. A lithe, brilliant, ferocious female the likes of which no firebird had ever seen. A savage hawk who surely would be wooed by the romantic peacock's wiles.

On his magnificent dancing mound, the firebird began to croon. Before the eyes of the astonished hippogriff, he spread out a massive fan of tail, utterly dazzling her. He danced a little to the left, and a little to the right—bobbed his head down low and up high, while wig-waggling his polished yellow claws. Clever golden eyes rolled fondly at the lonely mare, while the firebird opened his beak and trilled in glee.

One step at a time, Shaatra approached the mound and wonderingly began the silken climb. The firebird strutted excitedly up and down, always slightly out of reach, skipping and bounding up and down in dizzy ecstasy. He rubbed his beak against her hide, and she dimly felt herself reply, her feathers rising in wonder as she merged her voice with his song.

The firebird proudly swept aside his tail, and the hippogriff could only stare in awe at her prize.

A nest had been hollowed at the very top of the mount—a nest built from feathers of a brilliant orange hue. And lining the comfortable little home, there sparkled an empire's ransom in jewels.

Svarézi's treasury had been looted of its choicest sparkly things; there were polished copper coins and pieces of Lorenzo's mirror tiles, all intricately woven round with emeralds and pearls. Gold cups and burnished combs dazzled the hippogriff's helpless eyes as she felt herself drawn deeper into the hoard.

In pride of place, sparkling beneath the sun, there lay Tekoriikii's greatest prize, the best sparkly object in all the whole wide world. The Sun Gem twinkled its hypnotic message deep into Shaatra's eyes, singing the praises of the clever firebird.

With a cry of delight, the hippogriff turned three times around about the nest and settled into place among the jewels. With long lashes shading lovely eyes, she coyly hid her face behind a wing and made space for Tekoriikii at her side.

"Tekorii-kii-kii! Tekorii-kii-kii!"

A soaring song rolled out across the Mannicci palace, spilling up into the clear Sumbrian sky. All through the city, tired citizens stopped to listen as the sound of joy spun like magic in the winds.

For once, the roof tiles stayed in place, and Miliana's spectacles survived. She joined Lorenzo in gazing up at the palace with a smile, then stole an arm around his waist and led him on across the sand.

Behind them, the Blade Kingdoms at long last stood at peace, while the morning mellowed into a warm and gentle summer afternoon.

If you enjoyed *The Council of Blades*, try these other great **FORGOTTEN REALMS**™ books from TSR . . .

Elminster: The Making of a Mage

At last! The "biography" of the most famous wizard on Toril. From humble shepherd boy to powerful wielder of incredible magical powers, experience the life of Elminster as only **Ed Greenwood** can tell it!

Once Around the Realms

Author **Brian Thomsen** sends Volothamp Geddarm (yes, the famous "Volo!") on an light-hearted, though certainly epic journey across the FORGOTTEN REALMS. Why? There's honor at stake . . . and a bet. . . .

Cormyr: A Novel

Now available in hardcover! The history of Faerûn's greatest nation comes to life in this sweeping epic from the fertile imaginations of **Ed Greenwood** and **Jeff Grubb.**

Also by **Paul Kidd!**

Mus of Kerbridge

Enter a world of romance and adventure, a world where centaur ladies flirt with satyr musketeers—where rapier and pistol match their powers against ancient sorceries . . . where a small brown house-mouse becomes the king's most astonishing new cavalier!

Welcome to the FORGOTTEN REALMS, the largest and most detailed of TSR's fantasy worlds.

Look out from the high walls of Waterdeep, the sprawling, cosmopolitan City of Splendors. Beyond lies the Savage Frontier: the rugged mountains and endless forests of the Sword Coast, wilderlands that cloak the crumbling ruins of fallen kingdoms.

Travel with the caravans that cross these dangerous lands, heading east toward the kingdom of Cormyr, fabled realm of ancient forests, land of chivalry and romance. Stop over in the Dalelands, home of the crusty old wizard Elminster and the birthplace of many heroes and heroines. Then continue onward to distant Thay . . . and beyond.

In your travels, you will encounter many folk from highborn to low. Among the beautiful and deadly Seven Sisters are Storm Silverhand, the silver-haired Bard of Shadowdale, and High Lady Alustriel, the gentle and just ruler of Silverymoon. A third sister is the Simbul, fey and wild-tempered Witch-Queen of Aglarond. There are four more sisters, each beautiful and powerful in her own way.

If you meet them on the road, do not meddle with the mysterious Harpers, who work to uphold freedom and the causes of good throughout the Realms. You may, however, share a drink with the eccentric explorer Volo, and pick his brain for a wealth of information about your next destination. Beware that sinister-looking fellow in the corner of the common room. He may be a Zhentarim agent, gathering information for a takeover of the Heartlands.

Should the surface world not prove exciting enough for you, make your way beneath Mount Waterdeep to traverse the miles upon miles of tunnels and caverns known as Undermountain—but beware its deadly traps and skulking monsters. If you survive these hazards, press on to the subterranean city of Menzoberranzan, home of the deadly drow and birthplace of the renegade Drizzt Do'Urden.

When you return to the light of the surface world, you may want to explore the crumbling ruins of Myth Drannor, a storehouse of lost magic and deadly monsters in the heart of the vast Elven Court forest.

From the dangerous sewers and back alleys of sprawling cities, to glaciers, deserts, jungles, and uncharted seas (above and below the surface!), there's a whole world to explore in the lands of the FORGOTTEN REALMS.